DAWSON CITY SEVEN

Don Reddick

GOOSE LANE

Published by Goose Lane Editions with the assistance of the Canada Council, 1993.

Cover photographs: Henry Joseph Woodside/National Archives Of Canada/PA-16239; team photograph courtesy of the Yukon Archives/Joseph Forrest Collection.
Back cover photograph by Terry Reddick.
Book design by Brenda Steeves.
Edited by Laurel Boone.
Printed in Canada by Imprimerie Gagné ltée.
10   9   8   7   6   5   4   3   2

Canadian Cataloguing in Publication Data
    Reddick, Don, 1954-

    Dawson city seven
    ISBN 0-86492-158-6

I. Title.

PS3568.E34D48 1993   813'.54   C93-098641-5

Goose Lane Editions
469 King Street
Fredericton, New Brunswick
Canada E3B 1E5

For Ginny, of course

ACKNOWLEDGEMENTS

I'VE COME TO BELIEVE that our families allow us to be whatever it is we become; I'd like to thank mine for letting me write this book. I'm particularly grateful to my father, John Reddick, of Norwood, Massachusetts, for his support and for sending me back to Ottawa to complete the research, and my brother, Ken Reddick, also of Norwood, whose love of history and sport show up throughout the book.

I'd like to thank Lydia E. Watt, of Ottawa, Ontario, and Ken Forrest, of Marysville, Washington, who provided me with invaluable information regarding their families. My appreciation also extends to Ed Bennett of Woodstock, Bill Galloway, of Cumberland, Brian McFarlane, of Willowdale, and Kevin Kelly of Toronto, all in the province of Ontario, for their help in gathering the historical record. I am much indebted to the Yukon Archives in Whitehorse and the National Archives in Ottawa, without whose assistance this book would have been impossible. I'd also like to thank my editor, Laurel Boone, and designer, Brenda Steeves, for perfecting the book inside and out.

Last, I'd like to thank my four girls, Terry, Becky, Sarah and Allison, and all our friends — you know who you are.

Don Reddick, July 30, 1993.

DAWSON CITY SEVEN

1

NOW, I'M GOING TO LIE and wink. And I'm apt to exaggerate a little bit here and there, and I won't tell you when, and I do it because it makes a better story.

Who knows about this business? The Dawson business. And even though it's a long time ago — '05 it was — I'll be honest and tell you I remember every little bit of it, and I'll carry the sights and sounds, the living and dying, skates cutting that ice and the ungodly words from those guys' mouths — I'll carry it all to the grave. Course the hockey games was only a part of it, the gold mines, the store fronts, stump-mud Skagway with all the hooligans and cheaters and stealers, they was as much a part of it as any, and then the trip, the people in all the towns spread out across Canada, all cheering and crying for us to beat them Silver Sevens. People have asked me about it all my lifetime, if they hear I was involved and if they know anything about it, and since I'm old and probably dying now anyhow, I'm going to tell you the whole thing. If I may interject a bit, I think it's something that should be remembered, because we was David against Goliath, the underdog.

I was born not so far from here, and you're probably wondering how the son of a Confederate soldier came into the world in these parts. Daddy was from Georgia, a town called Milledgeville, which, you remember, was the capital of Georgia at that time. Daddy joined the Confederate army in Atlanta and fought with General Robert E. Lee, and to my Daddy that was the grandest thing he ever did. My Daddy always said the South would have won the war if it'd been close to an even fight, but I won't go into that.

Anyways, when the army disbanded in '65, all the Southern boys got home to just about nothing. A thirty-mile-wide trail of destruction was inflicted upon Georgia from Atlanta to Savannah, every last morsel of food confiscated, every last work place burned, and Milledgeville was smack-dab in the middle of it. You seen that movie *Gone With the Wind*? That touches upon it all, but barely. People actually starved to death in a land, on a soil that could grow food better and firmer than pride itself. My Daddy — he had my mother and my two oldest sisters Jenny and Babe — he was one smart Southern boy, because he realized things would be bad for a long, long time in Milledgeville, Georgia, so you know what he figured? Move north!

Now, in that day and time such a move was unheard of in Milledgeville, Georgia. But that tells you what kind of man my Daddy was, he was brave, thoughtful, and smart. He didn't care what those Yankees he hated so much thought, he knew he could farm and that's what he packed up and headed north to do, told my mother if they wanted the country together so damn much he was entitled to live where he wanted in it and the heck with what they thought. And that's how the son of a Confederate soldier came to be born on October 23, 1885, in the little farming town of Sudbury, Massachusetts.

I don't want to digress. I want to tell you the story about me going on up to Dawson City for gold, the team we formed to win that new Stanley Cup from the Ottawa boys, the whole thing, but I do like to talk about my Daddy. He was a little

Don Reddick

older than usual when I was born in '85, so I didn't get to know him as an adult, which has been my lifelong misfortune. But when I was young, he would set me on his knee, and he'd tell me what was right and wrong with the world and with men and even with women, which usually dismayed my mother. But I've got to tell you this about my Daddy, because it was the finest part of his life. On the third of July, 1863, my Daddy lined up with about twelve thousand other rebels, and they all run screaming about a mile across an open field at Gettysburg, in a movement gone down as Pickett's Charge. The high tide of the Confederacy it was, the grandest military charge in all North American history and probably of all time, far as I know, and you know what he'd say about it? He'd say he was so ascared he didn't even remember it except for the screaming — he was that honest — but he said he knew he was there and he knew he'd done it when it was all over, which was mighty darn quick. Actually, he told me one thing, he once told me he realized a little over half way up they wasn't going to make it, because he saw the Federals off to their right, which he didn't think no one else did at the time. They was flanked by that Stannard there, and that was that. He was one of about four thousand that made it back to the woods. But anyway, my Daddy fought for General Robert E. Lee at Pickett's Charge in Gettysburg, Pennsylvania, on the third of July, 1863, and he was damn proud of it and so am I.

Now Daddy, being a Southern boy, hated the cold, which I guess I must have inherited somewhat, and when I went to the Yukon I carried this dislike with me, much to my discomfort. It was just too cold there for normal human beings, and I'll tell you nothing bothered me more than men — and especially women — who said they didn't mind it, or that they got used to it, because that's nothing but a lie. Humans are meant to be in warm places, that's why they don't have fur. I know there's lots of animals around here and even down south that's got hair, but up in the Yukon, all the animals have double-hair, which is why we like to make coats out of them. Being cold ain't natural, plain and simple.

Being the son of a Confederate soldier that fought at Gettysburg, I lived through some situations as a youngster which enabled me to leave for the gold rush later on. Truth of the matter is, we was somewhat disliked and even shunned by people even in my memory. And winter on a New England farm gives you some extra time. Even though I hated the cold, I just couldn't stand the female yakking that goes on in a household with nine women and two men. Now I'm not anti-female — the missus and me was married fifty-six years — but the things women talk about and the things men talk about just aren't the same somehow. Like hens in a hen house, Momma and all my sisters were, so that's the main reason I'd leave the house and go out in the damn cold and strap on my skates, and that's how I'd spend my winter time, just wheeling and trimming and gliding up and down that river, one leg over the other. In all my remembrances there's no freer feeling, because a boy can move on a couple lengths of steel strapped to his boots, I'll tell you. As far back as I can recall I spent my winter days on them skates, year after year of my youth. Working on a farm and skating all winter long is what gave me my strength, and if I do say so myself I was a specimen of some regard.

Daddy died when I was twelve years old, on August 10, 1898. He was moving the rocks in the second field to the stone fence when something in him just quit, and we found him when he never came in for dinner. This happens. Truth is most people think they'll never die, and they live their lifetimes according. Not me. I knew I was going to die when I saw that heap of man lying on the ground in his own field, a man so big in my mind I never thought I'd see the day he didn't look me over and figure out what was wrong with the way I was dressed or what I was thinking. Truth is I think that was the day I stopped being a boy and realized someday I was going to be a heap of man lying in someone's field, figuring I'd be lucky if I died in my own field and not in some hospital bed somewhere. The point is, if you truly know you're going to die, you laugh a little more, you laugh a little longer, you decide to do things when the chance arrives that others who know they'll never die don't do, because they think they'll do it later on. Well, later on they die.

We're progressing to 1901 or so, I'm sixteen or seventeen, and I'm seeing all the Northern boys going up into Lowell or down into Brockton and working in the big brick factories, and that never settled right by me. A lot of families I knew killed a couple birds with one stone by sending off the children to work in them brick factories, not only one less mouth to feed on the farm, but a few dollars back usually. I was the only boy of eight kids and the girls was marrying off and, the truth be known, I knew I was going to die. The sight of that heap lying in that field soured me to something which at the time I didn't properly recognize.

I'd read all about the gold mines of Dawson and the Yukon Territory, I'd even seen some of the local fellows up and go themselves at the beginning in '98, and being young and foolish I knew if I'd go I'd be able to stand the cold and find gold somewhere, even though thousands of others were already back, stone broke. I knew I'd get rich. I'd busted my back for nine or ten years on a farm just to eat and save a couple dollars, I surely could go north and bust my back to get rich. See, I knew I was going to die. Soon. And so that's how I came about deciding to go to Dawson City.

Did I get rich? Yes, I did. Because I've carried something with me ever since, worth more than any gold any other fellow lugged out of that godforsaken place, because I still have all my riches. No one tries to steal your memories. No one barters goods and services for them. You can't hock them. You can't get drunk and lose your memories. And the only reason I got rich was on account of me being the son of a Confederate soldier in the North, not standing that female talk, and going to my skates day after day after day in the damn New England cold. I'd skate and skate and skate, the freest son of a rebel in New England, never knowing at the time it would give me moments in front of thousands of hockey fans, playing hockey with the greatest players of all time for a new trophy called the Stanley Cup, made in England for the club in Canada that wanted it most — yes, I got rich.

And this is how.

2

LIFE WAS MORE RIGID THEN. Today a kid can go most anywhere with a new job, or go to college for that matter, or join the service, but then you grew up on a farm in a farm community and most likely became a farmer. Followed a country girl and made her a farmer's wife. Our only alternative was them big brick factories in Brockton and Lowell. Leaving was hard, because it was very radical to leave home. End of the world for you, as far as your Momma and family went, but I was young and ready to run, and there wasn't much remaining to keep me home. I had to go.

So one day I just decided. I was walking down the road with a stick in my hand, batting stones like Ed Delahanty, and it just came to me to do it. Just do it, George. But be considerate, be gentle. I figured the way to do it was to ask Momma if I could go, sort of putting the shoe on the other foot, letting her make the decision herself. See, I knew she couldn't say no to me, her only boy and all. Apple of her eye, by the way. So I walk into the kitchen and says to her, "Momma, do you have a minute? As you know, I been thinking for some time now about things, and I've come to the thought that — with your permission of course — I'd go to the Yukon Territory to look for gold."

It was as simple as that. My mother looked at me and said, "No," and turned back to what she was doing.

"Momma," I says, "you're the greatest momma in the world. You raised nine kids and was good to Daddy, and there's just no way you ain't gonna end up in heaven." She looks at me with the dirtiest look you can imagine, because she sees what I'm up to. "And because of this I don't want to hurt your feelings by just up and going on my own, so I'm asking for your permission to do so."

"You'll go to hell if you go up there," she says, "I read the periodicals. There's whoring and gambling and robbing and stealing and all whatnot, and you're young and apt to be taken advantage of." Now, I didn't tell Momma that secretly these were half the reasons I wanted to go. Don't get me wrong, I certainly didn't want to be personally involved with that kind of stuff, but they're the kinds of things a young man just wants to see for his own. You might say it's something so real you just got to see it for yourself. So I says, "I won't get involved with that stuff."

"You got no money."

"I got two hundred fifty-seven dollars."

"That won't even get you there." It would, but I'm not arguing the minor points.

"I can work."

"They'll make you a slave. I heard if men lose all their money they become slaves and have to work all day and all night just to eat and keep warm."

"Ain't no slaves, Ma, that's crazy." I was tempted to say, Daddy lost that one, remember? but I was wise and kept my mouth shut.

"Nobody'll wash your clothes or make your meals."

"I'll wash my clothes and make my own meals."

"You ain't gonna have no meals to make."

"I'll find meals to make."

"You'll die if you break a leg in the woods."

"I won't break my legs."

"They'll make you a slave."

"Ain't no slaves, Ma!" I remain wise.

"Well, you just oughtn't to do it."

Now what do you say to that? When I don't respond she says, "'Sides, it's too cold up there." Now, that makes me frown. She knows I hate the damn New England cold, and she knows I'll just about die of it up there. But, see, I also realize she's using her heavy artillery now.

"I'll keep warm," I says, and she plops down on the kitchen chair and just looks at me with the saddest eyes. My Momma had the most beautiful, sad eyes. Eyes that seemed to capture all those things a mind won't let go, and then let them loose when she opened them. They were almost sad enough to prevent me from going. Almost.

"I'll keep warm," I says again.

"Do you really want this?" she asks, and looks out the kitchen window at the fields. So now I'm feeling a little guilty.

"Babe and Jenny are married now, they've got husbands that need work." My Momma waves that off, shakes her head ever so slightly. Wasn't that. She pauses, then turns to me and says the kind of words you don't forget.

"Your Daddy once explained to me about being a young man, about making decisions," she said. "Said a man ain't a man 'less he can make big ones. Course his was bigger than this, on account of having two kids when he left, and when he left we didn't neither one of us know if he was ever coming back. But he came back, a lot more solemn and sad and grown up, but he came back all right. And he told me once when you were only six or seven months old — I was holding you and talking to you and pretending you understood — and your Daddy just gets up and says, 'He'll be making big decisions someday.' And out he walks."

My mother is bearing down on me now with those sad, sad eyes.

"I guess this is your first big decision, then."

And that's it. She gets up and walks outside, without even putting her coat on. Let me have it good without letting me have it, you understand. Couldn't just say okay and be behind me, but she's gotta let me have it both barrels. And it didn't end there. Now I'm going, she's got to prepare me. *Prepare me.* Now, you must remember she's my mother and she born and raised me, which is why she's got to *prepare* me, not just let me go. But everything she did, which at that time annoyed me so, turned out to help, from the warm socks and mittens and hats she had the sisters mass-produce, to the talk she made me have with old Mr. Sullivan, an Irishman who lived by the railroad tracks through Concord that he'd helped build as a youngster.

"You go to old Mr. Sullivan, his younger brother Patrick went to the Yukon in '98 and he's got all his letters. You go up there and be nice and ask him to read you all them letters. You'll learn something from them, maybe you'll to come to your senses."

Course I ignored that last part, but I'm my mother's son, remember, so I go one Sunday morning up the pike to Concord and find Old Sullivan out back in his bean field, all stooped over and knees dirty, fussing with his bean poles. Now, the Irish at that time was kind of the niggers of the North, nobody really liked them much and wouldn't give them real jobs. They were just expected to be labourers, and most of them were. Irishmen built all the railroads in New England, and most of the paved roads and brick buildings, too. So Old Sullivan looks up at me in surprise because not many non-Irish folks called on him. But we was Southerners and somewhat outcasts ourselves, although not on the level of Irish people, of course.

"Mr. Sullivan," I says, "I'm George Mason and my mother asked me to come to you so that you might read me them letters you got from your brother up in the gold fields. It's my intention to go there and my mother feels it would be instructive to hear first-hand about it." Now does that sound like I spent the whole walk over rehearsing?

Well, Old Sullivan has a hard time straightening up and he says something that I've remembered since, he says, "Listen to me, young George Mason, I keep telling people not to grow old, but nobody seems to listen." All this in a terrible brogue, which I don't understand very well — as a kid I thought something was wrong with him. Old Sullivan wipes the dirt from his hands and nods toward his shanty and we go in, a small place but tidy, with a chair and a big bed and his kitchen, all one room. He pulls out a packet of blue-ribbon-tied letters from the top cupboard, and falls with a humph on his chair. There's only the one chair, so I loiter until he tells me to sit on the floor.

Now there's something different between men and women, and I've almost lived a whole life without putting a finger entirely upon it, but what Old Sullivan says next is part of it. He winks at me and says, "Your momma told me you were coming, boy, and she wanted me to explain how tough it is up there. Seems like she wanted me to discourage you some, but I'll just read you the facts." He smiles and winks again, and what it means is that he's just about going to do the exact opposite.

He takes off his hat and wipes his hands again on his pants and fumbles until he finds a date to begin with. Brings the letter close to his face and reads about a long train trip west, and a sea voyage on the *Amur*, with a capacity of one hundred crowded with five hundred gold-hungry souls — a squalid mess Patrick called "the Black Hole of Calcutta in an Arctic setting" —

Don Reddick

north from Seattle to places with names like Fort Wrangell and Dyea. Mostly these letters was about prices at first, wood is three and a half cents a pound, eggs is forty cents a dozen, flour eleven to twelve dollars a hundred pounds, whisky twenty-five cents a drink — three to four times their real price in New England, which was horrifying to me with my present money shortage in mind. Then, as Old Sullivan goes from letter to letter — he had maybe fifteen in all — Patrick goes up and over the Chilkoot Pass and relates another horrifying truth: that the Canadian Mounties guarding the border there ain't going to let in no one without a year's supply of goods.

I'm getting nervous, all I'm hearing is how much money I'm needing, and I'm not going to have enough. And I'm also wondering why Old Sullivan winked me into believing there was no discouragement here in these letters. These letters are anchors of discouragement. He keeps on reading, a word at a time because fact is he could hardly read at all, and there I sit sweating and frowning and hacking away at his brogue, and on he goes talking about building boats at Lake Bennett, which I know I can do, and raising a blanket on Lake Laberge and sailing on north, which I know I can certainly do, and riding down the long Yukon River and arriving at Dawson — and now my eyes are wide as full moons — and then another letter all about long trails into cold hills, and meeting Indians and men with long beards and hollow eyes and working until his hands were raw and all for nothing. I was impressed by the "nothing." It seems that Patrick put all his faith in the gold and nothing in the whole scene and sense of what he'd done, but through it all was Old Sullivan's twinkling eyes and his words of hard, long work and bitter cold and "nothing." When he finishes, the twinkle in his eye remains as he ties the letters back up with the blue ribbon, carefully replacing them in the upper cupboard. I could only wonder about the particular genius of a foreign old man who lived next to the railroad tracks in a shanty, who, before I left, showed me his bag of coins which were all flattened because he'd laid them on the tracks, believing they were worth more if they were bigger. I looked at this Old Sullivan and I knew there was more than the gold. But exactly what I could not know.

"The letters end off suddenly," Old Sullivan said, his face falling serious. "I have not heard from Patrick in a long, long time. Will you do me one thing, boy?"

"Yes, sir."

"When you go to the Yukon, will you send word of him? It's an awful thing not knowing."

I thanked Old Sullivan that Sunday afternoon in Concord so long ago, promised I'd send him a letter from Dawson with whatever I could find. I knew then I must go, and I was smarter for it all. I did need more money — Momma had been right about that. All the way home, as I swatted rocks over stone walls with a stick pretending I was Ed Delahanty, I thought how I'd get cash, and I knew in my heart — although at that very moment I didn't in my mind — that I'd have to go to Lowell or Brockton or Boston and work in them mills for a bit.

But as I've found throughout my lifetime — and it's a thing I think most find out — little detours like this often produce the best results, because I met a close friend in them mills that became a lifelong one, one that someday I'll lay down next to and be at home with once again. I ended up knowing her fifty-eight years.

Don Reddick

3

BOSTON WAS THE CLOSEST PLACE for me to make some money, and I came to the awful conclusion that I'd better put off going to Dawson until the following March, when I'd be better prepared. The decision near killed me, but I made it one day walking the fields where Daddy died. I was sure Momma thought she'd won the first battle and this was the beginning of me finding my senses. And I thought she was playing along when she had all the sisters mass-producing socks and hats and mittens and fixing Daddy's old boots and blankets, least I thought she was just playing along. Sometimes mothers'll fool you. She was somewhat reluctant about the Boston part, Boston, with its anti-slavery snobbishness and prim and proper liberal conversation, about as noxious to a Southerner as could be. But I was to work, which all good parents are for, and it wasn't all that far away, not as far as Dawson City anyway.

I knew because of Old Sullivan's letters there was a lot more to going up north and finding gold than I previously thought, and most of that cost money. Now in those days most people lived on farms, outside the cities most everyone did. There was no wages to be earned, or at least none to speak of, mostly you were paid by a roof over your head and daily meals and maybe some pocket change. Farm hands did make a little money if the farm they was with sold at market, but overall, at the turn of the century, if you wanted to make some cold cash you had to go to the city. I figured I needed a good five hundred dollars minimum to get up there, and that was bare-boning it, transportation and food and my outfit only. And I knew, with the two hundred and fifty-seven dollars to my name, I wasn't going to get that amount very quickly if I stayed in Sudbury. So again I approached my mother in the kitchen while she was doing something, I don't remember what.

"Ma," I says, "I decided I should maybe go to Boston to earn some money so as to afford to go to the gold fields."

"Look," she says, turning to me, and she's waving a big wooden cooking spoon in her hand for emphasis, "there's whoring and cheating and stealing in Boston and you're young and likely to be taken advantage of."

"C'mon, Ma, you know you raised a boy that can take care of himself." I'm using psychology now. I'm really saying, See, you didn't raise no timid dog here, Ma, you raised a man who can go places without restraint of fear — knowing this information will please her.

"They'll make you a slave in there," she says. Now, I'm saying to myself, what is it with this slave business in my mother's mind? Ain't no slaves anymore, Daddy lost!

"Ain't no slaves anymore," I said.

"There'll be nobody to make your meals or wash your clothes," she says, but I surprise her here.

"April's" — she's another one of my sisters — "April's husband's sister Mary lives in Dorchester, I've already spoke with her about it. I can stay there. A dollar a week." Which was a heck of a rate for even that long ago. My mother's a little taken aback, perhaps I'm really going to do it. But don't worry, it's only a small step, and them gold fields is really four thousand miles off, whereas Boston is ten. This is what I figure she's thinking, what I see in her eyes, but truth be known there's something in a mother's mind, in her eyes, with what she sees and feels and hears her own son say, that tells her truths the son don't think she knows. I figured it out way later, sitting on the banks of the Yukon River pulling on my skates and shaking off my sorrows, that Momma knew all along what was going on, even in my mind, and that's why she prodded my numerous sisters to mass-produce those socks and shirts and boots. She even had David, April's husband, clean and restore Daddy's gun properly, which, I somewhat dislike to admit, I didn't know how to do at the time. Didn't know how to prime and shoot it, neither. Never took it on account of that.

But the old woman knew what the young boy was going to do. I know this now, I didn't know it then. She prepared me. Made me always think responsibly about what I was going to be doing. That's why she sent me to Old Sullivan, not to discourage me — which I took for the reason then — but to make me understand what I was facing from one who'd been through it. Knew I wouldn't never listen to her or anyone else. And she was right. Mothers and daddies are always right. Always listen to them, because they're the only ones in the whole wide world that love you regardless. Will Rogers says it when he says, "Home is where when you go there they have to take you in." What he's saying is that no matter how much you screw up in life — and we're all going to screw up — the family will take you in because they love you regardless.

I moved to Dorchester on July 5, 1903. Paid my dollar a week room and board. The deal was made with my saving money in mind. They were helping me. More usual would have been maybe ten dollars a week, with meals. We lived in what we then called a flat and they now call a triple-decker. These were the normal buildings for the area, occupied by three families, one on each floor, with a broad front door and stairway inside, and out back three open porches, one on top of the other, where the women would string lines from one flat to the other to hang the wash on to dry.

Mostly it was an Irish community, Dorchester was, but there was a sprinkling of Poles and Germans toward Andrews Square, and some niggers over to the other side, and Jews over to Mattapan Square. But on Harvard Street it was mostly Irish. See, the Irish came in waves from the old country, seems like every time they ran out of food over there they came over here to eat ours. We'd a done the same thing if we was them, and come to think of it, which an Irish gentleman of my acquaintance once made me do, it wasn't very much different from my own Daddy moving his family up from Milledgeville when there wasn't anything growing in Georgia.

But Irish people was looked down upon in those days. My sister's sister-in-law Mary married a Cork man named Reilly, and it was his interest and vocation to sell and rent houses. Well, Reilly was an educated man though I'm not certain how, and he knew that in Boston there was no way that a man named Reilly was going to do business with any so-called respectable people — meaning the Protestants who had all the money. So, being made of pluck and ingenuity, he searched the registers and found a man named Weed and paid him five dollars a month just to use his name for business purposes. He run and owned Weed's Real Estate at the time I moved in and until he died some thirty years later, when the Depression came in, and he lost all his houses because the banks wouldn't accept his alternate proposals, a sad business for the family which I won't go into.

So anyways I lived with the owner of Weed's Real Estate, his wife and two little boys on Harvard Street in Dorchester. Mr. Reilly talked to some people and they balked at me until he told them my name was Mason. Honest, it was like that, that bad. I could see the disbelief in their eyes but I showed them the papers my mother sent with me and they shrugged, the boss muttering how strange it was for a Protestant boy to live in a Catholic neighbourhood. I learned something from all this though, I learned that outside of church and a few practices, usually at meal time, there just isn't all that much difference between people, and I used this realization my whole lifetime to my benefit. My family was in support of this, nobody ever uttered a bad word at all when my sister's sister-in-law Mary married this Reilly fellow, and I think it had to do with us being Southerners ourselves and understanding what it was like first-hand to be somewhat considered less of.

Don Reddick

Anyway Mr. Reilly got me a job in a box factory where they had all this sophisticated mechanical machinery that cut, formed, and stapled the boxes together. My job was to feed the sheets of cardboard into the machine and remove and stack the boxes after they was done, which sounds pretty straightforward, but Lord love a duck the darn thing broke down or cocked the cardboard wrong to back up all the others just about every five minutes. And the only way I could figure out how to fix it or prevent it was sticking my finger in there amidst all the moving mechanical parts, which put the fear of you-know-who himself into me with thinking about losing one of my fingers. And it happened in there, it did. Guys got their fingers crushed or taken right off more than you'd think. There was this old guy who'd lost half his hand — grotesque it was, watching him at dinner break holding a sandwich with one good hand and one stub, took my appetite away entirely the first time I saw it — but like everything else you get used to things like that. Course it never crossed my young mind I'd be seeing much worse than that when I went up north. And they called this guy Ouch.

At the time unions was a big issue, and while most plants just made things worse for the men who pushed unionizing, our place — it was the Chelsea Box Company — they thought otherwise and made things better for us. One thing that the unionizing men was going for was what we now call break times. The law now says workers must get a break, but then there was none at all. So my company sent a girl around with a box of apples twice a day instead of giving in whole hog to the new radicalized ideas. This girl was to make the rounds and offer apples for a penny each to all the workers, and guess who this girl in my part of the factory turned out to be?

Elizabeth her name was, Elizabeth Grady. She was of average prettiness, but the thing that got me, the thing I used to look forward to all morning long, was her smile. She had an exceptional smile, a broad, bare-toothed, go-for-it-all type of smile with a hint of mischief in it, and all morning long I'd be risking my fingers and sweating, piling up those boxes, thinking about nothing except that big, broad smile. Her eyes were of a pretty nature also, as though they were made special to go along with the smile. Back then girls named Elizabeth were called Lizzie and I used to joke and call her Lizzie Borden, who was famous back then as a murderer, although she was found not guilty in the courtroom. Made up a song about her and everything.

So she'd come along with the apple box strapped around her neck and all smiling and eyes twinkling, and I'd say, "Well, here comes Lizzie Borden, the city girl," and she'd say, "Well, here's George Mason, the country bumpkin," and we'd laugh. I was almost nineteen then and she was younger, and she wouldn't ever tell me exactly her age, which made me fear she was quite a bit younger, but to this day I don't really know. It don't matter now anyhow.

But I was country and she was city. This made me seem different to her than all the other fellows, and she was different to me. Different we was in numerous, small ways, hard things to describe, like how we talked and acted toward older people. When I told her why I was in Boston, she was amazed that I had the courage to go to the gold fields at such an age, and I was impressed by a girl who went to work every day like a man. We had a special year, or almost a year. We'd meet at the Public Garden and ride the swan boats on the little pond they have there, she'd make up bologna sandwiches and bring iced tea and we'd sit afterwards and watch all the well-to-do Protestants dressed up in their Sunday best clothes and walking about with their canes and top hats. Come to think of it, this is what proves the date, 1903. We attended every game of the very first World Series, Boston against the Pittsburghers, which we won in eight.

Now, my Daddy told me about baseball's beginning, how it spread across all the civilized portion of our land during the war. He told me of seeing Federal prisoners playing ball in the South. First time he saw it he went over, because he's the curious type, watched the men play with no gloves or nothing, and asked what the purpose of it was. He had conversations even with the Federals themselves, and he told me they said it was called baseball, that the Northerners played it mainly up around Philadelphia and Boston, and it was mostly played by the lessers, mostly the Irish.

But the Irish in the Federal ranks spread it to the other Federals, and they in turn, after they was captured, taught it to the Southern boys, so that the Civil War can properly be looked upon as the spreading point of the national pastime. Daddy became somewhat of a baseball fan, but he'd never go into Boston to see it played. Momma wouldn't go with him. He only studied the boxscores in the sports pages. There was leagues before the current two, the Players Association, the Federal League — a name Daddy hated — and others, the National League, of course, and Daddy would follow them in odd ways. He once made a list of all the professional players he could find who was born between '61 and '65 in the Confederacy. I don't know what ever happened to that list, but I remember the guy he talked about most, Robert Lee Caruthers, who won forty games twice in the '80's, once for St. Louis and once for Brooklyn. Caruthers owns the second highest winning percentage for pitchers ever in organized baseball, according to my almanac. Born in Memphis, '64. Quite the Confederate name, eh, Robert Lee Caruthers? Daddy would have been proud of a kid named Thomas Jefferson Davis Bridges, played for Detroit a few years back. Two presidents' names, and one the only president of his Confederacy. Would have liked that Kennesaw Mountain Landis fellow there, too, the commissioner who rightly banned the Black Sox in '19. See,

Landis's father fought with the Federals at Kennesaw Mountain outside of Atlanta in the war, and the battle left such an impression on him that he named his son after it.

Lizzie and I attended all four Boston games of the first World Series, and for the rest of our lives, whenever October came around and the boys played World Series games, me and Lizzie would look at each other with that special do-you-remember-when look, reminding us of being kids in Boston and falling in love.

Cy Young lost the first World Series game ever, played in Boston with me and Lizzie in attendance on October 1, 1903. Thing I recall most was I couldn't ever decide who was most impressive in that series, Young, who came back to win two crucial games in the middle — they played a best of nine then — or Big Bill Dineen, who won the sixth and of course shut out Pittsburgh in the final game to win it all. I kind of lean toward Young, but I suspect I'm influenced because of how he did overall in his career, which wasn't too bad if you haven't heard.

Ed Delahanty was my favourite player, the greatest baseball hitter of all time. Period. And one of the great attractions for me when I was moving to Boston to make money to go to Dawson City was I'd be able to go see Big Ed Delahanty play baseball — he'd just moved over to Washington in the American League in '02. But this didn't happen, because right after I moved to Harvard Street in Dorchester, and I mean within a day or two, Big Ed Delahanty, the greatest ballplayer of all time, died in the most bizarre and, when all the facts came out, most ugly manner.

Big Ed Delahanty got drunk on the team train in Buffalo, New York, got thrown off by the officers, and proceeded to fall off a train trestle he was attempting to cross, drowning, he did, in the Niagara River below. Went over the falls. My biggest baseball hero died because he was drunk. No matter how I turned or twisted the tale around that's how it come out to me, the hero of so many barefoot summers of my youth. It made my heart sink into despair about how unnecessary it all was. Delahanty was elected to the Hall of Fame in '45 I think it was. Maybe '46. End of the war.

But what I learned from his death is about the good falling in with the bad. See, after I realized that by drinking Big Ed Delahanty lost his baseball career and his life — I mean this is like Roger Maris or Mickey Mantle of those damn Yankees dying today — I realized that alcohol wasn't in the cards for George Mason. Not that Big Ed was my only learning experience in that regard, temperance was a big issue even then, though mostly with women like that crazy hatchet woman Carrie Nation, women who was sick of their men never coming home on payday. In the old days there wasn't nothing to help alcoholics like they got today. No A.A. meetings. Back then what men did was go to church and pledge not to drink. Called it The Pledge, and more than once you'd hear some kid say don't go near so-and-so's house, because the old man was on The Pledge and was being darn difficult. I decided long before — I heard all the stories and was read them letters, remember — long before I stepped foot on that first train that if I was fortunate enough to partake in the gold up there I wasn't going to be sharing it with no taverns. Called saloons out there. Let the taverns and saloons of the world govern the weak ones, not George Mason, no sir. And I kept true to that pledge, except once that I'm going to get to, which was understandable at that time, as I believe you'll agree.

Anyways, Boston. Big Ed never made it and I found a wonderful smile. I walked the streets of Boston at night and after work and on Sundays, and it was a scene of continuous movement. Sudbury ain't so far away from Boston but night and day couldn't be more different, one a quiet yawn-and-stretch-in-the-morning farming town, the other a giant brick and cobblestoned mass of people and horse carts and storefronts and teeming kettles and pans with the great smell of fresh cooked fish and potatoes and vegetables and all numerous sorts of German and Polish frankfurters.

And baked beans, it isn't any falsehood that baked beans is big news over in Boston. Properly fashioned — and Elizabeth Grady gave me the proper recipe, which was much to my advantage the following year in them gold camps — properly fashioned with a few strips of bacon or salt pork and a little molasses and baked in one of them big heavy pots for a long time — first the pea beans gotta soak the proper amount of time also — well, they smell as good as they taste, and on a Sunday afternoon in downtown Boston at the turn of the century the tremendous smell of baked beans flowed through the skinny streets like fried onions in the kitchen. Which reminds me of a small story my mother once told me about Daddy. Sometimes it occurred that supper wasn't ready exactly when Daddy come in from the fields, and you've got to understand my Daddy was one man who expected his supper when he came in, period. As though my poor mother should know exactly when he'd make his mind up to quit each day. Anyway, my mother told me one of her secrets. When he'd surprise her by coming in before she expected him, she'd just dice up a couple of onions and throw them onto the frying pan with a hunk of butter, and Daddy would walk in and sniff the air and say, "Hey, what's that you're cooking, it smells so good," and Momma would say, "Now, you just relax and wait a moment, I'm gonna surprise you." Daddy wouldn't never say nothing, he'd just sit in his big easy chair in the front room and put his head back, probably busy figuring out what it was smelled so good.

But Boston was a busy town, from the harbour traffic down by the Customs House to the merchants along those long grey-stone market buildings to the neighbourhoods full of youngsters playing baseball, with the country all full of itself after the Spanish War, beating down the Boxers in China, and Teddy Roosevelt agreeing to dig that ditch through Panama. Them Wright brothers flew their first plane that year, and 1903 was the year the first cross-country trip by automobile was made from San Francisco to New York. It's the year the first automobile made it onto the streets of Dawson City, and also the year Jack London's *Call of the Wild* got in print, which I'll attend to later. I wouldn't normally remember such things, it's just that when your special time comes you tend to remember everything.

In 1903 Lou Gehrig, Charlie Gehringer, Carl Hubbell, and down there in Bridgewater Mickey Cochrane were all born, and in Boston I fell in love, I gained the required money to head to the gold fields, and Ed Delahanty died.

4

IT'S FUNNY, WHEN YOU START remembering this stuff, what comes to mind. Delahanty and the rest. Most people don't know why there wasn't no World Series in 1904. See, the National League had been around forever, and had withstood all the other leagues that came along and challenged its authority. And along comes the American League and they talk the Nationals into playing a World Series against the best teams of each league, which wasn't a new idea, by the way. There had been other World Series before but they wasn't called that, between the Nationals and other leagues.

But what happens is this. All cocksure the Nationals was that they'd beat the tar out of any new American League team, so they agreed to the '03 series, and then they went and lost it after being up three games to one! Well, the men that run the National League was so embarrassed and upset that they picked up all their toys and went home, as they say. Wouldn't agree to a series the following year, which is why it wasn't played. But they resumed the following year and done so since. I think the only other professional sport to miss determining a champion since then was hockey, the Stanley Cup just after the First War, 1919 or 1920, the year half the world seemed to die of the influenza. The games was out west and tragic it was, because a bunch of the players fell sick and one of 'em even died, fellow by the name of Hall, if I remember correct.

Anyway. 1903 and Boston, Massachusetts, came to an end in one of those misunderstandings young people sometimes have. See, women are always falling in love immediately and wanting to get married, while men are more concerned with their finances. A man don't want to marry unless he's in a position to take full financial responsibility for a household, which is another way of saying it's the biggest reason young fellows use as an excuse not to marry. When they get cold feet.

Come Christmastime, which was a popular time then to propose marriage, Lizzie was apparently under the impression we had an understanding, meaning we were in agreement on marriage plans. She expected me to ask her father's permission to marry her, which was a good custom, one I think should have been retained by society, as it's a matter of proper respect. What a guy did was more or less come to an understanding with the particular young lady that, if he indeed got her father's permission, she'd then say yes to the proposal itself, otherwise it made for embarrassment all over the place if the father says uh-huh and then the daughter says uh-uh. So for some reason Lizzie thinks that we've come to our understanding, which I admit we touched upon, but I guess I just didn't quite understand our understanding the way Lizzie understood it. And not only that, but her daddy's got the understanding, too, which makes for a long, hard gaze from the old man Christmas Eve when I get up to go without approaching him.

Now I must be truthful here. Lizzie always walks me to the top of the steps — this was Marlboro Street by Commonwealth Avenue — when I take my leave at night, but this night she barely gets past the big front door.

"Goodbye, Merry Christmas," she says in a voice that would make Waterford the undertaker proud. Now I'm confused, I've waited until now, on her front porch on Christmas Eve, to give her some small present I had in my pocket, and I'm confused now and look at her, conveying my condition.

"Well, what do you think!" she blurts out and I move to her and grab her hands.

"What's the matter, Elizabeth?" I ask, using her full name which I did when we was serious. I'm also looking around at the folks walking by, after all I am a New Englander and this is quickly sizing up as dirty laundry.

She says, "What do you think is the matter?" And because I've missed the boat on this whole understanding we don't have, I stand there helpless and pull out the little present and shove it toward her and she just shouts something, runs inside and slams the big front door. And people saw it. Now, I've never apologized for this particular New England trait of not wanting the general public viewing personal problems. I believe in it greatly and have adhered to the principle my entire lifetime. You just don't do things like that in public.

I've met people, mostly men, from all over the world, and I can attest not everyone's of the same feeling. I've seen grown men cry, which is an experience of extreme mortification if you don't consider the reason too severe. I've often gone to funerals where men will do their utmost not to cry even though it's their own mother lying there cold, and you may find that stupid, or selfish, or careless, but I've always admired it, that a man will stick to a principle despite travails. Anyway the point is I got awfully mad at Lizzie for her flagrant disregard of my principles, which I had made clear to her as the duty of a gentleman courting. Not realizing her side of the coin, remember.

So I marched off mad as a hatter, without even a look back, trod down those snowy streets under gaslights, swearing I was becoming a foolish person to think I could get engaged at this young age while preparing for bigger things blah blah blah, and the further I got away the madder I got, and I determined then and there — I'm probably by where Fenway Park is today — that I'm not going to see her no more. And this began a very destructive period. When a boy becomes a man, he becomes like an animal. And I mean truly, just like the thick hairy ones we make coats out of, in that they're governed by new inner understandings about certain things, they follow certain instincts even though they bring problems and sorrows. Now the instinct I'm talking about here is Pride, especially when dealing with women. And if you don't believe me when I say young men, just remember that you don't see old men having fist fights over old women. Least not usually. Young men fight for their women in many ways, not just with their fists. They try to better themselves financially, they compete in sports to determine who's most attractive to the women watching. I've had disagreements over this last point, but I'll stick to it. Who has more women following him around, Ralph Kiner of the Phillies or Joe Blow at the corner drugstore? Joe can be better looking, smarter, gooder, but it don't matter. A woman's always going to want a man other men look to.

Anyway my pride came into play during that time. I'd decided I wouldn't be calling at her place no more, I decided I wouldn't be mailing any letters. I decided it was she who had to come to me and apologize, which was stupid and destructive because it almost ruined us forever. And the thing is it near killed me to be away from her and that smile, near killed me to

Don Reddick

think maybe she wasn't smiling, but inside me was this destructive voice saying, Don't do it, boy, make her come to you, show her how strong you are that you don't ever need her anyhow — and whatnot.

And that's how I left Boston to go to Dawson City in February, 1904. Where do I even begin to start this part? Leaving home was a solemn, unusual business. Going to hell. Going to the devil. Going. And there weren't many younger fellows like myself going, neither. You know there was a gold rush almost exactly fifty years earlier, the California gold rush, which, at the turn of the century, most people's grandparents could recall. Almost everybody went, I mean moms and dads and kids as well as the hordes of young men. You just got up all you got and left for California. Well, the Yukon rush was different. You needed to prepare for the cold, you needed to buy transportation, you needed to buy a year's supply of goods, and more often than not you needed to buy into somebody else's diggings, if you even made it up there. In other words, you needed money, lots of money for those times, and most young men just didn't have it.

Most of the people who went to the Yukon was men, and most of them was older men, from, say, twenty-eight to forty. Men that had some money. Course many young men was sent by older monied men that struck a deal, they was lucky. They could strut around all them outfitters' stores in Seattle just picking out this and that without frugality. And I think it hurt a lot of them, the carelessness this led to, but that's an old feeling I've harboured without concrete evidence. I wasn't one of them. I'd decided on my own to go to them gold fields, I'd gone to Boston to earn money to do so, and then I did it. I saved between two and three hundred dollars in Boston, I forget exactly how much, and I had my two hundred and fifty-seven.

February was cold and rainy in Sudbury, colder than real

cold because thirty, forty degrees with rain is always worse than twenty with snow. Chills to the bone somehow. But that's how I remember it. I'd gone home to be with the family and tie up various loose ends and collect all the articles of clothing my mother had everyone mass-produce, and also just to be there and walk the fields and help out in any small way I could to show I wasn't forgetting everyone by going. It was a strange week I spent there, all ascared and terribly excited at the same time, getting choked up thinking of leaving and feeling also somewhat guilty, though my rational mind knew this was not necessary. Figuring out all my travel plans.

We're at dinner, which means we got a whole line of people in that old household down one side the table and up the other, what with numerous sisters and some husbands and Momma, and there's a quiet because it's a fact I'm leaving in the morning, which is indeed serious business. So I says something to break the silence, the way you say just anything to try to make things seem more normal.

"Boy, these beans is special," I says, and there's several agreements up and down that long busy table, though I notice everyone's still staring at their plates. It makes me think something's going on in a way, but in the same way I don't. Then Momma looks up to me and says, "George, we don't want you to go to that godforsaken place, don't misunderstand. But we see you're up and gonna do it, so we put together some . . . thing that will help you. It's a family decision."

With that the woman reaches down under the big table and brings up her sack which she opens, and she pulls out a smaller sack and hands it to me. I take it with some hesitation, looking around at all the others, who now are all staring at me in suspended animation, then I open the sack and see a handful of dollars I don't even begin to count, and I look back up, realizing they put this money together for me when I knew they was against the entire idea. At least most were.

Don Reddick

Well, my eyes just water up, and you know how I feel about that. Already I had begun dreading the goodbyes, particularly with my Momma, and real concern I had that I'd handle my emotions properly, and then this is sprung on me. Well . . . I guess it was because of this I come to understand emotion ain't all that bad and you can live through it, because the truth is I started to cry at that table, which is a fact I don't think I told anyone for many years after, but I can tell it now because I'm old. I realize now not only was it okay to do that, but it was actually good that I did, to show everyone that I'm not some unfeeling old stuck-up Yankee who don't know a real right from a real wrong.

After that meal I left the house very quickly, my skates in my hands. Out the back door, over the stone wall and across the first field, across the second field where Daddy died, and down to the frozen river, where I sat for a bit in the coldness that had crept over the land that night, and I sat there numb to it all, thinking of everything, upset about what'd just occurred and feeling so much appreciation for all of them. I strapped on them skates and flew out over that river, thinking of everything still. I flew over that ice, my legs pumping, my arms flailing back and forth, flying, I'll say it, across that ice, flying! And the feeling this gave me, the flight, the freedom, the release from normal worries, it all came in on me, with the cold air pulling back the hair sticking out of my cap, leaning in on the curves so my body was close to the ice, turning, turning, gliding and striding — the freest son of a rebel ever skated in New England — somehow it came to me during those spins and turns that I'm bringing these skates with me. Who knows, I thought, maybe I can use them on the Yukon River if I come home during the winter, and so I decided that I'd be carrying them skates north with me.

I skated for a long while out in the dark, watching the house till the light in the kitchen was the only one left, which meant they'd all gone to bed. Then I sat in the snow and pulled off the skates and pulled on my boots and headed back up across the fields with that ricky feeling you get in your feet after you've skated hard. I was tired with the good kind of tired, with a great adventure lying before me and a great and wonderful family behind me. Only by keeping the thoughts of Elizabeth Grady away did I make myself feel completely wonderful as I trudged back across the fields to that old farmhouse.

But my Momma had one more surprise in wait.

"You've gone and done something wrong with the Grady girl, haven't you," she says out of the darkness of the living room where she's sitting alone. I frown with the loss of my wonderful feeling.

"What are you doing up?" I says, thinking equally about Elizabeth Grady and me making a fool of myself at the table.

"I wanna know what you did with the Grady girl, because if you did something wrong you're not going nowhere till you apologize to her. I'm not gonna have my only son behaving in the stupid man's way."

"I'm not being stupid," I protested, all the while shaking my head at how all women, whether it's your mother or grand-mother or wife or daughter, how they all seem to know when something's going on even though you ain't told them nothing.

"Well you haven't mentioned her name once in days and you're preparing to leave, so it seems awful odd to me that something didn't happen between the two of you. Now I want to know if there did, because you ain't going nowhere till you make a proper response to it."

So I sat down and sighed and proceeded to tell my Momma the whole story of the front porch incident, explaining well how I felt about it all. She just sat there quietly, understanding it all and saying nothing until I was done. And then she tore into me like a hungry dog after a spilled sausage, making me understand for the first time that Lizzie was expecting a marriage proposal, not some little trinket or whatever it was I brought her that night. And I just sat there nodding my head at the truth of this, and feeling a little embarrassed that I didn't understand it myself, which only made me more stubborn for that inner, instinctual reason of pride. Stupid. See, again, my Momma was right.

Tell you something else — I lied to her that night. She was coming down hard on me and even today I think her feelings about me leaving gave her scolding a little more edge than need be, and my head was exploding with all my emotions and the truth of the marriage proposal mess, and the fact is I just couldn't take it no more. Ma's insistence that I go and apologize to Lizzie was totally against my mistaken inner instincts, so I lied to her. I did and I can admit that today. I'm that honest. I lied.

"Then what I'll do is leave from South Station and go to Marlboro Street before and apologize," I lied, and she sat back in her chair, and though the whole thing took place in the dark I could sense her smile, as could probably every other ear in the house.

"And George," she whispers in the dark, "it's all right to cry once in a while."

"Aw, c'mon, Ma . . . "

"Grown men do cry, George. Your father cried."

"Don't say that!"

"I want you to know this. The first time I ever saw your Daddy cry was the night he come home from the war. He'd walked all the way from Virginia to Milledgeville, and out of nowhere up the front steps he walks wearing nothing but a quilt with holes for his head and arms, and just seeing his face made me burst with crying, but he didn't. And all evening long all he could do was pace back and forth across the bedroom, talking one instant about sowing crops and the next asking why Lee ordered Pickett's Charge, and then saying what the hell was we gonna do with no food and no work, and it just appeared to me he was all eat up inside, so I grabbed his hands and made him sit on the bed and tell me everything. Everything."

"What'd he say?"

"Well, he told me about going to Atlanta and then up north, and he told me all the fears the Georgia men had on the lines around Richmond, knowing that Sherman was marching on their homes and their women and children. He told me what he remembered of Gettysburg, and a charge he was in somewhere else on something called the Orange Plank Road, and the starvation at the end toward the surrender, and then back to Gettysburg, of course. But when he got to the wagon train in the rain after Gettysburg, all the wounded and broken men heading south in the rain, and he began to tell me the awful noise the hurt men was making and nothing anyone could do for them, your father just began to cry, and I mean howl, long awful sounds like an animal, and all I could do was hold his head against my breast and pet his head like a child's."

I didn't say nothing, couldn't, and thankful I was we was sitting in the dark because I could feel my own eyes again welling up with tears.

On the cloudy and cold morning of March 15, 1904, I left the Sudbury farm with all my belongings in the world, which amounted to just about nothing but the pile of mass-produced clothes my sisters had manufactured for me. Course I had money, but you didn't buy goods in the east that you could buy out west, even for a little more, to avoid the shipping costs on the railway.

The farewell went pretty much as expected. I kept a stiff upper lip.

"Well, you're going now," my Momma says to me. All the others gathered around, some of the sisters sniffling and whatnot, the husbands stepping forward solemnly to shake my hand. I think the husbands had mixed feelings about it all, on the one hand whispering to their various wives all the reasons it was just plain wrong, and on the other hand secretly wishing it was them.

"Well, you're going now," Momma says, and I nod.

"I'm going now."

"Be careful."

"I'll be careful."

"Don't let no one make you no slave."

"Ain't no slaves, Ma."

"Let us know if you go off and marry some Eskimo," brother-in-law William says, and my sister slaps his arm and looks up at him to kill. This naturally makes me think of Elizabeth Grady, but I manage a smile.

"I'll let you know," I says, and I figure this is enough of the small talk and I've made it this far without crying. I turn with a half wave to them all, and I leave. Actually brother-in-law David snaps the reins, because he's carrying me and my bags on the wagon into town, to South Station where I'll get my train. I had no intention of going by Marlboro Street, and I knew David couldn't make no reference to it because that would expose his portion of the eavesdropping that was so prevalent that night I came in from skating.

Secretly, and I mean even secretly from myself because I was bound and determined she meant nothing to me, secretly I hoped Lizzie would show up at South Station. I had gone out of my way to visit the box factory before I went home to say goodbye, and I made a point of telling several of our friends my new departure plans. Again, I see why now, but I wouldn't allow myself to see why at the time. The truth is I had decided to leave from South Station before I promised my mother. And it's probably a good thing Lizzie never showed up, because I would have nailed shut the coffin, I just know it.

So anyway we take the Concord Road up to the Lincoln Road and on in through Waltham, and we cross the Charles at

Watertown and on into Boston, the whole time David humming like he hasn't a care in the world and me practically paralyzed with fear. And something funny happened in Watertown, just before we crossed the Charles, something which struck me as representing the whole change of life I was entering. We saw an automobile chugging toward us on the road. I stared at it while David muttered about scaring the horses, I just stared, and on a ride I really don't remember much of anything else about, I remember staring at myself chugging, changing, while David talked.

"Advertisement in the papers says if you drive an automobile, carry a box of cigars to compensate for the chickens you kill on the road. I swear, cars without rails is gonna be wholesale slaughter."

I don't say nothing.

"Specially if they ever let women drive," David adds, nudging me in the coat, and I remember saying — I honestly said this — "Hey, women can't even vote, they'll never be allowed to drive automobiles."

But as the wind off the ocean came to us as we travelled down Commonwealth Avenue within a stone's throw of Marlboro Street and up over the hill by the Common, I seemed to tighten up with my fears. A lump in my throat formed and I couldn't even speak. I was learning, without being more than a couple miles from where I'd spent most of the previous year, what it was to contract homesickness, and my stomach turned with the knowledge that I'd be a coward to everyone and myself the remainder of my lousy lifetime if I ever did what my body now seemed to require me to do, namely turn back. I was a goner. Going, going, gone. Added to this were my worries about money and my hidden and crushing disbelief that Miss Grady hadn't bothered to show up. This was the lump of man, or rather kid, that got left off at South Station in Boston. David was very formal.

"I wish you a great, safe, and eventful journey, may you reap the rewards of man unafraid," he said, sticking out his hand rigidly, and I grabbed it, thinking, Now I know what he was doing while he was humming all the way in. He then left me to my reflection on how ironic his words were. Man unafraid.

I was homesick even before I entered the train. I was lonely as soon as I sat down, and I felt guilty the next whole year over leaving the farm and family and over what I'll explain later. All of which must be taken in the context of me telling you that the trip was the grandest thing of my life, changing me from a nine-teen-year-old kid to an instructed twenty-year-old adult, and that it was my first big decision. I stepped up into the train, and I paused to search for her one last time, attempting to look like I was really waving to David.

And I didn't see nothing.

5

FOR FIVE DOLLARS I got myself a chair in the coach, because this train was bringing me to Montreal where I'd get on the other one that brought people out west to Vancouver. I'd get a berth on that one, but not this one. At that time there was two major railway routes out west. The southern one is that American cross-country one with the golden spike that goes into San Francisco. The other one, the northern one that took most of the men to the Yukon, goes straight across Canada to Vancouver. That was my plan, which was just about the same as all goldrush plans of the day, take the Canadian train to Vancouver, then a short train down to Seattle to get outfitted, and then either a steamer or a sailing ship north to a place called Skagway, and then head inland. A very simple plan.

I had all my maps with me and I pulled them out as soon as I sat down. Despite the tightness in my throat and uneasiness in my stomach, I'm still greatly excited to be on my way. I'm not thinking of Lizzy Grady at all. I'm conspiring on what I'll do, how I'll approach someone with whatever proposition I come up with once I'm there, how I'll get along if there's no work or I don't find gold right away — I'm thinking things of this nature and studying my maps because the immediate countryside is familiar and of little interest.

This is how you have to be if you want to succeed. You have to figure things out in advance as much as possible. My Daddy once told me he mentally prepared for every bad thing that could ever happen to him, so that when it did he'd be able to handle it without getting all upset. And that's really how he was, the typical Southern country boy, quiet, strong as an ox, never getting loud and upset over nothing. Smart. The kind of man whose eyes were always moving while his lips weren't. Kind of man nobody paid much attention to until he spoke, then everybody hushed to hear what he said. He even told me once when I was a boy that he was prepared for me or Momma or one of the sisters to die. Said he thought long and hard about how he'd feel, what he'd have to do to transact the business end of dying, what would be required of him as a father and husband. Then he said he figured he'd even assume it was going to happen to at least one of us, and in that way he figured he was prepared. Of course this made him a more solemn and quiet man than most, and add to that he fought in the war, well, I'm just trying to give you a sense of the man, and trying to explain the importance of being prepared. None of us ever did die on him, he died on us. And none of us was prepared. So it was that I prepared myself on that train as we rolled north toward Montreal. I went over the route a thousand times, reading and rereading those names that bred fierce excitement in me — Montreal, where French-speaking people lived, Ottawa, which was a foreign Capital City, and then the far western towns, Winnipeg, Calgary, Revelstoke, Vancouver. Rogers Pass. I was going to roll through them all!

Then I pulled out a detailed map of Seattle, the streets and wharves and all. I pored over that, picturing what it must look like, figuring it probably looked a lot like Boston, being on the sea and all. Wondered exactly what street I'd eventually purchase my goods on. And then I leaned back and looked out the window at the rolling hills of New Hampshire and I allowed myself to think up things that might happen to me, good things, like meeting a fine girl in Seattle who decides to go north with me — I'm going to be three thousand miles from Sudbury and Momma, remember — and we strike out on our own up some uncharted valley with a beautiful, rushing stream through it and we hit gold, big nuggets you can pick right out of the water . . . and we build a little cabin . . . and then we'd have a large family I'd be rich enough to spoil, and Lizzie Grady would hear about it all. Or I'm in this gold camp, and everyone's asleep when this big grizzly bear invades us, trying to take our only food for the winter, and in the confusion I'm the one that grabs the rifle and places one through his heart, saving us all. Course real life never is like the life you think up while you're idle. Most women up north wanted two bits just to dance with you, and I recall thinking at the time that dancing with them women must be like dying — when your time is up, your time is up. And the only time I came face to face with a grizzly bear — well, I'll get to that when it comes around. I'll just say now it wasn't anything legends are made of.

But then I finish my maps and finish my thinking and, truth be known, finish with Lizzie Grady too, and I see we're passing over the Connecticut River at White River Junction, Vermont. Now I pay attention. I've never been to Vermont, and for the first time I see mountains, which seem huge to me but later will be put in a much more truthful perspective.

I'm on a train! For seventy years the sound and smell of the railroad was enough to make all young men dreamers, made them want to move and travel, became a solemn and special thing to use. And I wasn't no different. Whenever I heard the B&M — that's the Boston and Maine — going through Concord, it always made me stop and wonder, probably made a thousand souls in a thousand fields stop and wonder, made me think of exotics and faraway places and people, and probably had much to do with the formalizations of a mind that decided to go to the Yukon gold fields later. You've heard of Casey Jones, right?

But my favourite train story happened earlier, when things were cruder, and I heard it before our fireplace after supper one night when Daddy had an old war friend visiting. I always found a fascination when the old Confederates stopped by, which wasn't often, us being Northerners, of course. And whenever these men stopped by I'd always hang close to hear the stories they'd always end up telling, usually after being polite and not mentioning nothing during supper with all the women around. And the best times was when Daddy and his Confederates was alone with no sons-in-law even, just themselves and me, and their memories as pure and clear as spring water. Anyway, this fellow naturally gravitates toward the war after dinner, and Momma's gone after that look from Daddy, and the more the man drinks the more he gravitates, until Daddy and him are slapping knees and swapping stories, each one in his turn, each one funnier or sadder than the one before. And then this man tells us about Andrews' Raiders. I can still see him clear today, his eyes narrowed with alcohol, the play of the firelight on his stubbly grey beard, and his eyes piercing the room with shot-at memories.

"Was April," he says in that low, homespun Georgian voice much like Daddy's, "and was right after Grant defeated our boys at Pittsburg Landing" — and he looks at me with instruc-

Don Reddick

tion — "which now you read as Shiloh. Never agreed on nothing, Manassas was Bull Run to them, Sharpsburg was Antietam. Cripes, we couldn't agree why we was even fighting, they said it was the slavery, we said it was states' rights. I warn't there at Pittsburg Landing though, I was to Atlanta. And when the news come we started north on the railroad toward Chattanooga, which we figured would be next. It warn't garrisoned 'tall." Then, in a Georgian story-pause, he stops and stares at the ceiling and back down.

"We was stopped at Etowah, which lies by Kennesaw Mountain, and it was raining awful and rather mournful it was for most, and quiet with possible excitements of a future engagement at Chattanooga, when all outta hell comes running this man, screaming and a-hollering to git on the train there cause the train just gone through was all Yankees bent on burning all the trestles here to Chattanooga to protect Grant. Actually we didn't know that at the time, but it all come out by and by."

Georgian pause.

"Wall, we git to this train, *Yonah*, and proceed to chase them Yankees, hounding them all the way, not letting them have time to burn nothing, what with help from the rains also, but hair-raising it was, us highballing over sixty miles an hour, turning and weaving and all, any minute expecting them to ambush us, keeping our eyes lit for damaged track — they did this but couldn't derail us — all up past Adairville and Calhoun, up toward Dalton, every now and again catching a view and throwing a shot or two at them, seeing we're not giving 'em no time to ruin the track for us or burn no bridges. Up past Dalton is a tunnel which got us right ascaird, but we go through the tunnel without problems, and now we know we got 'em if they just don't turn their engine on us, which is privately what we all thought and feared they'd do. See, all they had to do was reverse the engine, jump off, and send it full speed at us, and we was meeting the Maker, but they didn't. Least not how it would kill us."

Georgian pause.

"They jumped all right, but by the time they decided to turn the engine on us their steam was near gone from lack of wood and water, and it caused us no harm 'tall." And then the old Confederate told the part that always bothered me, always made me remember Andrews's Raiders.

"We hunted 'em all down like squirrels in them woods, captured every last one of 'em. We never could understand why they didn't reverse the engine on us sooner and kill us all, and I asked one of 'em why later in camp as we was eating. Man looked up and told me cause it warn't part of their plan 'tall to hurt no one, they juss wanted to burn them bridges, is all. We executed near half of 'em."

I will never forget those Southern words before our fire, "We executed near half of 'em." They could have gotten away if they'd only killed the Confederates by reversing the engine, but they didn't because they didn't want to hurt no one, and so they got executed. I never understood why, whether they was saints, or naive, or just plain stupid. To this minute I don't understand why.

Daddy ended it the way he ended all war story nights, wondering out loud, his hands open to the ceiling, a pleading tone to his voice, saying, "Now why, why why why could he ever decide to charge? How could a general who made no other mistake in an entire war send Pickett and Pettigrew and Trimble across that field?"

They had a fiftieth anniversary get-together at Gettysburg. He would have gone. The 1913 reunion. And you know what happened? The Confederate veterans re-enacted the march across the field, Pickett's Charge. Daddy would have been one of them. They walked that mile of open field, men as old as me, just like they did fifty years earlier, all the Federal veterans of Cemetery Ridge waiting above for them like they did fifty years earlier. And you know what happened when them good old country boys reached the top? They started a fist fight with the Northerners, an actual fist fight, all sixty, seventy and eighty-year-old fools, still burning with excitement over being shot at fifty years previous. Honest to Peter.

Meanwhile my train passes through White River Junction, up past Barre and Montpelier toward Rouse's Point in Quebec. Vermont is a near perfect land, with small towns and roads tucked between the mountains, good stone fences well taken care of. The train chugs and squeals along, throwing steam and smoke over and around itself as it travels, the engineer's whistle announcing us to the numerous stops along the way. I'm getting tired by now, and a little hungry. I wasn't able to eat my Momma's big breakfast she got up early to prepare especially for me, what with my turning nervous stomach, so I haven't eaten nothing all day, and didn't sleep much as a matter of fact the previous night. I know I disappointed Momma, not eating that breakfast, a fact I'll always recall.

We stop at the Vermont-Quebec border and on up the steps come the Canadian officials. A big one comes down the aisle, broad hat and shiny black boots, checking everyone's story and looking in billfolds to assure himself they got money, because if they don't they go back. When he gets to me all I can see is the big handlebar mustache and smell the onions. And remember, smelling onions after they been eaten ain't quite the same as smelling them before they been eaten. And he leans down over me and says, "Where are you going, boy?"

"I'm going to Dawson City in the Yukon Territory," I says. The man makes big round eyes and begins to laugh. He gestures to another official, who strolls up, his boots clanking heavy on the wood floor. Now I'm getting nervous in one of those awful moments where you know you done nothing wrong and yet you still feel nervous and guilty for no reason. And it makes you angry although you can't show it.

"What have we here, John?" the new one says.

"He says he's going to Dawson, Yukon," the first answers in a voice that really says, Get ready to toss this one. He looks at me and changes his expression.

"Haven't you heard everyone's back from the gold rush, son? That's six years ago. Let me see your billfold." I fumble out my billfold and hand it to the man. He opens it and I can see his surprise at my money. He continues to peer through it, and I can tell he's doing it only because he's trying to figure a way out of what is fast becoming an embarrassment to him. His friend beats him.

"Leave it be, John, he's all right," he says, and good old Johnny stares at me and drops the billfold in my lap. I take it up and look away because I can't look him in the eye I'm so unnerved, and I hear the clank of boots and his gentler greeting of ladies behind me, and I sigh in relief. But I relate this because I saw for the first time that I was going to be dealing with grown men who might not like me, who couldn't care less about me, or what I thought or wanted or needed.

With this knowledge added to all my other woeful thoughts, you can imagine the feeling that began to drum out of the pit of my stomach. I became so fearful of nothing that I wouldn't leave my seat to buy something to eat at the depot for fear of calling attention to myself. It amazes me still, though I'm old and probably dying, to see what fear can do to a man's soul. And what to make of myself? Here I am, nineteen years old with the nerve to leave home to travel four thousand miles alone, and yet I've failed with Lizzie, I'm beginning to feel I've failed my family, and I lose my first mental confrontation with a grown man. I see myself in different ways, at once strong physically and mentally, but weak emotionally. And I think then of the tears I shamefully let fall at the supper table, and now I *know* I'm weak, and I'm despairing. Along with being tired and hungry and stiff from sitting so long.

We come to Rouse's Point on the flatland of Quebec and

change trains. It's here I buy a loaf of bread and some cheese from a vendor woman I'm disappointed can speak English because I'm wanting the foreignness of French, and it's here I become a bit encouraged with a little fresh air and movement, a little food and even a friendly smile. Even from someone taking my money.

The rest of the trip into Montreal was in darkness.

Such were the mournful beginnings of my great journey. Although my train ride through New England and into Quebec did open my eyes to mountains, it was still an extension of the Sudbury I knew. But when I headed west at last out of Montreal, all that changed.

My goodness did my eyes open! Despite my continuous frugality, I bought a berth for the train ride west to Vancouver. It was just too long a trip not to, though the sight of my precious money leaving me ached like a sore. I thought the man at the window understood my pain, but I've since changed my mind. He greeted me in French, but when I said, "No speak the French," his smile lost itself on a morose, tight lower lip and he spoke to me in English. I thought he disapproved of my frugality, but I've since decided, after being instructed by Albert Forrest, who was from Three Rivers, Quebec, that he just didn't like Americans. English-speaking people.

I slept at first, although the train lurched and had a particular bad bump at every length of track. I remember thinking with a smile that all they needed was another potato famine to correct that problem. But I slept the kind of mentally exhausted sleep that don't really refresh, only lets you wander a while before the shrill of the whistle and the screeching of the air brakes jar you to your unforgiving senses once again, the low, dark streaks of dawn peering sideways at you through them coniferous trees.

Opening my eyes under the covers that first morning out of Montreal, I began to fight the doubt. I learned from my Daddy and my own thoughtfulness the trait of never giving up. Daddy began it all with his talks of the Confederacy, a first-hand insight into what really went on in that war, what it was really like and what really mattered as far as winning and losing goes. Everybody wants to hear about Pickett's Charge or the Peach Orchard or the Corn Field at Antietam, or Fredericksburg, the Wilderness or any other of those awful fights, but the thoughtful, the ones that want to really understand the war look into the trains, the distances, the production of war materials and the potential for manpower of the two sides. What I'm saying is, Daddy told me about why the South lost, not just how. And the image I've retained, and under this image I built my own personal traits, the image is of the Southern boys, barely clothed, without ammunition, without hope at all, fighting at — oh, heck, was it Petersburg? — fighting against the guns of the Federals with rocks and sticks, never giving in until the very end . . . my eyes water at that sight in my mind, I saw my Daddy's eyes water at its memory . . . and that's how I became a resolute and disciplined man. Second Bull Run, that's where it was, not Petersburg, on the hill there with Jackson's men. And today, and probably for a long time to come, Southerners of all walks of life carry on the terrible pride of that army, and don't it seem strange? Well, I'll tell you why it makes sense. It's the image, same as my own, of a David against a Goliath, of never giving in. It's the pride of the South — never give up — and my Daddy's from Milledgeville, Georgia. And I'm my Daddy's son.

It is, therefore, my resolution and discipline not to give up in life, which is what began to kick in the moment my eyes opened up under that blanket. So what if I'm scared half to death and things seem wrong? So what? Go on, and know things will improve. I've seen men — specially where I was headed — who thought that way and did good, and I've seen men who thought negatively and always seemed to end up negative. So there seems to be something to it.

We came to Ottawa early on. It was exciting to me even though the town was indistinct, a low, brick town sprawling up on the south cliffs of the Ottawa River and off down the backside away, looking more like Lowell than much else until the grand spires of the Parliament buildings come into view. These solidified in my mind the foreignness of the place, and not a little time have I spent looking back, wondering what I thought as we came into that city, knowing what I know now about what went on there later. It's where the games were played against those Silver Seven, the greatest hockey team of all time, the experience of a lifetime for me and the other boys who came down from Dawson City the following winter. But how was the forlorn kid to know any of that?

We stopped in Ottawa and I ate something, I can't remember what. I moved around, I ate, I even took a stroll down the tracks a ways to get some exercise, but I didn't talk to nobody. I'm still a New Englander, now.

And here's where the first of the hardness that comes in my story occurs, it happens as I'm walking back up the tracks to the station with the warning whistle blowing. It's cold — but not cold like I'm going to see — and I walk quickly back on the railroad ties, noticing they're spaced just off enough not to let you walk right. Too close. But I'm walking back and I see kids running to the train from the side opposite the depot, they run, three or four of them, jump up and climb the ladders to the roofs and before you know it they're out of sight, lying prone on the tops of the cars, ready to ride. I remember it made me smile, for while many if not most so-called good people loathed the hobos, I did not, but saw them with the twinkle was in Old Sullivan's eyes when he looked at me.

On the spur of the moment I begin to make my first friend

on the road. I cross the tracks and am about to step up onto the platform when the yard dick, which is the guy who knocks the hobos off the trains, comes running up to me. He's out of breath and he stinks of liquor.

"You seen them kids running up the train?" he asks me.

"I didn't see no one," I says, and I feel kind of bad because I always want my lies to be at least literally true. Like I should have said, "I didn't see a one," which is a lie but really ain't because fact is I saw three or four, not one. Like once I'm standing in the grocery and this guy comes in and says to me, "Hey, you driving that red pickup truck?" but he says it in a way I consider inappropriate, rude, so I says to him, "Why no, sir, I'm not driving no red pickup truck," because what I'm doing is standing right here in the grocery, not driving my red pickup truck parked behind your car. But I lied poorly that morning in Ottawa, making me a friend I found out about too late.

The man looks at me queerly, as if he knows he saw them and he knows I must have seen them too, but all along not sure because he's got the remnants of alcohol streaming along inside him. He don't have the sense to believe his own eyes no more, he's drunk so much. Seeing he's not man enough to waste the truth on, it makes me feel better about the lie.

"Now if you'll excuse me, I'm on my way to the Yukon gold fields," I says, trying to express my new-found confidence. The man bellows out a laugh.

"I thought you was a fool!" he says, forcing himself to laugh more. "That's years over!" I walk away from him, stepping up onto the platform. His words bother me, not the part about the gold being gone, which everybody seemed to have to tell me, but the word "thought," he "thought" I was a fool, he said, which meant he looked at me before I said a word — or was it when I lied and his innermost undrunk instinct understood — and he thought me a fool. His attack on my Confederately inspired confidence angered me. But I turned it my way, I'd just have to show them all. Everybody fights the world, but some know it and some don't and some make it worse than it really is. See, that's my way of convincing myself I've got to accomplish things, to think I'm against them all. It's a trick I used all my life, made a stupid comment by a drunken yard dick anger me into resoluteness.

The train jerked into motion, leaving the brick city of Ottawa behind. We entered an immense forest, the likes of which I'd never seen before and didn't see again until I saw the forests of the Yukon, the deepest and awfullest of all. But as we slid into that dark land where there wasn't a soul or trail to be seen, I thought about them kids on the roof above me, wondered about their lives. Hobos was numerous in those days, the remnants and refugees of a half-century of hard times that started with the terrible war between the North and South. After that there was upheaval, what with the movement west and the money collapses and the general depressions that lasted years and years, so that by the turn of the century there was tens of thousands of people, sometimes whole families, riding the rails.

It made a profession for railroad dicks, men whose job it was to knock the hobos off the company trains because they looked bad and therefore was bad for business. Dicks was usually ignorant, mean fellows like that drunk in Ottawa — who else would take a job that required the daily beating of unfortunate poor people? That was the job, to intimidate the hobos bad enough to stay off by beating them half silly every chance they got. Sometimes shooting at them, sometimes trying to hit them.

But the dicks didn't stop them people from jumping the trains, they became a whole community of people who had their own way of living. They heard the lonesome whistle blowing and never came back. And although it was considered bad form to be a hobo or to think them anything more than dirt, I always had a place for them in my heart. See, I didn't know what was about to happen. I was wondering about them kids up there. I bought some salami and a loaf of bread in the dining car and when we stopped before Sudbury — Sudbury, Ontario — still deep in that bogged-down forest, I got out and went to their car and started to climb up. I heard them scurrying off as I did, heard them like you hear squirrels on a tin roof, sliding off away from me.

"Hey!" I called, loud enough for them to hear me but not too loud, "Hey, it's all right." But when I got to the top they was all gone off but one, a beady-eyed, tough-looking little punk with a cap pulled low over his eyes. He lay on his stomach about three feet from me when I came to the top.

"I'm Billy the Pickle," he says in a defiant, hard voice he tries to make lower. "I'm Billy the Pickle and I don't need your trouble."

"I'm George Mason, I'm headed for the Yukon gold fields, and I ain't looking for no trouble," says I.

He kind of looks at me the way everybody looked at me when I told them that, but unlike everybody else he doesn't tell me it was all over and I was a damned fool, he just looks at me in what I think is an odd way until I realize he is looking at the bread sticking out of my pocket. I take it out along with the salami and hand it to him. Now he looks at me like I'm really crazy, with suspicion in his eyes. He moves the cap around on his head a little.

"I believe I'll eat this," he says, as though questioning the reality of the moment, convincing himself it's true. Apparently he isn't used to people climbing up on trains and giving him food.

"Hey," says I, "strange things happen." Just then the whistle blows and I start down the ladder and I hear him mutter, "Holy Hell and God." And that's how I met Billy the Pickle. I met him but I didn't get to know him until later, in the mountains at Revelstoke, which is also important to my story

Don Reddick

because it proceeds down the path of sadness. And sadness, in all its big and small pieces that litter the roadways and railways of life, is what makes you grow up.

But the truth is after thinking about them hobos in the early parts of the deep Ontario forests, I forgot about them. Actually — and I've corrected myself all my lifetime in honour of the kid — Billy the Pickle was a bum, not a hobo, which he later was to explain to me. See, a hobo is a guy who roams and works, a bum is a guy who roams and drinks, and a tramp is a guy who roams and dreams. At the time I forgot about all hobos, tramps, and bums, though I began to feel like two-thirds of the group, as I was more than willing to work and dream. I wouldn't never drink — except once — because Ed Delahanty died from drink and I was a thoughtful, interested person. And disciplined, even in my youth.

We passed through the twisted wreckage of a primeval forest, all the deadfall straying about and leaning and rotting in confusion, with here and there long views of white lakes still frozen in. A lot of water, all frozen. Long stretches of nothing but dark woods and chugging, the odd little bumps at the rail connections, until I must have become mesmerized — just staring for hours at it all. I got tired of studying my maps, I got tired of planning my frugalities. I was tired of loneliness thinking of Momma and the others, and Lizzie Grady. Waking from my daydreams, I was either cocky in my Confederate confidence or scared to the hollowness of my stomach.

We passed tiny villages and small towns with names like Chapleau and Marathon, where we came upon a sight so amazing it broke me from my thoughts, the long, immenseness of Lake Superior breaking through the trees to our left. My goodness was it huge! And I recall the joke in the car, calling it Ocean Superior, in respect. This change livened me up so much I even spoke to the people I ate with the next morning.

Fort William and then Winnipeg. Somewheres around here

we entered the Great Plains. I must have been like a child with his face pressed to the window of the candy store, what with the hugeness and vastness of it all, the land all rolling away in one direction and coming around back at you from another, so that you could see for miles and miles and miles without restraint. At this time the provinces we know today as Alberta and Saskatchewan were still part of the Northwest Territories, along with areas named Athabaska and Assiniboia, and it wasn't until the next year that they was organized into Confederation. The men in the car began a game of spotting deer and antelope, with everyone pasted to them windows in earnest, trying to be the next to point and yell, "Antelope!" It was great fun for a long while, but like the enormous and unending deep forest of Ontario before them, the plains eventually lost some allure.

Truthfully, the allure of the plains did not leave me as soon as it did the others, probably because the prairie was so foreign to me. Which created an instructive situation. See, everybody else got tired of the view so I sort of went along and pretended I did too. It's one of those things in life you do to feel more in agreement with the crowd. And it's wrong, because it usually makes you look foolish like it did me as the train moved through the future province of Saskatchewan. Everyone seemed bored with the scenery, so to be in agreement I turned and said to the man seated next to me, "Doesn't it become such tedium to stare at it hour after hour?" And instantly the man brought home my foolishness by answering, "No, I don't think so. Do you know what happened out there?"

I shook my head, the foundation of shame in my thoughts.

"You're an American," the man said. "You think you're the only ones who've had a revolution. This is where the Canadian revolution took place." My expression showed my surprise and interest, and he continued, pointing across the long, unbent land.

"Louis Riel. Have you heard of him?" Again I shook my

head. I'm thinking that I know all the stories of the American west, but nothing of the Canadian west. Jesse James, Wild Bill Hickock, Promontory — I know most of that. Jesse James's daddy died in the California gold fields when Jesse was three years old, Jesse was shot and killed by Bob Ford in St. Joe's, Missouri, and Bob Ford was shot and killed by Ed O'Kelly in Creede, Colorado. See, I know these things.

"Louis Riel was hanged by the neck until dead less than twenty years ago out here." The man paused at that point and looked out the window, and I realized this was his particular style of story telling, to force me to ask questions. Everyone has their own ways of story telling. I think under normal circumstances this particular form would irritate me, but he spoke of hanging, which has been a subject of interest to me ever since that night by the fire when the old Confederate said, "We executed near half of them."

"What happened?" I asked. The man took a deep breath as though to signify the complete sadness of the tale, then turned to me.

"The railway — this railway — runs straight as an arrow across these plains, but there are many twists and turns to its story. It caused the Canadian revolution — some call it the Canadian Civil War but it wasn't really, there was never any attempt to form a separate state like there was in your country. It rightfully was a redress of grievances, very much like your revolution, but unlike yours, ours failed."

He looks out the window now until I dutifully ask the next question.

"What happened?"

"Do you know the Métis?"

I shook my head.

"Métis. They are the mixed-race descendants of the original voyageurs, mostly of French extraction. For generations they lived in this land, particularly by the Red and Saskatchewan rivers, and for generations they lived nearly as the aborigines lived, relying on the buffalo hunt for their subsistence, along with farming the riversides. The eventual encroachment of the white settlers affected them very nearly the same as it did the Indians, except they weren't considered as low as Indians. Man named Louis Riel was their spiritual leader, a big handsome man with an imposing beard, an eloquent speaker, and a man who felt God was directing him to save his people. He considered himself a kind of Messiah. There was earlier trouble in the '60s, and Riel was banished from the land. Then the railway was being built and the settlers came, and the old problems came back. The government was surveying all the land under new rules, dividing Métis farms and fields through the middle in some cases, and disregarding the old Métis boundaries which had existed for generations."

"Why didn't the Métis complain to Ottawa?" I asked, trying to show how smart I was to know Ottawa was the capital of Canada.

"They did, time and again. But the people who ran Canada were of British descent, while the Métis were of French. Ottawa didn't feel compelled to allow a group of half-breed people of French extraction to dictate policy. And while this was going on, Riel was teaching school in Montana, having visions of God telling him he was to lead his people in their fight for justice."

"You appear to be sympathetic to the rebels," I said. The man shrugged.

"I am a teacher myself," he said. "If you are to teach history, you must review the facts of history with impartiality. I like to think that by reviewing all the facts without allowing your own personal views to distort them, you come up with the truth. A teacher should only teach the truth."

I nodded my head in agreement — this man was ingenious in his outlook. He was already waiting for my next question, feigning interest in something outside on the prairie.

Don Reddick

"Then what happened?"

"Man named Gabriel Dumont, a fellow Métis, showed up one day in Montana with a few others and asked Riel to come home and lead them. Railway was bringing in more and more people, and things had become intolerable. Riel went back with them and again petitioned the government with their grievances, but Ottawa wouldn't see it. And then they decided to defend the honour of their culture by force.

"All along Riel was the spiritual leader, Dumont the military leader. But it was Riel who was the heart and soul of the Métis, it was he who could speak and move the masses. I truly believe there was something godlike in him."

He explained how the Métis started a revolution. Thousands of soldiers came, like they couldn't in the old days without the railway. The man felt that was the Métis' mistake — they hadn't calculated the railway's ability to move men quickly from one place to another. After a short and brutal war the Métis were defeated, Riel walking from the woods one day in surrender.

"His own lawyers," the man said softly, "claimed he was insane to save his life but Riel was too proud to allow that. Said he'd rather hang than be thought insane. At his trial the man spoke the grievances of the Métis with such force and persuasion that men bowed their heads in shame and women were reduced to tears, the jury — all white settlers — finally pleading for mercy for the man they found guilty of treason. But Canada, the same as your United States, wasn't about to interfere with its westward expansion. So in Regina, the exact same week that the Canadian Pacific Railway was being completed, Louis Riel was hanged, a martyr to all French Canadians. The animosity that hanging created between the French and the English was so great it exists still today, and, in my opinion, will exist for a long, long time to come."

"It's funny how things all tie in together," I said and the man agreed.

"No story is a story unto itself. In fact, the irony of it all is that the railway precipitated the final confrontation, and Riel's rebellion completed the railway." The man looked out the window.

"How is that?" I asked.

"See, the railway ran out of money. So difficult was the job of laying the track over the endless bogs of Ontario we just crossed, and then the impossible work through the mountains ahead of us between Calgary and Vancouver, that the whole thing went bankrupt. Then along comes Riel's rebellion, and the railway people made a deal with Ottawa."

"What was the deal?"

"Deal was, we get the government troops to Manitoba within eleven days, and you guarantee financing for the completion of the railroad. Ottawa agreed. The soldiers came, won the war, went home, and the railway was completed with the new government funds while Riel sat in jail for about a whole year, awaiting his trial and execution."

I whistled lowly at the wonder of it all, and the man nodded.

"Hanged the same exact week that the railway was finished across the country. It was a sad business." I thought about it all, looking out over that endless land that appeared so innocent. Then I remembered the other guy.

"What ever happened to the military guy, Dumont?" I asked. The man laughed oddly.

"Gabriel Dumont. He escaped to the United States. Last I heard he was in Buffalo Bill's Wild West Show."

Don Reddick

6

THE STORY HELPED PASS THE HOURS of the Northwest Territories, for even I, in the end, grew impatient with the long grass
outside. But as with any story of truth and history it allowed
the scenery and me to come to an understanding, and the
teacher went on to explain to me many of the ways and means
of prairie existence. But it was the Riel story which occupied
the largest area of my interest. I wondered how men like Riel
and Andrews's Ohioans could sacrifice their lives for their beliefs.

But isn't it a wonderful story? Riel in Montana having visions of being called to defend his people — and he *is* called. By
Dumont. And Dumont now in the Wild West Show! Nothing
more clearly explains what the railroad meant to both the Canadian and American wests, that men who played huge roles in
the development and relinquishment of their cultures in battle
ended up in a travelling show barely a few years later, putting
on mock battles of all they had done. That's how quickly the
west changed, how quickly the railroad changed it — these
were my thoughts as our train approached Calgary.

It was here I sensed strongly the foreignness of the land I
had entered, not just in the all-encompassing landscape, but in
the places we rode through, their recent histories of gunfights
and hangings. Why, Sitting Bull, the man who killed Custer
and his men at the Little Big Horn, had only surrendered from
his Canadian refuge a few years earlier, crossing the border not
far from where I now stood.

There is a wariness a person gets when he knows guns are
present. No one carried a gun back home in Sudbury, Massachusetts, at the turn of the century. The last gunfight in
Sudbury was way before the revolution, when Captain Wads-
worth and his boys was massacred by King Phillip's Indians.
April, 1676, according to the marker. But here I sensed an at-

mospheric change in the demeanours of men. It's difficult to describe properly, for on the one hand I knew the west had quickly changed and to what degree, but on the other the men still carried guns and probably used them easily. And on top of this all I was headed north, to the outreaches of even this crude civilization.

The troubled angles in my stomach reacted to this observation, giving me the sinking feelings once again, which quickly — as usual — grew to include my thoughts of Momma, home, all the sisters and Lizzie Grady. But Calgary provided more agreeable concerns to occupy my mind. I'd never thought much about the place until the day I set foot in it, a few rows of shacks clustered about the railway depot, lost in a million square miles of silent prairie. It was cold the day I disembarked to stretch my legs, though the sky was clear with sun.

And then I saw them. I'd been waiting and waiting, thinking about them as much as anything, ever since I saw the mountains of Vermont, and now, dead ahead at the end of the tracks was the Rocky Mountains, snow white and looming long over the horizon, a wall of snow covered rock stretching north to south. The Rocky Mountains! I couldn't see them before, because the rails go directly west toward them, while the windows searched out north and south. But now, stepping over the side tracks toward some shanties I hoped sold hot food, I stopped and stared at them, my hands on my hips like I was some explorer of renown, estimating my fame and fortune. They made me feel adventuresome, and the excitement I felt, knowing we'd be rolling into them soon, made me step livelier. I tipped my cap to the engineer as he walked about his engine, peering between the big wheels. As his men took on the water needed to create the steam, I crossed the side tracks and opened the door of a store named King's.

King's was a place I'd come to see a lot of in the north, a combination saloon, restaurant, dry goods store and general local hangout. You want something to eat in Calgary, you come to King's. You wanted some whiskey, King's. A shovel, King's. The latest rumour of a gold strike, you come to King's. And after you come you hang about bantering with the locals, and question all the travellers off the trains, particularly those heading east. I wasn't inside the door before all eyes was on me, including four belonging to two redcoated North West Mounted Policemen, one foot each on the brass rail, sipping whiskey.

This was momentous for me, for the Mounties were famous throughout all of North America as disciplined and honest men. This, I was to learn soon, was even more impressive considering the world that swirled around them and the opportunities it created for men in power. Bad opportunities. But to this day I'll tip my water glass toward them, though don't think for a second the men that kept drinking respectable in the north didn't have one once in a while themselves, as I witnessed in King's.

The eyes of a man will tell you a lot about him, I believe this. In King's that morning I got my first look from men that didn't say, Now what is a boy this age doing... or, I don't even know you but I ain't gonna take you serious. The look was of a quiet acceptance that I was to notice throughout the Northwest, this look that said, Maybe I don't know you, but you're here and I respect that. It's a hard thing to place a finger on, but there existed this attitude up there — and I saw it first in Calgary — that was based on comradeship, which was based on men relying on one another more than in civilized areas. It was another thinly veiled glimpse into the danger of it all, Indians and old soldiers, veterans of plains wars who still held that a life wasn't worth all that much, a climate that could kill about as quick, and the danger of passing mountains and waterways, on your own. It was a tough, keep-your-eyes-and-ears-open kind of territory.

I walked into King's.

"Good day, sir," one of the Mounties said, dismounting from the brass rail and strolling, his hand extended, toward me. As I shook hands with him I noticed that I had become the focal point of interest in the shop. There was several others besides the proprietor, two men in mackinaws and wide-brimmed hats playing checkers at a table, their coffee mugs aside, two more men drinking beside the Mounties, one foot each resting on the brass rail, and four or five others scattered amongst the tables, eating. They all watched us, listened.

"Nice to meet you, " I say, not knowing how one man greets another in the Northwest. The Mountie smiles and I realize with surprise that he isn't much older than me.

"My name is McConnell," he says, "May I inquire as to your name and destination?" He spoke in what we called the King's English, and that don't have nothing to do with King's of Calgary. A lost dog couldn't have bigger ears then than all the rest of the men.

"My name is George Mason, I'm from Boston and I'm headed for Dawson City in the Klondike to find gold." Course I learned later that by uttering the word "gold" I got the complete attention of the crowd. I hear one man, a checker player, laugh and slap his knee. I see McConnell smile again, give me a you-sly-dog look.

"Nome?" he says.

"Nome?"

He smiles again, looks back to his red-coated comrade and I see him wink. I don't get it. All I want is some hot food — and I can smell it and see it now — and I'm involved here in a discussion I'm missing part of.

"Where are you really going?"

"Ain't no gold left in Dawson," one of the drinking men says, a man with a long, drooping mustache. He says that, gulps down a shot and slaps the glass on the bar so it makes a pop. I shrug my shoulders. I'm getting it now, I'm remembering Old

Don Reddick

Sullivan's letters from his lost brother who complained bitterly of the lies and misdirections everybody bandied about when discussing gold and where it might be found. But I'm also getting the first-hand realization that, like people told me back home, Dawson City ain't the place I should be going. Nome?

I shrug my shoulders.

"Dawson City."

McConnell nods his head, satisfied somehow I'm telling the truth though it makes no sense to him. "Well," he says, "I wish Godspeed and the best of luck to you," and he turns, walks back to his companion who watches his face, smiling, as he approaches. I look about at the others, trying to read them, see a man with a plate of hot food in front of him wave me over. I sit down with him and the proprietor saunters over.

"What'll you have?" he asks, and I can't see no signs, so I look at the guy's plate in front of me.

"That," I say, nodding toward it and without asking the cost. The man walks away and my waver says to me — over oatmeal and hot bread I see — "You haven't been here before, have you?"

"No sir, I haven't."

"Dawson's played out, only Joe Boyle building dredges and a few diehards up there still. There's better prospects now, Nome, Fairbanks, somewheres that way."

Joe Boyle's dredges! I marvel today at hearing them words in Calgary that morning, knowing what I know now about them both. Joe Boyle. I shake my head even now when I think about that man. But here I look at my new friend. Here I don't know Joe Boyle from Adam.

"Have you been there?" I ask him.

"Been there and back several times. First over the Chilkoot and then the Dead Horse Trail back in '98, '99. It's easier today. The railway's in over the White Pass, which was the Dead Horse. It's the only way to go."

I lean in and whisper, because I don't want nobody to know if I'm asking a stupid question.

"Is it true, I mean, nothing's left at all?"

"Oh, there's plenty left, but it ain't placer and it ain't conglomerated in one place like the original stakes. It's dredge time now, although I'll say one thing. One thing that holds a little hope for you."

"What's that?"

"Nobody ever found the mother lode. It's gotta be there someplace."

We talked more and I ate cornbread and hot coffee at a reasonable price, all things considered, although how the proprietor got cornbread and coffee from oatmeal and hot bread I couldn't understand. I told the man in confidence that indeed it was the mother lode I was after, which was one of my more honest lies, as I certainly wasn't *not* looking for it. I think he believed me, but I'm not sure. See, I was involved with a conversation I didn't entirely understand, which makes sounding confident difficult. I didn't even know what a dredge was, and I wasn't going to ask, as that would expose my ignorance, which is another side of young men's pride. If I'd had the brains I'd have asked everything of this man, that would have been the best help for me, but no, my pride wouldn't allow it. It's why stupid men remain stupid forever, unless they learn better.

I managed to get two more cups of coffee in me before the whistle. Figuring on being smart, I thought there might not be many stops of quality in the long mountains ahead, so I bought a loaf of bread before I left. And outside, as I approached the train, stepping over the sidetracks, I happened to glance up and caught a head ducking down on top of the train. I was surprised, I never thought the hobos would come this far across the plains. How could they not be frozen? Being in a pretty good and suddenly benevolent mood, I rip off a good part of

68   *Don Reddick*

my loaf and yell up to them, then toss it up. I'm not sure of nothing until I hear the voice, sounding lower than it should, say, "Thank you, Sir Mason."

Sir Mason! It struck me that the kid had remembered my name and I was pleased, although there was no mistaking the part of it that was sarcasm. Just a part, an artful way of speaking, actually, incorporating equal parts sincerity and sarcasm. And from a kid so young he tried to make his voice sound lower. What was his name? Billy the Pickle, of course. As I step over the last side rail I reply, "You're welcome, Sir William." Equal parts. Back in the day car I settle in to a row by myself, figuring the mountains will require all of my attentions. I notice the teacher of Riel is gone, I notice the new faces, more women than men, which I find surprising. Quickly the shack town of Calgary falls away behind us, and to my dismay I remember the windows look only north and south, and it will be a couple hours before the train is swallowed by the monstrous jaws of the upended earth. But when we finally enter the mountains, I feel as though my life has changed.

Never in my lifetime have I felt the way I felt the day my train entered the Rockies. Remember, I'm really a naive kid — though I didn't know it at the time and really not for a long time after — a kid from Sudbury, Massachusetts, who marvelled at the mountains of Vermont. And now I'm smeared to the window of a train winding up amongst the picket-straight coniferous trees with the miles — yes, miles! — of rock streaming up through the sky beyond them, on both sides, so that the people in my car, including myself, rocked from side to side to capture every new and changing vista in our hearts. The change from silent prairie to eerie mountains was stunningly rapid, from small, swollen hills to the ripped-out earth in barely a few miles, so quick that if anyone had lowered his head to read for a spell he would have missed it, only to raise his head to this, a newest, wonderful fairy world. I was just plain stunned. The train chugged its way slowly along the track curving to the north and stopped a long while later, the brakeman running back through the cars calling to us all to follow him.

We stepped down from the train and the cold stabbed us like falling icicles, as if the scenery alone was not enough to awaken our senses. The place was a wood stop, badly needed after the infrequent ones on the prairies. While the crew tossed the wood up into the wood car, the brakeman waved us on, never explaining, up a well-worn path in the snow leading into the forest beyond the depot houses. The mountains rose precipitously above us, as though we walked at their bases, and I must say all of us revelled in that quietude, the only sound the squeaking of the snow under our boots and the puffs of our breathing.

When we had walked some way into the silent, snow-laden forest, our guide exhorting us to follow, the man finally broke and ran over a small knoll and appeared to jump for joy, and we hastened, probably twenty of us, to join him. And when I topped the hill I truly believe my heart fell from my body.

"Lake Louise!" our brakeman announced with a reverence bordering on love, and we strung ourselves out along the frozen edge of what must be the perfect lake of the world. On each side, falling to the ice were tree-covered slopes approaching angles of seventy degrees, and ahead, rising up beyond a point where the side slopes fall together, was the sheer mass of monstrous, sharp mountains, covered with a mantle of everlasting blue snow, all of it crowning this jewel of liquid, settled like a diamond flung down by the farthest star in this still remoteness.

We were all of us shocked to a stillness, with the lone exception of our brakeman, who had obviously been here many, many times. He chattered incessantly, pointing now to the tops of the mountains to the left, and now to the tops of the mountains to the right, a stream of joyful, patriotic banter cascading from his lungs, while the rest of us stared dutifully after his finger.

I moved down the lakeshore a piece and ventured out onto the ice, windblown free of snow and black as night. Black ice was a special thing back home in Sudbury. Being able to see right through it, though it stood many inches thick, made walking or skating upon it seem delightfully dangerous when it was not. This we always knew, and yet it had its strange allure, so that whenever nature found itself creating black ice we would always oblige with our skates. I thought of this now, at the top of Canada, and of my skates packed in my bag on the train. It was too special, this dreamlike place, this setting for the gods, and I knew I had to do it. I slid my way across the ice to the brakeman, who stood extolling the wonders of his very own Canada.

"Sir, how much time do we have before the train goes?"

"Ain't going nowheres without me, son," the brakeman replied, smiling. "Within reason, course."

"I've got skates."

The man lowered a suddenly sober, level glance on me.

"Get them."

I raced back through the woods to the train, jumped aboard and ran to my berth. There, from under my bunk, I pulled out them skates I'd decided upon taking on a whim, and returned to the lake.

"Can you skate, boy?" the brakeman asked, the others pulling together around me to see the shiny blades.

"I can skate like the wind," I said then truthfully, pulling off my boots. As I strapped them skates on the brakeman said, "This I got to see, folks. The grandest lake of the Dominion and a man skating on it! If only we had a camera!" I laced the skates as tight as I could and stood up, eager to skate for the folks but feeling the awkwardness of not using them for so long. But this feeling vanished after the first few long strides.

Out onto the lake I went, slowly at first and stretching my arms and legs, then grabbing my cap as it began to blow off my head. Encouraged, I built up speed and off I took across the ice, digging hard against the black, the wind whipping back my hair as my arms, one hand clutching my cap, swung back and forth before me. I fairly flew across that ice . . . and oh my goodness did I soar, as though my soul was lifted from my body and carried across the black ice of heaven, and only then, striding hard away toward the steep rockness of the sheer mountain did I hear the cheers of the others . . . and I turned hard and raced back at them at my highest speed, my legs pistons, my arms rods, firing away through the cold wind until I stopped in a sudden shower of ice chips that flew up and over their heads, their clapping hands. I took a deep bow and clomped up the slope and sat down, the men clapping me on my back, the women looking at me with admiration. Yes! I'll say it, they looked to me like I was a god all right, and the brakeman came to me and said, "You skate very well, son, have you played any shinny?"

Well, shinny is a Canadian word for hockey, which I didn't know at the time, but it didn't matter because I'd never played hockey anyhow. I shook my head, which made him shake his.

"Shame," he muttered, giving me a final slap, and he moved toward the woods as the shrill of the whistle blew tinny over the trees. The others followed, each man patting my back one last time, each woman turning one last glance as they trudged slowly back over the small hill toward the train. They left me alone for a few minutes, alone with the terrible raw beauty. As I caught my breath I looked it over one last, good time. At that moment I loved where I was, wouldn't want to be anywhere else in the entire world, and though I knew nothing of what was to befall me I was certain then and there that only the sweetest winds would ever fill the sails of my lifetime.

7

WE CONTINUED THROUGH THOSE BEAUTIFUL Selkirk Mountains, over Kicking Horse Pass and Rogers Pass, marvels of engineering at the time. I heard it said a man died each day working the railroad through, and looking at the trestles and avalanche sheds, looking at the slopes and cliffs the men perched on to work, it's not surprising. Here and there the old railway towns sat abandoned, ghost towns they'd call them today. Rogers Pass had one, just a line of false-front buildings along the tracks and surrounded by stumps, which was customary of all western towns. See a building, you'd see a bunch of stumps. Some of these ghost towns was old railway centres during the activity, and some was gold or silver towns which paid out quick or not at all, built quick and left quicker. Some of them became wooding stops for the railway because the thrown-up buildings was easy to pull apart for the wood.

These towns was of great interest to me — there are no ghost towns in New England. They seemed terribly stark and lonely as we rolled slowly past, covered with snow now and dead cold, romantic-looking places, framed as they are by the towering Selkirks. Empty. I wondered what they was like in their heydays, and became excited realizing that I'd be entering live ones just like them soon. Where I was going, unlike the settlements of California, men lived mostly a roving life, large numbers moving from place to place looking for the newest gold strike. They'd build a place up and leave it, over and over, so that the Northwest is dotted with these forgotten places. Maybe it's something cold in me, but seeing them starkly naked in the mountain winds, lifeless, forlorn and hopeless, kind of gave me hope, because that's how I felt about half the time myself, at once soaring across the ice of a Lake Louise or standing with my hands on my hips laughing at the mountains in Calgary, and then peering solemnly from my window, slumped, anxious, not knowing why I was here or really where I was going.

We pulled into Revelstoke with the dusk of a purple world, what with the sun long since gone behind the tall mountains leaving behind a semi-darkness, a coldness. We were to stay overnight in Revelstoke because of some malfunctions with the train machinery, and the conductor passed through each car alerting us to the fact. And although the cars was warm with the wood stoves burning hot, I decided to stretch my legs and left the train, walking alone in the near night.

Down away from the tracks I walked, watching the lights of small Revelstoke pop on here and there, and I came to the river which was crusted with snow and ice a third of the way in from each bank, the middle still curving and swimming west, toward the Pacific Ocean. Toward the Pacific Ocean! It was then, shivering in my mackinaw, with numerous mass-produced warming devices covering my head and feet and hands, that I realized we had crossed what is known as the Continental Divide. The Continental Divide is an imaginary dotted line drawn by map makers to instruct us map readers at which point all the rivers flow east into the Atlantic Ocean or west into the Pacific. It's information of dubious value, I believe, but we've used our tax money to mark it with signs all up and down the spine of the continent.

I saw the lights of their campfires from fifty yards off.

"Lizzie Grady, would you look at that," I muttered, stopping and staring. There must have been twenty of them, ragged, bearded, and seemingly filthy even at that distance. All of them wore caps, but I saw none with gloves, only a couple with decent boots. They huddled close to their fires and a few shook pots sitting on the coals, and it dawned on me, when I made out Billy the Pickle, that these hobos was all from our train.

I entered their camp and none called to me but looked at me dully, warily, in contrast to the men at King's in Calgary. I

Don Reddick

stopped, unaware of any impropriety, and finally caught sight of Billy slumped with his back to a tree, a matchstick in his mouth, and sure enough staring at me out from under his low-slung cap.

"Well, it's Sir George Mason, men, guy who gave me the food."

"Got any food?" a man sitting to my right said, turning. He was toothless, a grimy, ugly, and displaced animal. Big.

"I ain't got no food."

"Then get the hell outta here," another said. It's then that I recaptured my uncertainties among those faces of ignorance and need.

"I was looking for Billy the Pickle is all," I said, thinking of an excuse to be there. The grimy animal stood up and faced me square.

"What you want with him?"

The question caught me off guard, of course. I saw them all — there were two women and one small child amongst the men — glaring at me now. And in the seconds it took for my mind to work I understood that this is a sad, miserable lot, un-friendly and perhaps even dangerous. Fear built in my stomach, but I kept my voice firm. I think.

"None of your business," I answered, and Billy the Pickle jumped up and I saw I'd said something I shouldn't. And this is the most extreme example of stupid man's pride, to say something in defiance when in a vulnerable position as I was.

I swear the grimy man frothed at the mouth, but Billy the Pickle had moved.

"Get away there!" the frothing man yelled at him, but Billy strode quickly to me and grabbed my arm and pulled me along. I turned and stumbled, looking back at the grimy one who now yelled incoherently, waving a wooden spoon. I heard another yell at him to shut up as I was led back along the river.

"Let go of me," I said when I realized I was still being led by the arm. Billy the Pickle let go and stopped. He removed his

cap and pushed back his haphazard, dirty hair, and I could now
see for the first time he was just a kid. Fifteen, maybe. Fourteen.

"What the hell!" he said, his voice no longer low, and with
the accent on the "hell."

"Huh?"

"What, are you suicidal?" he asked, with a serious tone of
voice confirming my worst recent fears. "Last man who came
in like that was beaten silly. If you hadn't given me that food
you'd a been beaten silly too. What's wrong with you?" It was
a shock to be trimmed down by a kid four or five years
younger than myself, but it was happening, and there was little
doubt the kid felt allowed to do it. Which itself was odd. I
frowned.

"How old are you?" I asked.

"My God, you are stupid, aren't you," he says back. "You're
not used to out here, are you?"

I shake my head.

"You don't understand, do you?"

Again I shook my head. I began to feel very stupid, my head
wagging and tongue-tied and all. Billy the Pickle laughed in the
cold night. He clapped his bare hands and let out a long, winding wolf howl. The howl was echoed back by several drunken
voices from the camp, disturbing, spiralling against the purple
mountains.

"See, we're animals," Billy the Pickle said.

"You're a poor excuse for even a hobo," I said to him.
"Look at you, you ought to be ashamed of yourself, why are
you with such a morbid crowd?"

He gave me a funny look.

"What kind of accent is that?" he asked.

"See here," I said, trying to sound formal and in charge,
"you're filthy and you speak without respect. If I was your
daddy I'd beat you with a belt."

"I never had a daddy." He said them words with a blank

Don Reddick

stare which chilled my cold bones. It took me aback. "I come from nowhere," he said while I was still deciding what to say first. "There is no such thing as daddy, see, you don't understand. I'm the son of a man who never lived. Lucius is my jocker." He rocked his head back toward the camp, and since nobody else made any notice there I realized he must mean the disgusting, grimy man.

"You don't understand," he said again when I did not respond. I looked at him in confusion, so he said, "Prushun. Understand? Prushun."

"Prushun," I murmured, "Prushun . . . " and I turned the half-remembered word in my mind. I wasn't keen on hobo slang but you did hear the words now and then, and slow but sure I recalled, and recalled with horror. Remembered jocker, too.

"Prushun!" I exclaimed, and poor Billy the Pickle nodded.

I looked at Billy the Pickle that night long ago in the chilled darkness between the snow covered mountains, the river trickling along beside us. It was so quiet in them mountains you could hear lake ice cracking a mile off.

"You got to leave them," I said to Billy the Pickle. The look he gave me was his answer.

"I mean it," I said, "you don't have to put up with that kind of life. No one deserves that."

"You don't know nothing."

"I know what's right and what's wrong."

"You don't even know what a hobo is. You call me a hobo, I ain't no hobo."

"Well if you ain't no hobo, what in Sam Hill are you?" I said. And it was now that Billy the Pickle instructed me.

"Know the difference between a hobo, a tramp, and a bum?" he asked.

"Ain't no difference."

"Sure there is, and I'm going to tell you. But remember first you ain't no friend of mine, you're acting like my business is your business, talking about if you was my daddy, well you ain't. You're a stupid eastern fool that I'm gonna take one minute of my time to teach something to. Understand?"

I stared at the kid.

"A hobo wanders and's willing to work. A tramp wanders and dreams his dreams. And a bum wanders and drinks his drinks. Got that?"

"You won't work?"

"Hell, no."

"You dream?"

"Dreaming is for fools. I haven't dreamed that way since I was two or three."

"You're too young to drink."

And Billy the Pickle smiles at me now, baring a fine line of whiteness in his mouth amidst the darkness of his soul. It was a smile, a wink, that told me drinking was what he loved most. I reacted with appropriate disgust.

"You ever heard of Ed Delahanty?" I asked him.

"Second-best hitter ever lived," came his quick reply. This stuns me, throws me off my purpose.

"What do you mean second?"

"Keeler's the best. Everybody knows anything about baseball knows that."

And that was the end of our conversation. I was agitated, angry that he was a prushun and a bum and didn't know who the best hitter in baseball was, and he thought I was a naive fool from back east. I swore to myself I'd never attempt to help anyone again who didn't want to help himself, and I stomped away through the squeaky snow in disgust, Billy the Pickle doing his wolf howl behind. It was a narrow, darkened path I stumbled, and unknowingly a path of sadness.

8

I FORGOT TO DISCUSS CLASSICAL music earlier. I forgot to say that in the evenings at Lizzie Grady's house on Marlboro Street in Boston we used to listen to her parents' classical music. What we did was sit in the parlour and discuss what was going on at the time around the country and the world, like digging that ditch through the jungles of Panama, or what we were to do with the new possessions like Puerto Rico and the Philippines we got from beating the Spanish. Lizzie's father — I could never refer to him as Dad — Lizzie's father would lead these discussions, and when they ended he would play classical music on the phonograph.

"Well, I think we've done enough with the world tonight," he'd always say to end it, slapping both knees with his hands and rising, and he'd put on one of his records and walk upstairs with Mrs. Grady, leaving me and Lizzie alone. This formal time was pleasant for us because it was behaviour her folks, like most Boston folks, thought acceptable, despite all this Victorian business, and it definitely was courting procedure, regardless of what I might think of it. And we thought it humorous, us sitting across from each other like proper Bostonians, when outside in the streets we ran hand in hand.

And the music we listened to was classical, and it was strange to me. I said to Lizzie one evening that my Daddy once told me music wasn't music unless there was strings of some kind, meaning fiddles and guitars, and she laughed at me and explained that most of those sounds was violins. Well, I'd never heard a fiddle sound like them sounds off the phonograph, but I laughed anyways. My point is, I just had no appreciation of classical music. I tried, I listened, many a night during our magical year of '03, but the stuff just never clicked with me — until I saw the Rockies.

The shimmering snow, the crystal mountain streams froze

solid over the rocks, framed with the vertical climb of the cliffs — all of it a beauty I had never before visualized. These were the Selkirk, the Caribou and the Monashee ranges. And as my train, with hobos and tramps and bums hanging to the top, chugged over, around and through them, all I could hear was the chords of the masters I never before appreciated. And it all ended two days later when we rolled across the coastal flatlands into Vancouver.

Apprehension descended upon me as I stepped from the train at the depot, my bags in my hands, and it was discouraging that there was no one to receive me, no one to happily walk off and drink coffee with as I saw others do. I was alone and thinking such thoughts when I heard a great commotion beside the train. I ran down a ways with some others and looked between two cars and was almost hit by two hobos tearing through and past us, and behind them was the fisticuffs, the railway dicks beating up a hobo they'd caught and thrown to the ground, flailing arms, flying rags. I watched for a moment but could take no more, so disgusting a sight it is to see three men beating one. And of course Billy the Pickle came to my mind, and I shuddered. I turned in disgust and walked away, trying my best not to think of it.

Vancouver is bigger now, but in 1904 it was big too for the age, with asphalt streets and electric cars, row after row of brick businesses and monstrous hotels, like a good-sized New England town by the sea, only this was the western sea, the Pacific, surrounded here by mountains. The depot was downtown and there was liveliness around everywhere, and I proceeded to a tavern which, Calgary taught me, was the best location to learn facts. I needed the facts regarding transportation down to Seattle so I could buy my necessary goods, but it was then and there that the quirks of fate began their descent on me, though the final blow would not fall until Skagway.

Don Reddick

There's not much point in regretting it, after all, it was perfectly good advice. I just wished I'd never heard it.

Downtown Vancouver is on the waterfront, which lies just beyond the depot street and is lined with long wooden fish buildings, always mysterious to me as I wasn't a seafaring person. What went on in them I never could tell, all I knew was fish came in one side alive and kicking and out the other in tin cans, and after each shift out wandered the lost fish souls of the world, hungry for liquor and reeking of the semi-sick odour. It was this sort that inhabited the tavern I entered, whose name I've lost from memory.

Inside was hot from the numerous bodies pressed against the bar and all over the tables, a big black stove cooking away in the centre, the place alive with laughter and talk. A man with a long fiddle sat on a stool in one corner staring blankly, waiting to play when someone'd throw a coin at him. I went to the front and ordered water, which didn't appear to impress the men I broke through to achieve the bar. But they were friendly, gregarious people and we spoke to each other immediately.

"Where you going?" one man asks, hunkered down over his glass of beer. Others poke their heads around to see me, all eyes wondering at new people.

"I'm going to Dawson City to look for gold," I answer, and one man laughs, another raises his eyebrows, as much as to say, Well, it's not like I got any better ideas. And I inquire about transportation to Seattle.

"You don't have to go to Seattle no more," the hunkered-down man says to me. "That's years ago. So much stuff is up in the panhandle you can get it there. Stuff half the idiots just dumped when they gave up and come back."

"Is that right?"

"Go to Seattle then, I don't give a damn," he says.

"I'm sorry, I didn't mean to offend you," I say. The man

looks me over and sips his beer. The guy without any better idea peeks at me again over his friend's shoulder. The first man seems to realize that I'm okay.

"Don't go to Seattle. The whole kit and kaboodle can be bought at Skagway, you'll save the cost and trouble of getting it all up there. You'll want to go to Skagway, it's where the railway is."

"The White Pass," I affirm.

"The Dead Horse Pass," the man nods. He's referring now to the nickname the trail got in '98, when men misused a thousand horses in that place, and where most of their bones still lie. That sordid, cruel business left lasting, bad impressions on all who endured it who had a soul. Why, it even bothered Jack London, who published *The Call of the Wild* during my magical year of '03, and he was one legendary tough nut. The railway was built in '99 I think, to prevent the hardships of the two main trails inland, the Chilkoot over to Dyea, and the Dead Horse Pass at Skagway.

"You sound knowledgeable on the territory," I say to the man, and he nods solemnly.

"I was a pioneer of '98," he says slowly, turning to me, and I notice the respectful glances he receives, though there is no crowding in, which leads me to understand his story is known here. He's local.

"But I never made it to Dawson, didn't have to. I'm a seaman, I made my money getting the boats through Miles Canyon with Joe Boyle."

There is that name again, the name I heard in King's in Calgary. Joe Boyle, I know I remembered hearing it before, but I couldn't remember where. I imagine my eyes was wide as dollars as I listened to this man, though later I would realize he was winking when he spoke of Boyle. I doubt now this man ever laid eyes on the King of the Klondike, never mind worked with him.

"In '98 it's like now, you need a whole year's provisions to enter the Queen's territory, even if you was Canadian, which I am, eh? Now, do you realize what a year's supply of grub is?"

He looks at me and makes me shake my head.

"A year's grub consists of about eleven hundred pounds. That's only the grub, eh? It don't include candles, rubber boots, coal oil, rope, saws, files, hammers, mukluks. The whole of it covers two thousand pounds."

"One ton," the other peeks around and says.

"One ton," the pioneer of '98 nods. Now, I've learned these rules from Old Sullivan's lost brother Patrick, but with the weight of this man's look the weight of the goods becomes realer to me. All this stuff's got to be moved from point A to point B, which in the gold rush days meant Seattle to Dawson, but which I'm now instructed means Skagway to Dawson.

"We had to carry it all in, or hire someone or something to carry it. Today you just throw it on the railway," he says, a tinge of prideful disgust in his voice. He sips his beer. "And that's just the beginning. Then we had to build boats on Lake Bennett that had to be navigated over the Squaw Rapids after Miles Canyon there, and through eight hundred miles of Yukon River to that swamp town."

"But you never went there?"

"Hell no. I seen my opportunity right off when one boat after another broke up on the rocks because them city boys couldn't handle a rowboat, never mind them boats we built on Lake Bennett. And there were a thousand of them boats, and they all had to traverse the rapids. It's where I met Joe Boyle, we got rich together there that spring and summer."

"Why didn't you go to Dawson?"

"Because right away we began ferrying boats both ways, eh? They started coming back almost as soon as they got there, like for half of them getting there was the whole point, not working like a dog scraping frozen ground where there might or might not be gold. You got to remember, all the right spots was gone before word even got outside about the strike. You know what I read just the other day?"

"What is that?"

"I read sixty million dollars was spent by fifty thousand fools so forty men could extract ten million dollars in gold."

If the words were true, and I can assure you now with my *World Almanac* as proof it was close, it was a lousy-looking statement of the conditions up there. The doubts increased again in my mind, and I winced inwardly at the thought of attempting to do something that near fifty thousand others had recently failed to do. As stupid as it sounds, the advice of so many others who grasped this fact before myself came to me now, made me doubt myself the more. How many had laughed at me?

"But you know something? Nobody ever did find the mother lode." I drank my water and thanked the man, my confidence restored.

I made my way down to the wharves, inquiring for sailing ships or steamers, and was directed near a mile off to the correct wharf. As I walked for it I noticed the giant trees that lay stranded on the beach stones, great, dark red trees of enormous girth, floated down from some logging camp in the primeval forest. So large were they that I stopped to inspect them, read the initials carved into them, looked out to sea and then turned around to view the picturesqueness of the town, framed as it was with the snowy mountains above.

I booked passage on a steamer the next day. But don't think I squandered any money that night on any luxuriousness — which at that point meant anything not moving and with a roof. Frugal to the end as a matter of principle, I slept that night in near-freezing weather under my blankets on the stoney beach amongst them huge trees, the smaller bits made into my only companion that evening, my fire. I slept well, considering my body continued to rumble and clank with the train and was about to start rolling with the currents. Despite lying on the most obnoxious stones that beach had to offer.

I can't remember the name of the vessel I boarded the next day, but to my astonishment I saw Billy the Pickle and others of his kind on deck, their meagre belongings in a pile by the rail. Where'd they get the money? In one of them awkward moments our eyes met and we nodded but didn't say nothing, and I moved to the other side of the ship and stashed my gear against a corner.

I immediately considered my finances, the saving of money not only in not shipping all my goods from Seattle, but in the days I saved by not having to go there. To me every cent was sacred, it's why I drank water in taverns and ate bread and cheese on trains. It's not that I enjoy these basic foods, it's that in times of necessity a man needs to be frugal to a fault. It increases his odds of survival, and I revelled in every dime that remained in my pocket. In retrospect, it's part of the reason I got into so much trouble, this kind of responsible greed.

We steamed from Vancouver in the latter part of the month of March. Snow was still very much evident in the weather, and low, heavy mists floated across much of the ocean between the mainland and Vancouver Island. My bunk was on the deck, come hell or high water — literally — and my pack was my pillow. The steamer was uncrowded, unlike the mayhem Patrick Sullivan saw in the rush days of '98 and '99. I recall thirty or forty deckers, as we was called, and maybe twice as many passengers in the cabins below. Some were gloriously decorated with wide-brimmed hats and outrageous get-ups, others, like myself, rather nondescript, and still others like the Billy the Pickle people, ragged, dirty and unapproachable.

The kid weighed on my mind, as I just could not get the useless feeling of a wasted life out of me, and I found myself walking the rails, pretending interest in the mist-shadowed, secret mountains rising from the water's edge, but the whole time I was eyeing that crowd, determining how I could approach him. I think in honesty I had more than sympathy for Billy the Pickle, I was interested in their nomadic life and the confident toughness of a kid much younger than myself. See, I lacked confidence at times, and I found myself watching men who did not.

I felt this way in my youth, but as I grew older I came to the realization that in fact there were very few men who were really confident, the truth emerging that it was just a matter of appearing that way. I also noticed much of it had to do with the various successes or failures a man endures, which frequently involve luck or fate. And here is the sharpest point to this angle: confident men are often experienced with success, but failed men have the experiences that wizen a man, so that often in life it is not the beaming, striding leader you should turn to for advice, but the Old Sullivans — and Billy the Pickles — of the world, littering the railroad tracks and byways. It is from men like these that true wisdom flows, but because of their circumstances, few listen or seek. It's why I have optimism for this young Kennedy fellow, even though he's a Catholic. See, not only is he from an Irish family that did well back in the days when the Irish started out in the morning with two strikes against them and nobody on base, but he's experienced the disaster in life, too. Do you know his older brother Joe got killed in the war, a sister died in a plane crash, another one of his sisters is retarded? Can a family have more tragedy than that?

I remember an old Confederate warrior sitting at our table, the fire behind, sadly shaking his head about an old nigger he'd encountered on the side of the road after Atlanta. Said the man talked to him with such a wizened sadness, such a human outlook mixed with understanding and insights regarding each of their positions, that he went away troubled forever. At the same time he'd heard the speeches of Jefferson Davis, understanding the realities this kind of man had produced. The South, his whole land and life, lay in ruins. I remember the silence in the room after the old Confederate warrior concluded his story, and the hung heads of his fellow rebels admitting the truths of it, if only for the whiskeyed moment. And my Daddy breaking that awful silence by asking if anyone was ready for more, and all of them speaking up at once. I caught Billy the Pickle alone, leaning against the rail the first afternoon out. I came up and leaned myself, not saying nothing. After a long while he spoke first.

"Ain't saying Delahanty wasn't no good," he said suddenly, making me smile inwardly. "But cripes, Lajoie's just as good. Won the batting title last year, last man to hit four hundred, too. It's Keeler, though, that's best. Eleven straight years over three hundred. Twelve if you count his first year with only a few at bats."

"Delahanty hits harder," I replied, "averages about forty-five doubles a year. All Keeler does is hit banjo singles."

"Don't average forty-five no more, does he?"

This dig angered me but for once in my lifetime I showed restraint in discussing Big Ed Delahanty. But think of my position here, listening to a drinker putting a deceased individual down who died by drinking, while I'm propping him up. I sensed I was going to lose a battle here very quickly.

"Boston beat Pittsburgh, eh?" I said, imitating the Canadian's "eh" and referring to the first World Series Lizzie and I attended the previous October.

"They was lucky."

"Lucky? How can you say that? Dineen and Cy Young won near fifty games between them last year. They wasn't lucky, they're good."

"They was lucky."

I got angrier and just shook my head. Billy the Pickle said, "They're a scab team in a scab league and wholly without respect. I hope next year they don't play no American League team in a playoff, keep it strictly National."

Naturally I disagreed with him.

"They'll play, " I said.

"No they won't."

"Sure they will."

"No they won't."

"Well, why not?" I asked, exasperated by Billy the Pickle's mode of argument. And it was here that I began to see the depth of wisdom the young kid kept inside him.

"Baseball is becoming bigger business every day," he said. "The embarrassment factor is what they'll drum up, but in the meantime they'll wanna see if the American League fails like all the others, and also sign off as many good players as they can to nail down their own popularity. If they lose a World Series again in 1904, they're in big money trouble." I looked at the kid, amazed at his depth of perception, although I didn't necessarily agree with it all. I wondered how a boy like this, a prushun under a jocker, could develop such a mental constitution.

"How do you know so much about baseball?"

Billy the Pickle smiled and looked up at me. "You said you was from Boston, right? I been to the Huntington Avenue ball grounds. Seen the Pilgrims last year. The new park, stands with the twin peaks, right?"

I nodded my head.

"South Station ain't far from it. It's what I do in different towns, go to ballparks and sneak in. I seen Bennett Park in Detroit, the Polo Grounds and Hilltop Stadium in New York, South Side Park with the White Sox in Chicago. It's easy to sneak in. Easier to steal the food. You hold your hand up like you got your coins in it, they hand you the frankfurter or popcorn and you run. Easy. So many people milling about they lose you right away."

"You steal food?"

"No, I meet people like you all the time walk up to me and give me it. You just fall off the pumpkin wagon or what?"

"Look here," I said, "you can't see my strengths because of your warped outlook. You don't know me."

"Your strength is weakness," he shot back. "The only way you'll survive up here is on the sympathy of others."

My anger made me turn and walk away, and I heard him spit into the ocean as I did so. What to make of this kid? He no longer used his low voice with me, which I took to mean he no longer regarded me as a stranger. But his ability to say what he thought without fear impressed me, though at the time I felt only irritation.

We steamed north in the cold and I thanked the Lord my Momma had the sisters mass-produce the warm things they did. Two pairs of socks, two pairs of mittens. Two pairs of underthings hid beneath my wool shirt and mackinaw. All of it below my cap. I was outside and there was no getting away from the cold, which I made good in my mind as preparation for the Yukon. We sailed through the Queen Charlotte Strait at the top of Vancouver Island, through Queen Charlotte Sound, past the Queen Charlotte Islands, where, I was told, there was a town called Queen Charlotte.

It was a normal four or five-day voyage from Vancouver to Skagway, depending on the weather and the steam engines. Again my appreciation for classical music continued to resound through my soul, as we moved through magnificent scenery, rivalling the wonders of the Rockies. Great, snow-covered mountains fell into the sea on all sides of us as we entered the archipelago, a low mist and some snow squalls creeping up their sides and falling into their valleys, surreal and mysterious.

If I've ever been to an enchanted land, it was here. Around us swirled a million seagulls, and often we were surrounded by hundreds upon hundreds of porpoises, and occasionally whales were sighted and travellers would shout and point, as we had pointed at antelope on the train through the prairies. So engrossing was the scenery that I would forget my discomfort from the cold, staring for hours on end as we meandered our way slowly north, every turn drawing a dramatic new change in the view. We entered American territory — Alaska! — and stopped at St. Mary's Island, where all ships were required to check in with American customs.

Later we stopped at Fort Wrangell for an evening, and quite a sight this place was. Most of the houses stood on stilts, as the main street was covered twice a day with the tides. And many totem poles leaned here, standing sadly sentinel to some losing culture. I saw Indians, and no naivete here, as they bargained and bartered various goods and services as well as any Arab. Again I watched the hobo tribe, waiting for trouble, but none occurred. Word was they was headed for Fairbanks in the interior of Alaska, but no one knew by which route, so uncommunicative were they. I could stand it no longer. Finally I found Billy the Pickle where I could speak to him without the disapproval of his master, and offered him what I suspected he could not refuse.

"I'll buy you a drink," I said, and his eyes lit up in the remorseless manner of drinkers. We entered one of the multitude of saloons that lined the stumpy, mud-flowing alleys. Inside was warm, which was of great satisfication to me. A man banged away at a piano in one corner, a line of men cowered against the bar, still others played billiards in the middle. We sat down and I saw Billy the Pickle wince when I ordered him a beer and me a glass of water.

"You're embarrassing," he said, then yelled at the man to make his whiskey. He then turned to me with his knowing eyes and folded his arms, as if to say, Okay, now what do you require from me for this?

What I wanted was what I got. With a couple of drinks in

Don Reddick

him he opened up, told me as harrowing a story of youth as could be believed, growing up as he did under an alcoholic man he assumed was his father, who made him from the earliest he could remember go out and beg nickels so the old man could drink. He ran at age eight or nine, he could not recall, and had rode the rails since, becoming a prushun, though he would not speak of this. It was clear that the arrangement afforded him safety to an extent, but the whole business reeked of sadness, futility. He told it all in jagged sentences, shrugging his shoulders, swearing, seldom looking me in the eye the more he drank.

"How old are you?" I asked.

"I don't really know. That's why I don't know how old I was when these things happened."

"What are you going to do?"

"That's a stupid question."

"No it's not, you can leave." I hesitated a moment. "You could come with me."

I believe I saw a glimmer of hope in his eyes, but it passed as quickly, probably with the sadness of a history of lies that had been his lifetime. He did not know me, he was suspicious of me. But I saw a glimmer of hope.

"I should be where I am," Billy the Pickle said.

"I think you should consider my offer," I replied. "I think you should be honest with yourself and see how you're living, see how you could live. This is a place of free choices, you know. You don't have to live like this." I tried to say these words without the disgust I felt. Billy the Pickle finished his drink and placed his glass down on the table.

"Possibly you think too much," is all he said, and he got up and walked away, out into the Alaskan air. That's all that happened in Fort Wrangell.

Our journey, our glorious sea journey came to an end when we approached the long twin wharves of Skagway, jutting out to greet us from the mountain-crowded town, nestled as it was at the end of a long arm with the purple heights rising on all sides. Little did I know in my wild excitement that it would be here in this infamous mud town that my adventures would truly begin.

9

THE ADVICE I RECEIVED in the warm tavern in Vancouver proved truthful. Skagway was not the overrun town it was during the height of the rush, but the main street remained lined left and right with the numerous saloons and hotels, many of which were tents struck up behind the wooden facades. Every manner of gear was here, everything a man needed to survive in the hostile airs of Alaska or the Yukon. l cannot tell you how exhilarated I felt, inspecting every store I could, all the available goods, company prices, planning with frugality the savings I would realize.

I had most of seven hundred dollars. I needed food for one year, as the law stated. Sleigh service was now available to Dawson from the end of the White Pass Railway in Whitehorse, so I did not require the multitude of tools the original argonauts required to build their boats. I could travel much lighter, although transporting one thousand pounds of food was hardly a cakewalk. But I was mentally prepared. And the Indians proved plentiful in their offerings to carry goods, which eased my concerns on that matter. I held off buying until I could determine the lowest possible prices. And I ran into Billy the Pickle. He confirmed that his people were waiting the departure of the steamer, their destination the newer gold fields over toward Fairbanks. On a boardwalk we stood, the mud of the street below knee deep, and again I proposed to him his freedom.

"You can come with me," I said, knowing there was not much time to dicker. He glanced over his shoulder and blew on his hands to warm them. He appeared stuck betwixt and between, encouraging me, and again I saw the lonesome, love-starved stare of hope mixed with his customary mournful suspicions. He spat in the mud.

"Buy me a drink," he said, and I agreed, as it was probably my last possible chance to sway him. I knew I could help this poor boy, I knew with common sense instruction and leader-ship I could show him a proper way to live — such are the miscarriages of youth.

Everything that transpired this day drew me closer to the fate that lay in wait, like some Shakespearean play or some-thing. I put off my purchases to be with Billy the Pickle. We entered the nearest saloon, place called McGilvary's, and sat down, the wonderfullest strains of a violin falling from one corner, the usual crowd of men with one foot each on the brass rail, spittoons, billiard table, gambling devices and loud laughter. Billy the Pickle appeared very much at home amidst this debauchery, he stared keen-eyed at it all, nothing missing his alert mind. I bought him whiskey. I bought myself water. I noticed many of the men leaned in around one, a dark, short man with a long, drooping mustache. I turned to Billy the Pickle.

"Wonder who he is?" I said, and immediately a man at the table behind us tilted backwards on his chair.

"He's Tom Horey!" he said and nodded its truth, and I real-ized I should have appreciated this information, though I did not have the slightest idea who Tom Horey was. But where I would just nod and pretend to understand, Billy the Pickle shot back, "Who in Sam Hill is Tom Horey?"

"You don't know who Tom Horey is?" the man asked with incredulity.

"If I did I wouldn't be wasting my efforts with you, now would I?" Billy the Pickle said flat out. Despite the rudeness I could not help but admire the kid's ability to verbally stomp out a rival. So intimidated was the man that he replied, "Tom Horey's the man who caught Louis Riel."

With this information my mind went wild and I stared at the man holding court at the bar. He seemed very drunk and smiling. I also remember thinking that no one caught Louis Riel, he walked from the woods to surrender on his own.

"He's such a hero to the Mounties that he's the only man they let get roaring drunk and don't arrest up in Dawson," the man said.

"Who's Louis Riel?" Billy the Pickle asked. I briefly instructed him as I was instructed on the train through Saskatchewan. Billy the Pickle frowned when I finished.

"I seen Dumont in the Wild West Show," he said. "Saw Sitting Bull too. Annie Oakley. I heard Annie Oakley made it up to Dawson."

"You paid, I hope."

"Only a fool in this life pays when he don't have to. Seems to me you're gonna be paying the rest of your life."

I did not allow my infuriation to show. Here it was again, though. Despite me buying him drinks, why, he was beholden to no one. You could not court him, he only courted you. But then he turned.

"Seems to me Louis Riel had to die," Billy said, eyeing the bar. "See, he was a white Indian. Survival of the fittest, I say. All the French Canadians should be hung, but civilization won't allow it these days. To be civilized means to thwart evolution."

"Where did you learn that?"

"You don't learn stuff like that. You sense it."

"Well, don't be so surly about it. Someday I hope you'll find there's a whole other world out there, and it ain't stuffed with the hostility, meanness and hardship you see now. I saw a Win-

Don Reddick

chester cavalry rifle today, cost too much, though. I'd be complete with that, I'd give anything for that rifle."

See, I changed plans mid-stream. I did not wish to fight with Billy but free him, convince him to come with me. I realized mid-sentence I was leading us into another fight.

"Where?" he asked. He's asking about the Winchester.

"Two stores down. With the wooden Indian out front." He nodded and sipped his drink.

"I want to get drunk with Tom Horey tonight," he said.

"I don't think Tom Horey wants to associate with the likes of you," the man behind us said. I thought he was referring to Billy the Pickle's hobo looks, but that was hardly the case, and hardly the person he was actually addressing.

"Hey, boys," he called to the crowd surrounding Tom Horey, and they looked over. "This fellow here seems to think Louis Riel is some kind of hero or something." I realize now he is referring to me, and I instantly see the look in Billy's eyes, and the sound of general bad interest from these men. They come over to the table, famous Tom Horey weaving in front of them all.

"You defending Métis rubbish?" Horey says, and I stare at him with fear and confusion. The man himself appears to be a half-breed. Billy speaks up.

"It's all a joke, boys. We know who you are, Tom, we was just making a joke is all." I stare at Billy the Pickle as he says this, then try to smile myself. I can see these men have a hatred in them regarding this topic, and I understand immediately that being right in your outlook on a subject don't necessarily make you safe.

"I just said I want to get drunk with you tonight, Tom," Billy says hastily. "I was just saying we should hang all them Frenchmen. You know?" Tom Horey looks us over as indecisively as possible, his eyes dark and hungry to protect his shot-at beliefs.

"I guess this is all right," he says at last, and the men move slowly away, some with back looks that mean they weren't fooled like good old famous Tom. I try to act normal.

"When does your steamer sail?"

"It don't. Not today. Engines are being maintenanced. Captain said it would be sometime tomorrow, late."

I understand this to be good news, there would be no rushing out for Billy the Pickle. I feel the draft from the door as another group of men enter, the day becoming much, much colder. I want to get Billy out into it, as drunkenness would settle nothing this night. But Billy the Pickle won't let the thing go by without chastising me. He leans close and whispers, "You're a fool that'll kill us. Why the hell do you think I said them things? Do you really think I believe all French Canadians should be hung? You got to think before you speak up here."

I stood up, the whole thing shaking me with fear and anger. "I've got something to show you," I said then, and he followed me into the waning daylight without protest.

Over and into the freezing mud we stumbled, through the shanty town, until we came to the railway depot. Moving past it, we clambered up the hill beyond and stood looking down at the rails, at the town of Skagway nestled as it was amidst them cold, purple mountains.

"It's the train that takes us toward Dawson," I pointed, and Billy nodded. "It goes to Whitehorse, which is in the Yukon Territory, from Whitehorse we take the sleigh to Dawson. Ain't nobody found the mother lode yet, you know. It's gotta be there somewhere." Billy pulled up his collar with his bare hands against the growing cold.

"If I was to go — I know train yards," he said then. "The Abyss in Chicago is like home to me. If I was gonna jump this train, I'd do it this way. See them clumps of trees?" Billy pointed down to our right. "It's just far enough away from the dicks — they're lazy — and close enough so as the train ain't moving too fast. Them clumps of trees."

"Just grab onto the end?"

"Oh no, no no no. Never grab onto the end of a car, always grab onto the front. See, when you grab, your body flies back up against the car with the forward movement. You grab the end of the car and your body don't fly up against nothing, tears away your grip. You fall between the cars. Call you side-tracked, then."

I smiled at his knowledge and his joke. I looked at Billy. "We don't have to jump the train," I said. Billy stood numbly, shuffling in the coldness without replying.

"Getting awful cold," I said.

"Sure is."

"We wouldn't have to jump the train."

"We?"

"Well, why not, Billy? You can't go on living like this, you know it. We could search out the mother lode together. We can be partners, I got some money, we could make an agreement between us. We could work something out."

"You're not . . . you're . . . " Billy the Pickle said, and another one of them fateful things happened. See, I figured I had all night and most of the next day. It was a calculated reply I gave to Billy the Pickle then.

"Aw, go away then," I said with my most indignant tones. "If that's what you think of me, after I bought you food and bought you liquor and tried to instruct you straight — aw, the heck with you, Billy the Pickle, you can go to hell."

"You got it, pardner," was his reply as I stomped down the hill. I walked back into the outskirt ends of dark Skagway, confused and disgusted with the boy's unreasonable hesitation. And it was in this inflection of moodiness that I encountered the two men. Everything happened so quick this day, so successively, like a drum beat far away and steady in the night. I had made my way back into the fringes of the town, and passed the depot, when a man idles toward me from the side and hails me.

Just at this moment another man appears and hails us both.

"Johnson's the name, cards the game," he says, which sounds stupid here in 1962, but that's what the man said exactly in Skagway that evening in 1904. I'm a regular guy, I stop and greet them. The second man asks if either of us had been "in," which I took to mean in at the gold fields, and the first guy, Johnson, says "Yes," and he pulls out a massive bundle of bills, several thousands of dollars, I judge, and also a vial filled with gold dust, and my eyes must have gone full-moon wide at the first sight I had of gold. The other guy says to him, "How'd you come by all that?" and Johnson grins sheepishly and tells us.

"It's not a tale of fruitful labour, but it made my money back. I lost all the gold I'd worked two years for one night to a fellow playing the black jack trick, and afterward I told him I'd pay him one hundred dollars if he'd show me how he done it."

"How's it done?" the other man asks. Johnson pulls out his cards and picks out the jack of clubs.

"Now I'll just bet you — no money, now — I'll bet you can't pick out that black jack again." He fans the cards so we can't see them. The guy picks out a card and it's not the jack. He does it a couple more times but doesn't win, then he asks to see the jack to be sure it's all on the up and up, and when Johnson isn't looking, the guy folds just the tip of the black jack so it creases, and hands it back to Johnson.

This time he picks it out.

"Well, you got lucky," Johnson says. "Let's play for fifty dollars."

This all happens so quick, see? I mean, these men just appear from nowhere. The other man looks at me and raises his eyebrows. He pulls the jack. Johnson mumbles something about beginner's luck, but he hands the man fifty dollars. I laugh nervously, I don't know if the man will confess to his trick, and before I know it they play again. The man wins twice more, pockets the money, then turns to me.

"You try," he says and winks, and I refuse. It's an odd situation, a dishonest one, I see, but I didn't see the depth of dishonesty.

"Go on," Johnson says, "I'll bet you five hundred dollars you can't pick it out."

"It's easy," and I tick the tip of the creased card with my finger, and Johnson's face falls. He counts out five hundred dollars and hands it to me. The other man elbows me in the side, and I protest.

"I can't take your money, sir," I say, but both of them argue that fair is fair.

"Really," I protest further, "I don't want it, take it back," and I push it toward Johnson, but he won't take it. See, in my foolishness I refrain from admitting the truth for fear of exposing the other man. I don't want trouble with either of them.

"No, you're too lucky, you're bound to lose," he says, fanning the cards again, the creased one right in the middle plain as day. "Try again — double, for a thousand."

I began to shake my head but they both protest loudly. I make the mistake.

"It's this one right here," I say, picking out the creased card and turning it over — a two!

I'd been goosed but good, been had, and as I stood there shocked, Johnson asks for the thousand dollars. I think I got a "But — but" out, and the other man immediately chastises me to be fair and come clean.

I don't know what to do, so I hand Johnson his five hundred.

"Five hundred more," Johnson demands, and the other man looks at me like I was some sort of criminal. I actually think of running, I know they've skunked me, but I realize they're ready for it. I pull out my billfold and give him the money, leaving me with just less than two hundred.

"Try again," the other guy then urges, "get some of it back," and he winks at me again, which makes me think . . . Johnson flashes the cards both ways so again I see the creased jack, and I'll admit because I'm an honest man that I wanted to cheat him back out of my own money, so I said okay. In desperation your senses can leave you.

Well, do I have to tell you what happened?

They had the gall to leave me with words of condolence, having stolen all my money. I was stunned — me, Mr. Frugality himself — the guy who counted each penny like a gold piece, stone broke. And cold. Getting hungry. All in five minutes. In my despair I just whirled around, and then sought to calm myself. I'd have to go to the police. Tell them what happened. I still have my bundles of mass-produced clothing — but nothing else. Not a dollar. Can you understand the situation I was in?

And then pride kicked in. I couldn't go to the police, it would acknowledge my total foolishness and naivete. And then, like some awakeful nightmare, I recall Old Sullivan's lost brother Patrick describing the "sure thing" men that flourished in Skagway in '98, the men who played the confidence games on all the "young dumb ones." Yes, and the name Soapy Smith came to me, the Al Capone of his time and day in Skagway, dead and buried nearby, having fleeced one man too many.

"Oh my God, oh my God, oh my God," I moaned aloud, and stumbled aimlessly back into the mud, not caring if it swallowed me whole. How could this happen to me? How could I be so dumb — I'm not this dumb! They robbed me! But none of my various sinking afterthoughts brought my money back. I learned a lesson that evening but good, one I'd never forget, and one I realized I'd already been instructed on.

I remembered — not exactly then, but soon after — my Daddy once saying to me as we built the stone wall, "Someday, son, a man's gonna come up to you and tell you there's five aces to a deck, and he's gonna be right." That's all he said, never did explain it, and I never understood what on earth my Daddy meant by them words until after Skagway, when they came back to me with haunting proper good sense.

But the stars weren't done with me yet that night — nor with Billy the Pickle. The drum beat on. . . . I went back to McGilvary's but Billy wasn't there, I went to a place called Clancy's Bucket of Blood, but he wasn't there. In a moment of luck I spotted the kid walking the boardwalk in the darkness, his hands in his pockets and a matchstick in his mouth. I chased him, I told him in my shaking voice what had befallen me, and he looked sadly to the mud ground.

"You never heard of Soapy Smith?" he said, and even though I nodded, Billy continued, "He's dead. Guy named Frank Reid shot him dead the same second Soapy shot Reid, and then he died too. Those fellows must be old friends of his, though I'd heard this town was clean." My mind was a turmoil of disgust.

"What kind of a disgraceful man was that? How can people do this to someone else? How could this happen to me?" I ranted, I don't even recall what exactly I said, but I'll never forget what Billy said in reply, so controlled, so confident of its reality, and to a man who was distraught: "You believe these men are bad, and they probably are. But there's two sides, you know."

"What could you possibly be saying?"

Billy shrugged. "See, Soapy Smith and them guys, they're survivors like me, only on a grander scale. We're all like aspen saplings struggling against each other for some sunlight. You're like a full-blown tree standing alone in the middle of a field. Never had to struggle against no saplings for your sunlight, so you're straight and tall and filled out, while we're crooked and bent and searching. It's facts. It's why if you cut down all the other struggling saplings around us, we'd remain bent and twisted. Can't change how you growed. Soapy Smith got rich, but he couldn't change how he growed, so he was bent and twisted and turning to the end. That's all. You just shared a bit of your sunlight."

I turned in complete mortification at these words, and I stumbled away. Of course I was in no shape to consider these remarkable words from this kid, to consider how such stunning words could come from one so young. Aimlessly I wandered the freezing mud sands of Skagway, making my way slowly through the stump streets the way I had come, back to the wharves, as though I sought something I knew. Finally, sick with the world and myself, I grabbed my bags from the wharf and walked again to the edge of town and camped in the awful cold. And cold, cold it was, brutally so, with the wind whipping down the snowy mountains and mixing with the salt sea breezes, so that I curled up under a pile of the clothes I carried and somehow went to sleep.

I was awakened by kicks to my fanny. I sat up with half realizations including morning, men, froze, and stone broke, and I looked up at the circle of faces.

"This here's the fellow he was with in McGilvary's, the one talking for Riel," said a bearded man, his words billowing into clouds as he spoke. I drug myself to my feet, my various and sundry clothing blankets falling by the wayside.

"What's going on?" I asked, grabbing my shoulders in the early morning frigidness.

"Are you responsible for the kid you was with yesterday?" another asked, a man who seemed in authority. He had dark, heavy eyes and wore a huge bearskin coat and big red mittens. Huge fur cap. The others, five or six men, stood around me, the hot air from their lungs cloudlike in the cold.

"You mean Billy the Pickle?"

"You'd better come with us," the man in authority said, and

I stuffed my clothes in my bags and went with the men toward the depot. My mind constructed a dozen situations, wondering mostly how this had to do with the two thieves, because they was mostly on my mind. We crossed the sidetracks and approached the depot.

"You'd better prepare him," someone said, but no one did, nor I doubt that they could have. For I turned the corner of the white depot, and there sat the body of Billy the Pickle, back to the wall, a grotesque, open-eyed half smile on his fast-frozen face. Across his folded legs lay a Winchester cavalry rifle. And in his right hand an opened and empty whiskey bottle.

"That's the stolen Winchester," the man in authority said, pointing his mitten.

"Jesus!" I screamed in my horror and disgust, understanding, you see, the part the whiskey played in this tragedy, and mindful of the rifle and what it meant. I side-kicked the bottle from his hand, only to see it settle in the snow a few feet off, his fingers still adhering solidly to it.

Billy the Pickle sat grinning.

10

THEN THERE WAS BLUR. I can't adequately describe what I did after that, making signed statements and swearing testimony and whatnot — I honestly don't recall much. I do recall arrangements to bury Billy later when the ground wasn't froze. I do recall climbing into that clump of trees he'd pointed out, and running, slipping across the hard snow and grabbing onto the train as it sped by, holding on for dear life, visions of all lost innocence before me, Lizzie, Momma, all the folks from home now so distant and lost to me — and a Winchester rifle.

Yes, I was a hobo myself now — I was willing to work. I rode the White Pass rails into Whitehorse, Yukon Territory, and talked my way somehow onto the sleigh, promising to pay when I could, a deal the driver agreed to, reluctantly. He made me pay interest, as he put it, by having me cook them Boston baked beans I mentioned way back early. That and numerous other chores, carrying people's baggage and tending the horses, running alongside when the snow wasn't packed.

It all passed in a blur, the several hundred miles to Dawson, the scenery lost to me, my soul shattered and not yet mending, terrible revelations regarding my character imposing strict attacks on my confidence. I moved — and lived barely — by merely breathing from day to day, with some ration of hope left that I would be in Dawson soon, though penniless and without prospects. Without friends or family. Without.

I give myself credit for moving on, although I really didn't have much choice, I couldn't have afforded to get back home if I wanted to. At least by pressing on to Dawson there was hope, bleak as it was.

Cold as it was.

Sad as . . .

Lizzie Grady's image rode clearer into my mind, seeing that beautiful, warm smile under the sparkling eyes as she offered me apples while I stood proud before my box machine. Those days, our magical days of 1903, seemed so far behind me now, and I tortured myself with the knowledge that this proper, beautiful woman was right in shunning me. Why, look at me! Unshaven, thinning, harried, my eyes lowered, I was a sad spectacle, with little doubt. Whenever a man begins to feel bad about himself on the inside, he begins to look bad on the outside. I was looking very poorly.

I learned humility. My mind was not an ocean of young man's pride, but of wandering half-thoughts, sensing faults and fearing failure. My resolve, my confidence were there, working

Don Reddick

what they could, but for the first time in my life I experienced doubt, not the normal doubts about whether I'd make it, or find gold, or look stupid, or talk foolish, but real doubt that I might fall apart. I realized on a sleigh on the Yukon River that your mind will play with you when you're in trouble, it will harass and torture you unlike any human enemy, because while you can win a human attack, or run from it, you cannot run from your own angry, sad and distraught mind.

And I had terrible dreams, dreams that made no sense of my reality, but whose sole purpose appeared to be just additional mind-harassment. I dreamed hazily — several times — that I suddenly realized I was a murderer, had murdered these two men in a field, and somehow had kept this knowledge out of my real working mind. The feelings I awoke with, a nervousness and a terrible fear that it was true, haunted me, and increased the uneasiness occupying my stomach. In the dream I would walk by the field, glance left over the stone wall, and envision the two men, hunkered down over a pot, them looking up at me and finally me burying them in shallow graves, all the while sensing in myself a horrible truth that I could do such things and forget, carry on naturally.

This was one of two dreams I had over and over at the time. The other was shorter, of my going before a judge in a courtroom with a very bad friend, and the judge angry with us both — me included — misunderstanding that it was only my friend that was very bad and not me. But I couldn't speak up and correct his thoughts, and so I stood there, being looked upon with disgust by the judge, unable to fight it.

It was in this frame of mind that I came at last to the scarred city in the wilderness. Although I had not the luxury of watching the countryside on the way in, I was aware of the unending remoteness of the place. This indeed was the middle of nowhere. How men had found gold here at all, why they were here in the first place, was a common question newcomers pondered whenever they arrived at Dawson City. With the news that we were approaching, I abandoned my thoughts to view the long-awaited spectacle. Of course my travails had diminished my childish excitement, nevertheless I viewed our entry with keen, unemotional interest.

Dawson City lies huddled at the bottom of a sloping mountain cut from left to right and angling downward with a strange scar of exposed rock, some geological fracture of a sort I don't know. Built on a swamp, Dawson squats low against the ice of the Yukon River, barely rising above it, and now it was still snow-covered tight. The waterfront was makeshift and disorganized, though nowhere near as busy as it had been a few years before when boats lay tied three deep into the river the length of a mile, the transportation for the fifty thousand men who inhabited this strange place during the height of the gold rush. And a strange, strange place it was, a virtual city lost in the midst of a million square miles of wilderness, yet with every comfort and custom of civilization mixed with the raw, ruined manner of wilderness men and Indians, a flavour, a smell, and a sight all its own.

We approached, and many of the townspeople emerged to greet us. I could see the remains of numerous buildings which had fallen to the great fire, could see the false facades of Front Street with the raised boardwalks above the common bond of all Alaskan and Yukon towns, mud, and of course the stumps. I disembarked after squaring my meagre official owings. Owings now, not earnings. Disembarked without fanfare onto the cold ground of the cold town.

Though not near the rage it had been during its heyday, Dawson still bustled with the activity of prospectors and shopkeepers. It was a hearty, sad place to me, what with the ruins of the fire, the ruins of the abandoned boats along the shore, the strewn wreckage of tents and rotted baggage here and there, the lost dreams of tens of thousands, all of it littering the tents and

Don Reddick

log buildings of the town proper, which edged its way up against the base of the mountain.

I left my bags by the waterfront and walked along alleys trampled hard with crusted snow, looking in the shop windows and saloons, wondering already where I could get the cheapest meal. Do you understand? Here I am looking for the cheapest meal, and I don't even have money for that yet. I made my way from one end of town to the other in scarcely fifteen minutes, and back again, finding myself loitering by the river with nowhere to go, no one to meet.

So this is Dawson! God, how I dreaded my awful existence in this suddenly drab, isolated wasteland. Nothing around me showed any promise of wealth or gold, no jolly groups of working miners laughing and moving about the streets. Far from being the end of the rainbow, Dawson City struck me more as the bent end of the world. End of time. Of place, life, and limb.

The truth is I felt dizzy and ill, cold and forgotten. I stumbled along through the wide streets and cut across alleys once again, half as sharp as I would've been under other circumstances, until I came onto King Street, where I saw the post office. I joined the group of men reading the lists posted out front of persons who had letters or wires. Why I stopped there, why I would have any notion that anything might be there for me is an odd thing. I believe I wanted something to be there, some vestige of home, which in retrospect is rather frightening. I saw my name under Wires.

Now. I've told you the truth up until now, I've told you that a good story has all the many angles twisted about and mentioned barely, only to be brought up again at a crucial moment, I've explained all this. I've mentioned Joe Boyle twice, and I'm coming to him. I forgot to mention the classical music in a timely fashion and explained that. You'll notice I forwarned you somewhat about Billy the Pickle. But I haven't told you anything, given even the slightest hint as to what happened to me at the post office. I didn't on purpose, because I want you to feel the fear, the awful sadness and hollowness of the shock yourself here today, so you'll have an image of the reality that struck me down in my second hour in Dawson City, the goal of my great youthful adventure. And remember, it was the naive young boy that left the warm Sudbury farm, just a kid of nineteen who travelled across the bogs and plains and mountains of all Canada, who'd shipped up the cold, mysterious coast only to have himself robbed of every penny he had, and seen the froze corpse of the only one he'd tried to befriend. It was this lonely and wretched creature who withstood the cold outside that post office, then entered to receive his wire. I eagerly took the paper.

I opened the letter in the middle of King Street as I strolled, my excitement great, but suddenly there was no movement to my feet. And then, there, all my troubles, all my weariness and sadness and fears and self-disgust and naivete and loneliness dissolved into the truth that makes no one whole anymore: my mother was dead.

Momma is dead.

Ma is dead!

I read the words in that street, I mouthed them silently, re-reading the awful script, then whispered them to the soundless Yukon light — Momma is dead! Of course I didn't believe it, couldn't imagine it, denied it even, and reread the wire.

"Dearest George," is etched indelibly in my mind, "Dearest George, it is with regret that we must inform you of . . . " Oh my God, what?

A strange feeling engulfed me when I realized I had no more parents. The feelings I experienced when Daddy died — the thoughts of never having him look me over with a keen eye for right and wrong — they matched yet differed from my memories of a woman who'd steered me any which way she pleased, more often by refraining from words than by speaking them.

My Momma loved me as a baby, a child, and a young man as mommas do, unconditionally and with pridely eyes, and now she was gone. How does a woman die? It seemed manly, as absurd as it sounds, for Daddy to die the way he did, in his own field. I could always picture the Confederates dying in the battles I heard of first-hand before our fireplace, could feel the honoured souls of the newly lifeless forms on Daddy's awful retreat through the rain after Gettysburg. Men died all right, and died often, but how does a woman, a mother die? I could not begin to understand.

I didn't. I only understood that when your mother and father are dead, you stop looking up and start looking down. I dropped the paper to the crunching snow, saw the wind whip it up and away as I stepped back toward the beach. Through the awkward town I barely moved, frightened so badly I looked to neither side, but stared morosely forward, stomping rigidly, ugly, lost and confused. I remember I passed a laughing, kissing couple. I remember hearing the tambourine and drum of the Salvation Army people. I remember barely the charred, blackened face of a building peeking up through the sifts of frozen snow. I remember the low hills to the west across the river, denuded of trees, a wasteland.

I remember seating myself in the snow on the banks of the great river, and hanging my pitiful head. And I remember crying, emptying my soul in a torrent of anguish I cared not if anyone witnessed. I was beyond any pride. I had reached the goal of my great youthful journey, had encountered numerous and sundry obstacles and overcome them all, one after another, until I found myself, my head in my mittens, here on the shore of the great Yukon River.

Oh, I remember crying all right.

11

SO YOU SEE ME NOW and you can't understand, but if you're fortunate you will someday. Now, this may sound strange, but it all adds up — my Daddy telling me to be prepared, an old nigger by the side of some low Georgian dirt road explaining life — because he's seen it — to a losing Confederate who'd one evening tell his tale before my family's fire, wounded people called hobos and tramps and bums worthier than yourself. Least some of them. It all falls together, and if you're fortunate you'll digest the most nutritious of the sad morsels, building your own inner fibre and constitution.

Not a picture in the world could you have drawn of a more forlorn, hopeless wreck than I was at that moment, sitting and sobbing, my head in my mittens, on the banks of the thick-iced Yukon. It was a long time in the freezing cold before my head popped up, responding to a strange occurrence that somehow broke through. Behind me and down the trampled street was a man, had to be drunk, standing with a megaphone in his hand, calling out the day's news. So loud and deliberate was he that I'm sure he was heard at both ends of town, even across the Klondike River in Lousetown.

"Today is March the twenty-second," the man I came to know as the Spieler called, "and today in Dawson City, Yukon Territory, land of our beloved King Edward the Seventh and bastion of the Northwest, the Paris of the North I daresay, this is the news, everybody."

And the Spieler then recited who was marrying whom, who was leaving for the outside, who of note was arriving — my name was not heard that day — and what had happened outside yesterday that was news today in Dawson. It was the odd man — this odd man, don't let me mislead you into thinking there was only one odd man in Dawson — it was this odd man that raised me to my feet to peer at him, which made me realize how cold I was. How very cold I was. I knew the motion of my legs and arms was necessary to circulate the warming blood.

I wiped the last tears from my eyes and walked aimlessly about the town, passing this odd man, ignoring him, pondering my plight. My mother had died only days after my leaving, of a heart attack, the doctor said. There was no sense in my return, as she was long buried by the time I read the news. I loathed the response by mail I would be required to make, and then naturally my thoughts included my current situation, penniless and without prospects, and you can imagine my condition. I walked and walked, dazed and without any foundation whatsoever, until I came upon the sight which would change the remainder of my lifetime. Such was the tempo of the unending drums through the hills that these things occurred in rapid succession, dizzying me almost.

I'd reached literally the end of the road, or one of the roads, of Dawson. Before me, to my astonishment, was a flooded, iced area, hotly contested by flying men, ripping bodies, sticks in hand, with their teammates urging them on from the sidelines. The rink was adjacent to the Mounted Police barracks. Nearby stood Joseph Whiteside Boyle, the big Irishman, surrounded by his entourage of friends, advisors, and hangers-on, though I obviously didn't know who he was at the time.

I stood staring at the spectacle, getting colder by the moment, longing in my heart for the camaraderie I heard and viewed before me, my loneliness surging forward and lying at the top of my consciousness like a skim-top of swamp ooze. I wanted it gone. I was alone and I was empty. Angry, I was hungry. It's an oddity, but do you know I think there's a relationship between hunger and anger? It's not properly developed in my mind even today, and maybe I shouldn't mention it because I don't have the answer, but somehow the connection exists. Hunger and anger. The feelings in the pit of the stomach are the same, and they tie in with fear — a man only gets angry out of a reaction to fear. But I stood there amidst the crystallized coldness of the Yukon air, longing to play this game and burn the anger that occupied me, so much so that I approached Joe Boyle, who seemed to command an authority I could petition. I approached him boldly, having surrendered all shyness and doubt to fear.

"Excuse me, sir," I said, angling in at him from the side through the throng that surrounded him, their eyes cast disapprovingly at me, at my clothes. Joe Boyle looked at me, looked down at me, for he was a large, heavy-shouldered Irishman with a strong, thick face and hard eyes. He was covered with long robes of bearskin, with heavy mittens and a cap pulled low over his ears, but despite the savagery of his dress his elevated status somehow remained, perhaps from the regard the others showed him, as he was the centre of all their attentions. In brief, the man contained whatever it is that allows one to dominate the thoughts and expressions of those around him, a natural leader, the kind who'd enter a room and immediately rule it. When you hear what this man had done and been through, what he would go on to be and do, you'll agree with me the enormity of his resolve and soul. Joe Boyle was one of the immortals of Yukon lore, and here I was addressing him in my ignorance.

"Excuse me, sir," I said, "but I'd like to play."

All turned toward me, scrutinizing every thread of my mackinaw, every crease in my young, unshaven face. In the wilderness all men are interested in all other men — and especially women. They need to know who you are, how you came into being and what your prospects are. It's difficult to imagine today, but Dawson was ruled in those far-off days by a strict social code, a caste system almost, where all men had their place and few ever changed it. So it was with urgent interest that new arrivals were questioned and evaluated as either upper crust, merchant, labourer, or lastly Indian. It was apparent to these men immediately where on their evolutionary scale I hung.

"And to whom are we speaking?" one of his men asked icily, the tone of his voice chastising me for my ill-mannered directness. It seemed to me that most of the men held me in disregard immediately, except Boyle, who viewed me with penetrating, knowing, but sympathetic eyes.

I came to know the reason for this. Boyle, you see, was one of those rarities in strict Dawson who transcended class, his great wealth allowing him to socialize with the upper crust, his wealth of experience as a sailor, bouncer, bartender, fighter, and fight promoter more suiting him to the working classes he came from. Everything between was equally accessible. He looked at me now, unlike the others, those Victorian hewn timbers of social disgrace heavy with their barks, their disapproving clucks and glances.

"Who are you?" Boyle asked, turning full toward me.

"My name is George Mason, I arrived this morning from Boston. I'd like to play." I pointed toward the game as I said the word "play." Boyle glanced back at the athletes for a moment, thinking, then returned.

"Is hockey played in Boston?" he asked, and of course I didn't know then, but I know now that Boyle had a very direct reason for his question. I knew that there were hockey clubs in Boston, mostly collegiate clubs, the game having spread down from Ontario. I had seen similar games on the rivers of Sudbury and Lincoln where boys used sticks and balls, but it was a crude, unorganized business, unlike the stories I'd heard of Ontario, or what transpired before my eyes here. For myself, I'd never held a hockey stick in my life.

"There's a great deal of interest in hockey," I said to Joe Boyle, then with my wink, "and if you got any extra sticks I'd like to play." Now, why I wanted to play, how I could approach this stranger and ask to play, is up for conjecturing.

Looking back, I think it was the necessity to exert myself physically, to punish my body or someone else's for all the wrongs I believed had unjustly cascaded upon my shoulders.

"Do you know how to skate?" Boyle asked. This seemed somewhat absurd, as all the kids I knew around Sudbury could skate. Why, my Daddy had once read aloud from that Thoreau book, not the famous one there, but one of the others, saying he used to skate against the Bedford boys in his youth, which must have been near fifty, sixty years before. And in school I'd heard that Major Robert Rogers of the famous Rogers Rangers was an exceptional skater, who travelled with his men that way on Lake George and Lake Champlain near one hundred and fifty years ago. Before the country, even. So at first I found Boyle's question absurd, but this was the beginning of my realization that Dawson was a worldly place, with a man as likely originating from Tucson, Arizona, as Sudbury, Massachusetts.

"I can skate better than anyone out there," I said, nodding toward the melee. At this there was a great deal of creaking among the timbers. Boyle himself smiled and glanced at a couple of them.

"Well, if that's the case, put on your skates and let's see what you've got," he said, then added, "You do have skates, right?"

I left for the waterfront to retrieve my skates. I was on a mission to forget, to bust myself somehow. I returned and sat in the awful snow and tugged off my boots. Boyle brought me over to one of the groups of players on the sides and introduced me to a guy who ran the team from the sidelines.

"This is Boston. He'll play on your side," is all Boyle said, and hence my nickname came into being. I've always felt it was because Boyle forgot my real name, though I was to learn fast that everybody in the Yukon was known by some colourful nickname. I'd already run across the Spieler who daily stumbled from one of the saloons with his megaphone to shout the Dawson daily news; then there was a man in Dawson named

Donald Donald who was known as Twa Donalds, which always amused me, because I could never figure out if it was supposed to be Two Donalds, or whether Twa was for the French "three," which somehow seemed even more humorous. En, der, twa. And the innumerable "Reds" and "Kids," and one guy with a wooden leg they called Margaret, which I couldn't figure out at all until one night I suddenly realized it was the proper name for any woman called Peg . . . Swiftwater Bill Gates, Soapy Smith, some of the more famous ones. The Lucky Swede. I'll explain him later. Eldorado twenty-nine above.

So I was now, and for the remainder of my association with these people, "Boston." And I was standing two inches taller than normal with a fine hockey stick in my mittens, which I turned and inspected curiously. The play before me, now frighteningly close, was a mixture of hockey as I was sure it should be played and the more sinister football.

Men tore at each other with their elbows and sticks, frequently sending one to the ice who zigged when he should have zagged, without all his teeth left or with a badly swollen shin. The nets in the game were two large rocks with a log rolled in behind to stop the puck if it entered, and the sideboards was inches high. Pure pond hockey. The goalers were bundled up so as not to hardly move because they were stationary and freezing to death probably, while the skaters wore surprisingly light coats, mittens, and caps pulled low over their eyes. With my bird's-eye view of this carnage I felt the urgency you feel when you get excited physically, and I surged into the crowd when one poor soul limped to the side grimacing and holding his ankle, the boss on our side yelling, "Boston! Boston!"

I admit I near tore into that mess, my eyes ablaze, my new club cumbersome and unwieldy in my hands, it being new to me and I unable in any event to control it properly, so that I skated and skated, occasionally hacking at the puck when it bounced my way. Once or twice I remember breaking into the open and receiving the puck in a timely fashion, each time from a certain short Indian-looking guy, only to lose it in my skates each time. This would bring the hoots from the timbers on the sidelines and from opposing players, and the eye from the short man who sent it. I lost myself in the physical rigours of the game, striding, striding, cutting and stopping quick to avoid collisions with the clumsier ones, and I felt satisfied that indeed I could skate with any of them, though some were darn good.

The best ones, however, weren't necessarily the biggest, or strongest, or, as in my case, the fastest skaters. They were the players who had acquired an agility with their sticks, who could stickhandle, as they called it, and pass at full speed accurately, and shoot and hit the end of the log, who seemed to dominate. And one guy on my side, the short one, seemed to always be in the right spot, anticipating the movements of all the bodies and the puck, always appearing at just the correct moment to tip a shot or receive a pass, so that I soon recognized him as the best player on the ice.

Most, however, were nowhere near as talented as he, nor as fast as I, though I'm not in the least suggesting that we were therefore in the same category. It quickly became apparent that my inability to handle my stick properly sank me among the poorest players, despite my ability to skate. And there were many hovering at my level, mere brutes with long, full beards and crazed eyes, swinging away with their sticks as though they were battling Vikings, without the least idea of what they were supposed to be doing. Lumberjacks, we called them. These men caused most of the injuries, and there was several that day, from a lost tooth to a fractured, batted hand.

When it was over the men glided to the sides and fell to the snow exhausted, I among them, gasping for breath and feeling somewhat lighter. You get a strong, fulfilling feeling at this time, removing your skates, the body exulting in the physical

Don Reddick

exertion and challenge. This too is something primal in all men, I believe, representing the fight, the attempts at conquering and domination. It's why whole cities today follow their teams, so they too, they who conquer and dominate nothing, can recall the primal feelings as their team conquers and dominates.

There's a whole lot more to sports than meets the eye, and I'm not even sure myself at the extent of it, how deeply in our men's minds it runs. It is a compulsion, a necessity, the way men determine who among them is worthy, who should lead, something linked to rams and moose and whatever that makes them bat each other's heads in, determining who gets the girl bear, or girl elk, or girl whatever. Seems to me it's true of men too, and didn't I already say something about Ralph Kiner getting more girls than Joe the Shmoe at the corner drugstore?

See, I'm talking about things that women don't like to hear. Men don't like it either, I think because it shows clearly that they're really just animals too, and even though it's been a while since Darwin and the Scopes trial and all that, people still ain't ready for the news. It reminds me of something that happened when my Daddy was still alive. Daddy was a quiet man, as I have testified, and he read a great deal. He wasn't gone with religion, but he respected it. I told you he liked to read, and one day I came into the main room and Daddy was just sitting, staring out the window, a book lying on his lap. I spoke to him but he didn't answer, just kept staring out the window at the field we'd cleared of rocks, beyond which was the field he'd die in.

"Daddy," I said again, but he was somewhere else, and he got up without a word and walked outside. Well, this seemed awful strange to me, so I moved over to where he'd laid the book and picked it up.

"*The Origin of Species,*" I read aloud, and it was years before I understood what that was, or what my Daddy was staring at out that window.

"You can skate, sir," Joe Boyle said to me from behind, and I looked up at him. "But you can't play hockey."

I frowned with his assessment, though I knew it was more true than not. I saw behind him the knowing, nodding faces of the timbers, to my additional discontent. I didn't reply then, but looked down and continued untying my skates.

"Most of these men work for me," Boyle continued. "Either in my dredge preparation, or my sawmill, or my electricity plant. They all belong to the Dawson Amateur Athletic Association. We're here because the rink's occupied, scouting new talent. I think I'd like to see you come down here more often — tomorrow like — and work out with the boys. Do you have a stake?"

I shook my head.

"Do you have work?" he asked, and I shook my head again. I didn't look at any of them but I could imagine the glances they were throwing one another. "You know, I'd like to see you play tomorrow," Boyle said, then turned and led his entourage back toward the foggy town. I pulled off my skates and paused, huge billowing ice-breath falling from my chest, stared at the cut-up ice, the river beyond, the hills beyond that with the foggy cold mist closing it up like steam from a bean pot caught up in the stove awning.

Maybe because I'd held a civil conversation for the first time since awful Skagway with a normal human being, maybe because I'd participated in a team sport and exhausted myself in the stunning coldness of the Yukon, maybe because of this I felt better. I knew I'd find a meal and a bed this evening. But then, like a piercing splinter in my heart, I thought again of my mother. Never really stopped thinking about her, just kept it below somehow. And Billy: "Your strength is weakness, the only way you'll survive up here is on the sympathy of others . . . "

"Hey," the short, Indian-looking one who could stickhandle and pass like the devil said to me, his skates tied and slung over his shoulder, "I'm Hector Smith. The boys are going to the Club for beer. You're included."

They all laughed when I ordered root beer.

12

ABSENCE MAKES THE HEART grow fonder — out of sight, out of mind. He who hesitates is lost — patience is a virtue. Waste not want not — you can't take it with you. We have a host of contradictory sayings. It's like what Ben Franklin — or maybe Mark Twain, I forget for sure — it's like what one of those intelligent gentlemen said, ah, something like it's so great being rational creatures, as it allows us to rationalize anything we wish. But one philosophical saying don't have a contradictory partner, which makes it exceptionally wise and truthful: time heals all wounds. You learn to endure grief better on the one hand, and on the other the wounds heal all of their own, as your mind attends to your mental hurt the way your blood contends with your body hurt. And in the end the mental grief scars are very much like the physical scars — look into any mirror and you can see them both, the ones on your body plain enough, the others lodged indelibly in your eyes.

With every passing day I cured, day after dismal day at first, but then, with a week, two weeks, three, I came to a sort of compromise with my grief. With the passing days I recovered from the death of my mother, which completely overshadowed the stunning blows of my robbery and the death of poor Billy the Pickle. So much occurred of a humbling and embarrassing nature at first that I won't relate it, except to say that no one was allowed to go cold or hungry in the Yukon wilderness. I was offered help — it was called the Miner's Code — and I accepted it. The sympathy of others.

Joe Boyle was not one of my early benefactors, but only because Joe never understood my problems at the beginning. He would have helped me if he knew, it was an odd thing with him, you either loved him or hated him, and the same was true with his outlook on you. I know now that Joe Boyle was an odd man, of enormous energy and Irish pride, but never what one would refer to as a thoughtful, insightful individual. Joe Boyle was a man who got something in his mind and just did it, and the heck with what anyone else thought. He — but wait, I'll get to the famous Joe Boyle by and by. What I intended on saying, about overcoming my grief over my mother, was that I began to regain my sense of adventure, to appreciate that I was actually now in the infamous city of Dawson. My eyes reopened, as if I'd slipped into a long, grief-ridden nightmare, and had slowly awakened.

There never was a place like Dawson City. Built virtually overnight with the barest of plans, it spread along the Yukon River between the cold water and the scarred hill like mud pouring down a ravine. It spilled across the Klondike River and was there called Klondike City, or more familiarly, Lousetown. It was built of anything. It was built of everything. On the day I walked into town it had palaces of the grandest Edwardian architecture, filled with the worlds finest chinas and linens and tapestries; it had dozens of false-front saloons and eateries and hotels; and scattered among them all, sticking out at strange elbow angles, was hundreds of log cabins, and spaced among these was dozens of tents, all inhabited by the ungodliest crowd imaginable. Some buildings was boards, some was logs, one I recall was made of flattened gasoline cans. A wilderness will bring out the poverty in a man, and poverty is the mother of invention. Dawson was full of invention. Dawson was full of crazy men.

I've got to get this right. The place is so much a part of this story, such an unusual, never-like-it-again type of place I absolutely must convey to you the honest substance of it.

Okay. You're standing in Dawson, your feet's either on packed snow or in mud, your head's in the clouds, because this is the last great mining camp the world will ever know. Some call the whole thing the Last Grand Adventure, and you'd be hard pressed to find someone who was there that don't agree, though he might have some other apt descriptions in addition. There's gold, coarse gold and fine gold, called dust, everywhere, on the saloon floors, in bottles and packets and tin cans stacked behind the bars — each man's personal stash — it's in the streams, stuck on the bottom between the rocks, and it's all through the hills, half dug out and half waiting to see the light of day for the first time in a millennium.

There's gold, and there's men who've found the gold and men that want to find more gold, and men who want to find the gold already found, and in that respect the gold takes on alternate connotations. What I mean is, some are there for the real gold, while others want to relieve those first men of it after they got it out. They might be selling whiskey, or meals, or sawed board or electricity like the more organized and industrious ones — Joe Boyle, for instance — or any number of things that folks do to make money. I heard of one man who struggled in over the Chilkoot with a bunch of kittens, which everyone thought he was crazy to do, until he sold them all to the lonely miners out on the streams at a handsome profit.

These men fill the streets all day and most of the night, some moving with high heads and arms swinging like they know exactly what they got and where they're going, others milling around every corner, outside every saloon, sharing the news of the day and discussing which rumour could be trusted and which shouldn't, all of them shifty-eyed, surveying the newcomers and calling to the old hands, all of it in a coldness that blankets this godforsaken bent end of God's land.

And where did they all come from? Everywhere. Anywhere. I met men from Bangor, Maine, who thereafter hailed me as someone from home on account of our being New Englanders, men from Cleveland, Ohio, Tucson, Arizona, Monterey, California, and every white spot on the map in between, and then all the foreigners, many Swedes and Germans — why, Frank Slavin, Joe Boyle's early partner, was the former heavyweight boxing champion of Australia. They came from everywhere, and they came from all directions.

Men poured in over the Chilkoot and Dead Horse passes, they floated up on sternwheelers from St. Michael on the vast, solitary Yukon, they stumbled in over the Stikine Trail, were carried in from the Ashcroft Trail, and never arrived from the Malaspina. Once in Dawson, these men shared a common bond, having made it to Eldorado through unspeakable hardships and toils at first, before the railway was built. Even those that came by the so-called rich man's route — floating the Yukon — carried their own tales of hell, like being caught in the freeze-up and enduring the long Arctic winter in some stick hovel beside the river, freezing half to death and eating very poorly, suffering from scurvy and the harrowing tortures of the solitary, beaten mind. In truth I noticed three sets of people in this regard, each still part of the caste system.

The first group and the smallest was the original miners and wanderers that were spread throughout the Yukon before Carmack and Henderson found the gold. I've heard it said — maybe I read it — that there was fifteen hundred or so of these men, strictly silent and lonely, who for various unknown and sundry reasons left society behind to live in the wilderness. Some were bitten with the gold bug from California or the Cariboo gold strike in British Columbia, others were in trouble somehow, and still others were those men who inexplicably get up one morning and walk out the door of their well-structured lives, leave their women and kids, and just disappear into the

Don Reddick

sunset, on the other side of which lies the gold fields. I believe Albert Forrest's father may have been one of these men. But I'll get to that. These men included most of the ones that got rich on Bonanza and Eldorado, as they was closest to the scene when the action began.

This early and tough group seemed to have a fraternity all their own, were called sourdoughs, and tended to drink together and look down on anyone else, even the ones who had nearly starved to death, sacrificing their health coming in over the Chilkoot. Even the sourdoughs that weren't rich were pointed out in town and whispered about, as they was respected greatly by the newcomers, whom they called cheechakos, which is Indian for God knows what. Members of this first group included George Carmack and the unlucky Robert Henderson, of course, who discovered the gold in the first place, which is quite a story in itself about race and bigotry and greed. I have so many valuable stories I don't know if I'll get to tell them all. Swiftwater Bill Gates, the Lucky Swede, Lippy, they were all in this group.

To illustrate the esteem these men enjoyed, especially those that hit big, I'll tell you what happened one day. We were playing hockey, back and forth, up and down, so intense that a bomb going off wouldn't deter us from our concentration. One of the sideliners yelled, "Hey, there's the Lucky Swede," and all of us stopped dead in our skates, the puck sliding off and out of the playing area. We stared at the man as he passed in his carriage, a woman holding his arm with both of hers, him tipping his felt hat as the horses turned and walked them back onto Front Street. They was the royalty of Dawson, and the likes of me was the serfs.

The second group of people was those that came during the rush of '98, after Carmack and his Indian brother-in-laws spotted the gold on Bonanza. See, the rush started when the *Portland* docked in Seattle with numerous wealthy wildmen aboard. At that time there was poverty in the land, all across it, what with the crash of '93 and the lost legions it spawned. Why, armies of unemployed men marched on Washington in those times, and socialism was highly respected — Jack London himself was a soldier in the jobless army that marched on Washington. But what I'm saying is poverty ruled the land then, and people don't know it, or those that do don't like to admit it, but the fact is folks was starving to death in America at that time, so that when news of the fabulously rich gold fields came down with the lost miners into San Francisco and Seattle, the whole country just went mad.

I don't believe anyone knows how many men up and left for the Klondike, but in every town it seemed someone was going or knew someone else who'd already gone. Men who couldn't go themselves financed those who could, and watched with sad, envious eyes as their partners set off. I remember this well, I was what, fourteen or so, which back then was considered more of a man's age than it is now. I remember them going off, and it certainly got in my blood, though I had to wait. I remember Old Sullivan's brother Patrick going.

So this second group of men and women were the rush people, those that went up and over the Chilkoot and Dead Horse passes, mostly, and those other routes. They looked up to the sourdoughs, and then in turn looked down on the last group, which was mostly defined by those who rode the railway over the worst of it into Whitehorse. Naturally I was among this group, which included a wide assortment of individuals, tourists even, if you can believe it. See, we were looked down upon by most because we made it in too easy. But I shrug it off, because it's just the way of the world. If a man wants to be respected he'd better do something respectable, and loafing half the way in to a wilderness gold field on rails don't qualify.

Dawson's strict and somewhat complicated social order held

some surprises. I was surprised to find the Mounties weren't allowed in the upper crustiness, as they was thought of as common workers. And then you'd find the Joe Boyles of the world, Joe who could sip tea as politely as any government man, then whoop and holler it up out on the streams, jockeying with all the fellows. And you'd see Carmack's brother-in-laws, Tagish Charley and Skookum Jim — Indians! — but because of their wealth they was respected by all, the same as Dick Lowe and some of the other originals on Eldorado who were little more than animals.

And then this is Dawson: a man whose name I forget, he's just cashed his dust at the Bank of Commerce after spring wash up, he's got ten thousand dollars — ten thousand! — and he must have been full of himself, because he walks into the Northern on the corner of Third and Princess and plunks a thousand down on faro, I think. He loses. He plunks another thousand and he loses another thousand — this is after the darkness of a nine-month winter, of breaking his back in a smoky hole clawing at frozen muck sixteen hours a day, breaking his back months on end, dreaming of the day he walks out — and he proceeds to lose it all. He walks by the bartender and says, "I went broke, gimme a whiskey." He gulps it down, glances back at the table, walks outside into the sunlight and blows a bullet through his skull right there on the boardwalk.

And this is Dawson: men paddling their canoes into the saloons. Front Street is under four feet of water, because at break-up on the Yukon sometimes the ice acts like a dam, and when it busts it floods out a good part of Dawson. So there they are, paddling up to the bar, which is open, by God, and men toasting each other from their boats, the bartenders hopping the tops of kegs to serve them.

And this is Dawson: another man whose name I can't recall — I'm awful with names — living just doors away from the wealth and glamour of upper-crust Dawson, whose friendship he enjoys, dies of starvation in his cabin one winter because he's too proud to tell anyone he's out of money. They find his frozen body days later.

And this is Dawson: the Ice Derby, as it was called, the moment of the ice break-up on the Yukon River, which every Dawsonite and his brother wagers on. Most people I tell this story to kind of wink at me and smile, but this story's true. The break-up of the Yukon ice signified in a meaningful way that spring does come at last, so everyone bet on it. Dawson people bet on everything. And this is how they figured it, though there were changes, I understand, year to year. But this is the gist of it: a Union Jack was placed in the centre of the river and wires were laid in to Jenerette's Jewellery Store, rigged up so that when the ice moved exactly one hundred feet, a circuit would close and bells would ring. And when those bells rang, everything else would ring, because the circuit would also stop a clock, which would tell what time it happened, which is what everyone bet on. So this is the story no one believes: it's church time — course it's a Protestant church — and the minister's all worked up this beautiful Sunday morning about gambling. Gambling this and gambling that, everyone's going to hell and the whole bit, and just as the sermon's coming to its high-pitched climax, just when the minister's thumping hardest and his voice is rising loudest — the bells ring! The Yukon's broke, and everyone in the church bolts out the door, the sermon on gambling still ringing their ears, hightailing it down to Jenerette's Jewellery Store to find out who won the Ice Derby, and — honest to God — the minister's running right with them!

Ha! That's my favourite Dawson story and I get a kick everytime I tell it. But there's more — I was there! What a wonderful feeling in my soul when I say those words — I was there! It was my dream, my goal, my reward all in one, a solitary, cold, bleak drop in the bucket of the great unknown land, and it's still there today, I understand, with a few hundred lost souls still clinging. But I was there when Dawson was alive with dreams and tragedies, the focus of the world's attention, every winter the cold claiming another dozen unwary men along the diggings and streams, every year more millions in gold scraped out of the frozen muck . . .

I'm sorry. I lose myself in my memories. I once stood in the streets of Dawson City. It is the universal experience, I believe, of all who went there during those dark and light, awful and beautiful days, to look back with a certain lost longing. We temporarily forget in a sense — as I do, certainly — the single tragedies it sired, and instead recall the strength of our bodies, the hardness of our resolves, the beauty of young men with their strength intact. To stand strong, young, and tall in the streets of Dawson, our whole lives and loves ahead . . . Look at me, this is where it all goes, the trail always narrows and finally seems indecipherable, until you wander and stumble . . . I'm sorry . . . sharing the grandest, deepest emotions of my entire life takes its toll. How can I reach back through fifty years of time and bring them back? All men are young and that's how they remember themselves always, whether it's bulling over for a touchdown, or scoring a pretty goal — or standing on the ice, hearing the band play "God Save the King," nervously staring at Frank McGee and Harvey Pulford and those terrible Ottawa Silver Seven . . .

13

FRANK MCGEE! There's a name resides on the Stanley Cup and in the record book. Know that name? One-eyed Frank McGee? Joe Boyle. Hector Smith, Dirty Alf Smith, Harvey Pulford. It all began to come together, the hockey, though of course I was unaware of my impending adventure.

I began to assimilate into the Dawson existence, poking my way around here and there, constructing my bearings and inquiring as to work. There was plenty of work in Dawson at the time, mostly labouring jobs in the diggings, which radiated out of town up the rivers and streambeds in all directions. By this time men were chopping up the hills themselves, which at first made all the sourdoughs laugh, and Joe Boyle's dredges were being assembled, soon to whine away in that high-pitched screeching the great shovels and cables made.

I took work immediately in town, work agreeable to me as a carpenter, for several reasons. I wanted to remain with the most people to properly assess the gold situation, where to stake, what rumours were worth listening to — all of which proved rather fruitless, I was to find, as every available square foot of gold-bearing soil had long ago been staked and raked clean, it seemed. Also, to be truthful, I wanted to ease back into living. The last thing I could see myself doing was being alone in some godforsaken outback diggings, isolated with my receding grief. The town, the people, the hockey I played every late afternoon — these were the medicines which healed my awful wounds.

The confusion on the ice, too, began to settle somewhat in my mind, for every day I became more at ease with the boys, came to learn how exactly to tell a good player from a poor one, began to learn the tricks and moves which improved my own game. I recognized the others as individuals, learned who to steer clear of — those lumberjacks — learned who I could count on to land a perfect pass onto my stick as I raced up ice.

Don Reddick

Out of my very first paycheck I bought a hockey stick for seventy-five cents in Landahl's Emporium, over on Second Avenue. It surprised me what little guilt this expenditure aroused in me, such was the necessity by which I was drawn to this new sport. The perfect joy this game gave us is difficult to convey, the games starting early in the dull grey half-light afternoons and continuing late, with all the fellows arriving and departing as their work or laziness allowed, sometimes playing six, seven hours straight, exulting in the tremendous physical exertions.

I remember it best when I glided from the mess, huffing and puffing, my stick feeling good in my mittens and myself experiencing that contented, exhausted feeling as I looked around me, at the scarred hill above town, the misty Yukon River with the rolling, balded hills beyond, and all of it in a decided coldness the likes of which I'd never endured before. What a lovely, lonely feeling, gliding alone and dropping to the logs lining the ice . . . again those feelings of undefeatable youth claw my mind for its gold-bearing muck . . . I could see who the good players were, watched them from my cold log and remembered another bit of Daddy's advice, which was to find men you wanted to be like, study them, ask what they do to prepare, watch how they perform — those particular words his exact — learn, learn, learn. It's good instruction — if you want to be a hockey player, watch the best ones. Study the excellent players, Beliveau from Montreal, the Howe fellow from Detroit there, Lindsey, study them all, see the Rocket's red glare — and ever since I saw Rocket Richard play hockey I think of him when I hear those words — see how Richard concentrates on the ice and believes no one can stop him, and then watch him as nobody does. And see the sturdiness of that Howe fellow, game after game, season after season, how he plays every game hard. I studied my stars on the ice of the flooded lowland of Dawson.

As the evening wore on huge bonfires would be lit beside the ice, casting long shadows across the playing area creating an eerie, dreamlike picture in the valley. People from town, fresh from their work, would congregate by the fires to watch and socialize, Joe Boyle always there for a while it seemed, everyone festive with the display of athleticism, drinking coffee, whiskey, or frequently tea from heavy cups, refilled from blackened pots edged into the outer boundaries of the fires. Kids with frankfurters on sticks shielded their faces with crooked arms against the heat, trying to get close enough to cook the meat. People got acquainted with surprising ease, everyone it seems being lonely all day and gregarious all night, so that even the shyest of men showed up, smiled and smoked, finding someone to talk with.

I began to make the friends I'd keep track of for a lifetime, some of them the ones who shared my incredible adventure the following winter. Many interesting days and nights I spent there, learning from the whole world, as this was Dawson's blessing, to be inhabited by the entire earth, as it were. The stories about life and love and luck of all places and cultures, stories I would never hear back home on the farm in Sudbury, Massachusetts, stirred one world all together.

One evening Hector Smith mentioned Lewis Birney — I'll always recall this name — said "Lewis Birney rode with Custer the day he died." Some of the crowd seemed to know this particular fact while others, like myself, voiced interest mixed with mild disbelief.

"Lewis Birney died at the Little Big Horn?" someone said, and Hector and the others laughed.

"The day Custer died, not Lewis," Hector replied. "He lives at the end of Seventh Avenue, by Jack London's cabin, and for ten dollars he'll tell the whole story of the day." This, despite the obscene condition of requiring money — and ten whole dollars at that — to tell a story, was of great interest to us all. Storytelling on the frontier was like card-playing in the evenings back home in New England, everyone did it, and with varying degrees of skill, but the disgust at the man's audacity to charge was generally overcome by the enormous interest we all shared in any of the Wild West legends. And remember, Cus-ter'd only been dead twenty-five years.

"Me and several of the boys on ten below kicked in and heard it," Hector said. "It's worth it."

"What'd he say?"

"No sense me telling it, that's immortalness we're discussing. It properly should be told by Birney, he's the one was there." This pronouncement, made next to a fire in fifteen-degrees-below-zero weather under the brightest dark evening sky of the clear Yukon Territory, was generally agreed upon.

"Who wants to throw in?" Hector then said, and several did, including myself. It evolved that eight of us tromped up to Seventh Avenue, just before Eighth Avenue, which hugs the base of the scarred mountain at the back of Dawson, tromping up near Jack London's cabin, which even then was famous and visited by tourists who'd read his *Call of the Wild* book, past Jack London's and on to Birney's cabin, a rough-hewn affair but no rougher than a dozen other cabins within eyesight.

The whole troop of us hesitated before it, as though silently reconsidering the adventure. For my part, I was mostly recon-sidering the expenditure of a whole dollar for a story likely to be less than any number of real stories I'd heard through my lifetime from defeated Confederates before my family fire. But then, I thought, if it's true, this is a special story. As though we all participated in a similar thought, we moved together up Bir-ney's steps, and Hector knocked on the door. I heard a rapid, chair-rustling noise, and the man must have run to the door as it flung open immediately.

"What?" Birney says.

"We came to hear your story on Custer," Hector said, "There's eight of us and we throwed in a dollar apiece."

"Ten dollars. I tell the story for ten dollars," Birney says.

Hector looks at the ground and appears uncomfortable at having to argue with the man, and I sense both the necessity to hear out the story mixed with a certain contempt at the money required.

"Look, there's eight of us, we throwed in a dollar apiece and we think that's fair. We're not going to pay no more, right boys?" We all voiced affirmations. Birney's eyes got hot, his voice rose surprisingly high.

"Ten dollars," he says, "I'll tell it for ten dollars, it's part of history. I rode with the Seventh Cavalry the day it died, and now I live on Seventh Avenue in Dawson City, Yukon. You want to hear it or not?"

"We ain't paying no ten dollars."

"You're probably lying anyway," someone says from behind. I turn and see the sturdiest, most contemptuous look imaginable. For the first time I really look at Sureshot Kennedy. I look back at Birney and think he's going to burst his red face. Seeing the whole thing verging on collapse, I muster my courage and quickly say, "My Daddy charged Cemetery Ridge on the third of July in '63, and he never asked a nickel for that story."

Well, most of my group turned to me in surprise, and near reverence fell across the weathered, furrowed face of Lewis Birney. The others turned again to him and saw his mind working feverishly, and he mumbled, "Custer was there . . . " Then louder, "Well, I'm often apologizing to real gentlemen, I'm so often dealing with tourists these days. Eight dollars seems fair enough if your father fought at Gettysburg. Come in. Quick."

Keeping a door open for any length of time whatsoever was a problem in the Yukon, as the awful cold would suck out the warmth of a cabin in seconds. We hurried in and shut the door behind, the whole of us jamming the small cabin, all of us moving about and finding seats on the chairs, the floor, me on a windowsill. Birney himself sat before the fire and poked at it with a stick, then threw on two more logs to fight the new cold we'd allowed in. He fiddled with the positioning of the logs as we settled, then turned, slowly thumping the stick he held with both hands on the hard dirt floor. He sat on a stump, thumping, looking about at all our faces, preparing us, it appeared, for the momentousness he was about to relate. It struck me that he was an intense, structured storyteller, almost an actor, and that he must have told this story many, many times over the past twenty-five years to proceed so deliberately.

"I was twenty years old in 1875," Birney boomed, scaring us almost after hearing his high whining at the door, his voice now strong and low, heated, earnest, "when I left my home in Illinois . . ."

"Wait a minute," Kennedy says, causing Birney to turn red and glare at him. "You got anything to drink here?" Birney shot up to his feet and pointed at the door, then jerked his thumb over his shoulder toward town.

"You want a drink, go to a saloon!" he roared, and Kennedy waved his hands No, smiling. I saw the mischief in his eye, recalled the whiskey he'd had by the fire and prayed he'd remain civil.

"Jesus, Mary and Joseph," Birney declared. "I'm here telling the story!"

"I'm sorry," Kennedy said, wagging his head, the dull grin on his face. Birney sat back down and rethumped his stick on the dirt, repreparing himself.

"I was twenty years old in 1875 when I left my home in Illinois," he boomed, "and I meandered west to partake in its wildness, colours, and Injun wars." Birney then spoke at great length about himself and his family, establishing facts, as he put it, all of which I've forgotten and won't try to relate, it being as tedious now to you as it was then to us. So bad was it, Kennedy stands up after about a half hour of this and demands his dollar back.

"My little sister has better stories than this," he argues with the iron-glaring man. To my surprise Birney relents, agrees that he can get carried away, protesting only that he wanted to give us our money's worth. When he said that I was sure he was lying, but what he then proceeded to tell removed any doubt from my mind.

"All right, all right," he said, waving his stick, "this is it. Custer was as close a thing there is to an animal being a man. He was one of those crazed officers that led charges on horse-back in the war, fought for Sheridan, and he was the one in a hundred that didn't get shot down for some reason, which he believed was godsent. All of this affected his mind, so that he felt invulnerable. He knew nothing could beat him because he'd seen it — led his troops time after time, sabre in hand, and never got a scratch while those around him fell like flies . . . and through it all developed a man so hard he could kill you with his eyes.

"Do not misunderstand the nature of this man. He was as strong, cold and disciplined as any military man, was famous coming out of the war for being the youngest general, and was addressed as General always, though his rank was reduced afterwards. I would watch him — as everyone did — whenever he was near, he was a man whose experiences generated a flow of attraction around him, which made all men watch him and all women want him. But, God, he knew it and used it, and meanness and anger seemed as much a slice of the pie as not, so that he was never much liked by any of the men ever, never got along well with fellow officers, neither. A very difficult man, a complex man. A man you would charge into battle behind, confident of success always."

"What happened that day?" Kennedy asks.

Birney lowers his stare at Kennedy, and for the first time the room seems to tilt toward our storyteller, his eyes alive, his face and hands and body erect and rigid with his thoughts. He stared through Kennedy and said, "Sunday, June 25, 1876, came hot, dusty. We'd been travelling over a month from Fort Abraham Lincoln in Dakota, and everyone knew there was Injuns by the Little Big Horn.

"See, you have to understand we all expected a fight, and you also have to understand that we was behind a man who'd never lost, one of the few heroes of the war that was still fighting, and we was fighting an enemy that never fought a pitched battle. It was a three-pronged attack, Crook from the south, Terry, Gibbons from the northwest, and the Seventh Cavalry with Custer, Benteen, Reno and me down the Rosebud and across to the Little Big Horn . . .

"Everyone asks about the decisions. Well, let me explain the decisions. See, it all makes sense if you understand what I understand, which most importantly was what the date was. June 25, 1876. Ring any bells?"

No one said nothing.

"1876 was one of the biggest years in the country's life. The year Colorado was admitted as a state. The year major league baseball began, in April. The year Wild Bill Hickok drew aces and eights in Deadwood, the year the James and Younger boys made the mistake of riding into Northfield, Minnesota. The year George Armstrong Custer rode out to the Little Big Horn. June 25, 1876. Ring any bells?"

We continued saying nothing.

"Was a week and a couple days before the Philadelphia Fourth of July Centennial Exposition. Why, they even cut down one of them giant California trees and lugged it across the whole country for it, and here we are, in an election year, nominations due from the parties within the month, the Democrats meeting in St. Louis soon — do you all see? How about this: Custer'd been overheard more than once telling Injuns he was to be the Great White Father in Washington someday, and here we are, on our horses marching toward the Little Big Horn, and we all knew there was a large gathering, the signs was everywhere and most of our Injun scouts was scared near to death, which we could all see. Then, why did Custer and Reno and Benteen and Tom Custer and the other officers sing outside his tent the night of the twenty-fourth? Why did he allow us to travel at night, pots and cups a-banging, wagons creaking, making a racket no doubt — trying to sneak up! And the decisions . . . early on the twenty-fourth we stopped maybe ten miles from the river, and this is where it was decided who'd live and who'd die, because Custer here told Benteen to go south with three companies and look for Injuns, told Reno to take three companies and start north up the south side of the valley, while he hisself would take five companies with him — don't you see?

"Benteen didn't. He argued — I heard this exchange — he argued with Custer. Said, 'Sir, we're going to need every man possible with consideration of the size of this camp,' to which Custer glanced down at one boot like he had some bothersome insect in it and looked up as cold and calm as ever and says, 'You have your orders, sir.' Benteen don't like Custer, he turns quick and moves off, angry it is clear, but unable to bring hisself to argue with a man he considers stupid.

"I was in Captain French's M Company," Birney says, his eyes growing distant, the stick beginning to thud on the earth between his legs. "We went with Reno. That's all. That's all it was between me and immortality, but it wasn't like we escaped it all. Quite the contrary, the next three days was days already served in hell. The last I saw Custer he had on buckskins, a wide-brimmed hat with one side pinned up, his gaze earnest, his whole body tight with the smell of a fight. Everybody was intense, Injun scouts was leaving, convinced of bad medicine ahead, and they was certainly right.

"We followed Reno, about a hundred and fifty of us, over the hill and down into the end of the valley, and we rode toward the village and engaged the enemy. A miscalculation had occurred — we thought there wasn't no warriors in the village because none was to be seen, the mistake being they was all asleep in their teepees, asleep from dancing with Crook's men's scalps all night long. With our advance the teepees and huts came alive with the movement of thousands! Very quick, very sudden, we was seeing them at all sides, and thankfully Reno understood this, though he was in the midst of losing his mind now, yelling orders on top of orders, contradicting hisself, confused and scared to death like the rest of us. Off we break for the river where there's trees to hide in, the red devils falling in on us from all sides and behind us now, men screaming, throwing down their rifles in panic, losing their senses with the fears, the howling, the howling . . .

"I seen awful things, running, I turn and shoot but I don't know if I hit nothing, I turn and see one of us being hacked with a hatchet, another reeling with arrows in his leg and hip, screaming, trying to pull the one out of his hip, everyone screaming, the dust rising up with horses running every which way, gunsmoke hazily rising above it all — terrible confusion it was, deadly, and the river was no answer. We climbed up a dirt hill, what's known to history as Reno's Hill, where we'd spend two hellish days and nights fighting constantly, without water and barely no food."

Birney stops here, the chilled room covered with a silence of awe and respect. Even Kennedy is quiet, I look at him and see he's leaning in, wide-eyed.

"In truth, it was exactly what Custer went through some miles away near the same time, though they didn't get all of us. Benteen came, had orders to go to Custer but he helped us, we becoming near three hundred men. I lived, but I didn't believe I would, nor anyone else around me, and, after walking through the empty Injun village the next day and understanding its true size for the first time, I knew we wouldn't have lived if they'd not left. No one knew why they left.

"No one knew what happened to Custer. Where the hell is

Custer? We kept expecting him any moment. The Injun scouts was quiet, though, because they knew but didn't want to tell us. Finally some men was sent to find him, and as long as I live I'll never forget their faces when they returned. No surprise, no shock could have been greater than this awful news, men we knew, worked with, fought with, laughed with, played against, argued against, lived against . . . almost three hundred of us slain and naked and rotting on a nearby ridge . . . and nobody could speak.

"I was with the men who went up there to bury them. Words cannot describe the horror of the scene, now etched indelibly across my soul, for despite the responses given to wives, and newspapers, and even to friends by men who didn't want to remember, these men were butchered, every last one of them. I saw men with knives sunk to the hilt in their eyes, legs and arms lopped off, men scalped and their heads crushed to mush, man after man after man, men with arrows by the dozen shot in their backsides, all of them naked, cut, hacked, fingers off, eyeballs out, things I can't mention even to men in men's company, all of it amidst a stench beyond description, which made me and not me alone vomit . . . heads . . .

"Custer was shot in the head and the stomach, I saw him, my stomach dropping when I recognized his overgrown mustache, which is about the only way I could recognize him. His body lay on top of others, and he was no better or worse than the rest, though I've noticed since an almost silent league among the men who were there that day to proclaim him intact. Let me assure you here tonight in Dawson City, Yukon Territory of Canada, he most certainly was not. God in his utmost wisdom never created a more heinous and dark soul than that of the Cheyenne and Sioux. What they did to those men — and a thousand others across the history of the west — is beyond belief or description, and should never be forgotten."

Birney stopped and bowed his head against his chest. The

Don Reddick

room was silent. I envisioned it all, such was this man's ability, and I sat stunned like the rest, awestruck by a man who'd been in history. With Custer the day he died!

"And the decisions," Birney suddenly barked, his eyes hard, the fire crackling behind him, "don't you all see it now? It's clear to me, and I was there. Custer knew it was a large camp, knew for months even that it was. He wanted to be president, period. Knew Washington, Jackson and Grant got to be president through battlefield victory. Knew how this victory, this timely victory just before the Centennial Exposition — which he planned on attending! — just before the Democratic convention in St. Louis — knew this would lead to the presidency. This is what was happening on those plains on June 25, 1876.

"He didn't worry about Reno — I told you how Reno reacted in war — but he worried about Benteen, sent him chasing shadows in the hills where everyone knew there'd be no Injuns, to keep him out of the way. No sense in taking a chance someone else might get some credit — knew Injuns don't stand and fight pitched battles, knew once he charged the village they'd run helter skelter and it'd be he, George Armstrong Custer, who'd be credited with corralling Sitting Bull, Crazy Horse, Gall, Rain-in-the-Face . . . But he also was disturbed by the reports of their strength, so he led carols before his tent on the night of the twenty-fourth, let his men cook on open fires whose smoke could be seen and smelled for miles, moved us all at night amidst a terrible racket a deaf Eskimo in Nome could have heard, all to scare them off before he got there. Custer figured he'd catch enough of them to skirmish with, the rest fleeing into the waiting arms of Gibbons and Terry, his victory easy and complete. It would be he who captured the village and sent them fleeing . . . "

And then Birney, the great gift of storytelling obviously his, spoke in a whisper.

"Man named Martin was the last to see him alive. He's the

man Custer sent with a message to Benteen to come, he told us when Custer rode to the top of the rise above the valley and viewed the village for the first time — all four miles of village, now — he raised his hat, whooped and yelled, 'Now we got 'em, boys!'"

14

I'M GLOSSING IT OVER, of course. I just realized it, talking about Lewis Birney and Custer and the hockey and all, just like I did at the time. I attempted to make you feel as surprised as I was by not warning you, and then I just went into these other things like it was nothing, and it was near sixty years ago, now. Ain't that something? After all these years, I'm still glossing over my mother's death?

I'm old now, so I can say the truth, speak my mind. It's a luxury a young man don't have, either because of self-fears of a kind I've previously described in stern New Englanders, or just ordinary man fears of speaking plainly about necessary love . . .

My mother was orphaned at age six after being born in Milledgeville, Georgia, in 1841. No parents, no sisters, no brothers, just hardtack life in a orphan ward with the coldness that descends from paid day and night keepers, most more concerned for their pay than with the poor little lost souls in their protection. Through this grew a sad, tough young lady, and to this day I can imagine the look in her eye when she met the quiet young man Mason from across town — can only imagine because it wasn't talked of — can imagine them strolling down dusty, hot summer red dirt Georgia lanes, my father picking a peach off an overhanging branch and handing it to her, can im-

Don Reddick

agine the look in her eye that would allow the birth of seven daughters and then a son. By the time the guns were roaring up north they were married with two daughters, Jenny and Babe, and really still kids themselves. Daddy solemnly comes home one afternoon and explains it's his duty to go, and he does, riding the railroad into Atlanta to join the new Confederate army.

Can't you just see my poor Momma's face the day he walks off, young, huddled with two baby daughters, watching the man who saved her from the lonely darkness of the wards walking down the dirt road, turning, waving back? What must have gone through her mind at that moment, so long ago, why, almost exactly one hundred years ago now? My sisters were in school before they saw Daddy again, didn't know who he was until Momma ran through the door and threw herself around his neck and wept that day in the summer of '65. He'd come home, and come home in one piece even, unlike the Foster boy, or Terry Symington's husband, or the Bangston twins, or several hundred thousand other sons of the Confederacy, who now lay peaceful in far-off foreign places like Pennsylvania and Maryland, where they'd zigged when they should have zagged.

Daddy's always been a man to raise crops from the ground, knew no other job in his lifetime outside the army, but you can't sow crops in August. Daddy and Momma and my two first sisters nearly died of starvation that winter, as did many, many people in our old area.

Men headed west for Texas and California and Colorado, many of them wild with grief at the loss of their pride and the destruction of their homeland, many who never felt the sting of a bullet but scarred for life in their eyes at the cost of marching north. But Daddy wouldn't have it, no sir. Daddy, the silent, thoughtful man, told Momma he wanted his children schooled properly like the Federal men he'd talked with, said a man owed it to his children to improve their lot in life despite the cost. Told this to a woman who'd seen Sherman herself. And

Momma never said a word, which today might be criticized erroneously, for with her silent approval she stood by the decision her man made, with honour, because what Momma was was a loyal, strong, handsome wife and mother, who stood once and for all with her man and her family.

She was never one to talk too much of others, like many females. She never even wanted to leave the farm in Sudbury for a day in Boston, or even Lincoln. I think it was her lonesome, sad upbringing that made her that way, made her content with her kids and her husband, always busy it seems with preserving jams and knitting clothes and cooking suppers, never talking a whole lot but always directing you thoughtfully when she did, never allowing nothing to go under the table too long, but confronting it, which never allowed the petty arguments and jealousies of other families to fester. In my eye she was the prettiest woman on earth.

And she could be crafty, too. After Daddy died she somehow got it in her head to apply for a Federal pension. She never did think it fair that Federal widows was allowed pensions when Confederate widows weren't, and after the rules were expanded in '93 to include all Federal widows without consequence of whether their old husbands got hurt in the war or not, it really ate at her, I believe. Anyway, she applied for a Federal pension, knowing any application from Sudbury, Massachusetts, is going to look okay, and the family was full of winks and excitement, like kids sneaking up to the window to steal a pie, waiting for the word. At first the papers came back all right, but then the letter came informing her of her mistake, as they coldly put it, and that was the end of that. We never knew what really happened, Momma suspected it was the census papers she'd filled out which just happened to ask what colours your husband was wearing between '61 and '65, but it's her ingenuity I'm talking about here. But this didn't stop her, only made her more determined to assert herself as equal to any Northern widow. She decided it was her right to march in the Decoration Day parade — Memorial Day it's called today, began just after the war — so she showed up and stepped in and marched in the Decoration Day parade through town, her head held as high as any, which raised numerous eyebrows, let me assure you, but nobody got up the nerve to say what they thought.

And she's got her own brand of winking humour. Always called Reconstruction "deconstruction." Ran her hand through Daddy's hair one night as he sat in his armchair, fuming about the war again, and she comforts him, says, "Don't nobody realize everyone's truly Confederate at heart?" and Daddy stops, of course, looks up at her, wondering what it is she's meaning. And she says — she's running her hand through his hair, remember — and she says, "See, we all turn grey in the end."

Thinking back, there never was much time without hardship in her life, the orphanage, the lonely, young war years without her husband, the fear and adjustments combined with the subtle but certain shunning once they made it north, and the ensuing lifelong struggle to pay for the Sudbury farm. And all along she bore and raised eight children, lost a couple others at birth, and what did she get as her reward in the end?

"I wonder where your Daddy is," she said to me and looked out the back door toward the fields. It was October and the harvest was done, and Daddy spent his free days moving the numerous rocks from the fields to the stone fences, an endless job in New England, sometimes lifting a hundred and fifty and even two hundred pounders all by himself. I was in awe of the man's strength, the hands as hard as turtle shells, lifting rocks from sun up to sun down, with only a lunch hour and a few minutes here and there, setting down on the biggest rocks, in between.

He was silent when he worked except when he set down, his hands on his knees, huffing and puffing, and he'd look at me and say things, like someday someone would come up to me with five aces in his deck. He told me fragments of things which made me think, as if he'd been spending all those hours thinking them up.

"Supper's ready, I wonder where he is?"

"Ed Delahanty's the greatest ballplayer ever," he told me a week before, huffing, his turtle shells on his knees. "But in my heart I'll always like Robert Lee Caruthers most. Born Memphis, '64. But you know, boy, anyone who listens to his heart ensures it will be broken."

"He's always home by now."

"Daddy?"

"From a distance they all look alike, but your biggest decision in life will be which star to hook your wagon to, boy."

"George, you go find your Daddy and tell him supper's on the table."

"DADDY!"

"Suppose one day you understand you was wrong about the biggest thing in your life. Do you suppose it would be wiser to stick around and pretend to reinforce the wrong, or leave and face up to the hardship truth?"

"Momma?"

"Where's your Daddy, George?"

"Your Momma's the grandest thing ever happened to me, boy. Don't you listen to anyone says bacheloring's best. In the end all your good time friends'll be gone. Ain't no feeling in the world after a long day in these fields like tromping up toward the house and seeing your Momma's face through the window, over the stove . . . "

"Momma . . . "

And I saw the end, saw my Momma break across the second field at the sight of him, saw her grab up my Daddy's face and shove her own into it, her screams echoing down across the cold barren fields and into the coloured woods, wailing she was

Don Reddick

really, the way she described his crying when he tried to speak of the retreat of Gettysburg, and I saw her tears fall on his face and run down the crook of his eye, as though they were shared, and they understood both their hearts was broke now.

I loved my Momma. I haven't been the same since the day she died.

15

"I SEEN WITH MY OWN EYES Captain Harper of the Mounted Police climb up on the stage in the Monte Carlo, strip naked and eat a pound of raw beefsteak while standing on his head," Hector Smith told me one evening in the D.A.A.A. Club.

"He didn't do it," I protested. Hector nodded vigorously.

"Seen it with my own eyes. He bet a guy he'd do it, the guy said 'You're on,' and Harper sends one of his cronies out and sure enough he comes back with a slab of beefsteak. Harper proceeds to remove several layers of clothing until he's in his drawers, then he pauses dramatically, and he marches up onto the stage, the meat in hand, to an uproar of cheering and jeering. He flexes his muscles to one side of the hall and then the other, drops the meat on the stage floor with a thud." Hector paused to sip his beer, his eyes wild with the story.

"He didn't do it," I protested.

"He drops his drawers right then and there, stands on his head and proceeds to chomp away at that meat until it's all gone. I've never seen the Monte Carlo in such mayhem as I saw that night. When he's done he wipes his face with his drawers and puts them back on, gets off the stage and goes after his money, which the other man willingly forks over."

I shook my head and laughed. George "Sureshot" Kennedy leaned in.

"I seen Nigger Jim's dog sled and it has a bar built into it," he said, and I saw some others agree. Kennedy is a big man, one hundred and eighty pounds or so, and a childhood friend of Hector's. They'd come together to Dawson, pioneers of '98, from West Selkirk, Manitoba, which is on the outskirts of Winnipeg. Where Hector Smith was the fastest, shiftiest hockeyist in Dawson, Kennedy was more of a bull, tremendously strong and fearless, possessing "a shot like a cannon and straight as a die," as a newspaperman wrote later. I'd first noticed him the night we rode with General Custer, he'd been drinking whiskey around the campfires and acting up, and it was after that that I found he was a crackerjack hockeyist.

"He'll never be confused with Thomas Edison," Hector says to me after Sureshot leaves to lean over some stranger. "Know what he did last year?"

"What did he do?"

"Eilbeck runs the Civil Service teams — Eilbeck runs everything — Sureshot played on their hockey team last year with Doc McLennan, Norman Watt, Lionel Bennett. But did you know Sureshot's a great baseball player, too?"

I shook my head. Hector sipped his beer.

"Great ballplayer, centrefielder, played for the Idyll Hour, but Eilbeck offered him a government job at seven dollars and fifty cents a day if he'd come and play baseball with the Civil Service. Promised they'd take him on the hockey tour next winter, too. So what does Sureshot do?" Hector grins at me and I shrug.

"Do you understand what I'm saying? They're bribing him! Not only is it against the league rules, it's against the law! A government official giving out jobs to athletes! So what does Mr. Brilliant do? He walks out of the meeting and asks Gibson, his manager, if he can change teams, explains it to him! Naturally Gibson's upset and says no, and Sureshot storms out. He's all upset hisself now, for all he can see is the seven-fifty a day, so he walks up to some reporter for the *Dawson Daily News* and tells him everything!" We laughed and Hector pounded the bar with his fist, shouted, "Everything!"

"Next day front page headlines: 'Kennedy Asks To Be Released.' Caused a furore. And you know what? The fool still didn't understand. All he did that day was walk around with the newspaper, showing everybody his name in the headline." We enjoyed the laugh at Sureshot's expense.

I learned quickly that the flooded pond wasn't where the real hockey was played in Dawson City, but here where we sat now, the new arena Joe Boyle had built. An imposing structure, it had three-storey towers on each end of a covered rink, complete with stands and benches. It was built with New York and Chicago in mind, and money in hand. It contained dressing rooms, a gym, offices and an eatery which more resembled a saloon after games. The rink was wonderful, with a balcony around it all and heavy beams across the roof, where flags were draped.

It was here that the organized hockey was played under the adopted rules of the Ontario Hockey Association. It's where Hector'd brought me the first night I played with the boys, but in the darkness and excitement I hadn't even realized what the whole place was. Now — and we're talking about April, May of '04 — it's where I'd come at night after carpentering doors and staircases and whatnot, to watch the organized teams of Dawson play for the town championship. It was also where I realized why Joe Boyle and Hector Smith and Sureshot Kennedy showed such an instant interest in me. All the Dawson teams were highly competitive, and actively sought out new and better players. It must have been with a morbid fascination that they viewed me. Although maybe I couldn't keep up with Hector Smith, there was no other Dawsonite I couldn't out-skate, but my stickwork, my "head," just wasn't up to snuff at all. I was kind of like the proverbial pig dressed up in Sunday clothes, and they just didn't know what to make of me.

"I hear Eilbeck got a reply on that last one he sent," Sureshot says to Hector around me. We're sitting at the bar, the three of us in a row with me in the middle. The place is packed, it's after a game and all the players and spectators are jammed in looking for a drink.

"Wouldn't that be something," Hector replies, and I look at each of them. Sureshot saw my glance.

"You know about the challenge, don't you?" he says, and I shake my head. "Ever since McLennan showed up and told everyone about playing for Queen's, what was it, Hec, '95? I think that's what got the bug going. Specially in Eilbeck."

"Weldy too," Hector said. "And Senkler. Senkler's the goaler with the Civil Service. Great athlete. He toured Europe with the Canadian Association Football team several years ago. Doc McLennan was with the '94 Queen's tour, won thirty hockey games against clubs in the United States, Doc claims they only got one goal scored against them. Senkler and Doc telling stories about their tours, and then Boyle and Slavin toured, staged boxing matches — that's what got Eilbeck and Weldy going."

"Yes," I replied, "but what exactly do you mean?"

"The Stanley Cup."

Sureshot said it curtly, matter-of-factly, as if that explained all. I had never heard of any such thing in my lifetime. I was almost willing to let it pass, but I thought of Billy the Pickle.

"What the heck is a Stanley Cup?"

Sureshot groaned in disgust but Hector was generous. He ordered another round — two beers and a soda — then turned to me.

"I hear an all-Indian team out of Calgary is gonna tour," Hector said. "But it's the Stanley Cup, Boston, the grandest sporting trophy of them all we're talking about. Haven't you heard of it? It's all the rage in Canada."

I admitted I had not.

"See McLennan over there?" Sureshot said. "The one yelling? Mustache. He scored the last goal tonight, the two-on-one. He's a real doctor you know, and the best rover in Dawson, probably all western Canada. Best curler, too, he's a favourite to win the Jersey Tankard again. He played for the Stanley Cup in '95 for Queen's University. If we get a team accepted, he'll be on it."

"McLennan's good," Hector agreed.

"Hannay played for the Cup this winter," Sureshot said.

"Who's Hannay?"

"He was in and left last summer. Great hockey player, better than Hec here, maybe. He played for Brandon against the Silver Seven this past season. Lost, but he scored two goals."

"The Silver Seven? Who are the Silver Seven?"

Sureshot groaned again, making a game of it. Hector laughed and slapped me on the back.

"I can see we gotta get Boston into the swing, Sure. Thing is these Americans know everything, but they don't know the Stanley Cup, eh?"

"Americans, oh!" Sureshot agreed and drank. I tried to put together what they were saying.

"So you're saying someone's trying to organize a challenge for this Stanley Cup?"

"Ozzie Finnie — he's the clerk over in the gold office — I heard his younger brother Day Finnie might make the Seven this year," Sureshot said.

"I heard that," Hector agreed. "Goaler."

"Bouse Hutton can't play."

"So is somebody trying to challenge for the trophy?" I asked.

"His Excellency Lord Stanley donated the thing ten years

ago," Hector said, "goes to the best team. But there's rules. All games is played at the reigning champion's rink. So can you imagine if a team from Dawson wins it? It'll be here forever, eh? Imagine! The Stanley Cup in Dawson City forever!"

"Nobody'd come up here," Sureshot agreed.

I didn't bother to ask again. These two got talking hockey and there was no real discussing anything with them. Arguments always ensued.

"Frank McGee's the best hockey player alive," Hector would say, and Sureshot would counter — even though I'd hear him agree later with others — "No, no, Harvey Pulford is best. No doubt about it."

"The Ottawa Silver Seven are the best hockey team ever."

"No, no, the Victorias, with Graham Drinkwater and later Russell Bowie, was best, without question."

Such were the nights of my days, spent now at the rink with the fellows, getting to know more and more of them, skating daily after work on the pond, skating, skating. Work was a disappointment. After all, I had come to find the gold and here I am slamming nails, but none of this is real important — oh hell, I may as well tell you. It don't matter anymore. For years I never told no one outside about my general living conditions, they was so bad. I lived in a tent. That sounds worse than it really was, though it was bad enough. See, Dawson had lots of tents, so it wasn't all that unusual to live in one, though certainly it was the poorer folks that did so. But tell that to someone on the outside and they kind of look at you strange. I had no money, of course. I made about four dollars a day — a huge sum on the outside — but paid back, with frugality, near two to eat and sleep, and I figured I'd need about two hundred to get home, which I immediately began plotting, tell the truth. Plus I owed the sleigh. Two hundred to get home, after paying off the sleigh, two dollars a day times six days a week. There was no work allowed on Sundays. The sheriff, who was this fellow Eilbeck, and the Mounties, they were very strict about that, even the saloons closed down on Sundays. One of the stranger sights to witness in Dawson was the time leading up to midnight on Sunday night, when the boys would line up at the saloon doors, barely able to wait to squander their hard-earned gold. Funny thing, everybody used to go boating down the Yukon into American territory to avoid the Sunday alcohol bans, and one time I heard the boat conked out and didn't make it back for a couple days, the town nearly vacant and paralysed in the meantime without half its people. Anyway. What on earth was I getting at? Two dollars a day, yes. Six days a week, that's what? Twelve bucks a week. Twelve bucks a week times almost thirty weeks was what I'd need to get home, you can't save everything. Six months of slamming nails, that would put me in about late October, early November if I was lucky, and I'd better be because it wasn't easy leaving after that.

Skating took all this off my mind. The work never exhausted me sufficiently, so I was compelled to skate, up and down, back and forth. With the nerve-rattling experience of getting body-checked a few times, I learned to go up and down, back and forth with my head always up and my eyes always open — having someone throw a shoulder into your chest while you're moving twenty, thirty miles an hour, your head turned looking behind you so it's all a surprise, is one of the less desirable sensations in life. It makes you angry, makes you want to do it back to the guy that did it to you.

Joe Boyle, especially when talking with the newspapers, would always correct a man who said hockey was a contact sport. "It's not a contact sport," Joe would always say, "it's a collision sport." A collision sport where half the collisions were intentional. People that don't know hockey don't like the fights it spawns, but they don't understand this aspect of it. They say, well, in football the players hit each other every play, and there's rarely any fights in football, so why is there so many fights in hockey? Well, what they've misunderstood is that in football — which is a sinister sport — the players *know* they're going to hit and be hit on every play, they expect it, so it's no surprise or shock when it happens. In hockey, a guy *decides* to hit another guy, and in truth he never really has to. He *decides* to, which is the cause of innumerable bad feelings, specially when a player gets hurt. The hurt player always takes it personal, and just as you would be mad if someone came up to you and punched you in the mouth because he just *decides* to, so feels the accosted player. So he retaliates, and you've got a fight.

There once was an interesting and ingenious player on Hector Smith's team in the Dawson league. I forget the guy's name. Bernard something. "Bernard never got into fights, and he threw more vicious checks and elbows and stickwork than anyone," Hector says to me.

"How is that?" I ask him.

"He'd line up a guy and just ram him into the boards, slip a little hisself sending his elbow down on the guys head, and everytime the guy would turn, ready to fight, and Bernard would say, 'Oh, jeez, I'm sorry, Gloomy, didn't mean it, you okay?' and Gloomy would frown, swear a bit, and off he'd go. No hard feelings because Bernard always apologized and said it was an accident. We called him Saint Bernard."

"Nobody ever caught on?"

"No, but Saint Bernard got his comeuppance. Every dog has his day, ha ha."

"What happened?" I asked, not getting his pun about dogs until years later.

"One of the lumberjacks up and hacked out all his front teeth with a stick one night, and we just about all bust a gut laughing at him. He was incensed, incredulous that anyone would do such a thing to him, came back to the bench nearly crying, and honest to Peter the whole bunch of us was laughing at him. He quit that night and never played again, said it was all roughhouse with no integrity."

I love these stories the guys told when we were relaxing after games in the saloons or walking the diggings. Unlike myself, they've all played hockey for years, back home in places like Three Rivers, Quebec, where Albert Forrest was from, Cornwall and Ottawa, Ontario, where Doc McLennan and Gloomy Johnstone was from, Brandon . . . the guys loved to tell stories on other hockeyists, and if a guy brought up one, someone always seemed to think of another.

"I got thrown out of a game for lying once," said Norman Watt, a native of Aylmer, Quebec, across the river from Ottawa, after Hector finished his Saint Bernard story. This raised some eyebrows, and Norman leaned in.

"I played with a crazy man back home who always got thrown out for starting fights," he explained. "So one time he gets the axe, but instead of going out of the rink, he dives onto the floor by the bench when the referee ain't looking. The ref turns and sees he's disappeared, and he knows something's up because the doorway's far away and this crazy guy ain't had time to get there. So the ref skates over to the bench — the crazy guy's on the floor at my feet, trying to stop laughing — and looks about, perplexed, and says to me, 'Did he leave the ice?' and I nods, 'Sure did.'

"Well, then he hears the nitwit laughing, leans over the boards and sees him on his hands and knees at my feet, and jerks both his thumbs over his shoulder. 'Both of you,' he says, 'out of here!'

"'What did I do?' I protest.

"'You lied to me!' the ref yells," and everyone laughs and Norman Watt nods his head. "Thrown out for lying."

"I got a penalty for kissing once," McLennan then says, twisting the end of his droopy mustache with his fingers. This naturally brings the laughter and interest up. He leans in.

McLennan's the Doc, wiry, strong. He's a very good hockeyist, a rover, which in the old days of seven-man hockey was kind of an extra defenseman, usually your best one who'd be allowed to do much as he pleased. McLennan's got wild eyes, a lean, hawkish look to him, nothing remotely like what you'd expect of a real doctor.

"I got a penalty for kissing once," he says, "back home in Cornwall. I played for a nervous wreck, a man named François Lafrançois, a Frenchman from Quebec City. He ran the team, even bought equipment with his own money for the good kids who couldn't afford none. So we're in this big game, a tournament game, and sure enough I bust in over the left side and slide one by the goaler to put us ahead by one with only a minute to go in the game. Won the game for us. Well . . . I'm gliding back to my position for the face, you know, and I hear the people screaming, and when I turn here's fat François Lafrançois sliding across the ice — he's a big, fat, round guy with wide, wild eyes — he slides over, throws his arms around my neck and gives me this big, sloppy kiss right on my lips — right on my lips! — all the while doing his French gibberish because whenever he gets excited he forgets he's in English Canada, and sure enough we get a penalty for delaying the game. Off I go . . . "

These are the stories of hockeyists, and of course I'm relaying those mostly of the guys who went east, the Dawson City Seven, the team which did challenge for the Stanley Cup in 1905 in Ottawa. It all happened. And I was one of them, one of nine actually, with Hector Smith, George Sureshot Kennedy, Doc McLennan, Brother Albert Forrest, Archie Martin, Crazy Norman Watt, Gloomy Johnstone. I'll explain them all. Hannay.

I'll only tell you the good things about these guys, only the good stories. The funny ones. The reality being, of course, that we were all young, except Joe Boyle and Doc McLennan and Weldy Young who were in their thirties, and being young and away from home, well, there's bad stories to go with the good is what I'm trying to say. There's bad stories here, but I ain't going to tell them. What's the sense? When you're old and grey and nearing death like myself, you look back at the darker side and realize it don't matter all that much. And this is some testimony from me, the frugal, moralistic New England man, but it's what I feel now. I feel now that the small bad things a man might do in his long lifetime probably don't mean a damn.

Anyway. I found myself in crowded saloons, men arm to arm drinking, cursing, yelling, breathing and talking hockey, and I was young, and I was strong, and I found myself leaning into a wind whose gust sang my song. It was in the athletic club that I first met Weldy Young, who came right up to me and said, "Joe Boyle wants to see you."

Me? Me? A nineteen-year-old nothing, broke, without prospects, sad, called to see a thirty-five, thirty-six-year-old man, strong, keen, the whole of the Yukon in the palm of his hand? Joe Boyle *was* the Yukon, I'd learned since talking with him my first night. Remember, this is even before his First World War days which made him even more famous. Me?

"Joe Boyle wants to talk to you," Weldy Young says.

"When do I see him?" I asked. Young shrugged, picked up Sureshot's half-full glass of beer and emptied it. He stared at me hard.

"Ask me, I'd say he's nuts."

This is how I met the famous Weldy Young. I'd already got his story from the boys. Weldy Young was Dawson's most famous hockeyist, a veteran of nine years of senior hockey, and he'd played for none other than the Ottawa Silver Seven. He was as close to a living hockey legend as Dawson would ever get, a man who'd still be the great Harvey Pulford's defence partner had he not got the gold bug himself and left Ottawa in 1900, just before the Silver Sevens' golden years. Indeed, he was famous as Harvey Pulford's first defence partner, famous also as a guy who'd gone into the stands in his home rink in Ottawa after some overly critical fan, and he had played for the Stanley Cup himself. I don't know what part he played in the formulations of the Dawson hockey challenge, but he was friends with Joe Boyle and Jack Eilbeck and certainly had pull, and he was regarded not only as the natural leader of any team that might walk south, but also its best player. Weldy was thirty-two at the time, a tough negotiator, the son of an Irish father and Scottish mother, possessing, seemingly, the notorious traits of each of his parents' homeland. He could drink until everyone else had fallen, and he was as tight with a dollar as any man I've ever known. At the same time he was willing to work as hard as anyone, and he had that glint of confidence in his eye of a man continually on a mission. But there was no luck of the Irish in Weldon Young.

"Ask me I'd say he's nuts," is what he said. I pondered this exclamation for a moment. I was young, of course, but I entertained immediately what Weldy Young meant by his line, his tone. He was really saying, Joe Boyle, King of the Klondike, wishes to speak to you, whoever you are, nothing as far as I can see, you who can skate but can't hardly handle a stick, never mind play the game of hockey.

"What's Boyle want to say to him?" Sureshot asked. "He can't play hockey."

This, now, was another telling line. It suggested to me that Boyle's thoughts weren't always philanthropic. And I never understood why Weldy Young didn't like me. He didn't know me from Adam, other than seeing me play hockey. Hector Smith thought he knew why.

"Weldy don't seem to like me," I said softly to him one night at the bar. Hector frowned, shrugged his thick shoulders.

"Don't matter anyway, Boston," he replied.

"Yeah, but I wonder why he don't?" Hector played with his glass of beer as if debating something.

"Weldy's sort of a company man, eh? S'far as the country goes. Understand?"

Don Reddick

I did not. Hector pushed his glass back and forth between his hands.

"You're American," he said finally, and I realized the situation immediately. Dawson was unusual in yet another way, being a Canadian town comprised of two-thirds Americans. It made for lively, continual banter of all sorts and degrees between the two camps: who discovered the gold in the first place, George Washington Carmack of San Francisco, or lonely Robert Henderson of the Canadian Maritimes? The Queen's Birthday celebration on the twenty-fourth of May, versus July Fourth? Most of the arguing was good-natured, but nevertheless the feelings were real, and occasionally ugly. I personally tended more toward Sureshot Kennedy's assessment — "I get to eat two Thanksgiving dinners a year is all I know, eh?" he'd say, and smile his hungry smile. But to this day there exists a distaste for any American involved with Canadian hockey, even in the National Hockey League, though four of the six teams are located in the United States. These feelings have been around for quite some time and, according to Hector Smith, I suffered for it.

Course Hector's assessment didn't make it true, which is why I say today I don't really know why Weldy Young didn't like me. I don't mean to dwell on this, but it becomes important to my story, as Weldy was very much involved with the final selections of the team the following November, as you will see. At any rate, when you're a serf and the King of the Klondike calls, you answer.

Joe Boyle's headquarters were at the mouth of Bear Creek, between four and five miles from Dawson up the Klondike River itself, on what everyone called the Boyle Concession, that seven or eight miles of real estate Joe somehow wrestled permission from the Canadian government to prospect over with his monstrous gold dredges. The walk, over the famous gold fields themselves, was full of instruction and interest. Hector, who along with Sureshot Kennedy still worked the diggings, brought me there, which was fortunate because he understood and explained the whole business to me. He also began my instruction in racism.

"You seen Robert Henderson at all?" Hector asked me as we strode over the Yukon ice toward the mouth of the Klondike. I shook my head.

"Lean, hawk-eyed sort, tough. Don't talk much, less now after all that happened."

"I hear he discovered the gold in the first place," I says. Hector rolls his head back and forth, the puffs of steam billowing from under his hood as we walk briskly in the spring coldness.

"Yes and no. Maybe," he says. "See, it's a sad story, what happened, Henderson was inside for a long time, one of the original goldseekers, born to roam. He belonged to the Yukon Order, believed in its tenets. So one day he's prospecting on Gold Bottom Creek, and sure enough he finds gold. Not much compared to the big finds later, but enough to excite, so he rushes down river and who does he comes across but Carmack."

"George Washington Carmack," I says, and Hector nods.

"You heard of him? Course you have. He's a squawman, thought he was an Indian hisself, I hear, was lazy and good-for-nothing like real Indians, and he's fishing with Skookum Jim and Tagish Charlie, his brother-in-laws, at the mouth — why right here! — when they see Henderson.

"Now, Henderson believes in the Yukon Order, which says a man must share important prospecting information, so he tells Carmack about his find. Carmack scratches his head — everyone's heard this sort of line a million times before, remember — he scratches his head and says, 'Well yes, maybe me and my brothers here might wander up,' which is when Henderson makes the mistake that'll cost him a fortune." Hector paused and stopped, spread his arm across the land around us, the slow rising snow-covered hills, the flat river before us, crystallized.

"What did he say?"

"Do you understand how much gold was all around us then? Right here, eh? Wasn't even eight years ago. Can you imagine it? Millions and millions of dollars in gold, just lying in the streams for centuries, just waiting . . . "

"What did Henderson say?"

"I'm part Indian myself, obviously. Lots of Indian blood north of Winnipeg. Métis blood. You ever heard of the Métis? I know Indians, I can just see fat Carmack and Skookum Jim and Tagish Charlie, I can just see how they reacted. Carmack scratches his head and says, 'Well yes, maybe me and my brothers here might wander up,' to which Henderson — smart ol' white man he is — says, 'Well, I dunno, George, I don't want no Indians up on that river. You're all right, but I dunno . . . '

"This, of course, was normal stuff, but it didn't please Skookum Jim or Tagish Charlie much, didn't exactly endear Henderson to them, you understand. And then he compounds his error — he refuses to share his tobacco with the two Indians."

"And this is what cost him a fortune?"

"Hell yes. Because what happens is Carmack and his Indian brother-in-laws decide to wander up after all, and they find the serious gold on Rabbit Creek. Carmack never tells Henderson about it at all, who's working away just over them hills on Gold Bottom, never sends word to him, while the whole region rushes in and stakes out the richest gold creek the world will ever see. Never does because he insulted his wife's brothers, they just figure to hell with him. If you see him around don't talk about it, he searched all his life for the big strike, actually made it hisself, and not only didn't capitalize on it, but ain't hardly credited with the discovery to boot. He's a sullen, angry man now. Don't talk to him about it."

"He didn't make nothing at all?"

"It's worse than that. He staked on Hunker Creek — you understand the rules?"

"What rules?"

"About claiming. See, a discovery claim is worth two claims, and after that everyone gets only one each. Carmack, as the recorded discoverer on Bonanza — which is what they called Rabbit Creek after the strike — got two, though I heard Skookum Jim was the one did all the discovering. Carmack got two, Skookum Jim, Tagish Charlie and then all the rest got one each.

"So Henderson gets gold on Gold Bottom, over them hills, and on his way out he runs into Old Man Hunker, who shows him a better spot on the same river Gold Bottom Creek runs into. See, Old Man Hunker was too late on Bonanza so he went up to Hunker, which he named after hisself. He tells Henderson about the major strike. He tells him about the gold he's found here. Henderson's now in a bind, see, he can stake two claims as discoverer on Gold Bottom, or stake one claim on Hunker, which is richer. So not only was he out of the Bonanza rush, he don't even get a discovery claim on the poorer river. And it got worse." Hector paused and pointed to our right, where a white break in the low hills and scrub trees showed a river emptying into the Klondike, under a foot of snow, of course.

"Look," Hector says, pointing, "Bonanza Creek." This was an amazing sight for me, the source of this entire, crazed scene of the north, barely visible now and frozen solid in the deep cold, but clearly a centre of activity. Everywhere was the debris of gold seekers: pipes to carry spring water up to the diggings, heaps of rubbish, the discarded junk of gold rushes — broken picks and shovels, empty barrels and the piles of empty bottles and cans. Cabins. Mounds of frozen gold-bearing muck waiting for the thaw of spring, when eager gold men would shovel every last ounce through the sluices twice to capture the yellow specks.

"It's a beautiful place, eh?" Hector said, which made me impatient, but I appreciate what he meant now. The northland, despite the awful cold which I never got used to, was an awesome, silent presence in itself, as quiet as a moonless February night with no wind in Sudbury. Beautiful silence, if you can attribute a visual explanation to a hearing thing. We stopped in our tracks and looked around us, at the hills rising up gradually from the ice, the mounds of snow-covered paydirt, heard the tinny holler of workers now and then clanging across the rigid silence.

"So what happened worse for Robert Henderson?"

"You know there's two guys up on Dominion Creek got butlers in their cabins?" Hector said. I laughed and we stepped on toward Joe Boyle. "It's true. These guys that hit, they all went crazy. They all thought a thousand dollars was a fortune. I don't think half of them could ever understand the amount of money they was worth — and they all went crazy when they found out. So one guy up on Dominion gets a butler — answers the door and everything — and sure enough his neighbour got to have one too. Crazy."

"What became of Henderson?"

"Most sold out the first winter. Can you imagine that? Guys sold out for next to nothing, sold million-dollar claims because they thought a thousand dollars was the most money possible. God didn't have more money than that. So they sold out for ridiculous sums, eh? William Johns, a newspaperman, sold a million-dollar claim one half at a time, the first half for eight hundred dollars, the second half for twenty-five hundred. Lippy staked sixteen above that was abandoned, for cry-eye. Abandoned! I think it's the richest claim yet." Hector shook his head and howled. "And the Lucky Swede — you know that one?"

I shook my head.

"It's the best story of all. Shows what greed can do to a man. Al Thayer and Winny Oler — I seen Oler once — staked twenty-nine above Eldorado and figured for some reason it was worthless. They was at Fortymile in Jimmy Kerry's saloon and figured they had a sucker in Charlie Anderson, I should be such a sucker, eh? Anyways, good ol' Al and Winny proceed to get Charlie Anderson drunker'n hell, at which time they convince him to buy twenty-nine above for eight hundred dollars. Eight hundred dollars! Can you imagine? Good ol' Charlie, in a drunken stupor, signs the deed they drawed up on the spot." Hector laughed aloud and I looked over at him. We trudged on toward Bear Creek.

"What happened?"

"What happened? What happened? Charlie Anderson wakes up with a monstrous hangover, and sees this deed he's got, with his, Thayer's, and Oler's names on it, signed. Well, he realizes what they done — he spent every last dime to his name on this worthless claim. He realizes he's been duped so he marches down to the sheriff's to complain. 'I was drunk and they made me sign it,' he complains, 'I was drunk and didn't know what I was doing, I was drunk and these you-know-whats took advantage of me,' he says, but the sheriff just shrugs and points to Charlie's signature on the deed.

"'That yours?' he says, and Charlie looks down at the paper and back up to the sheriff, his eyes wide with his predicament. He nods his head and the sheriff shrugs.

"'All yours," the sheriff says, and off goes poor Charlie. He don't have no money, so he's got nothing left to do but go up and see what he's got. I understand he's taken out over a million dollars in gold now. Since then he's been known as the Lucky Swede."

I laughed with glee at this story.

"I seen Oler in the Monte Carlo in '98. When people realized who he was, they laughed at him and asked if he had any claims he was interested in selling. One guy got Oler so worked up he struck him. Things got worse for Oler after that, everywhere he went someone would say something about it and everyone else would laugh — he finally had to leave for the outside. Couldn't take it no more."

"Deserved it," I said.

"Sure he did."

"People generally get what they deserve," I offered hopefully, thinking of a couple of acquaintances of mine in Skagway. And then, shamefully, of Billy the Pickle. Hector did not reply. I gave up on any further information on Robert Henderson and we clomped along the frozen trail toward Joe Boyle.

"Nigger Jim has a bar built into his dogsled," Hector said. "Sureshot told me he saw it."

"I heard Sureshot say it," I replied.

"Heard about Dick Lowe? The famous fraction?"

"No."

"The famous fraction," Hector laughed. "Another good story. See, Oglivie is the surveyor. Named them mountains up north after him. That first year everything on Bonanza was staked out unprofessional so that claim boundaries wasn't all exactly right. So Bill Oglivie undertakes to straighten them all out, to end all the fuss. Dick Lowe is on the chains one day, and sure enough Oglivie finds a problem right smack-dab in the richest portion of the fields. Eighty or ninety feet of land that ain't part of either claim bounding it, so he's got a big problem. So he pulls Lowe aside and tells him about it, and off Lowe goes to register his new claim. Took out some six hundred thousand dollars from it I believe, the richest single piece of land per square foot ever in the history of the world."

"Does he still mine it?" I asked.

"Hell no, Dick's been drunk ever since, lost everything. A Mountie told me he's peddling water today in Fairbanks."

I shook my head again at the disgracefulness of the thing. Can you imagine, all the riches in the world falling into your hands and wasting the opportunities, drinking in the saloons? It's an awful thing, but Dick Lowe, like most of the other kingpins on Eldorado and Bonanza, quickly ended up stone broke.

We silenced somewhat as we trudged along the trail, the cold biting, the wind blowing gently down the river. After a bit Hector started up again, explaining to me the task of separating gold from frozen muck. He'd done it off and on for six or seven years now, his hands, his forearms rock hard, the veins bulging like steel wire wrapped around iron, testament to his toil.

"The gold was in an old creek bed, I believe. The old creek bed ain't necessarily the one that exists today, so you don't know where you'll find the gold. The streams uncover some of it, but most is down hugging the bedrock. Been there since ancient times, probably, before Julius Caesar and all that. Guys found gold everywhere here, on the benches, up in the hills, everywhere. Guys laughed at first when others started digging away up the sides of the hills, laughed until they saw the tin cans full of gold coming back down. What you do is sink a shaft to the bedrock. You either find it or you don't. If you find it, you tunnel in every direction, building fires or piping in steam to thaw the muck, then shovel it into the buckets and the windlasses carry it up and out."

"Why do they build up around the holes with wood?" I asked, and Hector looked at me in disgust.

"Why do you think? If you just start digging a hole and pile the junk around you, how you ever gonna get to the hole after a while?"

I shrugged. I don't like asking stupid questions and I shut up for a bit. But it's like this. They built square, wooden, chimney-like structures up about ten or fifteen feet over the hole. So when the windlass cranked up the muck, they dumped it over the side and it built up around the wooden structure without interfering with the workers. They'd climb up a ladder to get in. Understand? They did this all winter long, making huge piles of frozen muck all over the place, with all the little specks and nuggets of gold hiding in it, and then they waited for spring. In the spring, with plenty of running water, they sluiced the piles and found out how well they'd done.

A sluice box is a long trough with little boards along the bottom, set up at an angle. You pile in the muck at the top and then run water through it, and the gold, which is a heavier metal than anything, gets caught on the little wooden slats. Understand?

Hector and me took several hours to complete the five-mile walk out to Joe Boyle's, the whole of the way surrounded with gold mines. "Land of the rhyming elements," as Hector liked to say, "gold and cold."

Long before we came to it we heard the whining of one of Joe Boyle's terrible gold dredges, which turned out to be as monstrous looking as it was obnoxious sounding. It was newly built and being tested, gearing up to whine for the next forty or fifty years through all the creek beds of the Klondike. It stood on big legs that enabled it to move up the river water, a long arm with giant buckets strung out along it scraping up everything in its path and dumping it inside, where men worked like ants separating the gold from the muck. The thing looked like a huge, square, sailess ship. It was Joe Boyle's answer to the stray nugget. This machine missed nothing, tore up the whole river flow and left behind a pile of rubbled rocks where nothing would ever grow again. It seemed as evil as it was efficient.

"Dredge," Hector said, raising a mitten toward it as we passed. We came to a cluster of cabins beside a white spot in the hills which I took correctly to be Bear Creek. To the left was The Denver, a big log house with a single stove pipe up through the middle of the roof, a combination post office, saloon, and eatery. Sort of the King's of Bear Creek. To the right, past the cabins, stood the clapboard dining hall and bunk-houses for Joe Boyle's men, and beside them stood the office.

"Coldest spot around," Hector said to me as we entered the cabin area, a motley assortment of structures. We approached the clapboard office, unusual in this part of the world, and paused before the door. A sign, Office of Canadian Klondyke Mining Co., hung to the left.

"We skate here earlier than anywhere else," he said. "Ice freezes on an inlet behind the cabins in September. Norman Watt calls this Beer Creek." We knocked on Joe Boyle's door. "Don't say nothing against horse racing. Don't say nothing against boxing. And whatever you do," Hector whispered, "don't say nothing against the Irish."

I thought this interesting advice. I mean, how often will you get that kind of advice when calling on a man of enormous stature? Joe Boyle answered the door himself and stared at me.

"You stink now but I think you'll get better," he said. I stared at the man.

"Hockey," he said. "I want you to play on my hockey team, eh?"

Don Reddick

16

"HURRY UP AND CLOSE THE DOOR," he said, backing into his office. Inside I saw nothing remotely normal. Not that I'd been in many offices of great companies, but I entered the president's office of the box factory back in Boston once, and it was lavishly furnished, what with various shiny desks and chairs, thick, beautiful rugs that sunk a little when you stepped across them. Various important-looking documents framed on the walls. Here everything resembled the tent I lived in.

Joe Boyle, thick shouldered, iron jawed, eyes that would crack if he hardened them at you — this is difficult to explain — Boyle, for all his drive and all his energy, which resulted in all his companies and all his wealth here in the Klondike — he always struck me as an odd duck. Now, this is a man who attained enormous wealth, then forsook it all and became a legend in the First World War, so far be it from me to criticize him. I'm just giving you my impression of the man. I was a young man of considerable introspection. The Joe Boyle I knew couldn't have been more different. He was the type of man who believed in himself immensely, overbearingly confident, a man who decided to do things on a grander scale and then did them, damn the torpedoes. He was an enormous presence, a man automatically looked toward to lead.

"I don't beat around the bush, Boston," he said to me, motioning Hector and myself to sit down. "Hector here can attest to that fact." I looked at Hector and saw him staring into the fire.

"As you probably know, I was chairman of the Dawson Hockey Rink Committee, and the Athletic Association's my team. We had an accident yesterday on number one" — the giant gold dredge Hector and I had passed earlier — "and we now got a vacancy on the Association team." Boyle paused and threw a couple of split logs on the fire.

"We need a wing," he said, straightening up. He placed a

kettle on the edge of the fire to heat it up. "I been watching you, Boston, in those shinny games on the pond. I got a keen eye for talent, you know, I've organized more teams and tournaments than you can imagine."

"Tell him about Slavin," Hector said. Joe Boyle smiled but waved it off.

"All good stories in due time," he said. "I've watched you, Boston, you've got the legs, the wind, the strength of a great skater. You've got a talent not many have, and it's a shame you don't develop it. See, there's all different kinds of hockey players, ones that can skate like yourself but can't manage the other aspects, ones that can twist and turn, the puck glued to their sticks, but can't skate worth a darn, and then ones that seem to have everything but can't seem to do it when it counts — gutless wonders, the ones that shrink under pressure. And of course then you have players like Hector here — smart, crafty with a puck, skate like the wind, and don't fold at game time."

I know I saw Hector gleam with this assessment, though I wouldn't look directly at him.

"You've got half what's needed, Boston. You can skate. No doubt about that, eh? You might even be as fast as Hec here, stronger. What you need to do now is develop the other aspects, the shooting, the stickhandling. Bodychecking. Anyone can bodycheck, that just takes courage. Have you seen little Norman Watt play hockey? It's the other, the stickhandling, passing and shooting that takes practice. Ice time. I want to give it to you." He leaned over and placed his big hand on the kettle to test its hotness. He stood up straight and looked at me.

"We practise every day. Six to seven, before the games. That's when hockey skills are honed, Boston, that's when you try out all the tricks of the trade you learn from other players. You've got the strength, good arm strength is essential, you just need to polish the rest of your game. As for bodychecking,

168   *Don Reddick*

well, you can't learn courage, eh? We'll have to see about that."
Joe Boyle stopped again, stooped over to lay a hand on the
kettle.

"I'd be honoured to join the Association team, Mr. Boyle," I
said, and Hector laughed and Joe Boyle frowned.

"Don't call me Mr. Boyle. Doesn't sound right. Hector tells
me you're a carpenter, is that correct?"

"Yes."

"Well, we need help on the Concession. I'd be willing to
offer you a job if you need one. I've got Archie Martin working with me, you know Archie?"

"I know who he is."

"You'll know him. Never shuts up. He's on the team, too.
By the way," and Joe Boyle picked up the kettle and filled three
cups with the steaming water, "I asked you once about hockey
in Boston. Are there any good, qualified amateur teams there?"
In retrospect, I understand what Joe was getting at. I didn't
then.

"I ain't real sure, Joe." He nods and sips his tea.

"Have you heard about our challenge?"

I shook my head. Thing is, I never did get the whole story
out of Hector and Sureshot. Joe Boyle, in his manner, began to
pace back and forth, gesturing with his hands so that he'd spill
his tea even.

"Hec hasn't told you? We've made an offer to Ottawa to
challenge for the Stanley Cup. Eilbeck's handled most of the
correspondence. You know what the Stanley Cup is, Boston?"

"It's the trophy for hockey," I said, Sureshot Kennedy's disgusted gaze fresh in my memory.

"It's the greatest prize of all, and we're doing everything we
can to get officially recognized." He looked at Hector. "Last I
hear they're talking about an all-star team, not our championship team. Seem to feel our championship team wouldn't be up
to snuff."

This lightened Hector's eyes, he cast a glance at Boyle for confirmation. Boyle nodded.

"Why, that's excellent," Hector exclaimed. "That means . . . "

"We don't have to worry about who wins the championship any more. We just got to get together the best of the bunch. You, Sureshot, McLennan, Weldy of course. Archie Martin, maybe" — Boyle turned to me — "maybe you."

"Me?"

"What the heck do you think I'm doing this for, getting you on the Association team? You skate like a wild man, Boston, you skate as well as anyone — just about as well as anyone I've seen, you understand? The Silver Seven can skate like the wind, we need people who can skate with them. I'm the kind of man that doesn't leave anything to chance. You develop as a hockeyist, you hone those stick skills, and you're as good as anyone out there. I just wish I was younger . . . "

"Did you play hockey?"

"Course I did. I'm from Woodstock, Ontario, everyone played hockey there, Boston, it's our passion. That and lacrosse. And horse racing. And baseball, I was good at baseball. Do you know who I grew up with in Woodstock?"

"No, Joe."

"I grew up with Tip O'Neil. You ever heard of Tip O'Neil?"

"I most certainly have. St. Louis — '87? — had the greatest year in the history of all baseball. He played with Robert Lee Caruthers."

"That's right," Boyle said, with a degree of astonishment, "that's exactly right. Tip led the league that year in hits, runs, doubles, triples, homers, and average. Today they talk about a triple crown, well, what would you call that? He was a bit older, but I admired him, watched him practice day after day, learned a lot from that fellow. Greatest Canadian ballplayer ever. But what I'm saying is, I know sports. I know hockey, that's why I'm giving you this opportunity. See, I sense something in you that you yourself may not sense. I know men, Boston, I know eyes. I can look a man in the eye and tell you everything worth knowing about the man. Including hockey. I look in Hector Smith's eyes and I see motion as smooth as silk, high skills, the good touch, I look in Norman Watt's eyes and I see the reign of terror, I see courage far beyond his size, I look into your eyes and I see . . . strength, the broad back and heavy shoulders, I can tell by looking at you you've done work in your young life. And in the hockey part of your eyes I see splintering bodychecks at full speed, I see flag waving as a result of mere will! What do you say to that, Boston?"

Now of course I was stunned, staring gape-mouthed at the great man, experiencing first hand his presence, his overwhelming control. Confidence. I stuttered something.

"Anyways, I'm leaving soon. Business outside in Ottawa and Detroit. I'm going to talk to Weldy, and I'll be in touch. But I want you to develop, to talk to Hector here, do whatever you have to do to get better, because you're not so hot right now. And we'll know soon enough about our challenge, that should be incentive plenty. Can't you just see us bringing that Stanley Cup back up to Dawson City? Can't you just see us beating those Silver Sevens? Oh, God, I shake with the thoughts! And you know what? We'll never lose it, either. No team's going to come all the way up here to challenge for it, and that's the rules. Stanley Cup games have to be played on the champion's ice, with the champion's people in the stands."

"We'd never give it up," Hector agreed. "We could keep the Cup in the rink dining room. Above the bar."

"We could boil tea water in it!" Boyle shouted.

"We could serve walnuts in it!" Hector shouted back. I remember staring at each in turn as they shouted at each other, their eyes bulging, the veins on their necks arching against their skin. What was I witnessing, I thought to myself? The flow of emotion here was electric — it's the first I fully realized the importance this Stanley Cup had for these men. I got caught up in the excitement, but for the life of me I couldn't think of any use for the Cup here in Dawson that the other two hadn't already mentioned, so I kept quiet.

"Think of it, Boston," Boyle said to me, his tea flying from his teacup, his other hand clenched in a shaking fist. "We can do it, you know, our men are every bit as good as any team outside, especially an all-star team. McLennan's played for the Cup already" — "Queens, '95," Hector put in — "and Hannay played for it this year, though he lost."

"Who's this Hannay?" I asked.

"One of the boys that left last fall. He played for Brandon with Lester Patrick last month. Lost to the Silver Seven, McGee scored five in the first game and three in the second. Dirty Alf Smith got five in the two games. But it's Hannay's experience that will help us."

"Weldy Young played in one Stanley Cup game back in '94 against Montreal, and he lost, too," Hector said. "So that would give us three men with Stanley Cup experience, Weldy, Doc, and Lorne Hannay."

"Weldy's our most experienced man," Joe Boyle added.

"Will Hannay be able to play for us?" Hector asked.

"I'm going to do everything in my power to see to it," Boyle replied. "Why not? Just because he doesn't live here any more . . . " and both, then all three of us laughed. I didn't understand their laughter completely until later, when I found there was rules about who could play and who couldn't. We were bending the rules with Hannay, the man hadn't played in Dawson for a year. Boyle stopped suddenly and stared bug-eyed at me.

"You drink?"

"Not one drop."

"You smoke tobacco?"

"Not at all."

Joe Boyle smiled and dropped an arm around my shoulders.

Don Reddick

He drew me in tight, the size and strength of his arm impressing me. He smiled at Hector Smith.

"This is a good man here, just like Archie and Brother Albert and I. I just wish you and Sureshot . . . you take good care of my Boston here, eh?" he said. "You teach him everything you know, and he'll be on the team heading east next winter. Good talking to you," he said, withdrew his massive arm from my shoulders, threw on his coat and hat and walked out the door. Hector stood with his tea cup dangling empty from a finger, his eyes again mesmerized by the fire.

"Henderson," he said.

"Huh?"

"Henderson. You asked what could happen worse to Henderson." I frowned and cocked an eye at Hector, at his mysterious train of thought.

"Got robbed on the way outside. Robbed of all he had, what little he had. So disgusted he gave away his Yukon Order medal to Tappan Adney there. And you know what he said to Tappan as he gave it?"

I shook my head.

"I think it says something about his mind what he said to Tappan."

"What did he say?"

"Said he wasn't fit to live with civilized men." Hector paused. "What do you think he meant by that?"

My mind was still swimming with the whirl of Joe Boyle and the Stanley Cup, and when I looked at Hector, I saw the lean, hawkish face of sullen Robert Henderson and could not answer.

"I know we can win the Stanley Cup," he said.

I shook my head again.

"No?"

"Oh, no, I mean, I don't know. Sure we can win the Stanley Cup. Why not?"

We left the warmth of Joe Boyle's headquarters on Bear

Creek. Hector worked on one of the tributaries of Bear Creek, but he accompanied me back to Dawson, his day shot, as he put it, desiring now to partake of the nightlife that awful city could spawn. My hockey instruction began immediately.

"There's all kinds of tricks." Hector's breath billowed as we walked the frozen path in the twilight. "You can see at least one thing from every good player. Back home I played against a guy named Harras Kidder who slit the palms of his gloves so he could stick his hands through them and hold players without getting caught."

"How did that work?"

"Well, he'd reach through the slit and, say, grab hold of a guy's arm or a guy's stick at a crucial moment, and it would appear his hand was wherever his glove still was, which was far enough away to look okay. It infuriated us no end — we complained like hell to the refs but they just shrugged us off, figured we was just crying for the sake of crying. Kidder did that for years until a guy busted his jaw for doing it, and told him he'd bust his jaw every time he did it again. That effectively put an end to it."

I grinned at the trick, and truth be known, I swear I've seen that defenceman for the Toronto Maple Leafs — what's his name? — do it today. Brewer, Carl Brewer. I was at the Garden and I swear I saw Carl Brewer do it. So now you know, it's one of the oldest tricks in the book. Hector was talkative this day, as we trudged on.

"I remember a kid from Brandon also, an Indian named Nosilla, he figured out a trick and got away with it for almost a whole season before the refs caught on."

"What did he do?"

"What he realized was that the refs never call a penalty on the player in possession of the puck. Almost never, figuring any body contact was instigated by the other team racing after him, and him naturally defending hisself. Makes sense. So what

Nosilla did was every time he had the puck, he'd elbow and punch and kick just about anyone within reach, it got to be absolutely ridiculous, I mean, here he is, controlling the puck with one hand on his stick and flailing away with the other, and believe it or not he got away with it for the longest time before the refs finally got wise. But I give him credit."

"I'm surprised he didn't get the treatment that Kidder fellow got."

"Oh, he did. We busted his teeth all out, but it didn't make no difference to him. That's right! We called Nosilla Oatmeal because after four or five seasons of hockey he hardly had a tooth left in his head. Oatmeal."

"Good nickname."

"Yeah. I heard some pretty good hockey nicknames in my time. We had another kid come in one day, pretty fair player, rover, from eastern Europe. He's got an accent and Sureshot asks him what his name is. 'My name is Myles Ykeb,' he says. 'Where are you from?' Sureshot naturally asks, and Myles Ykeb just shrugs, says he dunno. 'What do you mean, you dunno?' Sureshot asks, giving the rest of us the eye as we put on our gear, and Myles Ykeb shrugs again. 'I dunno,' he says again, so Sureshot gives him his nickname right then and there. 'Well all right, Myles From Nowhere, have a seat.' That was a long time ago, and he's still Myles From Nowhere, though he ain't put on a skate in recent years. He got checked into the goaler one night and dislocated his kneecap and decided enough was enough. Sells oil paintings he does hisself now, a real lunatic, eh?"

We passed gold dredge number one, where the accident occurred opening up the space on the Association team for me. I stared up at the menacing, whining contraption with disgust and fear.

"What happened to that guy got hurt?" I asked Hector Smith. He laughed nervously, which I immediately understood meant the poor guy must have zigged when he should have zagged.

"How'd it happen?"

"Oilcan," Hector replied. "He fell into the gears that pull the bucket chains."

I said nothing.

"Call him Oilcan now."

17

MY FATHER'S BEEN DEAD now for over sixty years. I know this. I'm not obsessed with this knowledge, I'm not and never have been immobilized by it. Some men are. Some men lose their fathers and never really recover, but straggle and struggle along, never feeling right inside again, never fitting in again, never living properly and in earnest. You'll find these men in the saloons and barrooms of the world, dreaming away their waking hours, in jobs less than they should attain, in broken marriages. Worse. There's a difference between not being the same after a death and never recovering. A proper understanding and respect for the person and the flow of life will not allow you to forget, and carry you will and must your added knowledge. You're sadder. You understand where you never did before that you yourself are mortal, that we all are, and it makes you gentler with the remaining ones you love, and more tolerant of those you don't.

But what I'm trying to explain here is why I keep referring to my father. His presence, his influence over me are very much a part of my story. The apple don't fall far from the tree is a good saying, and to me it means more than the similarities between father and son. It means the learning between the two. See, this story is more than just about me going to Ottawa and playing for the Stanley Cup, it's really about me transforming from the farm kid from Sudbury, Massachusetts, into the man who could set up his household, though you'll have to wait until the end to understand that wholly. And to understand it wholly, you got to appreciate the teachings my father gave me.

"Longstreet didn't want to do it," Daddy told me one morning as we sat on the stone wall, the glistening dew-green of early summer reminding him of a July day a long time past. I watched as he slid the turtle shells up and down his thighs, as if removing a nervous sweat, watched his eyes focus wildly on the ground, intense, his struggling for correct words and sentences.

"Longstreet knew perfectly well what was going to happen. Did everything in his power to avoid it except flatly disobeying Lee's orders. Argued over and over to move the army around the flank instead and make them attack us, which made immediate sense. He knew we was going to leave a lot of boys on that field if he ordered Pickett to charge. He knew it! Lee knew it! So why'd he do it?"

My father looked suddenly at me. I sat speechless, my mouth open, unable to reason with this man who fought so many uniformed devils.

"We was in the fields behind Seminary Ridge, behind the artillery. Just setting there, staring at each other, fumbling with our rifles and ammunition. We all knew. No one really said nothing, I saw some pinning their names on their coats on scraps of cloth and paper like we seen other fellows do at Antietam. Others looked at their daguerreotypes. Fixed bayonets. I often wondered how we could've done what we did, knowing what Longstreet and Pickett and Lee and all the thousands of us knew at that moment, how we could march across that field . . . but you just do it, boy, you do it because everyone else does it and you don't want to look bad, though it'll probably cost you life or limb . . . you just do it. Seems to me a lot of things in life is that way. You just do it. You just grow up, you just work, you just get married. You just die someday. You just walk across a field and try to kill the enemy, for the cause. And there's always a cause, always a cause."

Daddy stopped, and at times like this, when his talking took deeper paths through woods I did not know, I remained silent, alert, waiting for his direction. Sometimes he'd just get up and it was back to work, soundlessly, sometimes he gave in and said more, let himself go, tried to instruct me, or himself.

"There was extenuated circumstances," he said suddenly, quietly. "For correct understanding, Lee felt a victory at Gettysburg would enable the South to sue for peace, would convince European nations to recognize us. This battle was of immense importance. So he felt the risk was justified for what it might bring. He did what he thought was right, regardless of the cost. Longstreet just saw the cost. In the end, we paid the cost, and Lee was wrong . . . and in my normal thinking mind I understand . . . but, my God, why'd he do that!"

"I don't know, Daddy," I said to him, and he looked at me then as though I'd surprised him, made him realize there was still two of us there.

"It's right to just do those things, you know," he said. "Don't think because you just do them, they're wrong. There's reasons we just do them, though we'll spend our lifetimes wondering maybe what exactly they were. Just do the things."

I found myself just doing things in Dawson City in the spring of '04. I went to work for the Boyle Concession but lived still in Dawson, skated every day at the twin-towered rink, exercised my wrists to shoot better, Sureshot Kennedy showing me how. He did it with a bottle, but showed me with a ball, how you take it in your right hand — I'm a right-hand shot, it'd be your left hand if you was a left-hand shot — Sureshot showed me how to squeeze the ball in repetitions of fifty, ten times in a row, five hundred in all, squeezing the ball as hard as possible until on repetition twenty-five or thirty my wrist and forearm muscles would begin to ache, and worsen it would, until repetition forty through fifty my arm would burn with pain. Sureshot told me he'd even do it until tears came to his eyes. What this does, of course, is make your arms like iron, able to fire a puck at the goaler with authority. Sureshot was the best at it, a shot as heavy and strong as in all Canada, I believe, and I was told, particularly by Sureshot himself.

"I got the hardest shot of all," he said to me on the ice one day, and I looked at him, my disappointment in his boasting mingling with my admiration of the fact.

"Watch this," he said, and quickly gathered the practice pucks, then cradled one on his stick in front of the north goal mouth. "Watch this." With one fell swoop, Sureshot shot that puck all the way out of the rink over the opposite end, over the goal and the boards behind it and all. It clanked against the back wall and fell to the floor, some kids racing each other to retrieve it.

"Watch this," Sureshot said, then flung puck after puck out of the rink, one after another, myself and all the others stopping to watch the display.

"Lemme try that," a kid named Johnstone said, and try he did, the puck ending up sliding into the net at the opposite end.

"Let me try," I said, and with my mightiest shove I got it over the net against the backstop, a pretty decent attempt. But nobody could do what Sureshot could do.

This performance went on under the watchful eye of Weldy Young, who I had come to see was an excellent hockeyist, on a par with Hector Smith, though nearly twice as old. I was encouraged by Joe Boyle's words, and I knew now the importance of Weldy Young. The rumours of the challenge for the Stanley Cup were becoming more and more frequent, and a realization came to me. This was a ticket home! Or at least close to home, Ottawa being, what, two days at most by train from South Station. Can you believe that? The greatest adventure of my lifetime was occurring, and all I could see was a ticket home!

Home!

How painful that thought had become, what with the awful news of my mother, and the seeming impossibility of ever getting there. See, when you're nineteen years old, a year working just to buy a ticket home was akin to hell itself, the time endless. I purposely avoided thoughts of home, of all my sisters who suffered, much to my later shame, for want of hearing from me, because I would not write. Somehow I convinced myself that if Old Sullivan's brother didn't write, I didn't have to, either. The sense of mysteriousness that my silence from afar would create back home also entered my mind, though this caused such severe shame I still regret to admit it. And Lizzie Grady. How painful it was to see the apple-tray smile gleaming like the jewels of heaven, the pretty, twinkling eyes — oh, Lizzie Grady, I loved you so! And in my heart, in my mind, in my gut — all I could imagine was Lizzie Grady taking up with some other handsome young man who knew himself and what he was about, forgetting that crazy Mason boy who lost himself in the unforgiving north frozenness. How could I think positive about these things, correct them, when there wasn't a chance I'd be getting home soon?

Nothing lasts forever, particularly those sights and sounds and happy times which bind men to women. Let me tell you something about love. It don't happen overnight, though this is much romanticized. How it does happen is through shared times, laughing on the trolley, holding hands and strolling across the Boston Common and Public Garden, sitting together in the stands of the Huntington Avenue ballgrounds watching Cy Young lose the first World Series game ever.

Listening to classical music in the parlour. Sitting down and re-membering these things you've done together is what makes love. And if you're not around to reminisce . . . well. Reminds me of those contradictory sayings that we use to justify what-ever it is we finally do — absence makes the heart grow fonder, out of sight, out of mind. Thinking of home meant thinking of these things, knowing I was losing her. Course, this all hung on my refusal to write, which was because of pride, as I have said. But what I mean is, Lizzie could either decide to have her heart grow fonder, or she could put the out of sight Mason boy out of mind. And considering he don't write, and considering he messed up on Christmas Eve, well, I came to believe I knew what Lizzie Grady was probably rationalizing. And so I just did things. Course, the main thing I did was practise hockey. Thank God.

The games at the rink were lively affairs, with the spectators paying a whole dollar to get in and all us players splitting the pot. There was much discussion and even argument about this making us professional players, which was a big controversy at the time. Back then you weren't well thought of if you took money for playing games, whether it was baseball, hockey, or even the sinister football. It suggested a link to wagering, for some reason, suggested a link to the devil himself. I think this attitude was part of the Olympics becoming so popular — after all, the Olympics only got going after all the other sports went professional. But a dollar is a dollar, and we certainly took what was offered. Why not? Dawson was always about making money, it's why the whole thing occurred. And I know a good story that illustrates the point.

Around this time one of Teddy Roosevelt's nephews or sons or something arrived in Dawson with the desire to work for a year by the labour of his own hands. Now, this is a rich kid, and a very rich one at that, and back east this was looked upon as an honourable expedition, the kid trying to sort out his place in the grander sphere of things, you know, considerations of a personal nature. And he arrives in Dawson and freely states all this. But the thing is, everyone in Dawson thought he was just plain crazy. In their eyes, this is a kid who already has everything they came north to find, so what the hell was he doing? See, Dawson was always about making money.

So what I'm getting at here is that this hockey business became something more to me because of the possibility it might get me home. I skated harder, strengthened my wrists with the ball, watched Hector and Weldy and McLennan, watched the good players to see what they did and how they did it, spoke endlessly in the saloons afterwards of nothing but hockey as all the players did, and of the Stanley Cup. At first I was lost on that rink, having never played where the puck would bounce back at you off the boards. I saw the many tricks that needed learning, how you could bounce a pass off the wood, how you could shoot the puck into the forward zone and just chase it, things like that. I got better. I learned to lead a skating player with my passes, where before they all ended in their skates, or even behind them. I learned, from painful experience, to keep my head up and watch for the lumberjacks, though there were fewer of them here in the Dawson league, the calibre of play much improved over the pond shinny. And playing with better players makes you play better yourself. I learned to shoot quickly, found surprise more effective than taking the time to spot a shot. I got a lot better. And by the time I got my best the summer came, if you can call it that, and the ice melted.

Hockey ended without my team, the Dawson Amateur Athletic Association team, or the D.A.A.A. as we called it, winning the playoffs. But the importance of winning these playoffs was negated because it appeared more and more likely that if our Yukon challenge was accepted, the team would be made up of all-stars from our league, not the champion.

The summer brought an end to hockey in Dawson, but

hardly an end to hockey talk. I was amazed at the intense interest it held over the Canadian community, and then amazed at how quickly my own interest developed. The sport captures your mind and soul, and I believe it's because of the sheer joy of playing it. Screaming up the ice as fast as an automobile — least in those first days of automobiles — winding up, leaning into the curves on them skates, the wind blowing back your hair, your eyes keen for the puck, there are no feelings that can match these in baseball, or the sinister sport. And to score! Well . . .

There is also a fairness to the sport. Anyone can play this game, anyone can be the best, regardless of size or strength or brains. Basketball, you got to be tall to be the best, in football biggest and strongest is best. Only baseball is similar, though if you're big and strong in baseball you can hit the ball further. In hockey, frequently the smaller guy excels, his elusiveness and quickness great contributions. A big guy can excel too, like Sureshot. Anyone can play who wants to play, who wants to practise enough to excel.

But anyway, just before the season ends, I'm in the rink saloon, it's after a game I scored a couple of goals in, we're shoulder to shoulder and it's actually hot, with the sweat of playing mingling with the heat thrown off by the open fireplace. And it's loud, the throng of tightly packed drinkers, fans and players alike, a few women, yelling bartenders. And I'm leaning one elbow on the bar drinking my root beer, when the Spieler forks sideways through the crowd and orders a beer. He notices me, knows me now as a hockeyist because he attends the games frequently, having to know everything that happens in Dawson for his general spieling. A spieler, by the way, is what you call the guy who calls out all the instructions during a square dance. And spielers in Dawson were the guys the big saloons hired to walk about and yell the attractions of their particular places, special attractions like a boxing match or concert. But the Spieler was unique. He decided during some glass of beer that he would be the self-appointed spieler of all Dawson. He paid for his beer and nodded to the bartender, then spied the hockeyist face next to him.

"Boston," he exclaimed, and patted my arm. "Good goals tonight, atta boy. Taking to the game, eh?" I nodded and sipped my root beer.

"There's things I ain't supposed to yell, eh?" he whispered to me sagely, his forefinger to his lips.

"What's the deal?" The Spieler — never knew his real name, doubt anyone did except himself — the Spieler again pressed his finger to his lips and leaned close.

"Eilbeck's making the official challenge," he whispered, and winked.

"That so?" I said, though I wasn't surprised in the least, in fact, considering all the rumours, I thought it'd been done already. But this was official news, according to the Spieler.

"How come you can't yell it?" I asked him. The Spieler shrugged.

"Nobody wants to look bad," he replied. "See, if we was turned down, we'd look second rate. No need for that. It'll all be official when the challenge is officially accepted. Joe Boyle's gonna handle things on the outside, set up the dates. Schedules. Weldy Young'll be in charge up here. It's all been decided. You know, Dawson City is Canada's largest city west of Winnipeg, but winning the Stanley Cup and hauling it back up here is gonna put us smack-dab on the map, eh?"

I agreed, though I wondered if the Spieler had forgotten Vancouver. I thought secretly of Weldy Young's apparent dislike of me. It was tempered by Joe Boyle's enthusiasm, but Joe Boyle was leaving for the outside soon.

"Who's going to decide on the team?" I asked the Spieler. Again he shrugged, but I realized this never meant he didn't have the answer, or didn't want to give it. He drained his mug.

Don Reddick

"I yelled good today, eh?"

"Yes."

"Did you hear me?"

"Yes."

"No one could yell better, I bet. Eh?"

"Doubtful."

"Beer makes me yell better, you know. It facilitates my vocal chords. Enlargens them. In order to yell properly your vocal chords must be facilitated."

"Of course."

"Why don't you drink beer?"

"Because I had an old friend who persuaded me not to. Had a bad thing happen to him while he was drunk one night. Neither one of us has had a drink since." The Spieler folded his face to think upon this. He nodded, coming to some silent understanding within himself, and waved toward the bartender.

"Bad things can happen, it's a fact. I'm sorry your friend had an accident, or trouble, or whatever it was happened to him. What was his name?"

"Ed Delahanty." The Spieler seemed to ponder this a moment. I watched him, amazed at how he could lose himself so completely in his thoughts, staring as he was toward the ceiling, while around us swirled the confusion of bodies and sound, beer mugs slapped on the bar, laughter, profanity. Screaming.

"Eilbeck's got influence," the Spieler said, lowering his gaze as though I'd just asked my previous question. "Boyle. Weldy." He shrugged. "Mostly it'll be obvious. There's five definites. Hector Smith, Sureshot Kennedy, Weldy Young, Doc McLennan. Lorne Hannay, if he's allowed. He's home in Brandon. So there's only three or four spots open, really."

"Who do you think?"

"Albert Forrest for the goaler position. That's a fact, I hear. Other'n that there's Norman Watt, Gloomy Johnstone, Paul

Forrest, Captain Bennett, Smiling Vince Keenan. You." I was young. I gave myself away.

"Me? Really?" I said, my eyes gleaming like full moons on secret nights. The Spieler thumped his mug heavily on the bar to notify the bartender of its emptiness.

"Funny," the Spieler then said, "used to be a ballplayer named Delahanty. Him and his brothers. His first name was Ed, too."

I didn't say nothing.

"Fool got drunk one night in Buffalo, New York, and jumped off a bridge, imagine that? Decided to try Niagara Falls without a barrel, eh?" The Spieler laughed heartily at his great joke. I said nothing again. The bartender replaced the Spieler's mug of beer and he thirstily gulped it up. Placing it down gently now, he looked at me.

"Ed Delahanty was the greatest ballplayer that ever lived. And you might play for Dawson for the Stanley Cup in Ottawa." I looked at my root beer and shrugged my shoulders.

"Willie Keeler is pretty good, too," I said.

18

ALL THINGS EVOLVE. Charles Darwin taught my Daddy this, and my Daddy taught me. Now, my Daddy didn't just tell me what Charles said in that book of his, but Daddy took the wisdom of that book and applied it to other things. At first I just did things, in the late winter and spring of '04. Then in an evolutionary movement I realized the possibility that hockey could bring me home, so I worked harder at it all, the skating, the shooting, the passing, keeping my head up, aching my wrists with the ball until they cramped with the bends. Cramps.

Don Reddick

And then again an evolutionary development — I got into it, as they say now. The earnestness, the hope, all the excitement about this mystical bowl of silver called the Stanley Cup, it found its way into my blood also.

During the summer of '04 it's all anyone talked about. That and baseball. Weldy Young wrote a letter to a man named Ross, who, along with a man named Sweetland, was called the curator of the Cup. As if it was a museum piece, for cry-eye. Boyle left in July, empowered on behalf of the Yukon Hockey Club to make arrangements, set dates, convince people of whatever it was they had to be convinced of. In August he wrote Weldy that the series would be okayed, but official word wouldn't come until a formal approval by some hockey board that ruled on all Stanley Cup challenges. Actually it worked this way: when Lord Stanley donated the Cup back in '93, he appointed these characters Ross and Sweetland as trustees — that's the word, not curators — trustees of the Cup. Gave them the power to authorize the various challenges — often there was more than one in a season — and to formulate further rules as they saw fit. It was all a very formal business, undertaken in the most proper Victorian manner. Phillip Ross was the editor of one of the big Ottawa newspapers, the *Evening Journal* I think, and Sweetland, Dr. John Sweetland, was the Sheriff of Ottawa. Joe Boyle had dealt with these men while he was petitioning Parliament on his sundry Concession businesses, and he wrote Weldy Young that our challenge would be accepted at their big meeting in the fall.

The word got out. If Joe Boyle, King of the Klondike, said the series would be okayed, well, you'd better believe it would be. This news was received with the greatest of elations among the hockeyists and our fans. I learned of it from Albert Forrest.

Albert Forrest was an eighteen-year-old French kid, round faced, innocent looking, small, and generally considered one of the up-and-coming hockeyists. For the last two years he had swept all the skating races at the spring D.A.A.A. carnival, winning medals in both the one and three-mile races, the most important ones, and also taking first in others such as the obstacle race, the backwards race, and the egg and spoon race. He usually beat out his older brother Paul in all these, except for the Ladies and Gentlemen race, in which a Mrs. Percival and Paul took first. And true to the family tradition, Emil Forrest, their kid brother, would win the boy's skating race. Brother Albert's greatest talent lay in baseball, however, and even though he was still in his teens, he was perhaps the biggest star in the Dawson baseball league. He played with the Amaranths, where he was known as the Boy Wonder. He was a tremendous pitcher, setting the record for strikeouts in a game with fourteen. He tore a muscle in his ribcage throwing a ball in the summer of '03, hadn't pitched since, which was generally regarded as a tragedy. Believe it or not he hadn't ever been a goaler, but his overall athletic ability, his stardom in skating and baseball, convinced Weldy and Joe Boyle to choose him as our goaler.

Albert's innocent appearance, however, was somewhat misleading. He'd come in over the Chilkoot with his family at age eleven, no small feat, of course. This after following his father to the California gold fields as a youngster and living north of Sacramento in the Grass Valley works, and then returning home to Three Rivers, Quebec. His mother had brought the whole family north in 1900 or 1901 in search of his father, who had disappeared after leaving for Dawson. He might have been one of those end-of-the-rainbow guys, for he was never heard of again. I once heard Albert speculate that he'd gone to Nome, but no one would ever know for sure. Enough said.

Albert stood in front of a goal set up near his cabin, glove and stick in hand. His brother Paul, a fairly good wingman with a chance himself of being chosen for the team, stood twenty feet in front of him, firing practice shots at him. These

Don Reddick

two had a wild rivalry between them, were famous for two incidents in particular, one of them humorous, the other not. In the obstacle race of '03 they were neck and neck for the win, when Brother Albert grabbed hold of Brother Paul and pulled him down from behind to the ice. Paul leaped back to his skates and did the same to Albert, causing them both to tumble to the ice laughing, allowing two others to skate ahead of them and win the race. The uglier incident has been talked about since, and probably will be for a long time to come. Brother Albert was catching for the Amaranths when Paul, who was captain of the Idyll Hour, came to the plate. One of them said something — neither will explain — Paul shoved Albert, and Albert replied with a right hook to Paul's mouth. Sureshot Kennedy played with Paul on the Idyll Hour, saw the whole thing and explained it to me later.

"They're both small, but they're both scrappers, tough as nails. Paul pushes Albert and Albert slugs Paul in the mouth, and all hell breaks loose. Both benches empty and there's a general melee, the Forrest Brudders the main event, rolling around on each other on the ground. I got four hits in that game."

They recognized me as I passed.

"Hey, Boston, you're Boston, right?" Paul Forrest, known around Dawson as Brother Paul, said, leaning his chin on the end of his stick. I stopped and nodded my head. He spoke with a heavy French accent.

"I'm Boston," I replied, stopping, "and you're Brother Paul, right?"

"Yeah, and that's Brother Albert," he said, angling his head back toward the kid in front of the net.

"You hear the news?" Brother Albert spoke up from the net. "Boyle wrote Weldy Young from Ottawa, said the games were on. You hear that?"

I admitted I hadn't. Brother Paul turned and shot a puck at

Brother Albert, Albert catching it easily with his gloved hand. It was easy to see, even in such a short moment, that the younger Forrest had the way about him, the quick hands, the movement and essence of composure that marks the good athlete.

"Weldy Young and Joe Boyle decided Brother Albert here would be goaler, even though he ain't played it before. They're smart hockeyists, they know great athletes can play any position. So it's Weldy, Kennedy, Smith, McLennan, Hannay if they can get him, and Brother Albert, they're for sure. Then there's Watt, Gloomy Johnstone, Captain Bennett. Jack Eilbeck. And me and you." Brother Paul turned then and fired a shot past his brother, slamming it against the side of his cabin, almost striking the window.

"And me and you," Brother Paul repeated and smiled, the challenge falling from his gaze, seething. I thanked him as politely as possible for the news, moved on toward my tent, barely containing my excitement. You see, I was going home! And I was going to play for the Stanley Cup! I decided these things then and there, and I entered my tent and counted my money.

Course, the Stanley Cup games weren't the only games we'd play. This was to be a grand tour of Canada and the United States, matches planned for Brandon, Winnipeg, Ottawa, Montreal, Saint John, Detroit — a whole slew of games. The Stanley Cup match was really just the crown jewel of the tour. The players would pay what they could — actually we was supposed to pay our own ways and get reimbursed from the gates, but the reality which was only whispered and joked about, was that Joe Boyle would make up any deficiencies. He wasn't about to let money interfere with the Stanley Cup. So, to be honest, more than a couple players — who'll remain nameless — suddenly got poor in the summer of '04.

I counted my money. With frugality I would have close to the cost necessary by December, which was when our team would leave. I realized that I'd probably have enough money to leave on my own anyway, but the Stanley Cup had inflamed my competitive energies. And there was also the possibility of making money — what if we sold out everywhere we played? This was not an unhappy thought.

I considered Brother Paul, the determination in his eye to beat me out. It was true there were only a few left, and there were others vying for the positions, Sandy Miller, Wild Billy Hope and Smiling Vince Keenan, as good and possibly better all-round players than myself. Actually, after seeing Captain Bennett play, I believed him a definite. I considered the practising Forrest boys, I thought of the instructions Joe Boyle had given me, and Sureshot Kennedy's ball. And from then on, even as I walked the streets of Dawson or sat down for a break on the Boyle Concession, I'd have that ball in my right hand, aching away my arm until it near fell off, confident that if I couldn't be the best hockeyist in Dawson, I'd be among the best skaters and shooters. I became a most determined young man, and it's a truth that determination often overcomes brains or brawn or even luck, so that if a fellow becomes determined, his odds of achieving his goal are greatly increased.

Of course this don't mean if you just convince yourself of your determination things will automatically fall into place. No. This ain't make believe, here. What it means is, if you're truly determined, you do the things required to achieve your desire. If you determine to become a Stanley Cup hockeyist, this is what you do: you think about it all the time, about all avenues you might follow, and then you follow them. You squeeze a ball until your arm goes up in flames to make your shot the best it can be, you walk and walk and walk in the summer to build up the important leg muscles, although they don't seem to be the same ones you'll use skating; you seek out and discuss strategies and tricks with those that play the best, the Hector Smiths and Sureshot Kennedys of the world. You watch what you eat and how much, to prevent slothiness from overtaking your body. You envision in your mind certain circumstances you'll see on the ice, envision what you should do, how you'll respond, and then see yourself doing it. You see yourself in your mind throwing your head left and cutting right. You see yourself looking up and passing the puck directly onto Hector's stick — you see these things and then you go on the ice and they become easier to do, for some reason. You see yourself receiving the pass, spotting the goal, and firing the puck into the net! Sureshot Kennedy scoffed when I told him I did this, but I think it helps. And then you talk hockey, talk, talk, talk, and if you do all these things, as hard and as best you can, you'll become a Stanley Cup hockeyist.

I did.

There was only one last important thing happened before the hockey months of '04 – '05. I worked on the Boyle Concession, that seven or eight-mile stretch of real estate on the Klondike River which Joe Boyle's monster dredge was readying to tear up looking for every last speck of gold. I still was a handy man sort, helping out here and there, shoring up what was falling apart and tearing down what had fallen apart. This was in the diggings, see, and I became familiar with the men and their claims, became friendly with most of them, as the Yukon seemed to draw men together in a way they couldn't, or wouldn't be drawn, outside. A tight society, or at least the sphere you belonged in.

It's a cold, bleak land that slowly works a charm on you, at least if you're a man. Women never seemed to rightly see the land the way the men did, probably something to do with nests and security and whatnot, where the men only saw freedom and independence. Men seem to crave that, that and a long horizon, and I know many stories of men who sent for their wives and sweethearts, only to find them aghast on their arrival at the wildness of the place. Truth is, a lot of women left husbands in the Klondike, and with the exception of some truly remarkable and hearty souls, most refused to live there at all unless they was making lots of money somehow. And most of them left after they made it.

I would stop work at times, and I'd just stare about me at the silence, the long, low slopes of the scarred, pocked hills falling away from the Klondike, the straggling trees stunted by northern coldness, the frigid, rushing waters soothing, a wonderful, melancholy life.

But I'd stand there and muse, conduct considerations of a personal nature, wondering about all I'd done, where I'd been, where I hoped I was headed. I felt proud, bettered somehow, encouraged by my ability to talk to people, even people I didn't know, more easily. Found out it ain't all that hard to say "Hi, how are you?" Found out you could fell great oaks with small strokes, go on long, hard journeys one step at a time and get where you're going, realized that just because Daddy said so didn't make Ed Delahanty's doubles better than anyone else's doubles. During one of these thoughtful times, as I leaned on my shovel thinking myself alone, Hector came strolling along the bank, whistling and then waving when he saw me.

He said what he'd been doing, which I forget, but it included his moving about the diggings and dealing with several men this cold morning. Late August. Explaining his travels, he said, "Up in Irishtown they said they's ready to quit."

"Irishtown," I say, "I never heard of that."

"Surprised, it's got Boston people there. I asked them long ago if they knew you but they don't."

"There ain't a Boston man there named Patrick Sullivan, is there? Brogue?"

Hector tilted his head in thought, then looked at me. I saw in his expression an attempt to sort out the proper words.

"I think sort of."

"What do you mean, 'I think sort of?'" Hec shrugged, said, "If you want, I'll take you there. There might be a man by that name."

We went to Irishtown the following morning, it being a long hike over rough hills. Hector was mysterious and quiet about the whole expedition, which made me think he was going to just point out lost Patrick Sullivan's grave, and say something like, "Call him Froze Sully now." But there were no graves on the path to Irishtown, which was over the hills on the down-slopes of the Indian River watershed. No graves with the name Patrick Sullivan on them, anyway.

Irishtown was an outback camp not unlike any of a hundred or more in the gold area, a group of earth-topped log cabins, awash in woodsmoke and awkwardly arranged, with the ever-present frozen mud and stumps between. An Ireland flag hung limp from a branch sticking straight out over one of the doors, with empty whiskey bottles stuck on the broken-off branch stubs. No one in sight, so Hector cups his hands to his mouth and yells halloo, and a young, sod-faced son of Ireland appears at the flag cabin door, his expression solemn and alert, friendly in a cold sort of way.

He says in the Irish way, "G'morning, gentlemen," and Hector and I nod our heads. Hector points at me.

"I got a friend of Patrick Sullivan's here from back home." The man looks tragically at me, frowning. It's obvious he don't know what to say, obvious that the personal circumstances of Patrick Sullivan ain't exactly normal. I sensed this with Hector but had refrained from asking, having learned long ago that it's usually better to keep your mouth shut and eyes open in this northland.

"You're from Massachusetts?" the man asks.

"Sudbury."

"I'm from Dorchester. Savin Hill. After County Cork, of course," and he smiles and the ice is broken.

"I lived in Dorchester last year, Harvard Street, met my fiancee there," I said, but immediately regretted it, because Hector looked at me strange.

"You never said you had an understanding," he said, and punched me on the shoulder.

"Well."

"When did you come in?" the Irishman asked.

"I came in last spring. Railroad."

"Prospects?"

"Nope." He waved his arm back toward the hills surrounding Irishtown. "We got colours, over and over, but nothing big yet. Mother lode's up here somewhere, hiding. Hide and seek. Peek-a-boo." The man smiled. "End of the rainbow," he said, circling his arm across the sky. All of which was oddly pleasant enough, but it occurred to me there was reluctance on everyone's part to get on with the business of the expedition. After some more small talk I made the point.

"So, where is Patrick?"

"You say you know him?"

"Well, no, I know his older brother. He read me all Patrick's letters about coming in, helped me prepare. They all been wondering why he don't write no more."

The man stared at me. Hector cleared his throat.

"C'mon." The man nodded toward the door, and we followed him in. The cabin smelled bad and was cold, no fire. Dark. It took my eyes a moment to adjust, and when they did I saw the man, saw Patrick Sullivan lying under a heap of old blankets.

"Patrick!" the man yells, and Patrick groans, turns about and peeks out from under.

"What?"

"Company."

"Who?"

"Man from home. Knows your brother." There was silence.

"Patrick."

"You know better than this," Patrick says.

"I didn't bring him, Hector Smith here did. I had nothing to do with the thing."

Patrick Sullivan sighed. He threw the blankets violently aside and swung his legs to the floor — and the sight of it dropped my stomach from my body, for Patrick Sullivan had no feet. When he laid his arms on his knees, I saw that Patrick Sullivan had no hands. What Patrick Sullivan did have was a twisted, godforsaken hatred in his eyes, a disgust for his situation he could not begin to hide. He gasped for breath, and I saw his eyes were sunk deep in his head, his body bruised, his face puffed out. He hadn't a tooth left in his head. Hector stood silent, his eyes to the floor, as I stammered something. Patrick Sullivan waved it off.

"So I've been found out at last, have I," he said. "Go on with you, then, spread the good word to all the loved ones. Patrick's alive and well and found his fortune in the holy land of gold. I hope you enjoy the notoriety of being the one to spread the good news."

"That's a wrong thing to say," I said, regaining my nerve. I looked to Hector for help, but he stared at the dirt, apparently feeling his part in the drama complete.

"Look, Patrick, I don't know what to say. I'm sorry. I didn't mean . . ."

"Don't apologize to me."

"I'm not. Well, I don't mean to, I . . ."

"Don't apologize to anyone. For anything."

"I won't."

"Anywhere." He lifted the stubs of his hands up for me to see clearly. "Think Robert Service'll write a poem about me? Think the ladies'll dance with me? Oh, Paddy Sullivan, why, you're the man of my dreams! Come, let's have a little dance."

"Why haven't you written your brother?" I asked, and the

stupidity of the question shone in all eyes immediately. I added, "You could have sent word."

"Word of what?"

"There's people that care about you."

"It doesn't matter. Besides, I didn't ask you here, I don't want you here, and you can go to hell for all I care. It's a fool thing you being here."

"I . . . didn't know."

Silence. Patrick Sullivan broke into an Irish ballad, the soft, old kind, and I turned to Hector. I could talk no more.

"Let's go." We walked from the rancid cabin and once outside I almost gasped for breath.

"I'm sorry he's that way," the sod-faced man said to us as Patrick's voice floated from the cabin. "He's got the scurvy now, and he won't eat the vegetables to fight it anymore."

"Can't you force him?" I asked, and the man shrugged.

"You can't force a man to do nothing he don't want to do."

"It's understandable," I think I mumbled, and we turned and just walked away. Hec and I just walked out of that terrible camp.

When we'd walked a silent mile or so I finally stopped and asked, "Why didn't you tell me, Hector? You could have at least warned me." Hector shrugged his shoulders and walked past me. "You could have," I said and he stopped. Hector turned and said something then I never forgot.

"Sometimes things is so real you just got to see them for yourself." I didn't protest this, as it struck me as a startling thought. But I had to know the story.

"What happened to him?

"Broke through the Indian River by hisself," Hector said, his eyes down, inspecting something in his walking stick. "Broke through and couldn't get out, so he took off his mittens to get off his boots so he don't sink, claws hisself out, and by the time he got back to Irishtown he was froze in his feet and his hands was gone."

I stared at Hector.

"Had to lose them all, or he would have died. There's some that choose that, you know. To die, I mean. Sometimes you wonder if they ain't right." We left unsaid that by refusing to treat his scurvy, Patrick Sullivan had belatedly come to the same conclusion.

We trudged back to Dawson and I determined that I would not now or ever be the one to enjoy the notoriety of spreading Patrick Sullivan's good news. The first thing I did in my cold tent was say a prayer for the man. And then I wrote a dozen letters home.

19

THINGS STARTED TO HAPPEN FAST. With the unofficial news of our challenge came a remarkable interest from abroad, numerous letters from towns and cities across Canada and the States, asking for a chance to play us. Montreal, New York, Toronto, Minneapolis, Brooklyn, Pittsburgh, Detroit, St. Paul — they all wrote, and many more. Winnipeg. Washington. I think the fables of Dawson's gold had something to do with our popularity, and a chance to see the goldseekers themselves, conquerors of the frozen north in the flesh, turned many minds northward.

On September 9, 1904, Phillip D. Ross, that trustee of the Stanley Cup, sitting in far-off Ottawa, officially recognized the proposed Stanley Cup series. Now, he didn't accept it officially, only officially recognized it, which was just as important, because, as Joe Boyle had instructed Weldy and Doc McLennan, if they bothered to officially recognize our challenge, our acceptance would be a mere formality. I doubt my words today can describe the euphoria this information created in our isolated land, even though Joe Boyle had already told us we were in. Men shot off guns and drank too much beer and otherwise used the news as an excuse to delve into promiscuity and unreason, most of which was overlooked by the Mounties. Dawson would win the Stanley Cup! The Spieler ran into the rink red faced and puffing with the great news. He nearly frothed at the mouth, I recall, yelling, not in his usual foghornish manner, but hysterically, high-pitched — "We're in! We're in! The Dawson hockeyists play for the Stanley Cup in Ottawa!"

And so it was. I remember standing between Hector Smith and Sureshot Kennedy when the Spieler ran in, and looking at Hector to see his eyes wild, his hand clenched tightly on his mug of beer, then at Kennedy to see the notorious look of self-confidence he paraded in times of excitement. The noise which arose from the rink saloon prevented any serious discussion, only slapping backs and winking eyes acknowledged the fuss. Then and there, beyond any homecoming thoughts, I knew I must go. I was hooked, lined, and sinkered. I wanted to win this Stanley Cup now as much as Hector and Boyle and Kennedy themselves, thought of nothing else. I was truly now a hockeyist!

There were complications in the following weeks. You see, the trip would cost an enormous amount of money, collected from us and then Boyle. We had scheduled several games en route which promised an opportunity to hone our skills in preparation for the great match, and also to get a good start on making money. But Ottawa said no. As a condition to the challenge approval, no games were to be played en route to Ottawa.

This devastated the potential hockeyists, who next to the Stanley Cup were most concerned about their personal money.

We officially responded that we were uninterested in previous games anyway, as they would take away from the spotlight of Ottawa. Privately we agreed that perhaps this was a correct turn of events anyway, for if we were to lose any of these games, our draw for the Ottawa match might substantially diminish. Believe me, all minds were on money.

Weldy Young announced try-outs for the team and a series of games against various locals. This activity sent all of us to practising, though the weather was not appropriate. The fall of '04 was warm, and the first ice, as Hector had said, formed on a side of Bear Creek, out where Joe Boyle kept his offices. Hector alerted me, and along with Sureshot we got a head start on all the others, who remained in Dawson, their skates in hand, waiting for the freeze-up.

We would stand on that ice in a triangle, three men covered with furs against the cold, under brilliantly starred half-nights and pass the puck one to another with precision. We'd skate hard and stop, reverse direction and skate hard and stop, doing what today is called wind-sprints. Our breath billowed in clouds from our tired, happy lungs, and it was magical, one of those rare times when everything in your little lifetime seems big, where your thoughts are tired but exalted, where you know exactly who you are and exactly what you're striving for. My God, if I was alone a tear could form in my eye in remembrance.

Hector Smith and Sureshot Kennedy were excellent hockeyists. If a professional league had existed in the far north at the turn of the century, they would have been in it, two strong, carefree souls who could pass, skate, shoot, and hit with the best. I admired them at the time, though in honesty Hector had some personal traits I disapproved of, and Sureshot was downright arrogant with the knowledge of his talent. But when I'm in a frame of mind to dwell on this, as I have been from time to time over the years, I sometimes decide that to be that talented, that good at anything, whether it's hockey or baseball or machine repairs or anything, requires arrogance. Without it, I can't for the life of me see Sureshot Kennedy bowling over anyone, scoring anything.

My disapproval of Hector, though don't mistake for a moment my affection for the guy, was because of his habits. Like most of the men still working the diggings, he drank and smoked and swore, pursued earthy pleasures and enjoyed simple thoughts. I can't bring myself to say he was dumb or unimaginative, it's just that he tended toward the immediate, grasping and gasping whatever he could, but to his credit with a wearied eye that provided some thoughtful insights into the calamitous world swirling around us. Like his comment on poor Patrick Sullivan.

"Weldy don't like me," I said to them one afternoon as we sat in the cold removing our skates.

"So what?" Sureshot said.

"So he's making the decisions," I said. "Hec here says he thinks it's because I'm American. That seems to me a wrong way to think."

"So what? You don't know Weldy Young very good, eh? He's an up and up sort of guy, and the decisions are too important anyway for anyone to fool with. He wants to beat the Silver Seven more than anyone, being his old team and all. He knows every single one of them except this Day Finnie kid, and don't think it ain't eating him all up that they out and won the Stanley Cup after he left. Won it now over and over. Cripes, he was on that team before even Harvey Pulford. He picks a friend or relative that ain't right for the team, there's gonna be hell to pay. Right, Hec?"

Hector shrugged, always shrugged when things only half interested him. Hector Smith, though his eyes often seemed concerned with things beyond the room, or mesmerized by some fire, always had his position in this Dawson scheme of things clearly in his sights. Hector Smith was going to play for the Stanley Cup against the legendary Ottawa Silver Seven. Everything else, including his job, it appeared, was of trivial importance.

"Boyle named us the Nuggets," he said in response. "Should have named us the Dawson City Seven. Got a good ring to it, eh? Dawson City Seven. Just like the Ottawa Silver Seven. Same ring."

"Dawson City Seven," Sureshot agreed. "This is what we can do, the same thing they done. They used to be called the Ottawas, they only named themselves the Silver Seven after they won the Cup a few times. So this is what we do, we go and win the Cup from them, and we change our names from the Dawson Nuggets to the Dawson City Seven, eh?"

"That's an idea, " Hector said, nodding, and he repeated the name in its new light. "Dawson City Seven," he whispered and laughed.

"Do you think I'll make the team?" I asked either of them.

"I heard some newspaper in Toronto or Montreal said our uniforms was gonna be laced with real gold," Sureshot said.

"People'll believe anything," Hector nodded.

"Said we was all millionaires, too."

"Anything at all, eh?"

"I'll be the first to make the team," I said to test if they were even listening.

"Probably the same papers that told everyone there was gold nuggets just setting everywhere on the ground in '98," Hector said.

"Probably the same papers that call the Ottawas invincible. Invincible, hell. McLennan told me we can skate with 'em all. Hannay wrote Weldy the same thing. So it ain't just make-believe, they've all played for the Cup."

"They all lost," I said, which I shouldn't have. Fact, I don't know why I said it at all. Possibly it was a gut reaction to Sureshot's overwhelming confidence, and sure enough Sureshot showed me his famous face of disbelieving scorn. They were listening.

"Brandon is a bunch of farmers, except for Lorne and Lester Patrick," he loathed, "and Queen's University is a bunch of school kids, except for Doc, eh? What are we, eh? What are we?"

"We got a tough bunch of boys, here," Hector said. "Let's face it" — he waved his arm across the freezing landscape around us — "Look where we are! Look what we all gone through to get here. Look what we do! Maybe some of us was farmers and schoolboys at one time, but we ain't no more. We're Yukoners! Nobody, not Pulford or McGee or Westwick — nobody! — is bigger and stronger than Sureshot here. And nobody's crazier than Norman Watt, nobody smarter than Doc McLennan. We can take these guys."

"You know we can, eh?" Sureshot added, looking for my agreement, demanding my agreement. It was my turn to nod, and I truly believed them, truly believed that an all-star group from a four-team city league lost in the frozen northland wasn't just equal to, but better than the best hockey team eastern Canada ever produced. Why not?

"Harvey Pulford's old now, too," Hector said. "He used to be their big star, but he's in his thirties now. Not what he used to be. Frank McGee's their big gun now."

"One-eyed Frank McGee," Sureshot agreed.

"Frank McGee only got one eye?" I asked.

"No, he's got both but lost the sight in one of them in a game up in Montreal. Stick."

"And he still plays?"

"He's their best. I heard Hannay say he's considered the best ever, maybe. By some."

"We'll see," Sureshot seethed.

Practices began on November fifth, and there was an important meeting on the twelfth to determine exactly how the team would be picked. At first the practices were on the open place where I'd met Joe Boyle, then on about the fifteenth the D.A.A.A. rink opened, and the first official practice occurred there the following evening. Two days later the Dawson Daily News announced that practice would continue there nightly until the team left for Ottawa.

I expect starting early at Bear Creek helped me considerably, as keeping up with Hector and Sureshot got my hockey legs and hockey wind in shape, where others, who arguably were my equals, showed up at the try-outs with virtually no practice at all. Cold. It probably made all the difference, and after several sessions, over the period of a week, at the end of one with everyone huffing and puffing and heading off the ice, Weldy Young glides up to me and shoves me with his stick.

"We got a schedule of three, four try-out games starting next week," he says, his eyes dead serious, unblinking. "We're going with twelve, thirteen men. You're one." And he skates off, steps from the ice and disappears into the locker room. I had survived the first cut, as it were, and I was elated. I took a few turns about the ice, dreaming of it all, what would happen in Ottawa, and I felt as young and strong and determined as possible. But when I entered the locker room I saw the flip side of that coin.

Jack Eilbeck, the deputy sheriff of Dawson City and one of the original promoters and writers to Ottawa, sat fully uniformed with his head back against the wall, staring blankly upward. He had been torn by the possibility of having to leave his post — whether he even could without resigning — and I doubt he ever envisioned the possibility the decision would be made for him. But it had been. He was out.

Brother Paul Forrest, anger in his eyes and movements, quickly dressed and threw his sack and stick over his shoulder and left, leaving no doubt as to his opinion of his situation. I looked to see the reaction of Brother Albert, the silent French kid, sitting quietly as normal in the corner, barely looking up to meet anyone's eyes. Smiling Vince Keenan.

Don Reddick

Twenty-one or so players had come, and now eight, maybe nine left in the same circumstance, including Ed Sears, Charley Thompson, Constable Rines, Sandy Miller. Wild Billy Hope. They went in near silence except for the dropping of a skate, as none of the remainder had the heart to celebrate with any last one of them present. And even as the last of the dying left us the dressing room remained silent, I believe with the certain knowledge that a few more would be joining them soon. Even the sure bets — and all acknowledged from the beginning that there were five — sat grim-faced, to their credit. I looked at them — Sureshot, Hector, Doc McLennan, Albert Forrest the kid, and Weldy Young — and I saw the faces of the others — little Norman Watt, big Captain Bennett, Gloomy Johnstone, Archie Martin, who also worked for the Boyle Concession and was close to Joe — mirrorlike expressions, all of us searching, then avoiding the eyes of the others. The scene finally was interrupted by Norman Watt, the crazed little man who feared nothing, who stood up and said, "Well, I believe it's time to try that beer, I hear it's pretty good."

This caused a wave of laughter, as Norman Watt was renowned for his affection for alcohol and frequently would announce upon entering a cabin or room or locker, "Hey, let's try some of that there beer tonight, I hear it's pretty good."

Because of this circumstance I had avoided Norman Watt, but in truth he was one of those wild-eyed characters with the most uplifting personalities, always smiling and joking and near impossible to actually dislike, the kind of guy who took a joke on himself well and was always plotting pranks against others. His story was good. At age seventeen, he'd run away from his home in Aylmer, Quebec, after his family refused to allow him to become a pioneer of '98. Working his way across the country he contracted a severe case of poison ivy and ended up in a Catholic hospital in Winnipeg, a charity case. This caused what most considered an odd bend in his character, for he would forever defend the nuns after that, in sharp contrast to his otherwise carefree demeanour. What occurred when the little man stepped on the ice would interest the Sigmund Freuds of the world, however. On the ice Norman Watt became mad, racing about with his eyes wild and his elbows pumping, creating havoc and mayhem everywhere, unafraid to take a check and certainly willing to throw one, and an elbow to boot if possible.

Hector confided the cause of this phenomenon to me while we sat on the bench watching Norman commit one of his atrocities on some hapless opponent. Seeing me shake my head in disbelief, Hector leans over and whispers, "Small man giving notice." Hector nods solemnly. "Same group out of Aylmer that didn't take Archie because he was too small didn't even consider Norman. Too small and too young. Besides that, he's always felt too small."

"You're short," I whispered back on that bench, "but you don't seem to mind."

"Hell, all people like me are small," Hector replied, "but Norman's from the white race, eh?" I frowned and nodded, appreciating if not totally understanding this insight into Crazy Norman.

The various personalities of what would be the Dawson Nuggets began to form clearer in my eyes with my closer association with them all. Hector Smith and Sureshot Kennedy I knew, already knew something of Weldy Young's ways, but now I saw him deeper, in a positive way. Sureshot was right, I didn't know Weldy too good, because what emerged now was a man, a little older than most of us, who was thoughtful and funny and serious, who drank but not too much any more, a guy intensely competitive on the ice and off. Fair. He had left Ottawa to find gold, had claimed out on one of the benches of lower Dominion Creek, and even made *Dawson Daily News* headlines in the spring of '04 as having the largest dump on the Creek. Well, having the largest pile of muck and hitting paydirt are two very different animals, but it was an indication of Weldy's work ethic that, of all the mines on Dominion, his was worked the hardest. It was also indicative of his general luck. He worked now in the recorder's office, an administrative job, which ultimately brought on his downfall. See, the year 1904 was a federal election year, December sixteenth the exact date, if I recall. Part of Weldy's duties was to prepare the election rolls for the election, which caused the whole problem. None of the Canadians would leave for Ottawa until they'd voted. Joe Boyle had done his most to put back the dates of the Ottawa games. Ottawa wanted them done by January tenth, but Joe argued we couldn't possibly get there in time. Course, in the back of his mind also was Weldy, who he knew couldn't leave until even later after the election, after the votes was tallied.

Ottawa responded by setting back the dates all right — to Friday the thirteenth! Now, I believe they did this in response to Joe Boyle's pressure. He was an old sailor, remember. I wished to gosh I could have seen Joe Boyle's face when he received that news, for Joe was as susceptible to omens and superstitions as any of us. I can only bet that Joe Boyle, proud man that he was, bit his lip and agreed, sweating like a beaver. I'm sure of it. But it didn't settle well with some of the others, particularly Joe's good friend Archie Martin, who was the most superstitious of all.

But anyway, come December first, it became clear Weldy Young wouldn't be able to leave in time because of the election. It was a great shock and loss to the Dawson Nuggets. It wasn't the last. The final team was announced on December ninth, which was humorous because on the following day, December tenth, Ottawa officially sanctioned our games.

These were days of great excitement for me, of course. My game was further developed than many of the others at the time, I was always a powerful skater, and now my wrists could fire a puck with authority and my passes ended up on the sticks of my teammates more often than not. I presented myself well in the practice games, scoring a few goals and checking without the fear Joe Boyle talked of. I made the team. And I got to know my new teammates better.

Jimmy Johnstone was a big, tough kid, hard as nails and silent, a dangerous man I thought at times. He was young, maybe twenty-two or twenty-three, worked with Norman Watt now in the post office after a stint as a constable, had come in in 1901. He was big and tremendously strong, almost as strong as Sureshot. Or me. He was habitually silent and staring, never smiling, as though he'd seen a whole lot of things that're so real you just got to see them for yourself. Gloomy, and it's what we called him, Gloomy Johnstone. I only knew him to express one slant of humour, when I heard him refer to a Mountie as "Your Royal Harness." This, of course, was a sarcastic reflection on King Edward VII, who in 1904 decreed the word "Royal" be added to the North West Mounted Police title. They were the Royal North West Mounted Police now. The genesis of this was that Johnstone was a Dawson constable, involved in the natural frictions and resentments one group of lawmen have for another. He was from Ottawa.

Actually, I remember something that proves Johnstone was human — I remember him as a quiet individual who thought too much. He was one of the drinkers, and whenever I saw him drinking during a sunset, I'd notice him drift away, look out over the colours and raise his mug silently. He once revealed, during one of his weaker moments, a scene on a high lonely road, receiving a dance lesson as the sun moved lower over the rolling hills, said he'd never forget it, became glassy-eyed and turned away. Raised his beer mug then to someone, someone who meant a great deal to him, in another place, another time.

Archie Martin neither drank nor smoked. He was from Aylmer, Quebec, from an Irish family, his father running out of potatoes in County Monaghan. He kept a lively step, was em-

Don Reddick

ployed by Joe Boyle out on the Concession, and was very close to Joe himself, probably because of Joe's family originating in Antrim, County Something. Archie told a good story about his coming in — among his numerous stories, for he as well as Joe had the gift — he told of being turned down by an Aylmer expedition because of his small stature, and of coming up by himself anyway. He had already outlasted all his bigger and tougher townies, and in truth would last another forty years before retiring to one of his brother's homes back in Aylmer. He was something of a black sheep in the Martin family, one of four boys, the other three being dentists. Four boys in the family, three doctors and one that went over the rainbow and never came back. You understand. Archie was thirty-two at the time, a funny, talkative sort who harboured tremendous superstitions. Played lacrosse in the Dawson league with the Hardwares, had won the Jones Cup for the championship in '03. This season he jumped to the Maple Leafs, playing with the likes of Doc McLennan, Crazy Norman Watt, and the four Scurry brothers. He also played hockey with me on the D.A.A.A. team, a steady but unspectacular player, good enough to go east.

So there, Smith, Kennedy, Watt, Johnstone. McLennan. Lionel Bennett had made the team. And Forrest. Randy McLennan was the Doc, a graduate of Queen's University, where he starred in three sports. He was famous in Ottawa for his hockeyist talents, a rover in '93, '94 and '95, winning the Dominion Championship in '93. Played senior lacrosse for Cornwall, played the sinister football, too. Toured the United States. Of all the Dawson hockeyists — besides Joe Boyle of course — McLennan held the most respect. More even than Weldy Young, I believe. He seemed accomplished in all he endeavoured, the three sports, doctoring, his personal way of carrying himself with dignity. Long, droopy mustache, lean and hard. A great man almost, learned in all things and a great reader, why, he even was treasurer of the Temperance Society in

Dawson. I looked up to him, but not as much as Brother Albert Forrest, who adored him. Tailed him about always, it seemed, McLennan taking the kid under his wing.

Brother Albert was only eighteen years old, round-faced and shy, nevertheless a great athlete, possibly the greatest of us all in the end, who would perform his best when the pressure descended. He played in the indoor baseball league now on the Violets with his brother Paul, baseball so popular in Dawson that the indoor league was established in the spring of '04. He was often alone, however, and I felt this was a consequence of not only his lost-father problems, but his isolation somewhat in being French Canadian, for there were few French-Canadian athletes in Dawson. He was a printer by trade.

There was some games, and some was called off. Brother Paul Forrest got together a group of cut players and a hundred dollars, hell bent on beating us, and Weldy accepted the game but declined the bet, his concern with the raging discussions involving professionalism foremost in his mind. On December fourteenth we played the Colts, with Brother Paul on wing and Emil Forrest in goal, and Clark, Swift, and Charley Thompson. We beat them four to one, thankfully, for none of us wanted to lose to men cut from the squad, and we all knew these fellows wanted to beat us badly. The night was a fund raiser for us with all the proceeds going toward our expenses, and a women's game preceded ours. The *Dawson Daily News* carried a story on us the next day, much encouraging us. Said we were "working like beavers" to accumulate our funding, which was the source of some sour joking among us, which I won't go into.

The women's game gave us an opportunity for much comic relief, for Crazy Norman Watt — as a surprise to everybody — came onto the ice to referee it in a dress and hat, the hat decorated with chrysanthemums. On his shoulder he twirled a sunflower-patterned parasol. This caused an uproar with our crowd — with everybody — and we called to him as Miss

Watt, and Doc noted he never did see such a helpful referee before, Crazy Miss Watt helping up any of the players who fell down close to him.

So only the last great shock remained for the Dawson City Seven. Lionel Gordon Bennett, Captain Bennett of the Mounted Police, was a big, strong, important part of our team. He was from Nova Scotia, and he'd captained the Civil Service championship hockey teams, skating with McLennan, Watt, Kennedy, Eilbeck and Johnstone, and was a star in baseball, hitting .321 with the City Eagles of the indoor league. In December of '03 his wife was struck by a runaway sleigh at the corner of 3rd and Queen, the horses dragging her near sixty feet, almost causing her death. She had never fully recovered from the accident, and I believe the news of the great Ottawa star Harvey Pulford's wife dying in November convinced Captain Bennett he couldn't leave his wife now. What a shock, as Bennett was very good and belonged on the team, but there it was. Two of our best players, the famous Weldy Young and the sturdy Captain Bennett, were out.

The Dawson City Seven: Hector Smith at centre, George "Sureshot" Kennedy at right wing, "Crazy" Norman Watt at left, Doc McLennan rover, Gloomy Johnstone at point, Hannay to be coverpoint. Albert Forrest in goal. Me and Archie Martin as extras, Archie in charge of other duties as manager as well. Nine of us altogether. Meetings. Money collected. Arrangements, sailing times, train schedules, hotels, everything gone over, studied. Newspaper reports. An obscure occurrence three thousand miles away made the Dawson papers, and I'm probably the only man in existence to recognize it years later, when its significance presented itself. The little town of Rat Portage, Ontario, changed its name to Kenora in October of '04. So what, right? So Kenora won the Stanley Cup in 1907, and but for that decision by the town fathers, the name Rat Portage would forever be inscribed on Lord Stanley's Cup!

Finally the time came. In near hysteria Dawson prepared to see off its heralded hockeyists, who no doubt would bring the Stanley Cup home to the north, where it would sit forever. Frank Slavin, former heavyweight champion fighter from Australia and one of Joe Boyle's early partners, came in over the trail from Whitehorse on foot, suffering badly from appendicitis. Told us there wasn't much snow nowhere. This was bad news for those of us who had decided to dogsled out, Hector, Gloomy, Sureshot, Archie Martin and me. The others planned on bicycling out the next day. Johnstone, when he heard the Slavin report, decided to wheel it out with the rest.

I woke up early that morning, having slept hardly at all. In the greatest of excitement I shouldered all I owned in the world, then for the last time walked the cold hard streets of Dawson, through the white tents and brown huts and woodsmoke-filled streets, now lined with miners and wives and children and hangers-on, all moving aside for me, clapping my back, yelling untold thousands of encouragements and advice. I walked, my skates slung over my shoulder for all to see, my hockey stick as my walker, and I marched in this fashion to the frozen riverfront, where I saw Hector and Sureshot standing amidst a large crowd, all smiles. Martin was nowhere in sight. I approached my friends, Hector's hand outstretched toward mine, Sureshot adjusting a pedometer he had acquired somewhere.

I saw McLennan and Weldy Young approach with Archie Martin, saw the dog teams, the sleds, the large carriage being piled high and secured. I saw the Spieler, speechless and hung over, tears in his eyes, standing with us all, a sadness to him which personified Dawson's sadness whenever anyone left for the outside, as more often than not they would never return.

I saw it all in that half-light morning, the brown, fur-covered men, the brightly coloured women, the kids running among our legs, touching our hockey sticks, and the tears of a young New England man came to my own eyes, for I knew I was leaving a special place, a historic place, a place I'd never forget. I shouldered my pack with the others, and with the howling, raging dogs I walked amidst the cheers of hundreds onto the ice of the Yukon, toward the wilderness. I'd been in Dawson less than ten months.

I left the last, the greatest gold camp of them all.

20

WE WEREN'T OUT OF EARSHOT of Dawson before Sureshot Kennedy pulled out a copy of the *Dawson Daily News* and called us to stop. This was my first hint of Sureshot's obsession with the printed page.

"'December 16, 1904, To leave tomorrow,'" he read aloud, his breath billowing the cold words, "'Dawson Hockey Men to Start for Ottawa, Will Lift Cup.'" He smiled his obnoxious smile. "'Hec Smith, Sureshot Kennedy, Archie Martin and Boston Mason, of the all-Klondike hockey team, will leave Dawson for Whitehorse tomorrow. The boys will hot-foot it to Whitehorse with a dog team, and promise to get there with the best developed set of leg and lung muscles ever built up for a hockey team. The other boys will leave by stage within a few days and overtake the mushers.'" Sureshot hesitated, said, "Blah, blah, blah," then, "'Most of them have interests or good positions to bring them back.'"

"Let me see," Hector said and pulled the paper from him. Archie Martin seemed uninterested, stared at the growling, yapping dogs. Actually yapping isn't a good description at all, for those northern dogs, closely related as they are to wild wolves, could not bark at all, but howled all their communications among themselves. I watched them all, the smiling, confident Kennedy, Hector reading the newspaper for himself, Archie gazing at the dogs.

"What's this stage business, eh?" Hec said and Sureshot laughed.

"They don't get nothing right. The Spieler probably told them that when he was drunk. McLennan this morning told me they was using bicycles."

"Bicycles won't last thirty miles," Archie said, surveying the low hills that crawled away from us in all directions.

"That's all right, we've plenty of time. The *Amur* leaves Skagway in what, twelve, thirteen days? Them bicycles could all fall apart and the guys'll still have time to walk to White-horse. It's only a few hours on the train to Skagway."

And with such definition Sureshot Kennedy reduced this three-hundred-and-fifty-mile trek from Dawson to White-horse, and the train ride from there to Skagway. From Skagway, the steamer *Amur* would transport us to Vancouver, where we would board the eastbound Canadian Pacific. After about five days, passage, we'd arrive in Ottawa with about a week in which to prepare for the great matches. Joe Boyle had planned it all to the day, even believing a day off in Winnipeg on the way was possible. Twenty-eight days before Friday the thirteenth.

"I figure ten days, thirty-five miles a day," Sureshot said, Archie nodded, spat on the ground, and we moved off then, a couple of us, I'm convinced, rather appalled by the schedule, or at least the immediate schedule. Thirty-five miles a day! With-out snow! My mind, practised at mathematics with the continual calculations of my money matters, figured further: thirty-five miles a day walking, perhaps three miles an hour what with the packs and sleds and the continuous untangling of the crazed dogs, that was twelve hours a day walking, fourteen with breaks and lunch. For ten straight days.

We soon succumbed to the unending silence radiating away

from us like spokes in a bicycle wheel, trudging along, our eyes on the ground before us, lost in our indistinct thoughts. My own reeled across numerous paths, my mother, my father, Miss Grady. The Stanley Cup. Home. Warm weather and faces and voices I know, the brick streets of Boston . . . the Stanley Cup. There was time to dream, and I did so, seeing Sureshot — to my unending discredit — hurt and taken off the ice, my replacing him and scoring the big goal . . . I saw Lizzie Grady with her father at the games, jumping up with celebrations at my goal, her eyes, her dazzling smile greeting my banged, sweating body afterwards. Everything works out in your daydreams, eh?

It turned colder, about ten below zero, and a dust of snow swept silently and unconvincingly across the land, and we trudged on through it all. The land itself is stunted by its northernness, the trees thin and bent, the rocks cracked with continual freezing, the air itself heavy with cold and half-lighted late afternoons. The trail was open and empty, and we yearned for the roadhouses that strung themselves out along at appropriate intervals, knowing that their warmth, with steaming hot soups and steaks of caribou and moose, would be waiting. We'd have places to hang our coats and boots, we'd talk with the lonely, strange keepers who endured their silent lives in continual vigil for the next travellers. The first one, Clark's, at twenty-five miles, we had deemed too short a day's travel. The second, Wounded Moose, at fifty-five miles, was too far. So the first night out we determined to sleep outside. All I remember is, fifty roadhouses between Dawson and Whitehorse, and here we're going to sleep outside.

We needed snow. Dog teams need snow to move smoothly, and there was almost none. It is a misconception that men ride in comfort on their dogsleds. In truth they do a great deal of running alongside, working the rig, so it's not as though snow would have eased our travels. But the dogs strained considerably with the weight of the sleds on solid earth, slowing us down. I'd heard it said seven days by sled to Whitehorse, I heard Sureshot say ten with what we had. I soon believed it would be more.

"Nigger Jim has a bar in his dogsled," Sureshot said at one point, but nobody responded, which was of greater significance. "Wish we did," I believe I heard him mumble, his scowl descending now, to rest on his face the remainder of our walking journey. On a few occasions in my lifetime I've come across written accounts of our trip, though for the most part the whole thing's been long forgotten. I've read nonsensical, supposedly first-hand accounts of us laughingly roving through the wilderness, having snowball fights and enjoying ourselves. Nothing could be further from the truth. Perhaps the only enjoyable aspect at all was our dreams, individual and collective, for all of us were headed for home, and all of us would play for the Stanley Cup. If my own thoughts are a sample, a lot of silence was devoted toward wives and girlfriends, family and old friends. For Hector and Sureshot they lay in West Selkirk, just north of Winnipeg, for Archie Martin in Aylmer, across the river from Ottawa, and for me, of course, Sudbury. And Marlboro Street.

We passed Clark's roadhouse, barely stopping to warm up, such was our excitement to be travelling at last. Sureshot, after consulting his pedometer, decided we should stop several hours later, and we did so, feeding the dogs and building the fire, and melting a lump of beans in the great kettle. I unfroze my sourdough by submerging it in the bubbling beans and I swear I never tasted a more necessary meal, it's what the cold does. We slept close, in a pile really, of dogs and blankets and men, with the Yukon cold of December covering us so that never was it possible to feel comfortable. But we slept. Soundly. I awoke to quarrelling dogs, tin cups clinking and the smell of strong coffee. It was well below zero, weather that makes a man mutter despite hot coffee and morning fires, and only moving along restored feeling to the extremities. Hector and Archie seemed chipper enough, but Sureshot was miserable.

"Only made thirty miles yesterday," he said to no one in particular, so no one responded. "We got to make it up today, eh?" He adjusted the pedometer on his belt. "We got to make it up today, eh!" he said again in his way that demanded a reply. His words irritated me, and I could see they did not please Archie Martin, but Hector, his old friend, cast a long, bored look in his direction. Sureshot caught it, some lifelong secret communication took place, and he quieted.

This day and the next we passed Wounded Moose and Stewart Crossing, bringing us deep into central Yukon, which is the middle of nowhere. A more forlorn, lost land cannot be imagined, a white spot on the map that sometimes hits fifty below zero in the deepest winter, which we were close to. There were no snowball fights. In fact, the land held little snow, though when we met the land stage they told us — after congratulations — that word had it it was snowing in Dawson and heading south, news our camp viewed favourably. This stage, with a group of four men, surprised us. We knew of Dawson's excitement, of course, but we did not know of the pride and good will the remainder of the territory held for us. The first greetings from these men's mouths were, "Are you the hockeyists?" Sureshot shouted we were, and I saw Archie Martin's eyes come alive with the excitement of this pleasant surprise.

"They're waiting for you in Whitehorse," the driver said.

"Who is?" Hector Smith asked him.

"Why," the man replied, in a tone which screamed, Don't you know? "Why, everybody!" Hector looked at me and I saw Sureshot cast his patented, glorious glare. For a short time our spirits lifted, Hector boxing the air and Sureshot even laughing, Archie Martin babbling no end of nonsense.

"We're famous in the whole Yukon now, eh?" Sureshot said, and we happily agreed. Famous in all the Yukon!

An astounding fact that was. Only a short time ago I had sat on the banks of the shrouded Yukon River, my face in my mittens, my heart and billfold broken. It was not even a year since I had left Sudbury. What had I seen? What had I done? Was this truly me trudging south through this remarkable wilderness, a pack on my back, the screeching dogs at my feet, my hockey stick in my hand as my walker — a veteran of the gold wars of Dawson?

Well then, I never had no turtle soup, but I had beaver tail at Yukon Crossing six days toward Whitehorse. We came onto this roadhouse earlier than we wanted to stop, but after one hundred and eighty-odd miles on two feet through frozen Yukon hills, you make excuses.

"We oughtn't to stop here," I said as we neared the two-storey log house, smoke and heat shimmering the air about the chimney, and everyone else muttered agreement as we walked in with no intentions of leaving. What luxuries — a roaring furnace, hot moose stew simmering lovely in the kettles, pegs to hang our coats and blankets. The proprietor, a small, bald-headed Frenchman with large eyes and a constant gap-toothed smile, knew us — famous we were, eh?

"I believed you was the other bicycle group, thought you'd missed me," he said, gap-toothed. "Word is the others ain't far behind, then." We all ate too much soup, then we ate beaver tail, which is somewhat of a delicacy up north, but which I hadn't yet had the opportunity to eat. It tastes good. Something like a tough, jellied beef, but nothing like that, exactly.

As we left early the next morning, Laroquette, the gap-toothed man, blessed us in the Catholic way and said to us he'd prayed to God we'd come back and show him the Stanley Cup. Hector and Sureshot assured him we would, which appeared to overjoy the little man, and we set off with pleased constitutions. Christmas Day was along here, at one of the roadhouses.

It was an awkward morning, none of us knowing what to say, and all of us feeling the lonesomeness the situation caused. Once outside the roadhouse, Sureshot came out with presents for us all, explaining he didn't have none for the keeper, so he'd waited. He gave Hector a cloth-covered pint of whiskey, he gave Archie a covered pint of whiskey which Archie promptly threw away in disgust, and he gave me a covered pint of soda. I thought it was a joke until he apologized, said he didn't know what exactly to get me. To this day I don't know what to make of that episode.

It was three more days of near freezing to death on that rocky trail, with stays at the Montague House, Hootchi, and Nordenskiold, before we heard the hollers of the others. The bicycle brigade, as Sureshot called them, had caught up. McLennan first, still on his bicycle. The others, he told us, had made it as far as they could until the bicycles had all broke down, and then walked. They weren't far behind.

"We're two days still," Sureshot mentioned, but the others and myself ignored him. It was too much, too hard to think of that much more toil. Seventy miles, more or less.

"We should wait for the others," McLennan said. "We should all go into Whitehorse together." We nodded agreement more out of respect for the man than any formal thoughts to the suggestion. McLennan, his breath froze in long icicles down each side of his droopy mustache, still held a commanding presence over the rest of us. With him about I knew there'd be less women, drink, and tobacco talked of, which pleased me. Crazy Norman Watt came up next, followed several hours later by Johnstone.

"Where's Forrest?" Crazy Norman suddenly yelled, setting up our biggest joke of the trip, for as he said it Brother Albert emerged from the trail, sitting comfortably upon the southbound Whitehorse sleigh. He was laying on the ground,

Norman was, his head on his pack, his hockey stick pointed up, shooting imaginary ducks for an imaginary dinner when he yelled. McLennan, wit that he was, made the joke.

"Well," McLennan says, "seems Norman here can't see Forrest for the trees!"

Norman broke into the biggest grin, shot another duck and said, "Forrest for the trees, eh?" amidst the laughter of the whole gang. It was a fine moment, our reunion, and after Albert removed his gear from the sleigh our spirits lifted and we made several more miles before camping and grub.

This night was still clear and very cold, pushing twenty-five below zero, and McLennan or Watt mentioned the barometers were falling at the Montague House, where they too had stayed. Not that we thought it much mattered, for we had made near three hundred miles without snow. It was a joyous time around the fire this evening, hockey once again foremost on our minds now the most difficult leg of our journey was almost over. McLennan told the first story.

"God-awfullest thing I ever saw was on the ice in Montreal back in '93. We had a guy named Weatherhead on our side, and we were playing the A.A.A. — they won the Cup in '93 and '94, actually they were awarded the Cup in '93, the first Stanley Cup games was in '94 — and I'm rover, and up ice we come and fire the puck in and Weatherhead races in after it, and the puck slides right to the Montreal goaler just as his point or rover comes in. They collide and down they go — just as Weatherhead glides in. He leaps over the two to avoid them, but his skate comes down on the inside of the thigh of the poor goaler."

McLennan pats the top of his inside left leg, the rest of us leaning up on one elbow, the flames dancing across our lost faces, our eyes stuck on droopy McLennan like burrs.

"Cut his leg so severely a patch of blood four feet wide appears instantly."

"Broke his central vein," Hector said.

"Severed his main leg artery," McLennan nods. "Luckily there were doctors there — I wasn't a doctor yet — and they slipped out over the ice and saved that boy's life right then and there, tied his leg up over the cut with a shirt and carried him off. Left the huge patch of blood there, which bothered a few of the guys. We sort of swished it around and mixed it with the ice chips to disperse it somewhat, but it sure was odd to go skating through it."

"What happened to the goaler?"

"Never played again."

"What kind of name is Weatherhead?" Norman asks, and everyone laughs.

Of course one story provoked another, as always. When one guy finished, all eyes wandered the fire circle, looking for the next story, and somebody would clear his throat and begin.

"Funniest thing I ever saw was Crazy Norman here last winter when Smiling Vince Keenan skated over his hand," Sureshot begins. We all look at Norman, who slides his flask under his blanket and smiles, happy to be the centre of a story, then back to Sureshot who nods solemnly, closing his eyes.

"Skated over his left hand, Smiling Vince did, I don't know, what happened Norman, you forget to put on your gloves or what?"

"Dropped it trying to swat Brother Paul!" Crazy Norman screeched from under his blanket.

Sureshot cocked his head toward Norman and rolled his eyes, then continued. "So he tries to hit someone else and misses, hits the boards instead and falls to the ice. Along comes Smiling Vince — smiling away — and slash! Skates right over Crazy Norman's left hand!" Sureshot laughs here, and the others join in, but I don't get it. This is the funniest thing Sureshot's ever seen?

"I don't get it," I says then, and the others laugh louder.

"I ain't finished yet," Sureshot says. "Norman looks down

at his hand and frowns, skates over to the bench, and we all can see he's bleeding and holding his hand, we skate over and Hector here says, 'Hey Norman, you okay?' and Norman raises his hand, then grabs the skin around the cut — and it's about two inches long and deep — and he starts moving the cut open and closed like it's a mouth talking, and he mimics, 'Why, I'm okay, Mr. Smith, I'm just a small cut.' We almost all died laughing."

And we almost do now, even I, at the thought of it all. I look again at Norman to see his eyes gleaming, his crazy smile, pulling his left hand from under his blanket to show his scar . . . all of this through the woodsmoke of a crackling fire warming one side of us only in the dark froze wasteland, where our words bounce back at us from the wall of cold.

A fine moment, captured in my mind like a snapshot, for I know Whitehorse is two days away at the most. One more day would find us over the Dead Horse Pass on the railway back into stumpy, muddy Skagway, Alaska, in the United States of America, and my Yukon days would be over forever. I was not among those with interests and good positions to bring them back. The only good position and interest of mine lay four thousand miles to the east.

Of course none of us, tired and circled as we were around that dot of a campfire in the long, black, wolf-howled wilderness listening to stories, none of us had the imagination to conceive of the turn of events in Whitehorse.

21

WE ENTERED WHITEHORSE on December 29, 1904, under greying skies which spit out occasional gusts of snow. Sureshot Kennedy's pedometer read three hundred and twenty-one miles, and we completed it in just under thirteen days, an average of what, around twenty-seven miles a day . . . on foot . . .

Whitehorse was a small town barely more organized than Dawson, froze against the banks of the great river. A surprisingly large number of humans existed here, and upon discovering us every last one of them appeared at our sides, slapping backs and shouting their encouragement, very much to our astonishment. It was one thing to reassure each other in the wilderness that we were famous throughout the Yukon after talking to a few sleigh drivers and roadhouse keepers, it was quite another to experience it here in Whitehorse, with people most of us did not know.

McLennan knew many, of course, having worked in other territorial government offices before being transferred to Dawson with Captain Bennett and ending up on the Civil Service hockey club. He embraced several men and women, all smiles and happiness, and our adventure turned golden in that half-lighted madness.

People unused to celebrity are apt to lose their senses to it. And it's not just celebrity. It happens, I've seen it, to any number of men and women who step up or achieve a higher degree of living, whether it's a better position at work, or more responsibility on the farm, or a newly married girl with her old friends. A giddiness surrounds their heads and clouds their eyes, so that they're somewhat taken with the importance of themselves, and they make mistakes. They can make asses of themselves. The younger they are, the worse it is, but with time things become clear, and normally a fellow understands what an ass he's been.

We was all young in Whitehorse. Young, strong athletes, hockeyists, thirteen days on the trail and dying, like a sailor long at sea, for living again. McLennan, our captain now that Weldy Young was left behind, didn't have a chance. Older, wiser, he was most probably above the ruckus, but he fell prey to it at the hands of old friends. And I witnessed myself the temptation to accept a stranger's free whiskey. Surrounded, we made our way to the hotel, whose name I don't recall. Once we dumped our sacks the music began, a fiddler, a piano player, a young woman whose voice rang with the sorried tunes of old, bringing tears to everyone's eyes with fallen thoughts of home. Whiskey found its way, I believe, into every hand but mine and Archie Martin's, even into the hand of Dawson's Temperance Society treasurer, despite Joe Boyle's instruction that liquor and tobacco were to be avoided once our travels began. I believe at least three hundred people filed through the hotel dining rooms to drink with us, speak with us, rub elbows. Grown men and their wives, their kids, young prospectors heading out themselves and awaiting the same morning train as us, pretty young ladies eager to see the hockeyists — so many eager, excitement-faced people all happy to see us.

For our part it was likewise delightful. Even with the large population of Dawson — Dawson had six or seven thousand people, and the whole of the gold region around it probably twenty thousand — we longed for new and different faces, the isolation of that remote outpost sullenly hanging over the whole like a leaden fog, particularly in winter. To speak with a pretty, unattached young lady was especially exciting, and we all did so, the young ladies revelling and competing for attention from us. Except I could not, probably on account of being sober, I could only think of lost Elizabeth Grady. Gradually, as the afternoon progressed to evening and evening to night, I withdrew to my own corner and watched the goings-on with a detached air. I don't know what it was precise, the young ladies themselves, the singing young lady, the sweet lonesomeness for my old pretty-smiled friend.

I felt sorry for myself.

It seemed the more everyone drank the less we shared, they seemed to take on different lives without our normal cares, and at the time I did not understand. Fact is, I did not understand alcohol in anything less than its tragic aspects. Even young Albert Forrest, barely eighteen, who never drank but occasionally smoked a cigar, was drinking and yelling, far from his normal demeanour, and I realized then it was his first time away from family. I thought of my Daddy.

"Never feel sorry for yourself," he told me as we sawed logs one day in winter. "It's selfish to feel sorry for yourself. And the way to overcome it is to do something for somebody else. Think of a kind word, or a kind thing, and do it for them. It will make you feel better about yourself because you done a good thing, make you stop thinking only of yourself in a selfish way." But before I could think of anything to do for anyone else, I was approached by a man who would make me angry.

"You're one of the hockeyists," the man said to me after idling over.

"Yes sir." I stuck out my paw. "I'm Boston Mason, of Massachusetts." The man limply swished my hand, a gesture of mortification to me. The limpy part. So I disliked this man — he was older than me considerable — I disliked this man instantly.

"Going to Ottawa, eh?"

"Yes, sir."

"Silver Seven."

I looked at him. I disliked him further for his abrupt manner of speaking. I didn't reply, which indicates my mood, because I'm not usually disrespectful, particularly to strangers.

"I say you're to play the Silver Seven," he said.

"Yes, sir," I said again.

"They are going to annihilate you."

He walked away, my eyes following him like a dog eyes a falling sausage. Apart from his absolute lack of manners, what on earth was that? My mind, furious with the insult, was spared further anguish by the sight of Sureshot Kennedy pulling out a Whitehorse newspaper. Several of us, McLennan,

Watt, Forrest, McLennan's Whitehorse friends, we all leaned over Sureshot's shoulder to read along as he read aloud.

"No water swillers, eh?" he said, frowning me down and snapping the newspaper shut, which I assumed was meant in jest, but with Sureshot I never knew. The others laughed and Crazy Norman Watt nudged me hard with his elbow, raised his eyebrows when I looked at him. I decided not to accept the joke, it was my mood. I turned, suffered a few pats on the back, and spotted the man leaning against the doorjamb to the kitchen, staring at us all, a drink in his hand.

I made my way through the milling crowd, noticed all eyes on me. Actual real admiration! It emboldened me, made me feel up to inquiring what he meant — like Billy the Pickle would. He eyed me humorously, I believe, as I came up to him.

"You don't believe me," he said.

"Why would you say that?" I asked him. The man shrugged, smiled, and looked over my shoulder about the milling, loud room.

"You ever seen Harvey Pulford play hockey?" he said. I frowned to his smile. "You ever even heard of Harvey Pulford?"

"Well, I heard the name bandied about somewhat."

"Art Moore?"

I shook my head.

"Frank McGee?"

"One-eyed Frank McGee," I said, desperate now. "Lost his sight to a stick end up in Montreal."

The man nodded.

"So you know all about Frank McGee. Frank McGee didn't lose his sight to a stick end up in Montreal, he lost it back when he played for the Aberdeens, in a game at Hawksbury, from a puck." He was doing something which is done frequently today, but not back at the turn of the century. He was humiliating me. And he didn't even know me. Before I could think of any snappy replies — I always think of good ones I should have used later — he spoke.

"This is the greatest team in all Canada, you know, this Silver Seven team. Alf Smith, their Captain, and Pulford are very good, but McGee, McGee's the best. Maybe the best ever. Billy Gilmour and his brothers are gone this season I think, and they got a new goaler, Day Finnie, who's better than Bouse Hutton. Finnie's brother Oswald works in the assayers office in Dawson, chief clerk there. Did you know that?"

"Of course I know that."

"Art Moore, Harry 'The Rat' Westwick, and Pulford are their defence. Pulford's wife just died. McGee, White, and Smith up front. This ain't the Dawson town league we're talking about here, son. This is senior hockey!"

"We play real hockey in Dawson," I protested, and the man smiled wide and raised his damn alcohol drink to me. I walked away.

McLennan, meanwhile, had wired Dawson and Joe Boyle in Detroit, extending the good news of our on-time arrival and our next plans, which entailed riding the White Pass Railway the next morning into Skagway. He told us he'd admitted that we were very tired. I thought this a mild expression of our condition. We were exhausted, if my own feelings were a sample of the rest. Exhausted, and only three hundred and some-odd miles into our four thousand mile journey. But, as I reinforced in my mind at this time, it certainly was the hardest leg, and it was over. From here on it was rail, ship, and rail. We would all have ample time to exercise, as Joe Boyle had instructed, and we even planned a day off in Winnipeg to skate a bit and otherwise relax. And then on to Ottawa for the grand matches, four or five days there in which to recover from our journey and to prepare. It seemed Joe Boyle's careful travel planning was panning out.

Now there's a Yukon expression. Panning out.

That stranger was the first man to express any hint of the Silver Sevens' superiority. It hadn't even occurred to me, among the confidence of the likes of Sureshot, Hector, and Doc McLennan. These guys, and Watt too, were all from the east, all must know what we were up against. Even with the loss of Weldy Young and Captain Bennett, which everyone took serious, no one's confidence had seemed wavering to me. So it was possible to doubt the man's wisdom and mental capacity, and I did so, yet with a nagging warning that all was not as it seemed. But I had become talented at mental suppression, and the deed was done.

What I remember most about that festival evening was the plain-spoken excitement of all those wonderful Whitehorse people, and despite my moodiness it left a good impression on me. Later, late, I walked outside behind the stumbling, laughing figure of Crazy Norman Watt, now full of whiskey, to breathe the frigid air of this Yukon place. We watched the snowflakes drifting about the silent, crunching town, looked about the sky as if it held some answer secreted away among its clouds to our obvious question: how much would it snow? But Crazy Norman said something about the young girls inside, and McLennan, his friends about him, broke out beside us, and these thoughts vanished. McLennan threw his arm around me.

"We're gonna win the Stanley Cup!" he nearly screamed in my ear, and in remembrance of his stature in my mind, I accepted his drunken condition. I smiled and I'm sure I yelled the same thing back at him. Norman Watt did a dance in the street, holding his palms open to the slowly dropping snowflakes, singing some song he'd heard the pretty young lady sing inside. All was well with the world of the Dawson City Nuggets. Our Dawson City Seven.

We retired to our rooms, I with Sureshot, Hector, and Archie Martin, and we promptly fell fast asleep, unaware that those slowly drifting, harmless snowflakes we had noticed were to become an enormous tragedy. We were awakened by the frantic knocking and yelling of Crazy Norman Watt.

"Get up! Get up!" he hollered, and as the others moaned and rolled, I jumped up and instinctively opened the curtain to see the problem. A good foot of snow had already fallen, and more and more swirled and slammed against the hotel window. We were amidst a raging blizzard!

Do you hear what I'm saying? A blizzard! Do you understand what we understood at that moment?

"A blizzard!" I shouted, which broke the boys from their haziness instantly. The four of us pressed our faces to the glass and stared, Watt and Doc McLennan and even others I did not know appeared, pressing in behind us to see.

"A blizzard!" was whispered from many lips, and we looked dubiously from one to another.

"What'll we do?" Norman asked.

"We've got to see if the train's running," Doc McLennan replied.

"Ain't no train running through this, boys," a man I believe employed by the hotel said solemnly.

"Sure it is!" Sureshot Kennedy said harshly, his glare questioning the man's sensibilities and manhood. "Sure it is." Sureshot's gaze dissuaded the man from backing his remark, but the fact of his words registered with us all, even with Sureshot.

"What are we gonna do?" Hector said.

"I've got to wire the *Amur*," Doc answered, and he moved toward the door. "I'll wire her to wait for us in Skagway. This won't last too long." And he was gone.

Famous last words. Sort of like Custer rearing up on his horse, his hat in the air, yelling, "Now we got 'em, boys!" The facts was this: wasn't no trains running, not this day nor the next. The snow fell in heaps across the landscape, shutting us down in the hotel, preventing even the townfolk from visiting too much. No less than seventeen snowslides were registered along the narrow gauge tracks to Skagway. The snow had caught us, and held us now as tightly as a snowball fashioned by a mean kid. A mean kid with bad intentions. It shattered our travel plans beyond repair.

Course we didn't know this for sure immediately. For two days we paced in our sudden confinement, arguing about our chances of correcting our schedule. Delaying the games, if necessary. On the third day the snow stopped and the railroad reopened. McLennan had wired the ship *Amur* daily, begging the Captain to wait for us, and he assured us he would.

"Are we gonna make it, Doc?" I recall Crazy Norman asking the day we rushed to the train depot. And I remember Doc's reply: "It's gonna be about as close as damn is to swearing."

It wasn't until we disembarked at the fateful Billy the Pickle station and raced to the long twin wharves that we found the *Amur* had waited twenty-four hours for us, and then had departed the day before. It now became absolute knowledge to us that we were in trouble.

"We got to wire Joe Boyle to get an extension on the games," Hector Smith told us all, and Doc nodded. There was no panic yet, for we all had faith in Doc and Joe Boyle. After all, no one could expect us to arrive the day of the games, after travelling four thousand miles by dogsled, steamship, and train, and play immediately without rest or practice.

22

IT WAS A CRUEL, CRUEL FATE that left us stranded in the stump-mud death town of Skagway for three more days. Think of our plight now, three days holed up in our Whitehorse hotel, a virtual igloo what with the heap of snow on us all, and now faced with the bleak prospects of three more days in the bleakest town of all. Where Billy the Pickle sat frozen, a grin on his mug and his fingers froze on a bottle several feet away . . . a Winchester on his lap . . . thoughts and reminders of a grim, heart-stabbing sorrow. I avoided certain sights and thoughts as much as a young man can. I declined the invitations to sightsee, declined the tramp to the rail station to locate the one man who seemed to know all the timetables.

As much as a young man can. The fact is a young man can't help but think about things too much, at least I believe so from my own experiences. Love to feel sorry for themselves, young men do, even if they aren't saddled with real woes and sorrow, as I certainly was. With the attempts at suppression of Skagway and Billy the Pickle came the faces of my Mother and Daddy, with the suppression of those images snuck back gut-turning sights and sounds of Billy the Pickle. No matter how far I stayed from the awful train depot the thoughts scarred my young mind. These Skagway days, upsetting as they were to all our larger travel plans, were hell to me. If there exists a hell on earth for me, Skagway, Alaska, is it. And forever since then, for over fifty years now, I've even referred to bad things or bad thoughts as my stump-mud things or stump-mud thoughts. I considered visiting the graveyard, but the thought of standing over the unmarked pauper graves, not even knowing exactly where the kid lay, was too much for me, and I avoided further thoughts on that.

The boys and I received much the same reception as we had enjoyed in Whitehorse. It seems the whole north was united behind us, and men from Dyea, or what was left of Dyea, and Juneau and even Fairbanks and Nome knew of us. It was as though all the frozen, forgotten outposts of the north found a rallying cry, a chance to root for a home team again, as in the old days of homes back east.

The boys put on quite a show. I admit that we revelled in our celebrity, and McLennan even led us on daily jaunts to the Skagway River, where we stripped to our drawers and plunged in, as though this somehow made us fitter. Actually, it was all more show than fitness, and I dreaded the awful exposure. But McLennan, sober now and I think wanting to reassert his earnestness and authority, insisted. Joe Boyle had him fill out daily records of the exercises we did, and with an absence of ice — skating ice — in Stump-Mud, it was near three weeks since any of us pulled on skates. The exercises became tedious — some of us weren't feeling too well, some legitimately so and some not so legitimately — and these three days dragged worse than a dogsled without snow.

McLennan made arrangements for us on the American ship SS *Romano*, which was scheduled to depart Skagway on January 4, 1905. Problem was, it wasn't going to Vancouver where the *Amur* would have disembarked us, but to Seattle, Washington. This further confused the schedule — another day lost, for we would have to backtrack to Vancouver to catch the Canadian Pacific, and as yet McLennan and Boyle had not determined how we would accomplish that.

Most of the boys spent their time languishing in the hotel saloon. Despite my abhorrence of alcohol, in them older days the saloons, or back here east the barrooms, were the men's social clubs of communities. So I went in and jostled with the rest among our fans, and water was free. I endured the taunts and jokes of friend and fan alike, and took it pretty well, I believe, despite my stump-mud moodiness.

Late at night interested me most in the saloon, as I was being educated to the actual effects of alcohol, and one of the startling things I found was that it could tend to make men, usually hard men, soft and talkative about subjects they normally avoided. Either that or it made normally sound, effective men crazy, crazy enough to fight even their best friend. Actually, our team was pretty much divided on alcohol use, with me, Archie Martin, Albert Forrest and Joe Boyle avoiding it, while Watt, Johnstone, Sureshot, and Hector did not. And Doc McLennan was treasurer of the you-know-what. It's how I found out Kennedy was human. We found ourselves secluded but still among the throng in a foolish old tent that charaded as a saloon, and he turned to me, hunkered down as he was over his glass of whiskey, and spoke.

"Like you," he said, his glassy eyes searching for something in mine.

"I like you too," I said, but doubted if I really meant it. I was feeling two ways about Sureshot Kennedy. I disliked tremendously his arrogance and confidence, his way of dealing with those he obviously considered less than himself. His sharp, quarrelsome tongue, his often bad disposition. On the other hand, I could only admire his skill and determination on the ice, where he reminds me now of a Maurice Richard, the very physical type of player who bowls over his opponents and scores with a relentless combination of strength and skill — and I admired that same confidence I hated, because I longed myself to feel that way and often wondered how it was people actually came to acquire it. Perhaps this was envy, which turns a positive feeling into a negative one. It was this George Kennedy that turned to me now.

"Like you," he said, his words slightly slurred from drink.

"I like you too," I replied. He put his arm around me and hugged me, to my mortification. I struggled free and he grinned, sipped his drink.

"We're a lot alike, you and I, eh?" he said, and I nodded agreement though I strongly disagreed, of course.

"We're both big and strong, good shots, good skaters — course I'm much better'n you — but it ain't the point. We're a lot alike. Both got girls back home, girls we think about all the time. Hec told me you have an understanding. My girl told me if I dig up a lot of gold, we'd have an understanding. She told me she'd marry me if I came home with a lot of gold. I ain't got no gold."

I frowned and listened only.

"So I don't know what to say to her. It may not matter, we ain't gonna have no time in Winnipeg like we planned anyway. It was there I'd see her. Me an' Hec are from West Selkirk, right above Winnipeg. It's where I'd see her."

"You could wire ahead," I said. I wasn't sure his of slant, whether he believed he would still marry this girl or not, and he shrugged and gulped his glass empty.

"I ain't sure I should see her." He slid his glass along the bar and nodded to the bartender.

"Why not?"

"Well . . . "

"Well what?"

"Well, I sort of compensated for my absence of gold."

"What does that mean?" I asked warily.

"Told her I had it."

"Oh. Well . . . how rich are you?"

"Very."

"Oh, Sureshot!" He shrugged and laughed, the laugh of a man who laughed only because alcohol allowed.

"You ever love a girl so much you'd do anything for her?" he asked. I nodded reluctantly. A properly reared New England man did not feel comfortable participating in such a conversation. Sober. Not that it didn't interest me, of course.

"I didn't think she liked me enough. So I told her one day I'd go to the Yukon and get rich, send for her. I knew Hec was thinking of going, so I figured I would too. Told her I'd dig up all kinds of gold and send for her and marry her. She said yes. We had our own sample of understanding. Problem is, when Hec and me got to Dawson, all the good claims was staked. All we could do was go to work on one of them for someone else.

And you know how easy it is to spend wages in Dawson." This I well understood, though I knew in Sureshot's case there was also a fair amount of squandering involved.

"So you told her you got rich?"

"Sure I did. I didn't want to lose her."

"I mean, you don't think she'll marry you anyway?" Sureshot shrugged, got handed another drink by Crazy Norman Watt, who stuck his nose in.

"Hey, Gloomy wants to know where wasted electricity goes." When neither of us replied, Norman asked loudly, "What are we talking about?" Sureshot looked to the straw floor, and I myself was somewhat disturbed that our conversation was interrupted upon.

"None of your business," I said.

"Oh, about Sureshot's wife, eh?" Norman said. Sureshot nodded solemnly.

"Forget her. You don't need lots of gold to get a girl, you just gotta be a hockeyist." Norman winked and off he went, cackling at his joke. We could not help but laugh with the crazy man. I looked back to Kennedy and found an amazing thing. I suddenly realized all his confidence and strength were fragile, were reactions to normal fears that normal guys had, but for some reason he had to hide. Boyle was that way, but I only realized it in the end, after he died in 1923. I'll explain that later. Now I looked at Sureshot Kennedy and actually sympathized with him, thought of Elizabeth Grady, the lost Bostonian, and such things.

"Maybe she'll surprise you," I encouraged, hoping that Lizzie would surprise me.

"No, would you marry someone who lied to you? Who told you he had two million dollars in gold, but really only had a hockey stick and a pack, and a chance to win the Stanley Cup?"

"Two million dollars?"

"Actually two and a half. I invested."

"George . . ."

"I thought about telling her I got robbed on the way out, but I couldn't figure out how to get robbed of those good investments I made, eh? You know, there's always something."

"George."

"What?"

"Tell her the truth."

"Right."

"Tell her the truth, tell her what you just told me. Tell her you love her so much you'd do anything to keep her, even lie, because she's so beautiful and lovely and whatnot you thought that'd be the only way you'd keep her."

"That won't work."

"Why not?"

"Because she's ugly and somewhat unlovely most of the time."

"Well . . . why do you want her so bad, then?"

"Why not? You got to marry someone. And it don't matter if a girl's pretty and lovely anyhow, what matters is how you feel for her. I love this girl, Boston, because she's right for me, we laughed together a lot. We did a lot of things together, went on sleigh rides, went to the farmers' market together. Held hands a lot."

"Well, if you can't tell her the truth, I don't know what to tell you. I still think honesty is a good thing. Especially if you're going to marry the girl. I don't know." Sureshot emptied yet another glass and grabbed my arm.

"You're a good guy, Boston, I admire you," he said. "No matter how much trouble I give you, I wish I was more like you. In some ways."

And he walked away toward the barkeeper. And I marvelled at his words. Sureshot Kennedy admired me? It was a bogglesome episode, and I watched him go with affection.

McLennan told us Weldy Young, when he heard we got delayed, intended to leave Dawson immediately to try to catch up. When the officials delayed the games, he would catch up to us in Ottawa and play. This was well received by us all, though it confused the plans to pick up Hannay in Brandon. Or did it? The thought did not escape me that Lorne Hannay might stay — he was excellent by all accounts and had played for the Cup already — leaving Archie Martin or me to possibly get dropped from the team. I kept these fears to myself, watching Archie Martin's eyes whenever it was discussed to see if he registered any reactions. But I detected none. Nothing really affected Archie, he was the kind of guy, like Norman Watt, who just didn't worry about too much.

The time passed. Finally we trudged down to the waterfront and walked the long wharf, the same long wharf where Soapy Smith was shot by Frank Reid and where Frank Reid was shot by Soapy Smith. We boarded the SS *Romano* at long last.

Wonderful news, eh? Great to be aboard, you think? Well let me explain this to you. It was a three-day voyage to Seattle, mostly hugging what is now called the inside passage, that normally calm, beautiful, symphony-like area I had enjoyed earlier on my way up to the Yukon. But Providence had not finished with the Dawson Nuggets yet.

Providence decided that a three-hundred-and-fifty-mile hike through the froze wilderness, a three-day huddle in the White-horse igloo, a three-day wait in Stump-Mudville wasn't enough. No, we'll teach these boys to steal the Stanley Cup and hide it away forever up in the lost north. And how will we do it? We'll make it the worst, sea-rolling, whooshing, fear-inspired experience they ever had. We'll roll that *Romano* to an inch of all their miserable lives, make them as deathly sick and vomiting as humanly possible, make them wish the ship would sink just to remove them from their miseries. And then we'll spit them out onto the wharf in Seattle to the gathered throng, where they'll have to keep their chins up and make a good show as they wobble on their sick sea legs from the ship to the train, which will lurch and rumble worse than their gone stomachs can take, back north toward Vancouver town . . .

And that's what happened. Continual, unremitting seasickness is a curse worse than death, period. Worse it is for proud young men who assumed they were immune to it, as if their strength and youth were some sort of inoculation against it. How wretched and sad to see these faces hung over the reeling rail, vomiting, vomiting what? After a day, no one had anything left in them to vomit, and none dared to eat a solitary morsel of food. Suffer we did, worse than imaginable on that violent, swollen and cursed sea. Truth is we were in honest danger of sinking, a not uncommon occurrence in those waters.

Again McLennan tried to be true to Joe Boyle's instructions, having everybody skip ropes — it's the only exercise we could figure on the ship. Everybody skipped ropes that first day, when we were still whole. But this, as all other activity, ceased with the godawful realization of what we were in for. It's a sight I'll never forget, McLennan, Watt, Martin, and Hector, all lined up side by side over the rail, four of the toughest, greatest hockeyists I ever knew. Kennedy was so proud, he tried to be sick where no one else could see him. Can you imagine that? Everyone on the whole ship sick as dogs, and he still didn't want no one to think he was.

When we finally spilled out onto the Seattle wharf, down the gangplank into that fair town, we were shrunken and lost souls, yearning for a good hot meal we could keep down and a warm, stationary bed where we could sleep. Sleep! We hadn't had a decent night's sleep since Dawson, and even the last evening there was mostly spent tossing and turning with nervous expectation.

The following day Sureshot Kennedy produced a Seattle newspaper while we milled about on the depot landing of the Canadian Pacific in Vancouver.

"'Nine husky, weather-beaten men walked down the gang-plank of the steamer *Dolphin* this morning and left Seattle on the Canadian Pacific train at 10:10 o'clock, on the longest trip ever taken by a hockey team,'" Sureshot read aloud, us all gathering about him and straining to see the words ourselves.

"Why the *Dolphin* and not the *Romano*?" Crazy Norman asked, but Sureshot kept reading.

"'These men are the pick of the hockey players of the Yukon country from Dawson on their way to New York and Montreal to play the best teams,' blah, blah, blah, 'and if looks count' — listen to this! — 'and if looks count for anything, Dawson will be well represented on the ice this year.'" Sureshot paused and looked at us, all grins and cheers at this absurd news.

"Get this! 'These men started out on their record-breaking journey with the idea of keeping in the finest possible condition, for hockey, be it known, is rougher than football or lacrosse, and is no game for children or girls.'" He paused again, and repeated, "No game for children or girls! Listen to this: 'They had with them a big coach sleigh' — uh — 'these hardy northerners rolled and tumbled in the snow like kittens at play all along the long journey, stopping occasionally for a snowball battle' — can you believe this? — 'If they failed to reach a roadhouse at night, they slept in the sleigh, so that the tramp was one long picnic for them.'"

"Who wrote this," McLennan asked, leaning in, "H. G. Wells?" Sureshot finished the article.

"'Seattle seemed hot to them when they came ashore this morning, although to the residents of this city the weather seemed a bit winterish. Most of the men are above average height, with the broad, heavy shoulders of the athlete, and the light, springy step of the man in perfect health.'" Sureshot closed the paper and Johnstone pulled it from his hands to read it again himself, Forrest looking over his shoulder.

"Springy step — why, we was lucky we didn't all roll over

off that gangplank into the water, eh?" Sureshot said and the others laughed.

"Yep, this trip is just one long picnic," Hec Smith said, and McLennan said, "Thick shoulders, above average height — did they see Forrest and Watt?"

"They were looking at me!" shouted Archie Martin, the hundred-and-thirty-five-pound man who was too small for the Aylmer gold rush gang.

"They couldn't see Forrest for the trees," Crazy Norman cracked, and we again enjoyed the joke. Tired, wrecked, we stood on the platform between trains, waiting for the whistle to blow. When it did, our entourage, which now included considerably more than our team, what with others who came down from Dawson earlier to go see the games for themselves, a few sportsmen who got caught up in all the excitement along the way, and an adventuress or two — we all boarded the Canadian Pacific train for the five or six-day, three-thousand-mile or so trip we had before us.

We undoubtedly all exhibited the light, springy steps of men in perfect health.

23

VANCOUVER TO ABBOTSFORD, Chilliwack, Hope, through Lytton on toward Kamloops and the rising tide mountain backbone of the continent — we were finally on our way home. Joe Boyle had rented an entire Pullman car for us, and the amenities it afforded, including our own cook, waiter, and porter, were among the most luxurious of the times, but in truth they were not conducive to complete restfulness. No train could be, what with the relentless motion and clacking of the tracks, the restriction of movement, the close proximity among all the boys.

Nerves, rubbed raw by continual walking and rolling and not a few too many drinks, frayed more easily than normal. Kennedy and Johnstone were at their worst, particularly Kennedy. I suspect the apprehension of a possible reunion with his girlfriend, coupled with his drinking, had much to do with his distemper. Gloomy Johnstone was a case in himself, but don't ask me why. I hardly was privy to the innermost mental conflicts whose battles were clear in his eyes. Of all, only Crazy Norman Watt, God bless him, retained the sparkle in his dubious eye, the smile on his face. The rest — including myself, Forrest, McLennan, Martin, Hector Smith — we more existed than lived, tired, sullen, but trying our best to be good men.

Teddy Roosevelt once said, "Be a good man to camp out with," and after my Dawson City Seven hockeyist experience, I understand his meaning. He meant everyone, anyone, can camp out for a day or two and put up with the unpleasantness that perchance arises; it is quite another thing to last for weeks, or in our case nearly a month, without losing your mind. Normal, petty little habits and occurrences became enough to send a man into convulsions.

One morning, I forget which in that endless progression of days, Forrest sat whistling lowly for hours beside Johnstone, when suddenly, without warning, Johnstone exploded, screaming at him to stop. So long had he endured it, so long had he sat silent that the rage built to a ridiculous level until it erupted. Forrest merely looked at him, the turmoil in his own mind, I believe, enabling him to understand, and he smiled and stopped whistling. But Sureshot Kennedy started whistling at the opposite end of the car, which was obviously meant to infuriate Johnstone. It did, but he only slumped in his chair and stared out the window, the rest enjoying the joke at his expense.

I tried hard to be a good man to camp out with. For the

most part I kept my mouth shut, spoke only when spoken to, although after more than three weeks travelling with these men I had lost all discouragement and fear of any of them.

"Will you look at this!" Hector Smith called, standing and peering out the front of the car as we rolled slowly to a stop at the Kamloops depot.

"What is this?" McLennan said, not understanding at first. Then I saw the smile flash upon his face as he turned to us and shouted, "It's for us! They're all for us!"

And once again the melee began, though brief, because Kamloops was a scheduled stop of short duration. We stepped from the Pullman to cheers and waving, our backs slapped and our hands wrung until they were sore. Banners were held aloft, the legend "Beat the Silver Seven" in bold letters across them, and now, here in the little village of Kamloops, we realized we were heroes on a national scale, all the people in every one-horse town across all of Canada rooting for us to beat them damn Silver Sevens. And as I said in the beginning, the roots of this was in the normal, everyday hatreds and disgusts people hold for the great winning team that ain't their own, just exactly like the New York Yankees today. It was a miraculous event for us, pulling us from our deep mental doldrums, forcing smiles even upon the faces of Kennedy and Johnstone. And there seemed no end to the amazement.

"Who are you? Kennedy? McLennan?" a young man perhaps my own age asks me.

"No, I'm Boston Mason," I reply, and as he shakes my hand his eyes shine and he repeats, "Boston Mason!"

"You'll beat them, you'll beat them Silver Sevens!" he says, echoing a cry that was to become familiar.

"Course we'll beat them," I agree, and others crowd me with the same refrains, "You'll beat them, you'll beat them Silver Sevens!"

"You'll show the Cup here when you return in the spring,

Don Reddick

won't you?" another asks, and another, and so it went until the whistle blew and we reluctantly made our way through the milling, cheering crowd up and into the Pullman.

"Yes!" Crazy Norman Watt shouted, shoving his arms in the air as he walked down the aisle, "Yes!"

"We're gonna do it, boys!" McLennan yelled, for despite his age and experience he again is caught up in the excitement every bit as much as eighteen-year-old Brother Albert, who even was moved to speak. He leaned over the back of the seat behind me and said, "Can you believe it, for us?"

"I believe it," I found myself saying, and added, "We're gonna do it, Brother Al, we're gonna win the Stanley Cup!"

And so our trip began in the land of British Columbia, enlivening us. After dinner and before the poker games, we found ourselves leaning once again into our group, listening to the hockey stories. The voices were livelier than they had been in days, the realization of our elevated status buoying all.

"Listen to this," McLennan said, and we listened. "We were playing I forget who in Montreal in '93 when I was with Queen's, and I roomed with a goaler named Hiscock. Good kid, kind of naive. So we get up, actually he got up first in the dormitory room they gave us, and what does he do but start making his bed, eh? Can you believe it? I'm laying there watching Hiscock make his bed. 'What on earth are you doing?' I ask, and he looks at me matter-of-factly and says, 'I'm making my bed. And so will you.'

"'I'm not making my bed,' I say as Hiscock finishes tucking everything up. 'I'm not making my bed,' I repeat, but he doesn't care to hear it.

"'Then don't,' he says with this voice that looks down on me like I'm on all fours. He leaves the room and I lay there staring at his bed that's made so perfect it don't look like no one even slept in it." McLennan stops here to let it digest, smiling and looking across us all.

"Like it wasn't even slept in!" he repeats, and it dawns on us and he nods.

"I'm looking at that perfect bed and I realize if someone comes in they're gonna think we slept in the same bed!" Everyone laughs as McLennan delivers an exaggerated wink.

"So what did you do?" Brother Albert asks.

"I think they really did." Archie Martin jumps up and exaggerates a wink himself. This brings forth additional laughter.

"What kind of name is Hiscock?" Norman says.

"I bet he made his bed," Sureshot says with his twinge of disgust, but McLennan shakes his mustached head.

"I tore that bed all to hell!" he yells triumphantly, and we roar with it all. And again they tumble, one after another, the stories of talking cuts, torn-up beds, lunatic hockeyists of old, all told with gleaming, wide eyes and the raised voices of punch lines.

"We had a championship lacrosse game back in Aylmer, '94, against Hull," Archie Martin says. "We didn't know, we thought this was the biggest thing we'd ever do. Had to win. So what we do is go over to Ottawa and get this kid named Bones Allen who's a star, and we kick off our worst kid, Serge Bedard, and we make Bones our new Serge."

All of us rustle with the potential of this story.

"See, the rosters are set, you can't add no new players, eh? So we pretend Bones Allen is Serge Bedard. So everything goes right, we score five or six, they get a couple, good ol' Serge Bedard scores a couple more, and then Serge gets clobbered over the head! Guy just clobbers him! Laid out flat unconscious, and everyone crowds around.

"'Let him breathe, let him breathe,' the ref says, though of course it's all in French. And this ref kneels down on one knee and says, 'You okay? You okay?' And Bones just lays there, his eyes half rolled up in his head, moaning, and the ref raises his voice and says, 'What's your name, can you say your name?'"

At this point we all get it and laugh, Archie nodding its truth.

Don Reddick

"The fool says, 'Bones Allen!'" And we break out louder, slapping knees and winking among ourselves.

"Bones Allen!" Archie screams with delight. "We forfeited that game right then and there!"

All across the continent this goes on, our punch lines rolling with the train. We couldn't see the Forrest for the trees.

Evening took from us most of the truly magnificent scenery, that of Mendelson and Chykosky, with the high slanted darkness. As the poker regulars, who counted among them McLennan, Johnstone, Kennedy and Watt, began to zip the cards with shuffling and the cigar smoke swirled — if Joe Boyle could see this! — I leaned back and in a silent manner reviewed the situations.

Kennedy and his millions. And his waiting girlfriend in Winnipeg. Hannay to be picked up in Brandon. Weldy Young starting off when he heard we'd been delayed, in hopes of catching us — and what would that mean to me? Or Archie Martin? I thought of home, and all my sisters, visiting the graves of my mother and daddy ... and Elizabeth Grady. I should have written her, I admitted that this night. Of all those letters I wrote the night I returned from Irishtown, I still couldn't find it in me to write to Lizzie. I should have listened to my mother the night before I left, done what I said I'd do and visit her to apologize. The shame of realizing that one of the last expressions I shared with my mother was a lie came to me, forcing a loneliness and sorrow hard to describe even today upon my old, roamed soul. And then there was the Stanley Cup. McLennan, who in my eyes had established himself as the master storyteller, had told us earlier a story most of the guys appeared to know. But we never tired of hearing it from a man who had actually played for it.

"Sir Frederick Arthur Stanley, Governor General of Canada in 1892, retired and went back to England, awaiting his successor. He'd been to several hockey games in Ottawa, was quite taken with the game, and was known to say there should be a trophy awarded for the best team. Felt it would put some regularity to the mayhem — typical Brit — and he decided to donate the Cup." McLennan leaned back to see the magic he held us by. All eyes were on him, and no catcalls, not even from Norman.

"The Cup was made in London and sent over, and it was first awarded in 1893 to the Montreal Amateur Athletic Association. Tom Paton was goaler, Jimmy Stewart point and Allan Cameron coverpoint, Irving, Hodgson, Haviland Routh. Billy Barlow. I remember them all, but it was back a ways, I don't think they were nearly as good as we are today. Maybe Haviland Routh. Possibly Tom Paton, the goaler. But these guys were awarded the Cup, it wasn't until '94 that the first actual Stanley Cup games were held. There was a three-game playoff, with Ottawa getting the bye because Quebec withdrew for some reason. Montreal beat the Victorias three to two, and played Ottawa, with Harvey Pulford and Weldy, for the Cup in Montreal. It was a close one until Billy Barlow scored for Montreal, and they won it three to one, becoming the first team to win a Stanley Cup series. It was the following year that the Montreal Victorias won the regular season and were awarded the Cup, but the Montreal A.A.A. had already accepted our challenge from Queen's University. This was the Stanley Cup game I played in, and we lost five-one, that damn Haviland Routh again getting two. I came close, though, I hit the arm of Collins — he'd replaced Paton in goal — I hit Collins's arm with a wicked shot but it didn't go in. That was the closest I ever came to scoring a Stanley Cup goal. I mean to get a few this time!"

"We'll all get a few, eh?" Sureshot yells, causing a cascade of shouts which only stopped when McLennan continued. By the way, Haviland Routh married Norman Watt's wife's sister in the 1920's, making them brother-in-laws. Anyway, McLennan continued.

Don Reddick

"Thing is, Lord Stanley never saw a Stanley Cup game. Cup's named after him — actually he named it the Dominion Hockey Challenge Cup, it's inscribed that way, only people started calling it Stanley's Cup and it caught on, but he never once saw a real Stanley Cup game." McLennan paused momentarily.

"I got news." He paused again to let the tension mount.

"Joe Boyle — I can't keep it secret — Joe Boyle told me over the wire Lord Grey is gonna see the match!" This was astonishing news, the new Governor General himself was personally going to grace our contest!

It now was beyond doubt — and comprehension — that our challenge for the Stanley Cup was a national event of epic proportions. The Cup series was already vastly popular, but for some reason this team from the Yukon, the Dawson Nuggets, was making it wilder this time. There was various explanations put forth among us on the train: Kennedy insisted that the country realized how tough we were, how good, and was welcoming us "home," Crazy Norman believed it was the gamblers and high-stakes professional owners who were promoting the game, a theory which caused the highest volume of arguments. But McLennan, I believe, brought forth the most reasonable and probable causes.

"It's the whole idea of gold," he said to me and Brother Albert and Hector, "the same feelings the whole race felt when it was first discovered. People worshipped the Yukon as the answer to all their personal and national problems, both Canada and the United States. And you know how it went — if you even made it to Dawson you achieved your goal, as if it wasn't really the gold after all, but just making the effort and succeeding with our arrivals."

"What's that got to do with the Cup?" Hector asked.

"Everyone who made it to Dawson and goes back home is a hero. We'd be heroes even if we weren't hockeyists. But combine it with the hockey, put all these people in a position to cheer for us — and themselves because they never went north! — and that explains a lot of it, if not everything."

"These people are cheering for themselves?" Brother Albert ventured.

"In a way," McLennan replied, "though they don't know it. And to cheer — don't forget this — to cheer for us is to cheer against those Silver Sevens, Pulford, McGee, Smith, the Gilmour brothers, men who've beaten their own teams for years, who seem and act invincible. People want us to beat these guys real bad."

I sensed the question on everyone's tongue-tip, even Hector's, Do you think we can? But nobody ventured it forth. To express doubt about our outcome would have been bad form, and none was courageous enough to advance. We all preferred the confident rages of Sureshot Kennedy, the constant encouragement and optimism of Doc McLennan, to any adverse considerations. But now and again, those words from the bad man in Whitehorse would seep through my mind, "They are going to annihilate you!"

God knows where he got it, but Sureshot Kennedy pulls out a newspaper and draws a crowd.

"Listen to this," he booms, his audience closing ranks behind him, peeking at the words themselves. "This is news from London. England. As quoted in the, uh" — and he bends the paper over to see — "in the *Ottawa Citizen*, December 22, 1904."

"Where the hell'd you get that?" someone says.

"'On The Side,'" he reads — that's the column headline — "'On The Side. The fame of the Dawson hockey team has spread afar, even to London, England. With the exception of a slight exaggeration of distances the *Express* has the facts pretty straight as follows: A rare enthusiasm is being displayed just now by a hockey team of Dawson City, in the Yukon Territory. The members will start next week for Ottawa to compete in the

amateur hockey championship of Canada. The team' — this is
the good part — 'the team will travel 9,000 miles, of which 900
will be walked, between Dawson and Whitehorse. The cost of
the trip will be $10,000, and it is expected that the team will
play a number of exhibition matches both in Canada and the
United States.'" Sureshot drops the paper to his lap and beams,
the others all talking at once.

"Nine hundred miles — no wonder I'm tired!" Crazy Norman says.

"Ten thousand bucks — no wonder I'm broke!" Hector
says, and now laughter fills the jolting car.

"Ten thousand bucks — does Joe Boyle know about this?"
Crazy Norman says, and naturally the air fills with shouts,
everyone trying to be heard over his fellows.

"We're gonna beat them!" Sureshot Kennedy shouts, his
adrenaline surging with every newspaper he reads, "We're
gonna beat them!" He jumps up at sudden occasions and
shoves his fist in the air and parades up and down the aisles
that way, glaring at each and every one of us and shouting,
"We're gonna do it!"

And it seemed that just when the excitement slowed and
quiet and reason once again visited our car, we'd again come
into a station and see the crowds. Small crowds in small towns,
big crowds in big towns. We knew now the importance people
attached to our chances against the Silver Seven, and our early
astonishment quickly turned to acceptance and stronger confidence. When we finally pulled into Calgary they mobbed us
at the trackside, the mayor or whatever the leader of the town
was called, standing out front with his arms raised, shouting
encouragement and praise.

We had time in Calgary to disembark and I did so, making
my way through the back-slapping, cheering crowd to old
King's, over the frozen, padded snow crunching under my
boots. I entered the same room, even recognized some of the

same faces I'd seen the previous spring. Only how things can change! When I last presented myself I was mocked and looked down upon as a liar and a greenhorn, considered unworthy of much attention. Now, with the pronouncement of my name and status as a member of the Dawson Nuggets, the whole room radiated around me like men about a campfire on a Yukon winter night. The very same eyes that barely glanced at me before stuck to me like skin to frozen metal, their eyes unable to look elsewhere.

What a feeling such worship instills to the soul! A considerable mountain of pride and satisfaction and accomplishment boiled from it, from its repetition at the various stops, until it created feelings of invincibleness. Never in my life have I walked stronger and taller than through the adoring crowds of Canada, on our way to our Stanley Cup match in Ottawa. Such tremendous memories of being young and strong and invincible!

"Which one are you?" someone asks as I step to the bar — actually I took everybody to the bar as the crowd moved in unison across the room with me.

"I'm Boston Mason," I reply, and the men nod, yelling among themselves this information.

"A toast to Boston Mason and the Yukon Nuggets!" a man hollers, the bartenders grow furious with the numerous pourings and glasses rise toward me through the dim light of the saloon. A man climbs up on the bar and waves his arm across us all, a whiskey glass spilling from the end of it.

"To Boston Mason and the Dawson hockeyists — may glory find you and the Stanley Cup together at Ottawa, may you bring the Cup west to the settlements forever!" And a roar goes up and men drink and slam the glasses to the bar. A whiskey is thrust on me but naturally I resist, I ask for water. The laughter goes up until they realize my seriousness, and then the oddest thing — respect! They accept my water drink without

Don Reddick

jeers and scoffs, but accept it from a member of the Dawson Nuggets!

We departed Calgary in triumph, heading east into those endless Métis plains toward Ottawa. McLennan, who was in touch with Joe Boyle at the stops, reassured us that the opening of the match, already delayed to Friday the thirteenth, would again be delayed. I suppose it is not necessary to bang out every individual stop we made, despite their remarkableness. Suffice to say that our reception was the same in them all, in Medicine Hat, in Regina, in Hannay's hometown of Brandon, crowds everywhere cheering us on with signs and banners, faces as excited as children on Christmas eve. We had become a national obsession. We picked up Lorne Hannay in Winnipeg. With him on the platform was his sendoff party, including all his family and friends and probably even his enemies, a young, good-looking lad with sturdy shoulders and a pirate smile. He greeted his old friends from the North with handshakes and embraces, happy to be among the excitement and the centre of attention. As the train whistled and pulled away from the platform, he hung out the door of our car, his hat held high above his head, waving to his admirers, as the whistle blew once again. Kennedy, I noticed with my heart sinking, stood behind the crowd arguing heavily with his poor girl, but whatever they said that day was lost among the cheers of the crowd and whistles of the trains, and Sureshot never again mentioned the woman in my presence. He had to run, break through the crowd, to make the train as she began rolling, busting by the hat-waving Hannay up the steps and striding into the car with his head tilted back, his monstrous gaze daring anyone to say a word.

A couple days later, after leaving the plains and traversing the bottomless bogs of Ontario, among long-rattled nerves and rising excitement, we finally entered the brick town of Ottawa. At four-forty-five p.m. on January 11, 1905, after twenty-five days of continual movement through the trails of the Yukon, the yanking narrow-gauge from Whitehorse to Skagway, the tossing and gut-turning of the sea passage, and then five straight days of train travel across all of Canada, the Dawson City Seven stumbled from the train into Ottawa's Union Station.

Four thousand miles in twenty-five days. I will never forget the look of concern on Sheriff Sweetland's face when he finally saw our boys dropping stiffly one by one from the train. If we truly harboured any feelings of invincibleness we only had to see old Dr. Sweetland's mug to dispel that notion. This man, fellow custodian of the Stanley Cup with Phillip Ross and our official greeter, was, to be blunt, aghast.

And he had bad news for the Dawson Nuggets: there would be no postponement.

24

I USED TO SIT IN FIRE-TOASTED rooms, listening to my Daddy and his Confederates, listening to things I didn't really understand until I grew up and stumbled among the realities myself.

"I'll tell you one thang," a crusted, greying son of the South whispered dramatically one evening, raising his half-filled whiskey glass slightly and holding it there, "I'll tell you one thang, and it's this: we didn't lose no war. We fought for the Constitution of the United States of America is what we done. Ain't it so the Constitution provides no provision against rebellion? Ain't it so? Don't the Constitution give states' rights? Don't the Constitution con-done slavery? Well, don't it?" The man sat still, his glass partially raised, the room as silent as the Gettysburg cemetery at dawn.

"We didn't lose no war, because you can't lose when you defend your own beliefs, your own Constitution. Winners write the history books, is all. Ain't that the whole thang?"

And I observed with studiousness the sombre nodding assent of the comforted lost, all grey-bearded now and glassy-eyed with liquor, all winning the foolish thang at last. Because that's what it really was, a damn solemn foolishness, no matter what they all convinced themselves of. I didn't know it then, that night, but I know it now, and I know my Daddy knew it then — I looked at him, as always, when words of interest passed, especially with such conviction as this man held, and I saw Daddy hunched over low, his hands clasped together and his elbows on his knees, staring at the floorboards. And yet he nodded with the others . . .

I found myself nodding as Sureshot Kennedy raised his hockey stick over his head with both his hands, still on the steps of the train in front of the milling crowd, yelling, "We shall crush the Silver Seven!"

The crowd cheered and jeered, and reporters with notepads and pencils — sports reporters! — found their way to our sides, asking questions, asking names, I saw the Ottawa boys among us, Johnstone and Watt greeting family and old friends, saw Brother Albert Forrest staring about himself in disbelieving fear of the pressing crowd. We made our way through Union Station to the Russell House Hotel, that four-storey brick and stone hotel which lay to our immediate left, where Joe Boyle had made arrangements. And, true to our new custom, the lines formed behind the bar in that small barroom, the lines formed at the door, and it seemed all Ottawa came to catch a glimpse of the Dawson Nuggets.

"Are we in the papers?" I heard Sureshot ask. "Beer? Beer? Why, I've heard it's a fine thing, I believe I'll try one," I heard Crazy Norman say. Albert Forrest bent toward a sports reporter, saying, "I was eleven years old when I crossed the Chilkoot with my family . . . " as the man scribbled madly.

Gloomy Johnstone, he of unspoken mental wars and complaints, stood smiling ear to ear in the middle of the room, gleaming really, with his father draping his arm over his shoulder, calling to all he knew, "This is my boy from the Yukon!" Doc McLennan stood with Hannay speaking with several gentlemen when Hector Smith nudged my elbow and nodded toward them.

"Quite the thing, eh?" he said. "Two men who've skated for the Stanley Cup." He looked at me. "Friday night they'll say the same about us, eh?" Then Sureshot got his newspaper and everyone gathered about him once again.

"Where is it . . . yes," he murmured, then raised his voice so all could hear. "'Hockey. The Dawson team should reach Ottawa on the Winnipeg train this afternoon at 3:30. Two days' rest should put them on their feet again after the railway journey, and it is probable that despite the fact that dispatches say the team desires a postponement of the first game, they will be in shape to go ahead on Friday night.'"

"Who wrote that, H. G. Wells?" Crazy Norman shouted, and he looked around with glee as everyone roared with laughter. Sureshot continued.

"'With the advertising done, tickets printed, it is rather curious that the challengers should leave it until the last moment to propose postponement. As yet the Ottawa club has heard nothing from them in this regard. A telegram' — and Sureshot's voice rose now — 'was received from Joe Boyle, who is managing the tour, yesterday to the effect that while he thought the team would want a postponement, if it was not possible they would go on and play as scheduled.'"

"Yesterday! He only telegraphed yesterday?" Sureshot wondered aloud, and the newspaper was pulled from his hands by others eager to read the story themselves.

"Is that all it says?" McLennan asked.

"So there's really no postponement?" Hector Smith asked,

and all at once this desperate bit of information sank in, despite Dr. Sweetland's previous announcement.

"Joe should have arranged for this last week!" Sureshot said.

McLennan nods. "I told him."

"Why worry, eh?" Crazy Norman shouts, "We're all in great shape!" There was nervous laughter. The truth seemed to be that Joe Boyle, despite McLennan's telegraphed warnings of our delays en route, had neglected to ask for the postponement until it was certainly too late. After all, the tickets were printed.

"What a bunch of junk," Hector complained. "It don't matter about no tickets. The next thing you know they'll protest Hannay. You know what I think? I think they're leaning on us every way they can, eh? We travel four thousand miles and they give us one day! I ain't had skates on my feet for weeks! This is nothing but a bunch of junk."

Course, Hector didn't say "junk."

Even in the early days which McLennan and Weldy Young told stories about, before the Cup took on its great significance, no team entered a match less prepared. None of us had been on skates in nearly a month. For myself, it was on December eighteenth, the day before we left Dawson. It was now Wednesday evening, January eleventh. Why, we hadn't skated since last year!

And the trip, the exhausting walk — I've gone over this already. We nearly fell out of that train, and only the vast excitement of being in that brick city on the hill at last, and for many the added excitement of greeting old friends and family, kept us going. For myself, I looked about that small barroom in the Russell House at the boys, seeing them roaring once again with glasses in their hands, and I began to worry about our prospects. I don't know what Joe Boyle would have done had he seen this, what with his abhorrence of smoke and drink.

I wandered away from it all eventually, numb in body and soul, and fell on my bed without so much as removing my clothes. Suddenly nothing mattered then, not Joe Boyle, not the boys, not the drinking excesses, not Elizabeth Grady. I fell on my bed — what a sweet, unmoving thing! — in complete exhaustion, and considered myself lucky at last to get a little sleep.

Albert Forrest came into the room, glanced me over but said nothing. He seated himself on the other bed, stared out the window, while I looked at this great athlete, this Boy Wonder of the baseball diamond, speed skating medallist, goaler, this quiet soul who nobody seemed to really know well. I thought of his family, his lost father, his poor mother struggling up in Dawson to hold it all together for him and his brothers. But I sensed above this all something else.

"Brudder Albert," I said, mimicking his accent in an attempt at levity.

"Brudder Boston," Albert replied, unmoving. I raised myself up on an elbow.

"We're here," I said, and he nodded without looking. He pulled a cigar from his pocket and lit it, puffed on it. He pulled it from his mouth and inspected it curiously. French Canadians are a silent, narrow people, set in their ways and confident of them. Serious. They're a lot like New Englanders.

"Are you okay, Albert?" I asked.

"I'm okay," Albert replied. "I'm just celebrating a bit before I go to bed. I'm very tired."

"Yes, it's something being here finally."

"That's not what I'm celebrating."

"What are you celebrating?" I asked, and he said the last words of the evening between us, words that seemed to bring home the awful loneliness and sorrow and worry and lost expectations of a whole generation that dropped their lives to search for gold in the hopeless north, words that still sting my soul today with haunting sadness.

"Today's my birthday," is the three words he said. They neither required nor sought a reply, I fell back on my pillow

Don Reddick

and studied the ceiling until I fell fast asleep among my numerous thoughts.

But there was no end to the absurdity of our Stanley Cup preparation. If you can believe what I'm about to relate, there was virtually no more sleep to be had in the thiry-six hours remaining until the first game. Morning was confusion. I awoke earlier than the rest, and I went outside to walk. How utterly strange it was to walk in the early morning light of Ottawa — and how warm! Twenty, twenty-five degrees — that don't sound like much to you, but it was a full fifty degrees warmer than several of our walking days to Whitehorse — and I walked about the brick place, my hands shoved deep in my coat pockets, my hat low over my eyes, peering about at the steam escaping the chimneys and sewers, smelling the sweet scent of wood smoke and hearing the jangling of horse harnesses, the horses shod in rubber to preserve the early morning silence, the ragmen's calls of "Rhaa-aggghgs! Rhaa-aggghgs!" in odd contrast. The chop of the new automobiles clanking on the brick streets.

Ottawa!

A warming smugness crept over my flesh, a self-confident, curled-lip smile over my face, for the Stanley Cup and all the adoration that followed could be ours in a very few hectic hours. As I strolled about the old town, as it gradually spilled its inhabitants worldwise into the dim streets, I come to a startling sight.

For there it was. Right in front of me. With barely a thin slice of glass between us, the Stanley Cup sat in the window of Bob Shillington's store. I stopped in my tracks and gazed at the "big liquid receptacle," as the *Dawson Daily News* so cleverly called it later in one of their articles on the games. Weldy Young had shown us pictures of it, with teams sitting around it, the Cup up on a stool in front. I don't know who, maybe the Shamrocks, young, grim-faced hockeyists, their hair all parted in the middle in the style of the day, staring out for all of history as old winners of the now famous trophy. I moved close to the window and pressed my hands against it to block the glare, and there she sat, maybe ten inches high, ten inches across, a silver bowl with "The Dominion Hockey Challenge Cup" inscribed like Doc said across the front, and smaller things scratched just under the top lip.

So this was the thing dreams were made of! A small pile of silver, fifty bucks worth, according to Weldy, sitting alone and staring back at me in the early morning cobbled-stone life of old Bytown. How startling, that this object created such monstrous behaviour in the normally mild men of Canada. It was near sixty years ago, the Cup only twelve years old, but already it was the passion of Canada, already dreamed of by young boys, already fought over by grown men with a ferociousness and desire unknown in baseball or the sinister football, as popular as they was at the time.

"Yes, sir?" a man said to me, approached from behind with a key in his hand. It was Bob Shillington himself.

"I was just looking," I answered, pointing toward the trophy. Shillington looked at it.

"It's something, eh? The Challenge Cup. Good for business to display it before the matches. Are you attending?"

"Why, I believe I will," I said with smugness.

"Have you got a ticket yet? It'll be sold out, you know. They went on sale yesterday, one dollar apiece, and the box office was mobbed. Are you familiar with hockey?" I shrugged, used my curled-lip smile. "I don't expect much of a contest, no one does." Shillington continued. "Weldy Young was a hero here, a tremendous player who'd probably still be playing if he hadn't left for that godforsaken land, but he didn't come. Who else do they have? Hannay? All he does is take long shots. Hannay and a bunch of miners. God save the King! By the way, you don't sound — where are you from?"

"Boston."

"Ah, Boston, yes. Is it organized in Boston?"

"It's very organized in Boston."

"Hockey, I mean. Are there teams?"

"Some."

"Ah. Boston. There's a fellow on the Dawson team from Boston. Boston Mason. An American! We've heard all about him, about them all. But pity those poor Yukonites. Yukonians. Whatever it is they call themselves. Dawsonites. Dawsonians. Do you realize Rat Westwick, Alf Smith, and Harvey Pulford have been playing together for almost a decade? Ten years! And Frank McGee's the best of them all, now. Do you know the Silver Seven?"

"Tell me about them."

"They're the greatest team ever. Ten years those three have played together, it's a shame Weldy left. Can you imagine how coordinated four men would be on the ice, having played ten years together? Weldy played before them all. I don't like this Finnie business, though. Bouse Hutton is an excellent goaler — it's all very upsetting. Bouse is a hard-headed boy, says he'll never suit up again even if we get him eligible."

"What's the situation?"

"He jumped to Brantford last year, which makes him ineligible. We could petition to have him reinstated, but it would be a messy ordeal, involving a whole team of guys who also jumped who we'd also have to reinstate, which isn't a popular idea right now. Also he's got quinsy, so it isn't worth the bother right now to even consider it. So we're going with Day Finnie. Name's Dave, but everyone calls him Day. Fine fellow. His brother works in the gold assayers office up in Dawson, by the way, helped us get a lot of information on the players up there."

"Who else they got?"

"Well, McGee is our best. Unbelievable hands, great stickhandler, a real bull with an eye like an eagle for the net. No joke intended — he's got blurred eyesight in one eye."

"So I hear."

"Got hit with a puck when he was a kid. Against Hawksbury. Don't matter though, doesn't affect his playing whatsoever. Greatest goal scorer I ever saw. Terrible temper. Art Moore's on defence. Him and Harvey Pulford are in great shape, they play for the Roughriders too."

"Who are the Roughriders?"

"The Ottawa Roughriders, our senior football team. Alf Smith is the quarterback and captain, Pulford's been a regular for years, and Moore. I play for the Roughriders. This year Joe Boyle, the manager of the Dawson team, played a couple of games."

"What?"

"Boyle. I'm sure you've heard of him. He's the King of the Klondike, a millionaire, and he's a sportsman. Tough nut, probably would be playing for Dawson but I guess he's not quite up to snuff on skates. He refereed some Roughrider games last fall, filled in a couple of times. Good sport. All our men are in great shape, Bones Allen and Rat Westwick are both lacrosse stars, Westwick one of the best. I hope these Yukonians are in top condition for this match, because our boys are."

"Bones Allen?" I asked in surprise, Archie Martin's story ringing back to me.

"Bones may play, maybe."

I mused silently on this information, and on Joe Boyle, a startling tidbit. It was all innocent enough, I believe, but in those days it was unusual to associate so closely with the enemy, is all. Boyle became clearer to me, I understood more than ever that his involvement was more of an adventure to him, a sideline to his numerous other occupations and investments. He was a sportsman, pure and simple. And he got along with everybody.

Don Reddick

"McGee's a big, strong kid. Smart. Violent temper if he's provoked. Pulford may not play tomorrow, though. His wife died recently, it's been terrible on him. Only thirty years old and his wife dies. Everybody's been worried about him, we all kind of felt the hockey season would help and all, but . . . Finnie's good, I'm not saying that, it's just that Bouse . . . Alf's the toughest. Alf Smith. I hope none of those northern zoners make the mistake of getting on his bad side — craziest hockey player I ever saw. Mean, hard, he'd check his own mother face first into the boards, eh?"

"Face first?"

"That's it. I can't wait. Governor General's going to attend. I can't wait."

"You seem to know a great deal about the Silver Seven."

"Oh," he said, as though realizing a social mistake, "my name is Bob Shillington, I'm the manager of the Silver Seven. It's how I get to display the Cup. In fact, I'm the one that gave them the name Silver Seven. For years we were just called the Ottawas, but since we've been winning the Cup over and over, we decided to change the name. Actually, it happened this way. I'm involved in the Cobalt silver mines up north — hit in '04 — and after we won the Cup I gave each player a silver nugget, and what does Harvey Pulford say when he receives his but, 'Hey, why don't we call ourselves the Silver Seven?' And that's how it happened."

"So how do you make the Yukon's prospects?"

"Palm trees will sooner grow in the Klondike," Shillington replied and laughed. "These people have no idea what they're in for. The very nerve of them — a bunch of miners — travelling here to take on the greatest team of all time. Can you imagine it? From the beginning I've felt it was just a publicity event Boyle concocted to help him win influence over in the Parliament buildings."

I wanted to blurt out that it was originally all Eilbeck's and

McLennan's and Senkler's idea, but I held my tongue. The information on Joe Boyle made me think, and I filed the information on the players in my mind to report to Doc McLennan. Then Shillington's wife — I assume it was his wife — banged on the window. She yelled something, "cakes" the only audible word. Shillington stuck his bag under his arm and extended his free hand to shake mine.

"And your name, sir?" he asked.

"George," I answered.

"Very well then, George. Perhaps I'll see you tomorrow night. G'day." And he entered the store which held the Stanley Cup. My eyes went back to it and I stared for a while. And I pondered Shillington's words, the worst words, "Palm trees will sooner grow in the Klondike." Pretty funny.

When I returned to the Russell House I found it already in turmoil, the mob in the foyer like the spokes of an automobile wheel revolving around one man — Joe Boyle. He'd arrived from Detroit on the night train and now he was excited as only Joe Boyle could be, animated, his arms waving and his eyes wild with expectation. Friend or foe, everyone who ever met him agreed he was the most energetic man that ever existed. His enthusiasm and willingness to move were unbounded, contagious. That's probably how a man could arrive at Dawson stone broke and see the land in terms so much larger than the rest of us did so that when he finally left, maybe ten years after Ottawa, he was immensely wealthy. All this while fifty thousand — probably a hundred thousand through all the years — left with less than what they'd arrived with.

Anyway Joe's eyes lit up when he saw me. As I approached he put up his patented friendly greeting, his right hand outstretched to shake mine, his left arm in an arc ready to fall like timber over my shoulders. "Here's one of my hockeyists now!" he bellowed in his commanding voice. "Here's Boston Mason now, one of my spares. Course it don't matter if he plays, our spares are as good as our regulars. Maybe better. Isn't that right, Boston?" and Joe squeezed the truth out of me with his long left arm.

"That's right, sir," I replied, and everyone nodded and immediately looked back at Joe. I saw the real Joe Boyle in action now, promoting the match endlessly, encouraging those without tickets to buy them soon, talking up the rivalry and the prospects of our lifting the Cup and keeping it up in Dawson forever. It was plain that his wandering years with Frank Slavin, arranging fights in the various towns and cities all across the continent to California, the experiences he gathered from those times, was useful now. Joe Boyle could make P.T. Barnum look timid, which reminds me, to further explain his abilities, something Hector told me once about him as we walked the diggings.

"I was only in maybe two, three weeks when me and Sureshot was hanging around town, looking for trouble. And that's when we first laid our eyes on Joe Boyle. He was in front of the Monte Carlo — it's gone now but it was most infamous in its time — there in front, on a box, was Joe Boyle, jumping up and down and swinging his arms wildly, yelling at the top of his lungs about someone he called the Sydney Slasher. Course the Sydney Slasher is Frank Slavin, former heavyweight champion of the Dominion and Joe's closest buddy for years — they met in a boxing club in Hoboken, New York — his closet ally for years and the man he came north with after they'd failed to make a living touring the country and staging boxing matches.

"And Joe's flailing away with his arms, his eyes wild, and at the time he had a full beard and mustache, like most the rest of those early men. And he's yelling, 'Bring him out! Bring him out! Why, if I even lay eyes on him I'll lose my mind! Bring him out!' and naturally we stop, like everyone else who happens into the street, to listen to this demention.

"'What's this about?' Sureshot says to the guy next to us, and he points to the sign in the Monte Carlo window. 'Boyle vs. Slavin,' it reads in bold letters, 'The Dawson Fight of the Century.'

"'This guy Boyle is gonna fight Frank Slavin, the heavyweight champion of Australia, tonight,' the guy says, and our eyes all fall back on Boyle.

"'I'll lose my mind! I'll lose my mind!' Boyle is screaming, and sure enough he stops, his eyes widen, and everyone's gaze follows his to see a man who obviously must be the Sydney Slasher emerging from a hotel across the street. Boyle goes crazy! He jumps from the box and runs through the mud at the guy, who walks fearlessly on, barely looking at Joe. Naturally, three or four men, one was Swiftwater Bill Gates, run up just in time and grab Joe and hold him back, all the while he's still screaming and pointing at Slavin, yelling things like, 'I'll get you!' and 'I'll murder you!'"

"So they staged it all?" I asked Hector, and he nodded vigorously.

"Course they staged it all. Sold all the tickets that way. Course, later when they buddied around it was all obvious, but no one held it against them. Dawson people will always respect making a buck."

So Joe Boyle, sailor, Concessionaire, entrepreneur, fight promoter, boxer — Joe Boyle stood in the foyer of the Russell House in Ottawa barking the new event of the new century. Wondering, no doubt, where the rest of the boys were and why they weren't exercising or otherwise preparing for the great match. When he finally felt he could let up he came to me and whispered, "Let's get the boys going, we've got a lot to do." Now, when Joe Boyle said you had a lot to do, you knew you had a lot to do.

The truth is nothing mattered anymore at this point. It's one of those things in life that you look back on and see clear as day, but you don't see it at the time. Things just happen. Things were all set. Our fate was cast with die-like precision the moment we took that first step out of Dawson, if you believe in fate. Nothing would alter our fates now. Not even the fact that we wouldn't sleep again before game time.

"The match of the century!" Joe Boyle yelled amidst the morning crowd, "Dawson's here for the grandest Stanley Cup match of them all!"

25

SURESHOT KENNEDY STROLLED into the dining room with a newspaper spread out before him, Johnstone and Hector on each side peering in. "'Hockeyists From The Yukon Have Arrived,'" he read aloud from the *Ottawa Citizen*, "'Challengers for the Stanley Cup Spent 23 Days en Route From Dawson City to Ottawa. Are in Fine Condition' — and that's just the headline!"

When the troupe gained the centre of the room, Sureshot continued. "'From Dawson City to Ottawa in twenty-three days, of which five were dead loss, is the story of the long expected Dawson City hockey team that reached the city at 4:45 yesterday afternoon.' Listen to this! 'All are in splendid condition. They possess some of the magnetism of the North Pole, from beneath whose shadow they come, for as the word sped rapidly through the city that they had at last arrived, the Russell House, where they registered, became a centre of unusual bustle, crowds thronging the rotunda and vicinity in the hope of catching a glimpse of the famous travellers.'"

"A glimpse!" Hector said. Sureshot scanned the rest of the article.

"Listen — 'They are after the Stanley Cup. They wish for nothing so much as to take the coveted emblem of the world's hockey championship north with them.' Ah, let's see . . . 'they

have endured great hardships and borne a tedious railway journey of 4,000 miles' — here we go again — 'tedious railway
journey of 4,000 miles without showing any ill effects, which
speaks well for their sound physical health. That alone, however, will not win them the Cup. They must win two out of
three games with the Ottawas.'"

Sureshot lowered the paper. "What's wrong with these people?
How come they always say what great shape we're in?"

"It's a conspiracy," Crazy Norman said.

"They're not accepting no excuses is all, eh?" Hector replied.

"I think that might be it," Johnstone said. "Last night my
father told me they was gonna submit a protest over Hannay
on account of him not being from Dawson no more. Combine
that with refusing to move back the dates, they're hedging their
bets in case they lose."

"And if they win they don't want no excuses about the
travel," Kennedy nodded. He looked back at the newspaper.
Joe Boyle came up and huddled over the paper like the rest.

"Am I in this?" he asked, scanning. "Here," he said, looking
toward the bottom of the article. "'Arrangements of referee,
umpires etc. are not complete yet, pending the arrival of Joe
Boyle from Detroit.' Hey, listen here," Joe suddenly bellowed,
"'As they said all the way East, their trip is no joke, and they
mean to show that they can play hockey tomorrow night. That
they will is the earnest hope of all, though' — listen! — 'though
their chances of victory are none too great.' None too great,
they say! None too great!"

And so it went that morning, catching up on the gossip in the
Ottawa papers, a reunion with Joe Boyle, and a meeting. The
meet-ing was held in Joe Boyle's small room, a raucous affair
with us all closed in tight, me, Hector and Sureshot, Hannay,
McLennan, Johnstone, Crazy Norman, Archie Martin, Forrest
— all us players — along with some others, Boyle's concessionaire partner Arthur Treadgold, known as the Treader,

Don Reddick

Johnstone's father who never seemed to leave Gloomy's side, vastly excited with his son in such national prominence, a couple others down from Dawson who I barely knew, Fred Congdon, Attorney McKinnon, Dan Stewart.

"This is the story, boys," Boyle began, standing up before us, his barrel chest out and his finger pointing for emphasis, "We're on for tomorrow night. I tried to get them to agree to an extension but they won't have it. So be it.

"Now, there's a great deal we must accomplish today and tomorrow. We have the rink for this afternoon's practice. I've also got the new uniforms and sticks on their way over from storage. We're to go to the rink directly after lunch, fit the uniforms and figure out the sticks, and I've got a photographer coming to take a team picture. I don't believe the light is good enough inside, so we probably will take it outside on Gladstone Street. We're also guests tonight for dinner, so no wandering off after practice." Boyle paused to catch his breath.

"I've been trying to get the rules committee to agree with me on a couple things, but I haven't had much luck. One, I tried to get any man that starts a fight thrown out for the game, but they didn't go for it. I also argued against having an Ottawa man referee, with greater success. I believe a man named Stiles, from Brockville, will be the man." And on and on it went, numerous little complementary actions and rules and whatnot, until he got to what today would be described as a game plan.

"Now, Weldy and I went over these people pretty solidly before I came out, and we've had correspondence since. Remember, Weldy hasn't seen these people for over five years, but he played here for seven, knows their system, knows most of them personally."

"When are we gonna rest?" Norman Watt said.

"No time for rest, Norman," Boyle said.

"Yeah, but we're all tired, eh?" Boyle ignored Norman.

"Listen, this is their line-up. In goal they've got the new kid

Day Finnie, you might know his brother, works in the gold assayer's office in Dawson. Oswald Finnie. He's a kid, this is his first Stanley Cup experience, and he's under a lot of pressure because he's replacing Bouse Hutton, who's very popular and very good, and who's won several Cups. Don't ask me why exactly, there's politics going on, I think they could have him if they wanted, but for some reason they don't. He's under suspension by the league for jumping to Brantford last year."

"Boston spoke with Shillington," McLennan says, "says Hutton has quinsy." Boyle nods with this information, seems to think about it a moment, then continues without comment.

"Pulford everyone knows about. Great all-round athlete, champion in several sports. Kind of up in the air, however, he's still quite upset about the death of his wife and might not even play at all. If he doesn't he'll be replaced by Bones Allen, who's a lacrosse star. Pulford's at the top of his game, he's got an awful lot of experience, get on him quick and make him rush. He stays near the net the whole match, and he's got an excellent backhand. Get on him quick."

"You all remember Serge Bedard, right boys?" Norman says to additional laughter, particularly Archie Martin's.

Now before Joe Boyle goes on, I should explain a little bit about hockey in the seven-man era, the era of the offside forward pass. Let's see if I can make sense of it. You could never pass the puck to a teammate who was ahead of you. What you could do was loft the puck up in the air, down past everyone to the opposition's end, and have your own men skate themselves onside, thereby allowing them to play the puck. This caused terrible confusion for the referee, who tried to keep track as best he could of which of the fourteen players was onside and which wasn't, because if someone was offside they didn't blow the whistle like they do today. Biggest problem a ref faced was sorting out the numerous arguments over this. Anyway, my point here is that the style of the game, then, was for the defencemen to stick tight to their own end, and whenever the puck came down to them, they'd lift it mightily up and over the whole crowd back down into the other end, with everybody chasing it. This made for rather tedious play, sometimes several minutes of one team lofting it one way followed by the other team lofting back, back and forth with little other action but the poor forwards chasing it. But this was Harvey Pulford's specialty, his ability to loft the puck down the ice.

"He has an excellent backhand loft, get on him quick," Joe Boyle is saying. "Art Moore's the coverpoint, big, strong lad, been with them for several seasons. Not flashy, not spectacular, just steady as she goes. Not much at scoring. He's in great shape after the football season, like Smith and Pulford. Don't let him lull you to sleep.

"Rat Westwick is the rover, and he's having the best year of his career. He's fast, he can skate like the wind, he's played with Pulford and Alf Smith forever. He can pass with the best of them. Excellent athlete, the best lacrosse player in the province. You're gonna have to keep your eye on this guy all the time, he's better than Smith. What do you want now, Norman?"

"Nothing," Norman says, which breaks us up for no reason. I doubt to this day that he listened to a word Joe Boyle had to say. Boyle ignored the foolishness.

"On the forward line you got Alf Smith at left wing — Sureshot — McGee at centre — Hector — and White at right wing — Norman." He said the names of our fellows who would line up against each, to gain special attention from them.

"Alf Smith's an oldtimer, he's like the guy on the dock who's been around so long he knows everything inside out, and acts it. He's not so fast, doesn't pass as good as Westwick, but he's a battler from way back, tough as nails and he'll hit you every chance he gets. Keep your head up around Alf. He's dirty. I don't expect him to score as much as I do Westwick and McGee, but be forewarned, he comes to play.

"I don't know much about this White. But he's playing so he must be good. He's taking Suddie Gilmour's place. Gilmour's up on the Gatineau timber limits, and normally his brother Billy would replace him but he's attending McGill. Good place for Suddie, he's one of the best, him and his brothers. But White's playing so he must be good. And the last one is McGee." Boyle paused to consider his words.

"Frank McGee's only got one eye, but don't let that fool you. He set a record for goals in a Stanley Cup game with five against Toronto, and then he did it again last year against Lorne's Brandon team. He's the real thing, he can score better than anyone else in senior hockey, and Alf Smith says he's the greatest hockey player he's ever saw. I hear the same thing from others. Keep on this guy all the time, keep your stick under his, keep your body between him and the puck. He's a bull, very, very strong, and if you rile him he's even worse. He can skate as well as Westwick and he's a stickhandler. We stop McGee, I believe we stop the Silver Seven. They had their first regular season game last week, and McGee scored four goals and he hurt his wrist. But don't even think about that, I'm told he's fine."

"How'd they make out in that game, Joe?" McLennan asked.

"They beat the Wanderers, nine to three. McGee scored four, Westwick and Smith got two each. I'm told Finnie was nervous, but he showed up with the goods." Joe Boyle paused and there was a general shifting.

"These boys are excellent. They are defending Stanley Cup champions, they've won five consecutive Stanley Cup challenges, and despite all the ruckus about professionalism, I think they're all getting paid somehow, but don't quote me — that would just create problems that might prevent us from arranging other games. But even though they're good, we're better! Who's from the Klondike? Who left their homes and families to travel a million miles, suffered all the sufferings, worked their tails off in the frozen wilderness, to better themselves?

Who" — he looks at Archie Martin and Hector Smith and George Kennedy and me — "who broke their backs in the frozen woods heating up muck for the gold? And who travelled twenty-five days, four thousand miles, to just get here?"

"I dunno, who?" Norman says, which breaks Joe Boyle's argument and makes him mad. But he don't stop, ignores Norman completely. Nobody dares laugh with Joe the way he is.

"It's us! The Dawson Nuggets, the Dawson City Seven! I know you want to call yourselves the Dawson City Seven, but we've got to win first. We didn't come all this way for nothing, did we? We can beat these boys and if we do we'll carry that Stanley Cup back over the CPR and dogsled it up into Dawson and we'll keep it there forever!" Sureshot Kennedy jumps up at this point and punches the air.

"We're gonna do it!" he yells, and everybody, even Norman, joins in, and we all jump up and yell and scream and act terrifying.

Boyle brought us to Cassidy's for lunch, for "exposure" he explained — Cassady's, the location for one of the greatest sporting blunders of all time two nights later.

What happened there? Well, let me tell you what happened one night later before I tell you what happened two nights later, eh? Eh? Heard a funny explanation for the Canadians' use of that expression, by the way. Walking the trail out with the dogsled boys, I comment to Hector about it, he turns to me, his face all covered with seriousness, and says, "You know why all Canadians say eh? We learn it when we're little in school. Teachers teach us to."

"They teach you to say that?" I say, frowning and falling into his joke.

"Teacher says spell 'Canada,' and she says 'C — eh? — N — eh? — D — eh?'" We bust up laughing, one of the few times we did so on that long, desolate, wolf-calling walk.

So. We had lunch at Cassady's, the sports hangout in Ottawa. All the big hocus-pocus hung around there, the Silver Seven, and it's where I got my first sight of Pulford, McGee, and

Dirty Alf Smith, the hotshot young lawyers and the political sidekicks, you know the type.

Then we went to Dey's Rink down on the corner of Bay and Gladstone streets, down on the backside of town away from the river. We sat in the locker room and watched as the crates of sticks and uniforms was broke open, saw the beautiful blue sweaters with gold pants, brand spanking new. I don't suppose you can visualize ten men fresh from the sordidness of the filthy wilderness, with eyes that looked like they spotted nuggets in the streambed as they rummage through the brand new clothes. I imagine none of us had a new piece of clothing like this in a year or more. Depending when they went in. Of course with the exception of Joe Boyle, who I believe was already a millionaire.

We argued over who got what and what fit who, then leaned on the new sticks Joe Boyle had got, scraping the floor in imagined shots at imagined goals, cross checking and poking each other in fun. Then Joe Boyle says the photographer's here and we troop outside with all our new gear on, even our skates, and Joe Boyle says, "Hey, boys, get your gloves and sticks too," and we do, and again we troop out and line up. But something happens now which never settled right with me — Joe Boyle says it's the seven starters only that get taken, which leaves out me and Archie Martin. It was the custom of the times to photograph only the starters, as is testified in any number of old photos of Stanley Cup winning teams, but nevertheless, after all we'd been through together, it bothered me then and it still does. Archie Martin looks at me and shrugs, he doesn't seem to care. I know Archie and Joe Boyle are close, which makes it easier for me to accept. Nothing personal, eh?

But the photograph is a marvellous thing, I brought my copy and I want you to look at it now. Look at it . . . and think about it. In back there's Hector Smith, Indian-looking guy on the left, next to him is Sureshot Kennedy, then Hannay, then

Johnstone and then Crazy Norman Watt on the right end. In front is the kid Albert Forrest with his goaler pads on, Joe Boyle in the hat with Doc McLennan, mustache and all, on his left. This is the Dawson City Seven! But look at it closely . . . do you see what I see? This picture's worth a million words — do you see it? This is a photograph of eight men who are about to contest for the Stanley Cup in front of all Canada, and look at them. Do you see one smile? Look at Sureshot, even his disgusted gaze is a tired disgusted gaze, look at Johnstone's dead eyes. Norman Watt isn't even grinning, for cry-eye. Albert Forrest, the nineteen-year-old kid — as of yesterday — looks fifty, with the eyes of a man who's seen things you sometimes just got to see for yourself. It took me time to understand the whole business, but the picture says it all . . . the truth is exhaustion had overtaken us, had probably overtaken us as we stumbled numbly into Whitehorse so long ago.

The skate was an illumination of dreadfulness. I don't believe I mentioned it, but we'd been able to skate a half hour or so the evening before, and the soreness that comes to your legs after your first skate in a long while crept up at us from below, our breath was laboured, all our actions awkward. We were in awful shape! Joe Boyle watched it with disgust, arguing with Doc McLennan who he'd instructed to make us exercise throughout the trip, which obviously we hadn't done. Doc argued back just as much in his frustration at the whole situation. When it was over — I thought it would never end — we crawled off the ice and I believe Norman Watt even got sick, though he wouldn't admit it.

Our team dinner was held at the Russell House, which now, on the eve of the Great Match, was in near bedlam. All sorts of people came by, staring at us as we ate, men with their wives and girlfriends, men with their young sons holding short hockey sticks in their hands, men with their men friends, all coming around to see the famous heroes from under the shadow of the North Pole, or whatever that silly newspaper said. Magnetism.

Young, unattached women came, which was a shock to me, and perked up several of the boys, particularly Sureshot and Norman. We had turkey for this dinner, we had turkey and stuffing, roasted potatoes and milk, with coffee and cigars offered around after, which caused many a wink and smile, what with Joe Boyle's aversions.

After dinner there was speeches, Joe Boyle standing up, of course, and explaining how tough and hard we were, how cold it was up "home" and whatnot, how we would gladly entertain challenges for the Stanley Cup once it was up in the Dawson Amateur Athletic Association rink with the twin towers, and on and on. Sureshot's famous gaze returned, Norman made everyone laugh, Johnstone sat with his father and his father's friends, McLennan with his family up from Cornwall, Archie Martin with two of his three brothers, over from Hull. I believe the only people without family or friends there was Brother Albert and myself. But with the multitudes willing to talk and laugh, we were not lonely.

Of course this was the worst possible activity, you understand, for a team preparing for a great match the next night. The atmosphere of the previous night descended over us again and evening led into night, with more toasts and chair-standing joke deliveries as the party wore on and the bartenders' pockets grew heavier. Even Joe Boyle, who had a constitution of iron, melted into it all, which should surprise no one who ever knew the gentleman, for Irish Joe Boyle was ever one to storytell with the best of them. A crowd surrounded him at all times, such was his spell, and he enjoyed it.

Oh, I could go on and on. I remember the laughter and the faces and the bartender with his curlicue mustache and Hector winking at me and Brother Albert peering nervously at the merrymaking . . . I believe I relented upon myself and went up to the room about three-thirty in the morning.

I was the first to leave.

Don Reddick

26

WE STOOD IN LINES ACROSS from one another, on what today would be the blue lines. There weren't any blue lines in the old days, just one line across the centre of the ice splitting the rink into equal halves. I stared at the lean, scarred faces of the Ottawa Silver Seven with combined fear, awe, and nervousness. I remember Dirty Alf Smith and Art Moore best, Smith because of the absolutely evil disposition of his face, the quick shrugging of his shoulders as though arranging his sweater to give freedom to his arms, his glare as it covered us left to right and back. Moore had more of a deadly, blank, and totally professional, distracted appearance, at once aloof and concentrated. Intimidating in a cold way.

I saw the others also, of course, though they seemed less chilling. There was twenty-four-year-old Frank McGee, of slighter build than the others, fine-faced and blonde with the lazy dead eye, there he was mostly with his head down and his feet sliding fore and aft in his nervousness; there was Bones Allen, looking every inch the great lacrosse player, though I'd never seen a lacrosse player before and never seen a game of it before or since. I thought of Archie's story, but I was incapable of any smiles. His presence, of course, meant the great Harvey Pulford would not be playing, which much heartened us.

Next to him was Harry "The Rat" Westwick, another imposing specimen. This is the greatest lacrosse star on their team. I thought his nickname might have something to do with his looks, but as I stared at him now I doubted it, because Westwick was a fine-looking young man, thirty-one years old, lean and handsome. He stood very much alert, his eyes darting about — he looked ready.

Who else? Ah, Finnie, Dave "Day" Finnie, the rookie goaler in his first Stanley Cup match with a team that had won it over and over. He was downright nervous, looking at us, up into the

crowd at his family and back, at Westwick to his left and whoever it was on his right and then slamming his goaler pads with
his stick, sweat already dripping from his chin. His anxiety, of
course, was multiplied by his replacing Bouse Hutton, a great
favourite and proven performer. That was all a bad business
which whispers said had to do with being paid, but I don't
know the whole truth and won't speculate. All I know is what
Shillington told me, and that Hutton never played again.

White stood there, a relative newcomer, replacing a kid
named Suddie Gilmour. Those with knowledge claimed we
were lucky he was up on the Gatineau timber limits. I can't remember White's first name. He made no impression on me. So
these are the great ones, I said to myself. They were quite in
contrast to their magnetic visitors from under the shadow of
the North Pole, opposite them.

Where Day Finnie was the only blatantly nervous one of
their bunch, all of the Dawson City Seven were in a state of
near mortification and panic at the entire proceedings. No matter how much Joe Boyle prepared and encouraged us, speaking
with hard, direct words about courage and faith and whatnot,
he could not relieve the awful nervousness from our tight
bodies.

Out onto the ice come the high news people, Joe Boyle for
us and Shillington for them, and P.D. Ross, the Cup trustee and
editor of one of the big Ottawa newspapers. Then Earl Grey,
the Governor General of Canada, daintily walks and slides toward centre ice. He's a pretty good-looking man who's been
around — Rhodesia and other places — and who likes sports.
Later he himself donated a winner's cup for the sinister football
championship of Canada, and they still play for it today. The
Grey Cup. This particular habit of Governor Generals donat-
ing cups was of course established by Lord Stanley. Actually,
cups were very much a part of the sporting scene of Canada.
Up in Dawson they had the Jersey Tankard for the curling

Don Reddick

championship, which Doc McLennan's rink won while we were in Ottawa, and in 1906, Joe Boyle, caught up in it all, donated the Boyle Cup to his hometown of Woodstock, Ontario, also for curling. To this day it's still contested for.

Two men named Murphy — and I don't know if they're related — are with His Excellency, one of them the president of the Ottawa Hockey Club, the other a member of parliament. They're all at centre ice, and Ross says a few words I forget, and then Grey says something like this: "It is with the utmost admiration that we welcome our friends from the Northland here tonight, for as everyone knows they have travelled a remarkable distance in a very short time to compete this evening. Not a finer group of young men could our Yukon Territory produce, and I believe it is heartily agreed that we wish them the grandest of luck in their quest for Lord Stanley's Cup."

The crowd cheers when he steps back, though they couldn't possibly have heard him clear, the players tap their sticks on the ice, and Grey turns and waves to all corners of the humming, packed building. Dirty Alf Smith and Doc McLennan, as captains of our teams, glide over and remove their gloves and shake hands with the man, who then turns and shakes hands with the referee Stiles and says something amusing to him as he does so, as Stiles breaks out in a smile. Norman leans close to me and whispers, "Hey, maybe if I clobber Bones over the head he'll play hockey like Serge Bedard."

Stiles hands His Excellency his whistle, and all of them troop off toward the side, both teams giving Grey three cheers. Then the players turn and dash around the nets in one last warm-up, and off me and Archie Martin go to the bench. This is when I receive a satisfaction, for Shillington, sitting on the Silver Seven bench with a puck in his hand, meets my eyes, and I can see the shock my appearance produces. He turns away immediately with a gesture that tells me he's mad. With my smuggest smile, I float with Archie back to our bench and step in.

Boyle paces back and forth, alternately staring at the Silver Seven and scanning the crowd for some smoker he thought he'd seen — smoking, much to his approval, is prohibited in the rink — Archie yells as usual. His Excellency stands on the ice by his box, whistle at the ready.

Stiles, the lone official, carefully places the puck between the two centres and backs off, glancing over his shoulder at Grey, signalling for the whistle. The crowd howls with anticipation and everyone rises to their feet. I see Hector, eyes wild, leaning in and tense as a kitten camping on a mouse. Westwick's the same. Grey blows the whistle!

Immediately it's apparent why Westwick takes the face instead of McGee, their usual centre. As soon as the whistle sounds across the ice, Westwick pokes the puck back through Hector Smith's legs and practically hurdles over him, retrieves it and passes it left to Dirty Alf who feeds it right back to him. Wham! He fires it on Brother Albert, who makes the save. That fast, that coordinated, and the game is on!

This is a marvellous realization to me, of course, and I stand wide-eyed at the side boards hollering my encouragements and disappointments with Mr. Stiles, Archie screaming right along with me, Boyle pointing, shouting, throwing his arms up when something goes wrong.

Johnstone bats away Westwick's rebound, McLennan picks it up and lugs it away, passes to Norman Watt who breaks up ahead. Norman shoots wide of Day Finnie, Bones Allen picking it up and trying to clear. Hannay bats it down, Hector grabs it and fires, and Day Finnie gets his first save.

This is how the game starts, very fast, very nerve-wracking, and the minutes creep by, all the players skating their hardest, minute by minute passing. We're keeping pace with them, Brother Albert making stops on McGee and Westwick, Finnie on long shots by Doc McLennan and Hannay, who's famous for them, having scored one that way in his previous Stanley

Cup series. This is when the first of the ugliness starts with Norman Watt.

I saw the whole thing and I'm still uncertain whether Dirty Alf Smith meant it or not, I was told later this occurred frequently with him. Norman and Smith collide heavily and Norman goes down, a nasty cut on his forehead. Now, you got to remember Norman's nickname, and, if what Hector told me was true, his fears about his stature. Norman jumps up and starts belting Dirty Alf Smith's head, a right and a right and a right, and Smith ducks his head down and flails back and we've got our first fight.

Stiles asserts his authority and prevents a melee, sends them both off for ten minutes, which is time for me to explain one more thing. In those days — and this causes a funny thing Stiles does later — in those days it was up to the referee to decide how long a penalty was. For your everyday slash or trip, you had a minute coming, if a guy intentionally tried to kill someone — which Norman tried to do later — fifteen, twenty minutes wasn't unusual. And you didn't come back on the ice if the other team scored like you do today. No sir. You stayed in that penalty zone until your time was up, period. And then you only got out when time was called because of a goal or something.

But the game's on! What a sight, the red, black and white stripes of the champions streaking among our blue and gold, such a dazzling display of athleticism, the tremendous speed, particularly by Westwick and Dirty Alf Smith, who is much better than any of us had expected. McGee is good, but he seems distracted, not performing one hundred percent. I remember thinking his wrist must be bothering him.

Hector shows spurts of his own speed but seems somewhat out of sorts . . . nervous maybe. Kennedy barrels up and down his wing, but he too seems unable to unleash his full capabilities. On it goes, eight, nine minutes into the match without a score, the stands rising and falling with each clear scoring chance, until McGee scores.

Kennedy had fed McLennan who popped one on Finnie, and Rat Westwick picks up the rebound and flies up ice with slant-eyed McGee, passes it to him just over the line. McGee, using Johnstone as a shield, fires the puck past Brother Albert for the first one. The crowd roars its approval, the Silver Seven congregate about McGee and pat him on the head and rear end. Two and a half minutes later Dirty Alf Smith takes McGee's pass and puts one in the net to make it two-nothing.

This precipitates the most hectic, industrious stretch imaginable, tremendous hockey skills exerted, with Day Finnie making great stops on McLennan and Watt, and then Hector Smith is positively robbed of a goal! At the same time our boy Brother Albert Forrest is called upon to stop cold both Smith and White. And then it happens, Westwick scores from passes off the sticks of Alf Smith and that White fellow.

Three-nothing.

This is particularly disheartening, coming around the middle of the first half, but we have virtually no time to ponder it, because right off the face, Hector gains control of the puck about mid-ice, wheels and passes it to the Doc, and McLennan fires and scores! What an explosion of hysteria this produces in that long-lost little building, McLennan mobbed by the team, little Norman Watt diving up on top of the huddle, as though we had won the Cup itself!

Now, you're probably wondering when the old man sitting here before you got in the game, but I'm going to remind you: in them old days of seven-man hockey there were no substitutions unless a man got hurt bad. Spare men like me and Archie Martin seldom got to play at all — we were for insurance purposes only. Fact of the matter is, I didn't play a second of this first game, but I'll warn you that events soon to transpire would change all that for the second.

Don Reddick

But the game's on! It's three to one now, and hotly debated still. These men know they have to skate a full sixty minutes, but they go all out anyway. After Doc's goal, the game becomes more controlled, with several lifters back and forth by the defencemen, the only excitement being Hector Smith missing a breakaway. At nine-thirty the half whistle blows, and we all tromp off to the applause of a grateful, excited crowd.

There is much commotion and emotion under the stands. "We're in the thick of it!" Joe Boyle yells, and agreements resound all around. We sit on long benches, Boyle handing Archie Martin a bag of apples — in mid-January! — and Archie passing them out. Others pop into our dressing room, Arthur Treadgold among them. The players pant and perspire and throw the apple cores on the floor. When Archie's done with the apples he looks at the floor, notices all the crossed sticks and corrects them, under Sureshot's disgusted glare.

"We can beat these boys!" Sureshot yells, and affirmations cascade. Hector, obviously taken up in it all, for he's normally subdued, jumps up and hollers, "We're from the Yukon! We gotta do this for every Dawson man ever scraped that froze earth, every Dawson woman ever cooked that meal we tumble home to! Let's do it, eh!" and again everyone shouts his serious agreement.

"Westwick married Peg Duvall's sister last year," Norman yells, "and Peg didn't make the team this year. Bother him about that!" Heads nod.

"And McGee's sister is a nun in Montreal," Sureshot yells, but before he can finish Norman stands up and points at Sureshot with his stick and says, "Don't be making fun of the nun." This confuses Sureshot, and he argues something I don't hear.

Joe Boyle hushes us up now. "There's some guy doing Indian club exhibitions or something out there, so rest up, they'll probably give him ten or fifteen minutes. I want you all to breath deep and relax your muscles, rest as much as possible.

We're in this game, boys, there's no doubt about it. McGee's not doing much. Watch out for Westwick and that dirty one Smith, and White, who is this guy White? Keep Westwick toward the boards, defencemen — Johnstone and Hannay — drive them all to the outside and make them pass back to the middle, and the rest of you run back and get those passes."

Boyle goes on and on and on, his mind all excited and working about a hundred miles an hour. Sureshot rests his head back against the wall, his face glistening like a freshly bobbed apple. Lorne Hannay's alert, probably on account of him being in decent physical condition compared to the rest of us. Beside me sits Brother Albert Forrest, as quiet as quiet gets. Suddenly silent Albert jumps to his feet and stuns us all by yelling — yelling! — "We can do it, boys, we can beat these sons-a-guns, we can do it, *let's go!*" It stuns us all. There's a split second of incredulity before the loud affirmations, and Brother Albert plops back down next to me, leans close and whispers, "Pretty good, eh?"

"Okay, okay," Joe Boyle says. "Now let's remember everything and make crisp, excellent passes and hard, accurate shots. Sureshot, I'm expecting big things from you this half. Hector, look for your wings breaking. Jimmy and Lorne, stay back, don't be caught up ice. Let's go!" And we hustle out the door and run onto the ice, the low murmuring of the crowd breaking into roaring cheers and applause.

The mighty Silver Seven make their entry and the sound doubles, and the two teams skate in circles among one another. Believe it or not, I get a slash across the backs of my legs, and I see Dirty Alf Smith shoot by, pretending to doctor the end of his stick. The whistle blows, and I return to my bench, shaking my head at it all.

"What do you think, Boston?" Joe Boyle says to me, and I answer, "We can beat 'em," and he nods seriously. The man wants to win so bad. Like everything he's done in his lifetime he takes every bit of it seriously and studiously, and I remember marvelling at his intensity that evening. How he must have wanted to play himself!

The second half starts slowly, lifts from one defence to another, Bones Allen to Hannay and back, the forwards scurrying back and forth, their heads skyward watching the black disc, back and forth. For the first time I see the hesitation in our men, the exertions required just to stop short and reverse direction . . . and then that dirty little Alf Smith breaks our backs.

First he picks up the puck out of nowhere right in front of Brother Albert, whirls and fires it home. Our spirits momentarily lift and then sink when Doc McLennan misses a good chance, then Norman Watt, his head down, breaks in alone but don't see Day Finnie charge out of his net and bang the puck away. Then Dirty Alf Smith scores again, this time after White steals the puck from Sureshot and passes it clear across ice to the breaking little devil. And then again he scores. I'd say it all began to unfold badly for us here, the score being six or seven to one. We just stop skating.

Our frustration shows when even Albert Forrest gets a penalty for slashing White after he comes in too close to the net, hacking at his own rebound. Hannay fills in at goal as Albert serves his time in the penalty zone and gets scored upon twice more. And then the ugliness in Norman Watt emerges.

This time Norman trips Art Moore, the heavy-shouldered hulk on defence, from behind, and Moore slashes him in the mouth for his efforts, which obviously hurts Norman. He goes down in pain, his glove to his mouth checking for blood, then rises, madness in his eyes. He charges after Moore from behind and clubs him over the head, breaking his stick, as nasty a performance as I've ever witnessed in a hockey rink. Moore collapses in a heap to the ice, unconscious, and it is a miracle that referee Stiles prevents a large fight.

Approaching the timekeepers, who were directly to our right, Stiles says — and I heard this with my own ears — he says, "Watt is off for fifteen minutes, and he's off" — he's pointing to Moore's prone figure across the ice — "he's off for two minutes. What's his name?"

"Moore," replies the timekeeper.

"Moore? Is that Moore?" Stiles says, "Make it three minutes." And off he skates. Both benches bust out in laughter, but in a nutshell the incident displays what kind of game he called that night. Several of their goals appeared offside even to me, but I thought little of it until afterward, when Joe Boyle explained the loss to us.

I can't say much about the rest of the game, except we score once more, the last goal of a nine-to-two game, when almost our whole team, Hector, Sureshot, Doc and Norman break together down ice, Watt shoots and Day Finnie saves, only to have Sureshot ram home the rebound. But it was very much too little too late, as they say, and the game was called short a few minutes later when it was apparent to all that we could skate no more.

Joe Boyle's only words in the dressing room was, "We've got to win Monday."

27

NO GROUP OF MEN IN THE HISTORY of sport lay more unconscious after a game than we did. The *Ottawa Evening Journal* the next day said it best: "At the end of the game Yukon were so tired they could hardly stand on their skates and they went to their hotel as limp as wet rags."

This rag attests to it, for never in my lifetime, what with the physical and emotional distresses and upheaval, have I experienced such all-consuming fatigue. And I didn't even play! We indeed returned to the Russell House, and most of us didn't even eat, but fell on our beds and died until late the next morning. Even Joe Boyle knew enough to leave us be, though he had arranged for an afternoon hour in the rink, which he intended to use despite Doc McLennan's objections.

The loss stung us numb. Nine to two! I heard a few objections after the game, Joe Boyle railing about the referee Stiles, who he insisted missed four offside goals by the Silver Seven. Forrest claimed he missed six, though he had personal integrity at stake and exaggerated somewhat, I think. But there was something to the complaints — even the *Journal* felt three were scored by offside men.

The next day, bolstering our wounded confidence, the talk increased. Two of their goals were scored on Hannay while Brother Albert sat in the penalty zone for slashing White. Watt had spent twenty-five minutes — nearly half the game — in the zone, creating what is now called a power play for almost that whole period of time. And added was the indisputable: our awful stress in attempting to play after so long a journey without rest. As that article in the *Journal* put it, "It was only when the Yukonites tired and showed the effect of their long journey that Ottawa began to pile on the score." Indeed, at the half it was just three to one and still anyone's game, and we had skated with them stride for stride.

We struggled our bodies into our wet uniforms and practised that afternoon, put on a good front for the fans that came to watch, and again nearly fell across our benches in the dressing room afterward. But Joe Boyle was all business. Despite the fact that he had not participated in our long journey or the game, his enormous energy displayed itself now.

"All right then, listen to me," he said in that magical, magnetic voice which immediately silenced any room. "We lost last night nine to two. It's no secret we're tired, it's no secret they refused to delay the games, as any gentleman would, to allow us time to prepare. And four offside goals — I'm not going to allow Stiles to referee Monday. I'm insisting he's replaced. Watt . . . Norman, you've got to hold your temper. Paper today said it hasn't seen anything like it since Murray hit Harry Ketchum in that Shamrock-Capital lacrosse game. That's bad, Norman, bad for you and bad for our reputation, never mind we played short for most of twenty-five minutes because of it."

"Moore got three," Norman objected meekly, and Boyle ignored him.

"This was no nine-to-two game, boys! Lorne let in two that Albert would have got. So take away those two, take away four offside goals, and right there you got a four to two game, and that despite losing Weldy Young and Lionel Bennett, no practice for Lorne to feel comfortable with us, and having no rest for a month of Sundays." Joe Boyle paused to let it all sink in. Norman Watt burped and everyone laughed, but Joe Boyle's glare stopped that short.

"Wait a minute," he said, recalculating, "that's a three-to-two game. Three to two! Think about that! And think about all the good scoring chances we missed! Now, Monday is a different story. There'll be no skate tomorrow, we're going to be fully rested. Fully prepared. I got word today Weldy is on the way. We win Monday and he'll be here for the third game. We can still win this thing."

Then I got the first inkling of my fate: Doc McLennan stood up and I saw him wince, favouring his left leg. McLennan had had an old hockey injury, hurt his knee a few years before. He limped over to his clothes and painfully pulled on his pants. I did not fully realize at the time that this was my road to playing in a Stanley Cup game, but it was. Sunday found Doc's knee swole so bad he could barely walk at all. But I'll get to all that. In the meantime, it was unfortunate that Joe Boyle

Don Reddick

couldn't prepare us in another fashion — schooling us to keep our mouths shut.

On this Saturday night we packed up and headed out the door past Joe Boyle, who was covered with sports reporters, and I heard him saying that our strategy had been to get into shape the first game, take the second, and with Weldy Young, the hero of so many old Ottawa games, with Weldy Young in our line-up we also would take the third game and win the Stanley Cup. They scribbled it all down. He also said, and I quote from the article that appeared the following day, "The boys are improving rapidly and they will show it Monday. Even their flesh seems different after their wholesome, comfortable sleep."

Back at the hotel Sureshot got hold of a Montreal newspaper and bothered anyone who would listen, reading lines about himself such as, "'G.A. Kennedy, the bravest on the team, one hundred and eighty-five pounds, is by no means the slowest. He plays right wing. He starts a bit leisurely, but will be a hard man to stop. He shoots like a cannon and straight as a die.'"

"Hear that?" Sureshot yelled, "'Shoots like a cannon and straight as a die!'"

This delighted him, of course, though he wasn't going about quoting the *Ottawa Evening Journal*, which said, among other things, "Big Kennedy on right wing was expected to do more effective work than he did, and can do. He played a game that was remarked upon as clean. For such a big man he used his weight very little. In shooting he lacked accuracy . . . "

That same article found Hannay and Brother Albert the favourites of the crowd, called Doc McLennan the hardest worker, Hector Smith the fastest, and — not surprisingly — Norman Watt the craziest. A "cruel blow" they called his disgraceful attack on Moore. The paper also saw Dirty Alf Smith as far and away the best all-round player on the ice, and added, "McGee did not exert himself much." This assessment was shared, unfortunately, by many, and most unfortunately by Norman Watt.

Several went their separate ways this evening, Johnstone taking Albert Forrest along to eat and visit with his proud parents, McLennan also entertaining family and friends from nearby Cornwall, Norman Watt and Archie Martin crossing the river into Quebec to visit their old haunts of Hull and Aylmer. But only for a while. Norman eventually showed up at Cassady's, where Hector, Sureshot, and I had eaten dinner, with a troop of eager, arm-bending followers. Hannay and Joe Boyle were nowhere to be seen.

The youngish crowd at Cassady's sports cave stood elbow to elbow, spilled out of the barroom and into the dining area, infringing on the tables. A mist of cigar smoke hung low across the rooms, the official hangout of Ottawa's athletic elite. Sam Cassady oversaw it all, a funny, good humoured fellow, slim and athletic looking himself. He stood perpetually by the door, shaking hands and slapping the backs of those that entered, shaking hands and slapping the backs of those leaving, always smiling.

He recognized us and ushered us to our own reserved table, and I recognized a few of the Silver Seven at the bar. Art Moore, the hulking defenceman with a bandage across the back of his head where Norman tomahawked him, left early on, leaving Rat Westwick and Dirty Alf Smith. Westwick barely nodded to our waved greeting, and Smith refused to acknowledge our presence at all. In those days you didn't fraternize with the enemy, period. Unless you were Joe Boyle.

We ate dinner, I had hot bread and butter, pea soup and a slice of ham. I remember these things. Real good slice of fresh ham, something I hadn't had in a long, long time. With pineapple slices, a rarity during the winter even in Ottawa. You've got to remember, we was only a month out of the wilderness, and train fare hadn't been exactly Momma's cooking, you understand. Hector and Sureshot both had pieces of roast beef with gravy and roasted potatoes and green beans, and they drank free beer from Cassady, and then from other anonymous fans. Saturday night at the turn of the century wasn't unlike Saturday night here in 1962, men were out with their wives and their future wives, dressed up and carrying the extra dollar, drinking a beer or two more than they would on a workday night. Cassady's had a wonderful atmosphere, for a barroom, of which by this time I had seen sundry. The buzz was about the game, of course, and we were once again the centre of attention for many men and even a few shy, peeking single women. Sureshot smiled at them all, I saw, but Hector was Hector, silent, staring into space. They asked Hector about being Indian, they asked Sureshot how he became so wealthy.

"Boston," a young man said to me earnestly, "that's over there in the Maritimes, eh?" and I nodded my agreement, of course. Maritimes. It was talk like this that made me favour conversation with my teammates.

"What are you going to do after?" I asked neither of them in particular. The question appeared to confound them, as though they had given it no thought whatsoever.

"We're playing Queen's," Sureshot replied, his tone screaming, What do you think we're going to do after?

"After the tour, I mean," I said. Just then a small boy manoeuvred his way between Sureshot and Hector and asked for our autographs, which was a source of immense amusement to us. When the deed was done, with a pencil on one of the newspaper articles, Hector steered the conversation clear of any abstract thoughts such as I was attempting to introduce.

"McGee didn't do much," he said, "considering everyone warned us he was just about the grandest thing to come along since the Gatling gun."

"Smith and Westwick were both better," Sureshot agreed. "But you know what? Bones Allen must be a better lacrosse player than he is a hockey player. I'm afraid Pulford will play Monday instead."

This concerned us. Harvey Pulford had been the best defenceman in all Canada for the last ten years, and the thought of additional obstructions to our offense was sobering. No one showed it.

"He's older now," Sureshot said. No one said McLennan, or Archie, or Sureshot was just as old, or that Weldy Young was even older. We dwelt on the positives, as well we should.

"That was a three-to-two game, you heard Joe," Hector said, though it sounded like a remark more likely to come from Sureshot. Remember, this is the guy who figures sometimes things is so real you got to see them for yourself.

"If we get on Westwick and don't retaliate on Dirty Alf Smith, we spend the whole game with a man up instead of them, and Westwick won't have no room to skate. He's a hell of a skater, eh? See him jump around?" We nodded.

Joe Boyle strutted in and gave us loud, haughty greetings, keeping his hand on Hector's neck and declaring to all around that we were indeed the famous Dawson Nuggets. He leaned over our table and whispered, "I heard from Weldy. He arrived at Vancouver yesterday and he jumped the next CPR. He'll be here in time for the third game."

This became a lively topic of conversation, and Joe Boyle eventually left us to our table and moved along to some expensive-looking men. And Norman Watt and his entourage finally arrived from Aylmer, and our table quickly began to accumulate beer bottles.

"Where's Archie?" Sureshot asked.

"Beer, eh?" Norman said, approaching our table with his patented disarming smile. "Beer? I hear it's a fine thing, that beer is, I believe I'll avail myself of some." We all laugh. Free drinks brought by Cassady himself arrive and I see Norman notice Dirty Alf Smith and Rat Westwick leaning on the bar. I also notice the guy next to Smith is almost his exact duplicate — I found out later it's his brother, one of his six brothers, Harry Smith, who would join the Silver Seven in '06 and become an instant star. It's quite a story, I don't have time to go into it, but all seven Smith brothers eventually tried their hand at hockey, with a younger brother, Tommy, the best.

Anyway, Westwick and at least two of the Smith brothers lean against the bar and confidently discuss their own one-game-up situation with anyone who'll listen while we sit around our table, Norman having pulled up chairs with his boys, joining us and us discussing our one-game-down situation. What happens next, though none of us know it, is the beginning of one of the historic moments in all sports history, an event that would be recalled for decades in any number of coaches' final instructions before big games. It happened in a smoke-filled barroom named Sam Cassady's in Ottawa in January of '05, a place arm to arm with sporting men standing on floorboards sticky with spilt beer, and it happened between Crazy Norman Watt, who was spilling his share, and iron-eyed Dirty Alf Smith, consuming his fair share. And I heard it all. Everything's normal until Norman drinks too much.

He's cut on his mouth, remember, from the stick of Art Moore. He's bruised so badly from his collision with Alf Smith he might not be able to play the next game. And he stares at Smith now, and his voice rises.

"We're gonna beat them Silver Sevens," he says loud enough for them and half the rest of the patrons at the bar to hear. I view this as inappropriate, but Hector and Sureshot enjoy it, encourage it with smiles and winks.

"Yes, we was just warming up and getting in shape last night, eh? And half their goals shouldn't count." I look over and I see Rat Westwick ignoring it all, but Smith isn't. A cagey veteran of more than a decade of senior hockey in Ottawa, renowned for his toughness as well as his dirtiness, he glares over his shoulder when Norman speaks. His eyes, chiselled along with the other features on his lean hockeyist face, speak volumes of disgust.

"Yes," Norman continues, his eyes alive with the knowledge he's irking Smith. "Why, everyone knows they're scared of us, they officially protested Lorne Hannay in case they lose, they wouldn't delay a few days to let us rest. It's all obvious, eh?"

This brings snickers across the crowd, and there's no doubt in my mind that Smith's hearing every bit of it. Norman keeps it up until Rat Westwick leaves, which triggers something in him, I guess he was fearful Smith would leave too, ending his game. Norman starts again in earnest. "We thought Stiles was impartial, but I dunno . . . " He sips his beer and eyes Smith. He raises his voice a notch, and breaks the camel's back.

"And McGee, famous Frank McGee, he wasn't much. All we've heard for ten months is how great he is. He wasn't much at all. Fact, I'd be surprised if he isn't replaced Monday anyway, eh?"

Dirty Alf Smith slams down his empty mug and makes his way toward the door, much to our men's delight. He pauses, Sam Cassady leans in, and then Smith leaves, his brother and a couple of others in tow.

"I told him, eh?" Norman screeches, producing his famous smile which makes all others smile. He empties his mug in tribute, and Joe Boyle reappears, introducing his brothers Dave and — I forget. The party lasts into the night, all of us mindful of the day off we had coming. I enjoyed it all, though I didn't drink a drop of alcohol, of course. I had learned to enjoy myself among drinkers, which is not easy, having no other choice unless I wanted to spend all my time alone. When I left Cassady's I had Dirty Alf on my mind, and as I passed the smiling, slapping Sam Cassady I paused.

"What did Alf Smith say to you when he left?" I asked him.

Don Reddick

"Did you say something to him about Frank McGee?" Sam replied.

"Norman Watt did," I said, throwing my thumb over my shoulder at the figure who now held himself up at the bar, his back to us. Sam Cassady shook his head and smiled.

"That explains it. All Alf said to me was, 'They'll know Frank after Monday.'"

"Did you go last night?" I asked.

"I sat behind His Excellency," Sam replied.

"Well, what about McGee? Was he off-colour?"

"Frank McGee scored twenty-one goals in eight Stanley Cup games last year against the best opposition in all eastern Canada. He's got the goods. You didn't see the real McGee last night, no. But remember, he hurt his wrist last week against the Wanderers."

I nodded. My mind was busy, so I did not take his remark as something extraordinary. I mentally shrugged it off. I imagine I figured knowing Frank McGee after Monday wouldn't amount to all that much. But all the hockey world, until the end of it comes, would know Frank McGee after Monday.

28

THE TRUTH IS I BELIEVE players are better today, though I warn you there's many old timers that'll disagree. Don't listen to them, they just want to believe everything was better back then, but it wasn't. Just because the hockey players are better today don't mean if the old timers were to be young today with them they wouldn't be as good, or vice versa. If you put Maurice Richard or that Howe fellow there, or, say, Geoffrion from the Canadiens — if you were to put them back there in Dey's Rink in 1905, they wouldn't be any better than Frank McGee and Harry Westwick. Back then a senior season was only ten or twelve games, and to be good at something, particularly athletics, you got to compete with the best and do it often. Today the National Hockey League plays sixty games or so, and then playoffs. And because of the organized nature of the land, with trains and planes, the best hockey players are all in that league. In the old days you'd have McGee and Westwick in Ontario, and Ernie Russell and Russell Bowie further east in that Canadian Amateur League, and Art Ross and Tom Phillips out west, all in different leagues. Do you see?

So yes, today's players are better, but only because they play more against the best players throughout the continent. Today Frank McGee would be scoring forty, fifty goals a year, and Ed Delahanty, why, with that rabbit ball, Ed would be hitting what, a hundred doubles? Well, that's better than anyone does today, but that's because Ed Delahanty was the best baseball hitter of all time. Him and Willie Keeler and Babe Ruth.

On Monday night Joe Boyle is beside himself with excitement as we wait for word to go on the ice. He paces back and forth, whispers to Archie Martin and McLennan, looks at his timepiece. The rest of us sit with our hockey sticks before us, leaning forward, nervous once again. McLennan stands up, and every-one's eyes follow him. He's not dressed. In his uniform, I mean.

"All right boys, this is it. This is the game we've got to win, for Weldy's sake. He's going to be here, it's definite. Wired from Vancouver and said so. We've had our rest, and even though I can't play it doesn't matter. Boston's taking my place."

This stuns me, it's the first and only information I hear about the whole situation. We knew Doc's knee was bad, and when we saw him standing in his street clothes without his gear on we knew he wouldn't be playing. But since I hadn't heard

Don Reddick

nothing, I assumed Archie Martin had got the call, and when I saw Joe Boyle whispering to him I believed that proved it. And I wasn't angry at the decision. Now I sit stunned.

"You're rover, Boston," Doc says, and he twists his curled mustache with his fingers as he says so. He's disturbed deeply he's not playing, but he's Doc McLennan and he don't show it. Stiff upper lip.

"Get in Westwick's way," he says. "And don't swing back at that Dirty Alf Smith. And don't underestimate White, he's better than we expected. Moore's hurt but he's playing. Bones Allen is being replaced by Harvey Pulford" — I see Sureshot and Hector exchange glances — "and the rest's the same. Day Finnie in goal, McGee at centre. By the way, Brother Albert says when he wired Dawson with his report on the game for the *Daily News*, Constable Rines told him Ozzie Finnie was boasting we'd be beat bad and was betting against us. Just another item to bear in mind when we go out there tonight."

"The hell with Ozzie Finnie," Hector yells, "he's been cheating us for years!" This of course refers to Finnie's position as chief clerk in the gold assayer's office in Dawson, where all the miners brought their goods to be graded and weighed.

"He's gonna lose his dust!" Sureshot shouts, and it's on. Everyone jumps up and shouts, even Albert Forrest once again, even myself. Joe Boyle put up his hands to silence us.

"It's important to remember who we represent," he says, and he takes the time to look each of us in the eye. "I can't adequately convey how important we are to the Yukon Territory. All Canada is assembled here with the new government, and we're emissaries from our great northern land. Every time you speak to someone, every time you sign an autograph, every time you don't retaliate at Alf Smith, you're crediting our Territory. Every time . . ." and on and on he goes, his mind churning out situations and ideas none of us even remotely considers.

The truth about Joe Boyle is probably that he cared deeply

about the sport involved in our tour — after all, he was a former pugilist and had toured previously in that capacity with Frank Slavin, the famous Sydney Slasher. But the truth also is that Joe Boyle was an extraordinary businessman and concessionaire, and in this capacity he saw the threads as we did not, the connections between politicians and sports and reputations and emissaries. But in the end he did care, and I can prove it, which I will when the time arrives. But now he finishes up his pregame oration, his barrel chest out and his right hand puncturing the air for emphasis.

"You will win tonight for Yukon, for Weldy, for all the miners on the creeks, for yourselves, for Lionel, for Brother Paul and Smiling Vince and all the others who would have given anything to be here tonight. All of Dawson will be at the telegraph office for the running account. You will win for all those people across the land who came out to cheer you, all those little towns, all those crowds — we're gonna win it for them! Do you realize the whole country wants us to win? Everywhere, from Saint John to Vancouver, they're cheering for us, pulling, hoping and praying we beat these Silver Seven, and we can! We've got to draw out the greatest game we possess inside us. Sureshot, you'll shoot straightest and hardest you ever shot, Hector, you'll skate and jump as quick as ever, Brother Albert, you'll be as keen-eyed as a cat tonight and make your family proud back in Dawson — they'll be with all the rest at the telegraph office getting the running account. Lorne, you know what to do, Johnstone, be tougher than ever, and Norman — Norman!" Joe Boyle shouts his name to make him look up. "Norman, keep your temper tonight, play the greatest game you got without penalties," and then Joe Boyle looks at me, frozen as I am with fear and anticipation on that hard bench.

"Boston!" He looks at me now with lightning eyes that convey the whole story between us, of our meeting for the first time at the outdoor pond with the bonfires and the Victorian social timbers after I'd learned of my mother's death, of his employing me, of his encouragement and instruction in the skills of hockey, it's all in his eyes now, as deep and true as the freshest well. "Boston!" he says, "You've been called upon unexpectedly, and I know your strength, your character, I know you'll do the job out there, I know you have what it takes to reach down and grab hold of what's necessary — I didn't bring you here for no reason, Boston!" At this point I hear Crazy Norman say, in a stage whisper, "Boston'll be all right — even his flesh seems different after his wholesome, comfortable sleep." Joe Boyle doesn't hear it, but he sees Johnstone and even Doc turn away to smile. He ignores them. I'm too scared to appreciate any humour. He looks out the door and his eyes go wilder. "All right, let's go!"

We jump up roaring and charge out onto that bright ice, the crowd deafening in its roars, seemingly on top of us they were so close, men hanging over the boards wild-eyed and shouting at us. The Silver Seven, with their tiger-striped jerseys of red and white, come slowly and confidently out of their room, I stretch my arms and legs, bend over to release the tensions in my back muscles, limber up with the others. It's all terrifying to me now, the brightness of the lights reflected off the ice, the overwhelming din of the crowd in our ears, my own inner desire to perform well and fear that I will not, all of it forcing my stomach to turn and my legs to feel like rock.

A fellow named Butterworth would be the referee for this game, Joe Boyle, true to his word, had removed Stiles. Ernie Butterworth, I think his whole name was. After we warm ourselves he gives a snappy whistle for us to line up for the face, and he confers with the timers and the goal umpires, the umpires perched behind the nets with their flags, ready to signal the goals. I watch with sadness as Archie Martin alone skates to our bench and climbs over the boards to join Boyle and McLennan, of all of us who came so far he would be the only one not to play at all in the great match.

The front line, the centre and wings, line up — the same as they do today — across from their opposing centre and wings. Behind them the rover places himself — I'm rover now, re-member — places himself wherever he sees fit, usually to the backhand side of the centre on the opening face. In a face inside an opposing zone, the rover normally positions himself to take a good shot. The point man stands a ways before the goaler, closer to home, while the coverpoint stands even closer to the centre, but not aligned straight. We glide now to our stations, eyes meeting concerned, interested eyes, nodding as if to say, Okay boys, this is it . . .

The great roar of the barn rises as Butterworth places the puck between Hector and Frank McGee — they'd pulled their West-wick trick and now installed normalcy with McGee back at centre — and Butterworth backs all the way to the boards, then blows!

Fast and furious the battle begins, and several times in those frantic first moments I catch myself watching more than playing, each time correcting myself with a few quick strides in some direction. In the first couple of minutes, their great ones fly down the ice, but Johnstone and Hannay break them off to-ward the sides, myself, Hector, Norman, and Sureshot firing back like pistons and breaking up their passes, just as Joe Boyle and Doc McLennan told us to do. Hannay makes a great rush and misses. Albert makes saves on McGee and Smith, then Westwick and Smith again. It's wild, fast, and exciting, the crowd jumping up and screaming at every good chance, laugh-ing at every misfortune. And then Westwick scores.

It's a pretty goal with sharp passes between McGee, White, Smith, and finally to Westwick, who merely taps the puck behind the tangled Albert Forrest at four-thirty. I hear Joe Boyle scream-ing from the bench though I can't understand his words, and we go.

Again the pace is electric, stressful, I see I can skate with them all except Westwick, but they've honed their passing skills to such perfection that each knows instinctively where the others will turn or when they'll break. Their stickhandling, particularly McGee's, is also of the highest order, making it difficult for us to bother them.

Westwick scores again. Time: seven-fifteen. This is a goal that shouldn't have been scored, and Hector glares about, and Kennedy shouts at the top of his lungs at someone, then at Butterworth. Hannay bumps me and says, "Pick him up!" which annoys me, and the pitch grows ugly. We go at it again.

This time nothing seems to go right. These devils manufacture four good scoring opportunities, and but for Brother Albert we're in deeper trouble. Then Albert saves on White, Kennedy swats the puck to me, and I'm up ice! I skate as hard and fast as I have in my lifetime, pushing the puck ahead, and I can hear that Dirty Alf Smith huffing and slamming the ice with his stick right behind me, calling for a drop pass — I see Hector racing up and half way in I roll it back toward him. He reaches, cradles it and fires — and he scores! Hector scores!

This is a remarkable turn of events. The crowd howls madly, we swarm Hector, and he grabs my neck with his gloved arm and hugs me. "Good pass, Boston!" he yells, his eyes crazy wide. We glide toward the face, Boyle screaming, Archie Martin on his feet and banging the boards with his stick, McLennan with his arms raised in the air — and I see Frank McGee.

He's not seething, as Alf Smith is, but he's already at the face, bent over, his gaze at where Butterworth will place the puck — he's ready in a way, with an intensity we'll only understand later. But it's two to one almost ten minutes into the game, and again, just as in the first part of the first game, we show we can skate with them when we're not tired. All the talk of the five or six illegal goals, no Weldy Young or Lionel Bennett, no rest — all those reasons for losing sound awful good right now and I can see the fire in everyone's eyes — I even see worry in Moore's, I think. Right here we know we can do it!

"Attaboy, Boston!" Joe Boyle yells, gaining our attention by slapping a puck against the boards, "Attaboy, Hector Smith!" I nod to Joe Boyle and again to Hector as he twirls around before the face, and off we go!

But something is dreadfully wrong. It's as though we weren't really tired after our journey, or during that first match, or after, it's as if all that was all merely a slight weakening of our souls compared to what happens now. Westwick scores again, and it's three-one.

For no good reason other than luck, fate, and Brother Albert Forrest, it takes seven more minutes for one-eyed Frank McGee to score his first goal of the game. Ten seconds later Rat Westwick scores again, his fourth of the game, and at that moment it would have been absurd to think that the man would hardly be remembered as a hero of this game.

Thirty seconds later McGee scores again. All these goals are clean, crisp, smart attacks ending in solid, undisputable goals, without an offside in sight. Tiger red and white thundered over, around, and through us like locomotives, our breath spent, our legs iron and our arms water. Thankfully the half whistle blows at Silver Seven ten, Dawson one. Even Hannay spends the last few minutes mostly standing and turning, watching McGee score two more, watching the rest fly by. There is no hope.

Ten to one!

The dressing room is a morbid scene. Our heads down or back against the walls, our tongues out, and a rain of sweat across our faces. Joe Boyle is silent, brooding, slapping a fist into his hand, but he knows it's over, and he's a gentleman. Archie Martin leans over and uncrosses two sticks — does he really think it matters? — and Sureshot Kennedy makes a half-hearted attempt to rally the troops. There are no affirmations called in response, only the solid, sordid silence of embarrassment.

Ten to one!

I see Hector with his face in his gloves — he's so tired he don't even take them off — and I'm worried about the man who wanted to win the Stanley Cup more than anyone else — I see Lorne Hannay staring straight ahead, his second chance in two seasons fading before his eyes — I see Norman Watt gasping and coughing up phlegm, his face twisted and agonized. I shake my head and close my eyes. At the end Joe Boyle speaks very softly to us.

"We're all in, boys," he says, "we're all in. You've got nothing to be ashamed of. We've got to go out there now and show them what Klondike is made of, show them even in the jaws of defeat we hold our heads high and try our damnedest. So let's go out there and finish it up. Hey, who knows . . . "

McGee scores thirty seconds into the second half. He seems possessed coming from the dressing room, scoops the puck at mid-ice right after the face and stickhandles through me, Hannay, and then Johnstone before firing the puck into the upper corner of the net. Watt and Kennedy had barely moved from their face positions. White scores next, leading up to the most bizarre stretch of hockey the Stanley Cup will ever see.

Frank McGee becomes animated, indestructible, performs with such swiftness and precision as I've ever witnessed, before or since. McGee scores two goals within thirty seconds. He scores a minute later. He scores ten seconds after that, now that's four goals in a span of about a minute and forty seconds. This is not counting the four goals he's scored in the first half, or the one he scored to start the second. He's got nine goals now. People go crazy in the stands, chanting his name — no one's ever scored nine goals in a senior game before, never mind a Stanley Cup senior game. In fact, McGee already holds the record for most goals in a Stanley Cup game, with five. Two times. And then what does he do?

He *is* possessed. He stares at the face spot before Butterworth even puts the puck down. He don't even acknowledge his teammates or the fans, and we're just gaping at him, beyond exhaustion. He scores two minutes later. He scores again ten seconds later. Ten seconds later again! Something odd happens and he don't score again until a whole four minutes pass.

He scores again thirty seconds after that.

Frank McGee scores eight consecutive goals in a Stanley Cup game in a shade over eight minutes. They were his, what, sixth, seventh, eighth, ninth, tenth, eleventh, twelfth, and thirteenth goals of the game. The score is twenty to one!

Debacle is too generous. Humiliation doesn't even begin to describe what we felt standing on that ice — and standing is about all we could do at this point — and it's not over. Dirty Alf Smith scores, and a couple of minutes after that Frank McGee concludes the most incredible night by a hockeyist in the history of the sport, to this day. It won't be surpassed, period.

Frank McGee scores his fourteenth goal, taking passes from Rat Westwick and Dirty Alf. Westwick concludes their scoring three minutes later, their twenty-third goal of the game and his fifth, making him the second man ever to score five goals in a Stanley Cup game. And believe it or not, and I still don't to this day, Sureshot gets the puck off that last face and bursts past Pulford — Pulford! — passes the puck back to Hector Smith in the middle, and Hector fires it past Day Finnie for a goal, his second of the game.

As I skate to him — the crowd roars enthusiastically and honestly — I see the tears in his eyes, removing all joy from the event. A minute later, Butterworth calls the game early, with perhaps two or three minutes to go.

There are not words to describe the dressing room. This was annihilation beyond anyone's fears. Twenty-three to two.

Twenty-three to two!

Hector Smith sobbed in his arms. Johnstone could not look at his father when the older man entered. Joe Boyle and Doc

McLennan hugged one another, not releasing for a long moment. Sureshot Kennedy sat with his head back against the wall, his arrogance and glares drained, Norman Watt, doubled over, coughed and coughed. Archie Martin kicked a stick which lay across another. Only silent Albert Forrest seemed serene in his exhaustion, the nineteen-year-old kid sitting, staring straight ahead, appearing the most poised of us all. My mind was blank. Playing sixty consecutive minutes of hockey in the old game was the true test of athletic endurance, leaving all who tried it exhausted. Never mind — but oh, let it rest once and for all.

The Dawson Nuggets, the Dawson City Seven as we wanted to call ourselves, had lost by an accumulated score of thirty-two to four. So there would be no Stanley Cup for Dawson City.

Ever.

29

MY DADDY OWNED A STORY that hurt him so bad he couldn't tell it, not in its entirety. Fortune must have accompanied me in my youth, because despite the outcome, there was a satisfication on my part for where I'd been and what I'd done. What I'd seen. I love to tell my story, it makes me young and strong, tears away my soul again. But at least I can tell it!

There's more — I'll tie it all up. A banquet was held in honour of both teams. We congregated with the Silver Seven that night in Cassady's, and that's where we learned of Norman Watt's folly. Alf Smith, who believed Frank McGee was the greatest hockey player there ever was, had indeed become incensed by Norman's inappropriate barroom remarks and repeated them to McGee, enraging him. Now it's traditional common athletic sense never to talk down the enemy before the war. In fact, you'll even see the opposite by thoughtful coaches and players — "We have total respect for the opponent and expect a mighty difficult time" etcetera, etcetera. Why, you lull a lion to sleep before you face him, you don't throw sticks!

So you learn . . . At this dinner I caught the image that remains with me always, and that is the sight of the Stanley Cup — it's just a bowl now, remember, not that big ugly thing you see today with all the added bands — with Dirty Alf Smith, in his best suit and loosened tie, the Captain of the mighty Silver Seven, emptying two bottles of champagne into it, one in each of his big hands, a grin splashed irretrievably across his scarred, crooked face. And then the Stanley Cup, rippling with the stuff spilling over its edges, is passed from hand to hand and the boys all tip it back and drink.

And do you recall when I said I'd only partaken of alcoholic beverages once in my entire lifetime? Without restraints of any nature, I confess now that it's here it occurred. Hector himself drinks from the passed bowl, looks at me next in line and stops in confusion. But when I grin and nod, I observe the most beautiful expression on his face, and I take the Stanley Cup from Hector and tilt it up! The only time in my entire lifetime I drank alcohol was from that Dominion Hockey Challenge Cup, Lord Stanley's Cup.

There were speeches, big speeches, by Joe Boyle, gracious and gentlemanly, and by a man named Dickson, who shocked all present with his views on professionalism. Funny songs were sung, several toasts — "The King, God Save the King!" one man called, and glasses were raised. "The Dawson Hockey Club!" Joe Boyle stands up and says, "The Ottawa Hockey Club, no matter what Montreal or Toronto may say, plays hockey and does not hold the Cup by hook or crook, but by playing the game."

The Reverend speaks, the president of this speaks, the president of that speaks. I look for the Stanley Cup only to see Art Moore carving his initials into it with a fork. "The Yukon!" is called and we drink, "The Press!" and again, and then Day Finnie and Art Moore stand up together and propose "The Ladies!" which brings a wild cheer, and Sureshot and Hector jump up and respond. It was all talented and proper, a most happy occasion for us all, with no pressure of games ahead. The games to be played now were only for money.

I see Doc McLennan deep in conversation with Dr. Sweetland, both Doctors and both graduates of Queen's University. I see Frank McGee, somewhat taken with liquor and arm in arm with his brothers, calling out over all, "Party at our house, 185 Daly Avenue!"

After some hours I excuse myself from my smoky table and step outside to gasp some of Ottawa's cold night air. As I step outside I'm confronted by none other than Harry "The Rat" Westwick himself. This was good fortune, for despite the coziness of the dinner inside, both factions primarily kept to their own side of the room, the welts and bruises on our bodies and minds still aching from our match.

"Boston Mason," he says, extending his hand, and I shake it, and then I learn this solid, good-looking young fellow's gentlemanly nature. "You played a fine game," he says to me in his quiet, steady voice.

"We did our best," I reply, and we discuss the various problems my Dawson team had, what with the schedule and delays and player changes. Westwick is a thorough gentleman and good sport, not once making any mention or gesture acknowledging the complete embarrassment his team had inflicted upon my own. We talk of the games, the various turning points, Frank McGee. Norman Watt. Joe Boyle.

"He's quite a man," Westwick says of Boyle, "but I'm not sure I understand him correctly. On the one hand he's so force-

ful, confident, overpowering even, and on the other he's so . . .
naive. So honest he believes everyone else's as honest. First he
insists no Ottawan referees the first game, then he insists Stiles
not referee the second game, and agrees to Ernie Butterworth."

"I'm not sure I understand."

"Ernie Butterworth grew up across the street from me!"
Westwick laughs, and I do also, wondering privately exactly
what he means. But the games are over and I let it pass. I look
at this man as we speak, see the reason and intelligence of his
soul, and wonder again about his nickname. The Rat. I had expected a rattish-looking person, but Westwick is as handsome a
young athlete as Ottawa produces. I then believe his ratlike
qualities will emerge in conversation, but as I have testified, his
manner is that of a complete gentleman. So after we chat further, I finally give in to my curiosities.

"Tell me, Harry," I say, hoping I'm not crossing some unpleasantness, "how is it that you're nicknamed Rat?" Westwick
laughs, laughs hard with his head rolled back. He looks at me
with the gleam in the eye that allows a man to take a joke on
himself.

"A sportswriter from Quebec City gave me it after we
played a game up there in February, '95. Ten years ago. It was a
terrible game, a game in which Weldy went wild, got into several fights that spawned several others. After the game — we
won 3-2 — the Quebec crowd was so out of control they chased
the referees and caught them, brought them back to the rink
and tried to force them to call the game a draw! The whole thing
caused the Quebec team to be suspended for the rest of the
year, but anyway in the next morning's paper this sportswriter,
while evilly dispatching our entire team, refers to me as — and
I quote — a 'miserable, insignificant rat.' Naturally after the boys
read it I never heard the end of it. Called me 'The Insignificant
One' or 'The Miserable Rat' for the longest time, until it just
became plain 'Rat.' I don't mind it, though, heard a lot worse."

We shared this joke and further pleasantries, and I have corresponded with Rat Westwick on and off through the years. Our meeting produced a genuine friendship that allowed me to follow some of these hockeyists' lives. He wrote me of his teammates, of men that are now considered among Canada's greatest athletes of all time. Harvey Pulford, Frank McGee, Alf Smith, and Harry Westwick himself are all in the Hockey Hall of Fame. Bouse Hutton, too. And that Gilmour, the one that didn't play against us. He's considered a member of those famed Silver Sevens. The one that went to that Gatineau timber limits, whatever on earth that could be.

"Dirty Alf, as you call him, isn't all that bad a fellow, sort of Ottawa's answer to Norman Watt," Harry joked that night. "Really, he's very humorous in his own way, but growing up tough the way he did, well, that makes him more understandable. He's the quarterback and the captain of the Roughriders, too, but hockey means everything to him. It's his life. And he's got brothers that can play, Harry and Tommy. His family — he's one of fifteen kids — his six brothers and his father have a standing challenge to any other family for the Family Championship of Hockey, as they call it. They're thinking of touring themselves. But no one's tougher than Alf Smith.

"Frank, he's turning into the greatest hockey player of all time. We opened a week ago against the Wanderers and he scored four goals, and he got his wrist hacked so he can hardly close his fist. He was taking it easy until Alf told him what Watt said in Cassady's, he's too proud a man to let something like that slide.

"Harvey, well, Harvey's Harvey. He's simply the greatest athlete Canada's ever had, great in lacrosse, rowing, football, hockey, anything he wants to play. He's been our rock on defence for eleven years now, except when he broke his collarbone playing football for the Roughriders in '99. Missed that whole season. Started out with Weldy Young back in what, '94, played there ever since, and I don't think he's near ready to quit yet."

"What was Weldy like in the old days?"

"Oh, Weldy Young was a hero here, one of the toughest, craziest hockeyists of the times. Went into the stands here in Ottawa, over in the Rideau rink, after one of our own fans who'd become exceptionally vocal during one game. Nearly caused a riot. Had his share of fights, was probably the first defenseman ever to rush the puck from one end to the other. Why, during those years he played with Harvey, he outscored Harvey maybe eight to nothing. I'm surprised he never told you that, he told everyone else around here at the time. It was all a sad business when he announced he was off for your gold fields. Are you going to McGee's after?"

"I don't think so," I replied, imagining what that would be like, with both teams, particularly Dirty Alf Smith and Crazy Norman Watt, being late into the liquor.

A loud shout of laughter went up, reminding us of the festivities inside, and we rejoined our teammates in their revelries. I recall seeing Norman with Frank McGee and his brothers sharing a laugh, and recall it with a chill, knowing as I do now that they were all shot. It closed soon, with all the athletes shaking hands and exchanging well wishes, the Silver Seven wishing us luck on our tour, our men wishing them luck with their senior season. It's then, late at night as we head back to the Russell House, that the odd thing occurs.

"We could have won, eh?" Sureshot says as we stagger home through the streets of darkened, cold Ottawa, and I'm shocked to hear the agreement.

"No sleep in a month, no good food, no time to practise or rest once we got here," Hector agrees.

"Hannay never got a chance to get used to us, and we lost Weldy and Lionel right off," Sureshot says. Albert Forrest says, "Six, not three or four, but six of those first-game goals was clearly offside," and it hits me all at once how I've seen this before, been here in this field, the rocks, the stone wall, my father sinking to his knees and then falling back against the wall too hard, and I stop rolling my rock, concerned.

"They didn't understand," he says, the strain choking his words, and I realize his silence has been spent unwisely in thinking. "I got home, and there was nothing! Nothing! No fields planted, no sound fences, no laughter! They'd taken all the food, all the valuables the women tried to bury in the woods, half the houses. There was nothing, boy!" I sank to one knee and stared at my father. He glanced, bewildered, to his left, off toward the trees. The sunlight crossed his face with scared shadows, sneaking off when he turned back to me.

"They wanted to celebrate Thanksgiving. Warn't even no food and they wanted to celebrate Thanksgiving! They been there. They saw what I saw, did what I did. Don't you understand?"

I looked at my father.

"Do you know how I celebrated the first Thanksgiving? We was on the lines around Richmond, and we was suddenly required not to use much ammunition no more. We all knew what that meant, everyone knew our ammunition was manufactured in Atlanta. We heard about Lincoln proclaiming Thanksgiving. And then we heard, the very same week as that first Thanksgiving, that Sherman had marched into Milledgeville. Into my home! I ate nothing on that first Thanksgiving and almost died worrying about your mother and the girls. That's my Thanksgiving. Then I come home to nothing, your Momma and your two oldest sisters starving to death, some people already starved dead. We'd get together to smoke and drink, all us war heroes, and you know what they'd say? Said we should've won that war, said we was better'n any damn Yankee factory boys, said if this happened then or that happened here it all would've changed — do you see?"

All I could see was the tears falling from my beaten father's eyes. Momma hadn't shocked me that night before I left about Daddy crying, because I'd seen it myself in the fields. It wasn't until years later, on an old cobblestoned Ottawa street, that I finally heard his words.

"This war ruined my land, the whole of the Southland, and for what? There was nothing! And I listened to them boys, some without legs or hands or sound minds no more, and I listened and they just didn't understand! And I knew all was lost, much more than just the fight, and it's then I needed to go home . . . "

"Is that why you came north?" I asked. My Daddy nodded his head, then his face fell to his hands and he sobbed, God love him, the man sobbed, a man so physically strong and sound I knew then that life required more of us than that kind of strength, and then it drained it from us.

"I've got to go," I said to Joe Boyle in his hotel room. He looked up at me thoughtfully, clasped his hands together and leaned his chin on them.

"I was going to have to tell you the same thing," he said matter of factly. I sat down on the edge of the bed. "Weldy's coming. Hannay's the best we got, and Archie, well, Archie will always be on my team. You understand. You've done yourself and the Klondike well, Boston, and I'll be forever grateful. I'll take care of the arrangements to get you home." I did not protest, but looked at Joe Boyle with true pride and admiration.

"I'm an honest man, Boston," he said, "and I want you to know why I liked you so, why I spent so much time trying to help you."

"Why is that?" I asked.

"It wasn't the sense you have for not drinking or smoking, which I'm sure you've heard some of the railbirds sing, but it's Skagway, what happened to you there, and what you did." My

Don Reddick

mind swept back among the awful sights and sounds of my robbery, and Billy the Pickle.

"You know about that?" I said, and he nodded.

"Everybody knows everything up there, Boston. Do you know what happened to me in Skagway?"

I shook my head.

"Me and Frank Slavin arrived with fifty cents left in our pockets, and we split a cup of coffee and were broke. Not a red cent to our names, and you know what I did? I found a broken banjo, tossed off by someone who found it unnecessary among his goods, and I took that banjo down to the corner, threw my hat on the ground and started singing every song I knew, Frank keeping time patting his thighs next to me, and we raised the money to go on to Dawson. Weldy left a situation here in Ottawa as an athletic star to go to Dawson. Archie made it there after being turned down by that knuckle-headed Aylmer group because he was too small. He outlasted all of them. And Norman, Norman's family wouldn't allow him to go, so he ran away to get there. Ended up in that hospital, broke, in Winnipeg on the way, and still made it up. Do you understand? You were broke in Skagway and you made it to Dawson. That's why I've always respected you, why I've respected all the boys, why I knew you could do anything you wanted to do, learn to shoot, to pass — anything."

I stared at Joe Boyle now with respect for his humanity. This was a rich man, and here he was spreading honesty and reason and strength of character to me, George Mason.

"I'm ready to go home," I said.

30

I HAD MY DRIVER STOP short of the farm, and I got out and he tossed my bags to me. There was no snow, and as he puttered off in his jalopy I stood at the wall and stared across the sweep of my farm, my fields, my house, all the scenes of my lifetime so familiar, all the while my insides quaking, fearing and rejoicing at the same moment, and I didn't even have the dramatic satisfaction of surprising everyone because brother-in-law David spied me and started hollering to wake the — well, you know.

But it's all a messy thing for a proper New England man to relate, even sixty years later. Let it suffice to say I was home, among my family and in my own bed, next to the field where my Daddy'd died. At dinner that first evening there was looks and various winkings among my sisters and their husbands. April clears her throat and announces during a lull that Elizabeth Grady had inquired as to my wellbeing. This was important and exciting news to me of course, but the truth will always remain that I'd decided to pay her a visit, however humbling it might be, to ask forgiveness for my indiscretions of that previous Christmas, and also, if I lasted long enough, for neglecting to write. I had arrived at this decision at no certain point, but a conglomeration of understandings descended upon me somewhere during my hockeyist experiences. I became certain that pride was a wasteful, sad emotion, capable of ruining sunrises and sunsets, and before I stood looking upon my farm, my Sudbury home, as I had this afternoon, I knew I would be going to Marlboro Street.

This dinner was an event long remembered by my family, for the lost boy was home at last. One after another my sisters hugged me, including in their tightnesses that special extra squeeze for Momma, the men, David, William, and Ronald — new Ronald — waiting patiently to shake my hand with proper seriousness. When we all first sat down and started passing po-tatoes and string beans and roasted chickens, an audience formed for me, all of them looking at me, until April finally says, "Well?" You see, they all wanted to know every last bit of where I'd been and what I'd done, and I drew a deep breath and began with my biggest news.

"I played for the Stanley Cup in Ottawa," I say, and stop to gauge their reactions. They range from April's politely blank face to David's concerned, if confused, demeanour. Silence. Not a single soul responded to my pronouncement, but all stared at me, awaiting some explanation.

"What the heck is a Stanley Cup?" David finally asks. I sud-denly realized that no one could appreciate what I'd done and where I'd been, that the whole thing was only for me. The whole long, tragic, uplifting experience was nothing more than lost time of the most nutritious sort, to be digested and com-manded by my innermost resources. It was something so real you just had to see it for yourself. I never once again men-tioned the Stanley Cup to my family, nor did I ever utter a word about Billy the Pickle or lost Patrick Sullivan, of course. These were now things for a proper New England man to hold solely for his own solid, appropriate constitution, and I did so. There was enough of the rest, the travel, the Canadian Rockies, the characters and gold of Dawson City, enough of these things to satisfy any of my inquisitors.

I took the carriage into Boston the next morning. Not being totally without fears, I avoided Lizzie's father and waited up the street for Lizzie to come home after work. I was willing to take the consequences of her wrath, but not his. But my anxiety all dissolved when her eyes met mine, for Lizzie Grady's blew wide open with excitement and joy when she saw me. She dropped her bag right on Marlboro Street and ran to me and hopped into my arms and grabbed my head with her arms and squeezed me until I near couldn't breathe!

"My God my God my God!" she kept screaming, and I hugged her back, giving me a feeling of . . . what? How do I explain it when you finally know deepest down in your heart that everything's all right with the one you love? So remarkable a moment it was that I forgot all the people walking around us staring, forgot the inappropriateness of the scene. Now doesn't that adequately convey it all, that I could do that?

"I'm home," I said, or tried to say through her stranglehold. Finally she let go and dropped down and she wiped the tears from her face, cast her eyes down in embarrassment, then grabbed me again and we embraced for the longest moment, and I figured, why not?

"Can we have an understanding?" I whispered, and I felt her body go still, then tremble. She did not move. "I won't have no more misunderstandings like Christmas. If you feel we can have an understanding, well, there's a question I got in mind to ask your father." And Lizzie Grady pushes back now, looks up to me and releases her magical smile, the one matches so well those eyes, and . . . I'm sorry . . . and . . .

Hold on.

Okay.

Okay, well, you understand the gist of it. I'm sorry. It's just the memories of that moment, these times I had under the new stars of the new century, these were the days of my young life. As I've said, people always see themselves in their youth, and I see Lizzie that way too, young, smiling, as vibrant and clear-eyed as any young woman has a right to be, not the way she was those last few months . . .

See this? See the tear? Tears is just something you lose from the inside when you've lost something on the outside. It's an equalizer of sorts and I don't know exactly how it all works, except when you lose something very great on the outside, you usually got to compensate with an appropriate amount of tears from the inside. That's how it works. I don't think there's been

Don Reddick

a day gone by since Lizzie died I haven't lost some tears, but they get less and less as time goes on, equalizing it all inside. But the biggest, grandest thing you ever had in your lifetime will cause real, frequent tears. And you know how I feel about my tears now? I feel like my loss is so great I don't give a damn what anybody thinks and I just drop them. And that's the way it is.

So I want to end my story by explaining exactly what happened. The boys went on the tour. They won more than they lost, finally getting in shape and playing some hockey. Hector hurt his leg and ended up in a Montreal hospital, Sureshot lost a front tooth, they played a game for Brother Albert's sake in his old hometown of Three Rivers. A Toronto newspaper accused Joe Boyle of running a professional team and Joe responded by offering to play anybody and donate the proceeds to charity, but nobody took them on. The tour finally fizzled out in Brandon, more than a month later, in some sort of fiasco I don't remember, Sureshot Kennedy the only man to play in every game. Albert Forrest was the first to stumble back into Dawson City, with Sureshot, Crazy Norman, Doc McLennan and Gloomy Johnstone close behind, Sureshot boasting of the professional baseball contract he was offered in Seattle.

In Georgia in 1862, James J. Andrews, caught behind enemy lines in civilian clothing, was hung by the neck until dead with seven of his men because he didn't want to hurt no one during the war. In Montana, on June 25, 1876, George Armstrong Custer, the man who never lost a battle, raised his hat over his head and yelled, "Now we got 'em, boys!" In Saskatchewan of the old Northwest Territories, on November 16, 1885, Louis Riel, leader of a vanishing people, was hung by the neck until dead because he was too proud to pretend he wasn't crazy.

In Sudbury, Massachusetts, on August 10, 1898, my Daddy's heart finally broke after thirty years of breaking.

In Niagara Falls, New York, on the evening of July 2, 1903, thirty-five-year-old Big Ed Delahanty, the greatest ballplayer of all time, drank too much alcohol, got thrown off the team train and fell into the Niagara River and drowned.

In Skagway, Alaska, on March 22, 1904, the fourteen or fifteen-year-old prushun philosopher and baseball fan named Billy the Pickle finally found the ability to dream, and froze to death, an empty whiskey bottle and a Winchester rifle in his arms.

In 1916 the great trench war called The Somme occurred in France between the Allies and Germany. Occasionally the bones of one of the hundreds of thousands of men who fell there still turn up under the plough of some local farmer. Walking the site of such horror, through the sweet pastures and woodlands that now quietly rule, it must be hard to believe that under those silent grounds lie the body of hockey's first immortal, Frank McGee. He'd enlisted with his two older brothers, Charlie and William. Charlie was killed at Festubert in May of 1915. Frank was wounded in December, sent back to England to convalesce, then rejoined his battalion in time for its advance. September found the daily casualty lists exploding in the Ottawa newspapers, until on Saturday, September 23, 1916, the poor folks at 185 Daly Avenue received yet another visit from a member of the Canadian Expeditionary Force. Lieutenant Frank McGee, star of the immortal Ottawa Silver Seven, was killed in action on September 16, 1916.

Joseph Whiteside Boyle also answered the call, but in a slightly different manner. Told he was too old to serve, he forced himself on the war, forming and equipping at his own expense a fifty-man machine gun battalion of Dawson's ablest men. Faced with further rebukes from Ottawa, he went to England and harried officials there until they relented, sending him to Russia to assist in the organization of that ruined country's railroads. Once there, it was as if all his varied life had merely been in preparation for what he now saw, and he threw himself headlong into the effort, earning medals from Russia, England, his beloved Canada, and Rumania. Indeed, he became the man called The Saviour of Rumania and the lover of Queen Marie. So extraordinary was this man, so strong and hard and correct, that some of the harshest figures in world history bent to him, acceded to his thoughts and beliefs. But so hard driven was he that he suffered a stroke, and, ashamed at the loss of his immense physical powers, retired to the home of an old Dawson friend in Hampton Hill, England, just outside of London. Joe Boyle, King of the Klondike, sailor, horse breeder, pugilist, bouncer, concessionaire, promoter, hockeyist, and finally war hero, quietly died of heart failure there on April 14, 1923. Queen Marie, in testament to where his heart truly roamed, placed a stone on his grave with the inscription drawn from Robert Service's poem, "Law of the Yukon": "Man with the heart of a Viking and the simple faith of a child."

Dr. Donald Randolf McLennan returned to Dawson after the tour. He became a principle in the Yukon Silver-Lead Mining Company, staked the Frog and Faro claims on Keno Hill in 1919. Doc eventually moved to Mayo, where he married Margaret Kenney, a nurse at the Mayo hospital. There he succeeded Gloomy Johnstone as postmaster and ran a drugstore until his death on December 12, 1935.

Weldon Champness Young, that unlucky soul, hurriedly copied his south Dawson registration lists for the government instead of tabulating them correctly when he heard the team was delayed in Whitehorse. He promptly left Dawson and tried to catch up. His misdeed was discovered in January, shortly after the games, and he could never show his face in Dawson again. He settled back in his home province of Ontario, refereeing senior hockey and opening a life insurance business, which he operated until his death in 1944.

Norman Allen Watt also returned to Dawson, where he was

employed in the Civil Service for ten years. In 1916 Norman enlisted with the rank of Lieutenant in Joe Boyle's machine gun battalion. On October 11, 1918, a month to the day before the war ended, he was shot and seriously wounded near Cambrai. Norman was hospitalized in England, where his fiancee Dorothea Acheson, a nurse with the Canadian Red Cross, came to care for him. Norman and Dorothea were married upon their return to Canada, in April of 1919. He resumed work with the Civil Service in Victoria, and he came to be known and trusted as one of the finest Civil Servants in British Columbia. Norman Watt died of a heart attack on January 9, 1946.

James K. Johnstone also returned to Dawson after the tour, but I don't know much about the man. Never did. I know he was the postmaster in Mayo for a time. Gloomy was the only one of us to live in Dawson City at the end, which came to him on May 23, 1948.

Brother Albert Forrest, kid star of several sports, received a hero's welcome when he returned to Dawson. He was a man I've always believed could have played two professional sports had he lived at a different time and in a different place. He became a linotype operator in the print shops of Dawson and later in Juneau. I know Albert married a Dawson woman named Parmelia Joyal, and had four kids. Later in his life, after his wife died, he moved south to Everett, Washington, where he died at the age of sixty-nine on July 28, 1955.

Archie Martin continued as a prospector in the Klondike until 1945. He lived in Keno for thirty years before retiring to the home of one of his dentist brothers back in Aylmer. He'd been a printer in Ottawa before the gold rush, and besides goldseeking had worked at numerous and sundry jobs up north, a helper on the Boyle Concession, later a guide, as well as taking a hand in the print shops along with Albert Forrest. Archie's still alive and kicking, I understand, up in Aylmer, and he must be what, ninety-one years old now. Born in 1871, so that's about right. He'll probably outlive even me. After all, he didn't sip the champagne out of the Stanley Cup that night, and I did.

I never have heard what happened to those two from West Selkirk, Manitoba, my best friend up north Hector Smith and his unforgettable buddy Sureshot Kennedy. As for Lorne Hannay, Lionel Bennett, the Spieler, Brother Paul Forrest and any number of other characters I knew up there, I've also lost them to time, as happens in this life. Sometimes it's better that way, because it allows them to remain to me what they were, and not what they probably are.

Well, I enjoyed this. Forgot to tell that bear story. Forgot to lie about Jack Frost there, what's his name, Service. Robert Service. And that Jack London. Nobody needs to know London was there and gone before me and I was there and gone before Service. Oh, cripes! Did I say it was Will Rogers that said home is where you go and they have to take you in? I did! Robert Frost said that, not Will Rogers. But I guess that don't matter.

What's important to me is that I walked down the road with her. I told you about our days in '03, the baseball games and Cy Young, the classical music, the swan boats, those sandwiches. Bologna sandwiches and iced tea by the pond with the swan boats. We did all right. We knocked our heads against the wall a few of those years, but so what? It don't matter all that much in the end, does it. I believe the grandest thing I ever did in my lifetime was walk beside her.